THE GOODBYE GOVERNESS

UNEXPECTED LORDS
BOOK FOUR

SCARLETT SCOTT

HEA

Happily Ever After Books

The Goodbye Governess

Unexpected Lords Book Four

For more information, contact author Scarlett Scott.

https://scarlettscottauthor.com

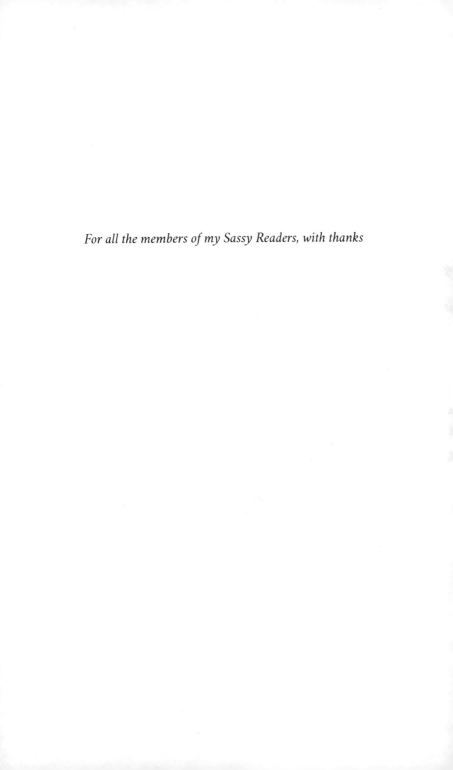

For all the members of my Sassy Readers, with thanks

CHAPTER 1

YORKSHIRE, 1886

*S*omeone had drawn on his face whilst he was sleeping.

Grimly, Knight surveyed his visage in the looking glass. One of four someones, specifically, had committed this abomination. Given the lack of skill in the comical eyebrows which had been applied above his own to create an expression of perpetual surprise, he would wager a guess it had been the youngest of his nieces, five-year-old Mary. And she had used what appeared to be…

He rubbed his face, smearing the right eyebrow.

"Boot blacking," he muttered.

Where had the little devil managed to get her hands on that?

Knight poured some water into a basin and scrubbed at his face, cursing his brother Robert. There had never been a modicum of fondness between them. They'd been enemies from the earliest of Knight's memories. And now, the selfish, smug arsehole who had delighted in tormenting him in life continued to do so in death, via the medium of his wayward offspring.

Who would have supposed that four young ladies could be so much bloody trouble?

Not Knight. But then, he'd not had to even contemplate that sort of thing when he had been across an entire vast ocean, happily living the life he had carved out for himself in America. He was The Bruiser Knight, renowned boxing champion. Women loved him. Men alternately feared him and wanted to be him. He had spent every day in unabashed worship of the credo that a rolling stone gathers no moss.

Until the day a telegram had arrived from England almost a year ago, telling him he was the newly inherited Earl of Stoneleigh after his brother had failed to recover from a sudden illness, joining his wife Martha in the hereafter. And leaving Knight the sole guardian of Robert and Martha's daughters.

Hellions was a far more appropriate description, he'd discovered upon his arrival at Knightly Abbey just three days before.

Grumbling to himself, he reached for a towel and blotted his face dry before assessing his reflection once more. The worst of the damage was gone, but faint traces remained, making his visage appear oddly dirty. It was going to have to do.

He stalked to the door of his chamber, intent upon finding his nieces and forcing them to confess which of them was responsible for this nighttime atrocity.

A torrent of icy water rushed over his head as he crossed the threshold.

"What the bloody hell?" he roared, looking around to find a pail had been hung over his door and rigged to pour water on him the moment he pulled it open.

Muffled chuckles hit his ears as he blinked the water from his eyes.

"Mary," he growled, searching around for the source of the levity.

The little wretch was hiding somewhere about. He knew it. But where?

And, more importantly, where was the damned governess?

Scowling, soaked, and furious, Knight decided to pay his first morning call to the newly arrived woman who had been hired to get this damned house in order so he could return to America. Her train had been late, and he had not bothered to meet her the day before when she had finally turned up. She came highly recommended by her previous employer. A most important distinction, for his nieces had chased off every governess who had taken on the sorry task of keeping them from running wild all over Knightly Abbey like the cunning little termagants they were.

He had been desperate. When Robert's steward—now his steward—had telegraphed with the suggestion they hire the latest governess, he had agreed. He'd been in the midst of long-overdue travel to return and hadn't taken the time to pore over the details.

But he was less than impressed with the woman.

He came across the housekeeper, Mrs. Oak, before he found the governess or any of his mischief-making nieces. Perhaps a bit young for her position, the brunette woman was eminently capable, and thank Christ for that. He needed all the help he could find.

"Good morning, Mrs. Oak," he said.

"Lord Stoneleigh." She dipped into a curtsy. "Is something amiss?"

"I reckon it looks as if a pail of water was dumped on my head," he drawled, a headache thumping to life.

It had taken him nearly a year to force himself back to

England following Robert's death. And this was his dubious reward.

"Yes, my lord." Her eyes were wide.

"Because it *was*. To that end, I am searching for the new governess. Have you seen her?"

"No, I haven't seen Miss Brinton yet this morning, my lord. You may wish to try the nursery."

"Apparently, neither have her charges," he observed, nettled. "Thank you, Mrs. Oak. I will indeed try the nursery."

Now that he thought upon it, the nursery should have been his first stop. But he was not accustomed to dealing with children or governesses or estates. His chief concerns for the last few years had been boxing, traveling, and bedding women. In precisely that order. And what a glorious life it had been.

Would be again.

All he had to do was find a governess worth keeping and abandon his brother's hellions to her care.

Scowling, Knight stalked through the great hall, back up the staircase, and to the nursery. By the time he reached it, even his shoes were squishing with water that had run down his trousers and pooled about his feet. Mary was going to pay for her misdeeds.

And so was Miss...Miss...whatever the hell her bloody name was. Mrs. Oak had just said it, had she not? He ought to have remembered. Perhaps he'd taken one too many fists to the upperworks.

He threw open the door to the nursery without knocking and bustled directly into a soft, feminine body. The impact of their collision took him by surprise. Knight's reactions were honed from years of perfecting his craft. His hands shot out, landing on her waist, steadying her. Through the layers of boning and silk, she was soft and curved every way a woman ought to be. Her drab, shapeless governess weeds hid a decidedly delectable figure, and he couldn't control the effect it had on him, as instantaneous as the water upended over his head, and yet with an opposite sensation. Heated flame rather than a cooling shock.

"Oh!" she gasped, clutching his wet shirt, eyes wide and round, fringed with thick gold lashes.

Her hair was woven into a Grecian braid that emphasized her high cheekbones and the lushness of her mouth, the color of which reminded him of roses. *Damn.* It wasn't just her body that was tempting. The new governess was beautiful.

This was going to be a problem. A very big, very tempting problem.

One he could avoid, naturally. He hadn't returned to Yorkshire so that he could lust over governesses. Not even ones with burnished-gold hair, full, kissable lips, warm eyes, dimples in their chins, and the most bewitching smattering of freckles he'd ever beheld on their noses.

"Steady?" he asked, the gentleman within demanding he make certain she would not go sprawling to the floor if he released her.

The man in him not wanting to let her go.

She nodded, smiling as if they were sharing a joke. "Forgive me for my lack of grace. You may release me. I promise I shan't topple over."

He set her away from himself as if she were a funeral pyre, for she may as well have been.

"The governess, I presume?" he asked, remembering his position and, belatedly, his reason for seeking this woman out.

His shoes were *soggy*, for Christ's sake. Where were his nieces?

"Yes," she said, her smile fading. "I am. And you are?"

"Stoneleigh," he said, the title an abomination on his tongue, still so foreign, so unwanted. "Your employer."

HER EMPLOYER.

What an odd notion. One Lady Corliss Collingwood was not accustomed to at all. Seasoned governess, *Miss* Corliss *Brinton* would be, however. And she knew that if this ruse was to be accepted, she had to act the part of the devoted, experienced governess she had claimed she was.

Which she decidedly, wholeheartedly, was not.

Remembering herself, she dipped into a curtsy. "My lord. Forgive me. I hadn't realized you wished an audience this morning. I would have been better prepared."

That was a lie; she would not have. For nothing could have sufficiently equipped her for meeting the Earl of Stoneleigh. When she had conceived of this plan, her mind had conjured a picture of the earl—he was perpetually dressed in tweed, and he sported an elaborate, waxed mustache which curled at the ends and wore small, gold-rimmed spectacles. He had bushy eyebrows and was pale, thin, and tall, at least twenty years her senior, and he frowned a great deal and spent far too much time potting orchids in his orangery.

However, she had been wrong.

Very stupidly wrong.

Because the Earl of Stoneleigh was wickedly handsome in a way the aristocrats of her acquaintance and imagination alike were not. He wore buff trousers and a white shirt, which clung to tremendously broad shoulders and strained over his chest. He sported a small neck cloth—quite informal, really—and not a hint of country tweed. A finely trimmed beard decorated the sharp angle of his well-defined jaw. His eyes were shockingly blue, like a summer sky over her family's estate, Talleyrand Park, and unobscured by spectacles.

He was not pale at all, but kissed by the sun, looking far more like a laborer than an aristocrat. Indeed, he did not appear as if he had spent any time at all within an orangery, potting orchids or otherwise. The earl was lean but not thin, decidedly not twenty years her senior, and he was frowning, but that was perhaps down to the remnants of something dark on his handsome face and the fact that he was wet.

Dripping, in fact.

It looked rather as if someone had poured a pail of water over his head. Perhaps someone had.

Oh dear.

She had a feeling it was one of her wayward charges. The youngest, Lady Mary, was the likely culprit.

"Can you not imagine why I might wish an audience this morning?" Stoneleigh asked her, sounding grim.

She bit her lip, not wishing to point out the obvious. It was plain from the expression on Stoneleigh's countenance that he did not like her much. She couldn't countenance what she had done that merited such enmity already. But then, his reaction likely had far more to do with the soaked state of his person than with Corliss herself.

"Perhaps you wished to welcome me to Knightly Abbey," she suggested brightly, before belatedly recalling that she wasn't a guest here.

That she wasn't Lady Corliss Collingwood here. She was not even her pseudonym, C. Talleyrand, here, which had already graced the three books she'd written and published previously.

Instead, she was Miss Brinton, the capable governess. A young lady of fine breeding who had fallen upon unfortunate circumstances and had been forced to earn her bread, not one of the cossetted and beloved daughters of the Earl of Leydon. To further research for the latest novel she was writing, which she was determined would be the novel that granted her the financial independence she so longed for, Corliss had decided to become the heroine.

"Welcome indeed," Stoneleigh said, the words steeped in sarcasm. "Have you any notion where your charges are?"

Drat.

"Of course I do," she lied, watching as two droplets dripped from his hair to the carpets. "I was just on my way to gather them for today's lessons."

He raised a brow. "I presume you are wondering why it looks as if I were wandering about in a rainstorm."

"It isn't for me to question, my lord," she murmured, yet again reminding herself of her position within this household, so unlike her everyday circumstances.

That was how *Miss Brinton* would answer such a question.

He leaned closer, as if he were imparting a great secret. "I'll tell you why. It's because someone planted a pail of water above my bedchamber door, with the intention that when I exited, the pail would empty itself on me."

Oh dear.

Had Lady Mary done something so wicked? Corliss bit her lip to stifle the startled laughter threatening to burst free. The notion of a child intending to make so much mischief was quite laughable. She and her twin sister Criseyde had been quite the hoydens in their youth. But not even they had ever dared such a prank.

"Are you amused, madam?" Stoneleigh growled.

She swallowed hard and forced herself to think of something that didn't involve intrepid girls who rigged a bucket to fall on their uncle's head. "Of course not, my lord. I merely... have something in my eye."

Biting her lip to tamp down her mirth, she dabbed gently at her eye with the back of her hand.

The earl's gaze had narrowed on her. Truly, his height and well-muscled form were breathtaking.

"Where?" he demanded.

She blinked. Surely he could not mean to help her with the imaginary dust mote in her eye? "I'm certain I managed to resolve the problem, although I do thank you for your gracious offer of assistance."

"The *children*," he elaborated through clenched teeth. "I was asking where they are. You said you know where they are, and I wish to have a word with Lady Mary myself. As I'm sure you will agree, this manner of misbehavior is reprehensible. It cannot continue."

Oh. Her cheeks went hot. What a goose she was, overwhelmed by one handsome earl. Skin tanned from the sun, large hands, and compelling eyes should not so entrance her that she lost her sense of purpose. Coming here had been a risk. One she may not have the opportunity to take again. If she wanted to accurately portray Miss Brinton, she had to cease being such a ninny, her head so easily turned.

"Naturally, I agree, my lord," she said, aiming to placate him in the hopes his ire was reserved for his niece and not for herself. "I will have a stern word with Lady Mary concerning this outrage."

As soon as I can find her.

Naturally, Corliss didn't say that aloud. Because admitting she had no idea where her four charges were on her first day as a governess seemed poor form indeed. Not the sort of mistake a formidable governess like Miss Brinton would make.

"Thank you." He was frowning, considering her with a shrewd gaze she could not help but to fear saw too much.

"You are aware of the reason you were hired, are you not, Miss..."

His query trailed off, and she realized he either had forgotten or did not know her name.

"Brinton," she supplied. "Of course, my lord. Please rest assured that I will not tolerate ill-becoming pranks whilst the ladies are in my care."

He inclined his head. "I have been told you have wrought miracles in your former situation. I am afraid we may be in need of a few miracles of our own here at Knightly Abbey. My nieces have been running wild since their mother died, and matters didn't improve with the death of my brother. They have run off every governess thus far. Nonetheless, I am sure you are made of sterner stuff. Lead the way to the hellions, if you please."

"As you wish, my lord," she said faintly, wondering if she had been too effusive in the praise of Miss Brinton which she had written in her own hand. Likely so. Why had no one mentioned before now that her charges had chased away her every predecessor? "Come with me."

Pretending as if she knew where to find them in this unfamiliar estate, she glided past him with confidence that was entirely feigned. Down the hall from the nursery she went, surreptitiously peeking into opened chamber doors along the way. She reasoned that she could make a perambulation of the entire edifice with Stoneleigh trailing in her wake if she must. Sooner or later, she would have to find her recalcitrant charges.

All four of them: Lady Mary, Lady Henrietta, Lady Beatrice, and Lady Alice.

Four ladies could not possibly keep themselves hidden.

Could they?

As she progressed down the hall and approached the staircase, she began to worry her deception would soon be obvious to the earl. Until she heard peals of laughter fluttering up to her from below. Young, feminine voices she recognized from her brief meeting with her new charges the evening before, just after she had arrived late from the train in York.

"Alice has won again!" cried one of the girls, punctuating her announcement with a rather unladylike giggle.

"Do let us have another race! I am convinced Alice cheated."

"My ladies, I do not think it prudent…"

The chiding voice of the housekeeper, Mrs. Oak, reached her next.

Followed by a delighted exclamation from one of the older girls. "On the count of three! One, two, three!"

Grimly, Corliss hastened her pace, descending stairs two at a time as the scene unfolding below was revealed to her. At the base of the stairs, near an anxious-looking Mrs. Oak, stood Lady Henrietta, the eldest girl at nine years old, and Lady Beatrice, who was second oldest at eight years of age and appeared to be leading the affair. The younger two girls, Lady Alice, who was seven, and Lady Mary who was a spirited five, were sliding down the banister, one on each side.

Racing, apparently.

Her heart leapt into her throat as the youngest girl slipped and nearly went toppling from the polished rail before she dismounted and landed with a graceful flourish that belied the peril she'd so recently faced.

"My ladies," she snapped, hoping her voice would possess the same stern lash her own governess's had. "I demand that you cease this dangerous nonsense at once!"

Corliss gathered her skirts in her hands and practically leapt down the remainder of the stairs, not caring about decorum. But then, when had she ever been concerned with something as boring as proper comportment? Her parents had always been pleased to allow her life to be governed by her own rules. And what rules they had been. They'd led her here, to this latest—perhaps misguided—chapter, after all.

Four faces turned toward her, eyes the same vivid blue as their uncle's blinking and wide. They all looked so very similar that it was plain to see they were sisters, all brunettes with curls framing their heart-shaped faces.

Laughter died.

Excellent. She had their attention now.

"Sliding down the banister is dangerous," she warned them sharply, even though she had done the same on many occasions at Talleyrand Park as a willful young girl. They needn't know *that*. "And it is most certainly behavior which is unbecoming to ladies."

"I hadn't reckoned the first order of the day would be a lesson on the finer points of sliding down banisters," drawled a voice at her back.

Her shoulders stiffened, for Stoneleigh was challenging her authority before her charges. But then, he was her *employer*, she reminded herself, schooling her features into a mask of impeccable sangfroid as she turned toward him. To do so was his right.

"Would you care to join us, my lord?" she asked him, offering a polite, if not precisely welcoming, smile.

For a moment, the span of her heart's frantic beat and no more, he stared at her. That astounding gaze seemed to sear her soul.

And then he clasped his hands behind his back, strolling forward with the stride of a man who was powerful and well-muscled and *knew* it.

"I would like a moment with my nieces before your banister lesson continues, if you do not mind," he said.

Her *banister lesson*.

As if she had ordered the four of them to conduct races

down the grand staircase. If only she were Lady Corliss. She would have given him a sound upbraiding for his cheek. But she was not herself. Lady Corliss would never wear such a hideous gown, and nor would she rusticate in Yorkshire attempting to coerce four wayward hoydens into behaving as ladies. Lady Corliss would never dream of taking a meal below stairs, and she would not be sniffed at by the house-keeper, who had made comments about her youth and appearance upon her arrival.

"Of course, my lord," she said magnanimously. Through clenched teeth. "Whatever pleases you."

Lady Corliss died a bit inside just then, shriveling like a summer rose caught in the first autumn frost. An indication that perhaps this post would not be as much of a boon for her novel as she had hoped. She hadn't anticipated the burdens a governess faced, nor what it was like to be a member of the servant class. She was already gaining a new appreciation for the governesses she had known in her life.

The earl raised a brow. "Take care with what latitude you grant the members of this household, Miss Brinton. Let that be *your* first lesson."

She had a feeling it was far more warning than lesson.

CHAPTER 2

*K*night grimaced at the stack of correspondence on Robert's desk—a desk which he refused to think of as his own—and rose to his feet, abandoning the seemingly ceaseless pile for now. He'd had a letter from his old school chum, the Earl of Anglesey, who had recently married. Knight had called at Barlowe Park on his path north, but Anglesey and his new bride had been honeymooning. He had invited them to pay a call to Knightly Abbey when they returned, and the earl had accepted.

A familiar face—and trusted friend—would be most welcome now. The rest of the correspondence, however, had blurred together like watercolors in a painting. He wasn't accustomed to so many people requiring so many different things from him. Boxing had been much simpler than being an earl was proving to be.

And Lord knew he'd never wanted to be an earl.

He'd become a prizefighter to reclaim his life as his own. The second son, in search of something more for himself than the limited options available to him in England. And yet, ironically, he'd been forced to return to a life of duty and responsibility he'd never wanted. His life, once again, was at the mercy of an endless and dubious line of obligation. Obligation, tenants, improvements to be made, land to be sold, land to be bought, mining rights, *sheep*.

Christ, the sheep.

And nieces who were hellions.

And a governess who was…

No, he wouldn't think of Miss Brinton now. He'd learned her name. He'd learned, too, the way her hips swayed as she walked. The musical lilt of her voice. Allowing her to occupy any more space in his mind was a dreadful idea.

Passing a hand over his jaw and sighing, Knight stalked across the study, drawn toward the bank of windows overlooking the Knightly Abbey park. If he couldn't be outside, at least he could provide himself with the illusion of the freedom he had once enjoyed. Until he could escape this blasted prison.

A knock sounded at his study door, and a glance at his pocket watch revealed it was likely time for more mundane, relentless tasks.

"Come," he called grimly.

The door opened to reveal Robert's steward, Mr. Smithson—for Knight would not accept the man as his responsibility any more than he would the furniture—hovering at the threshold.

The older man bowed. "I've come to review estate matters with you as planned, my lord. Does the time still suit you?"

Of course it didn't suit him. *Never* would be far more agreeable as to when they might review estate matters in greater detail. But Knight couldn't say that. Instead, he stood in a slat of unlikely sunlight creeping across the fading Axminster, allowing it to warm his shoulders. He couldn't help but to feel chased by all the burdens threatening to choke him and the irritating attraction he shouldn't feel for the one woman on whom he had pinned his hopes for abandoning Knightly Abbey.

"The present will suit, Mr. Smithson," he said with the greatest of reluctance.

The steward entered, discreetly closing the door at his back, bringing with him a stack of documents which he placed on the desk by the interminable pile Knight had just abandoned. Mr. Smithson's brown hair was perfectly combed in a neat part down the middle. His spectacles were perched on the bridge of his nose, and he was regarding Knight as he imagined the man might look at a fearsome insect which had just descended from the heavens to eat all the crops in the tenants' fields.

An odd combination of fear and uncertainty, Knight thought.

"Have we many matters to discuss?" he asked, dreading the answer.

"Countless of these matters have been delayed for far too long, given the length of time between Lord Stoneleigh's death and your return, my lord," Mr. Smithson said, sounding regretful. "A great deal needs to be attended to over the course of a year, particularly given the tenants. Candlemas is approaching in but a few months, and the tenancies must be reviewed."

Ah, here was the scold. Not that any of the men and women in his employ would dare to gainsay him. Nor would they ever directly give voice to the apparent consensus they all shared—that he should have returned to Knightly Abbey immediately upon receiving news of Robert's untimely demise. But it was there in their solemn gazes, in the careful manner with which they all chose their words.

"Why can you not review the tenancies?" he asked Mr. Smithson. "Did you not do so last year?"

"His lordship had already made his advisements before falling ill," the steward said, blinking behind his spectacles in a way that rather nettled Knight.

Was there something in the fellow's eye? Surely not a tear at the reminder of his former employer. Robert had been an arsehole to everyone who was unfortunate enough to know him, Knight was reasonably certain.

"How good of his lordship," he said wryly, thinking it quite ironic that his brother continued to haunt him in death as he had in life.

"His lordship preferred to review them," Mr. Smithson added.

"I am decidedly not my brother," Knight pointed out.

For one thing, he was a head taller than Robert had been, and larger in every way, his build made to be a prizefighter. For another, he had never swilled himself to death. Oh, no one had admitted the cause of Robert's illness. But Knight wasn't a fool. His brother had been a great many things, and he had shown a stern face to the world, but he had been a drunkard since the age of fifteen.

"Of course, my lord," Mr. Smithson said agreeably. "Forgive me. I didn't mean to imply you were. I was merely attempting to relay the manner in which I am accustomed to proceeding with the tenancies."

Knight didn't give a goddamn about the tenancies. Or about Knightly Abbey. If the blasted estate weren't part of the entail, he'd have happily sold it and forgotten he had ever once walked its halls. It was just another burden, as far as he was concerned. Another bitter memory from a past laden with hurt, disappointments, and failure.

Another impediment to returning to America and the life he'd built for himself there and to upholding his championship title. He could not answer a challenge when he was mired in Yorkshire with four hoydens and a nettlesome steward.

And a governess he wouldn't have minded bedding, had she been anyone else.

Never mind that.

He sighed again and decided to try a different tactic. "Thank you for your diligence, Mr. Smithson. As you are no doubt aware, I'm woefully unprepared for the duties facing me. However, I'm confident in your abilities as steward to guide me in the proper direction. I give you leave to make all the decisions on my behalf."

"But my lord, I cannot do so," Mr. Smithson protested.

He resumed pacing. "Why not?"

"Because I am not the Earl of Stoneleigh."

Knight almost blurted that he wasn't either, but he stopped himself. Because he *was*, damn it all. He ought to have feigned his death in America. Let his noxious cousin claim the title. The thought had crossed his mind more than once, but The Bruiser Knight was too well reported on in the American newspapers for such a plan to be feasible.

"Very well, Mr. Smithson," he conceded. "Prepare a report on the tenancies. I'll review it."

"I have already, my lord, and it awaits your perusal."

Of course he had.

"Are there other matters which must be attended today?" he demanded, feeling restless and itchy.

His fingers flexed at his sides, opening and closing into fists. Thank God he'd found a few overgrown stable lads who suited as sparring partners. He couldn't unleash the full fury of his fists on them, but at least he could have a means of easing some of his frustration and keeping his body agile when he wasn't training.

"There is an iron and coal company desirous of a mining

lease," Mr. Smithson announced. "The former earl advised that he was amenable to such an arrangement being made."

In Knight's mind, he was already in the stable yard, feinting right and blocking a blow. But the steward was awaiting a response.

Knight rolled his shoulders. It wasn't good for his form to allow himself to be as tense as he had been since his arrival in England, and he knew it.

"Excellent," he said distractedly.

"You are in agreement then, my lord?"

Was he?

He pulled at the collar of his shirt, which suddenly felt too tight. "Prepare a report on the benefits to the estate, please. I'll review that as well."

"Very good, my lord." Mr. Smithson was nodding, relief in his voice. "There is also a horse farm of five hundred acres which borders the estate and has been offered by the land agent. Would you care to purchase it?"

"No," he said instantly.

He didn't want to acquire any more land than that which he already had to contend with. Six thousand acres were quite sufficient at present, thank you.

"But my lord, the land is currently valued at five-and-twenty pounds per acre, however, it should fetch one hundred pounds per acre if the mining lease is granted and becomes common knowledge."

Bloody hell.

He blew out a breath. "What does the property entail?"

"A house and several farm buildings which may be of use," Mr. Smithson reported.

"And what did the former earl advise concerning this land offer?"

The steward pushed his spectacles up the bridge of his nose. "The former earl's death preceded the land offer."

A headache was beginning to thump to life behind Knight's eyes. He rolled his shoulders again, grimacing at a familiar twinge of pain he'd been suffering ever since that last bout with Billy O'Brien.

"What is your recommendation for the land offer, Mr. Smithson?" he rephrased, trying again.

"In my opinion, the investment would be worthwhile, despite landed property at present being an unprofitable endeavor for most."

Investments. Those were long-term endeavors which denoted an intention to remain dedicated for years. In the case of an estate such as Knightly Abbey, a lifetime. Knight's mouth went dry and his throat constricted at the prospect.

"I will defer to your expertise in the matter," he told the steward. "We'll purchase the land. Is there anything else which is pressing? If not, I have some other matters awaiting my attention."

Matters such as using his body for one of the two divine purposes for which God had made it. The first was fighting. The second was fucking.

In this instance, he intended to let his fists fly and work off some of the tension coiled inside him like a watch spring.

"Decisions must be made concerning the draining as well," Mr. Smithson said.

"Later," Knight said. "Tomorrow."

The steward pushed at his spectacles again, his expression concerned. "As it pleases you, my lord."

There was the rub. Nothing about this godforsaken place or the bloody responsibilities weighing on him pleased him.

"Thank you, Mr. Smithson." Gathering what was left of his wits, Knight left the study, restless and in desperate need of losing himself.

~

FOR THE SECOND day in a row, Corliss had lost her charges.

She wandered through the quiet stillness of the nursery, looking beneath every piece of furniture, lest the hellions were hiding themselves somewhere. Two days into her tenure here at Knightly Abbey, and she was already exhausted from attempting to lead four girls who had apparently trampled over every governess preceding her. She couldn't help but to think of herself and wonder whether she had been so troublesome for her own governess. But then, the girls had been orphaned, their little hearts terribly bruised, their worlds torn asunder. She had come of age with both her parents doting on her.

"Lady Mary," she called. "Lady Alice?"

No answer.

"Lady Henrietta? Lady Beatrice?"

Not even a giggle to indicate they were anywhere nearby.

She heaved a sigh. The morning had begun with such promise. And when she had granted them a break from their reading, she had returned to find them gone.

Being a governess was far more difficult than she had supposed. And if she did not take care, her post would be over before it had truly begun. The earl had made his disapproval of her more than apparent the day before when they had caught the girls racing each other down the banisters. If he were to discover that she had no notion of where his nieces had disappeared to today, she shuddered to think what his reaction would be.

And she could not afford to be sacked.

She needed to immerse herself in the role of governess so that she could make her Miss Brinton as sympathetic and realistic as possible.

One thing was certain. Her charges were not within these four walls. If she wanted to find them before Lord Stoneleigh did, she would have to go looking for them. With a weary sigh, Corliss left the nursery and began her search of the surrounding chambers. Predictably, the girls were nowhere to be found. Nary a wardrobe nor a bed was overlooked. She stopped short of his lordship's chamber—she would most certainly not trespass within the earl's private domain.

At a loss as to what had become of the miscreants, Corliss descended the stairs, ears and eyes attuned for the slightest hint of her charges. But as always, her mind was whirling. Thinking. Perhaps a turn of plot such as this would heighten her novel. In addition to a brooding, handsome lord with dangerous secrets, Miss Brinton could also face charges who were recalcitrant.

She was so lost in her mind that she nearly collided with Mrs. Oak in the great hall.

"Miss Brinton," the woman said coldly. "You should take care with your haste."

The chastisement stung. And it shocked her to realize that no one had chastised her as Lady Corliss. Not ever. The sensation—being reprimanded, taken to task—was unfamiliar. Uncomfortable. Tears pricked the backs of her eyes, and she furiously blinked them away, thinking she would likely endure greater hardships than a sharply disapproving domestic over the course of the next few weeks.

She forced a smile she did not feel. "Forgive me, Mrs. Oak. I should have been watching where I was going."

"I would imagine your haste has something to do with Lady Mary, Lady Alice, Lady Beatrice, and Lady Henrietta having gone out to the stables," the housekeeper said, her voice clipped, her lips pinched.

The stables? What in heaven's name were the girls doing in the stables?

She was careful not to allow her surprise to show. "Yes, of course it was. If you will excuse me, Mrs. Oak. I'm off to fetch them now for the remainder of their afternoon lessons."

"Indeed, Miss Brinton. I suggest you keep a tighter watch over your charges in the future. His lordship will not be pleased if I'm forced to inform him of your dereliction." With an unkind smirk, the housekeeper continued on her way, presumably to visit her unfortunate personality on another unsuspecting member of the household.

Gritting her teeth, Corliss hastened to the doors and let herself outside into the cool, late-autumn air. The moment she crossed the approach, her feet beating a hasty path to the stables, she regretted her lack of wrap. The air possessed a definitive nip, and a particularly vindictive wind whipped at her skirts. The sky was leaden and gray, but it wasn't raining yet.

As she reached the stables, a cacophony of sounds reached her.

"Show us how you bested Billy O'Brien in Mississippi!" shouted a male voice.

"Punch him in the nose, Uncle," called a youthful, girlish voice in a most unladylike fashion.

Good heavens, what was happening in the stables?

"No," said another feminine voice. "Punch him in the breadbasket!"

The breadbasket? *Punch* him?

As she stormed inside, she drew to a halt at the sight before her. The Earl of Stoneleigh had squared off with one of the grooms. They stood between rows of stabled horses, surrounded by hanging tack and the familiar scent of horse-flesh, squaring off on a floor strewn with dirt and hay.

Both men had their fists raised. As she watched, the groom took a swing at the earl which he easily sidestepped, chuckling as if he found the notion of one of his servants attacking him amusing. And ringing the entire spectacle were grooms and all four of Corliss's missing charges, cheering.

"What is going on here?" she demanded, quite forgetting in her horror at the scene before her that she was Miss Brinton.

And a governess must not demand anything of anyone save her charges. Particularly not the earl who had given her this position. Even if he was currently engaged in a bout of fisticuffs with one of his grooms whilst his lady nieces cheered him on.

"Oh, Miss Brinton," Lady Beatrice said with a grin that told Corliss the girl had likely been the leader of this particular scrape. "How good of you to join us. Uncle was showing us how he defeated Billy O'Brien in Mississippi!"

Corliss didn't know where to begin.

Many pairs of eyes were fixed on her. Gawking grooms, troublesome young ladies, and one wickedly handsome earl. Their gazes clashed, and she felt the connection as surely as a touch, his mocking and hard as it meshed with hers. How had she managed to forget that wide, slashing jaw shadowed with a dark, neatly trimmed beard? Her eyes dipped to his mouth, which was currently flattened in an expression of disapproval, as if she had once again committed a sin for which he would judge her later. He was rugged in a way most lords were not, brawny and muscled.

Despite the damp chill in the stables, he wore no coat, and he had rolled the sleeves of his white shirt up to his elbows, revealing strong forearms. His hands, still clenched in fists, were larger than she had realized on their previous meeting. She struggled to remind herself that she wasn't meant to be admiring the Earl of Stoneleigh's dashing figure. She was meant to be playing governess to his wayward nieces.

"Have you come to watch as well, Miss Brinton?" the earl asked, his tone taunting.

As if he dared her to say that yes, indeed, she had come to watch. To watch *him*. She had to cease staring. Lord Stoneleigh was the sort of man who knew precisely the effect he had upon women.

Her ears went hot, and she was sure her cheeks were red. "I was seeking Ladies Mary, Alice, Henrietta, and Beatrice, my lord. They are overdue for their next lessons."

A dark brow rose, his full, sensual lips twisting. "Surely not more banister lessons?"

"Lessons of the ordinary sort, my lord," she said, forcing another smile.

Likely, it resembled a wince more than aught else. Yesterday's folly had not been forgiven, it would seem.

"Oh, but Miss Brinton," Lady Mary said, pouting quite prettily. "I wanted to see how Uncle bested O'Brien!"

Her curiosity defeated her common sense. "Who is Mr. O'Brien?" she asked, just a touch more crossly than she had intended.

"The Boston Brute," Lady Alice informed her, as if the fellow's name should have already been known to her.

"The Boston Brute?" she repeated weakly.

"The champion," said one of the stable lads, grinning crookedly.

"*Former* champion," corrected another groom, giving the other a good-natured jab with his elbow.

Corliss wondered grimly if she had somehow stepped into an alternate universe in which it was perfectly ordinary for an earl to be squaring off with a groom whilst his lady nieces watched on. She had no notion of what the girls and the stable hands were speaking of.

"Who is the present champion?" she found herself asking weakly.

"Uncle is," Lady Mary said proudly.

Her gaze flew back to Stoneleigh, who was watching her

with a stare that made her feel flushed despite the cold damp hanging in the air.

He shrugged as if the appellation hardly mattered. "For the moment."

"Show us, Uncle!" Lady Mary exclaimed in pleading fashion, clapping her small hands together in her excitement. "Show us how you defeated O'Brien."

"It was with a few right punches, was it not, my lord?" asked one of the lads. "Less than eleven minutes till you bested the Boston Brute."

Stoneleigh was a pugilist? And a champion one, at that. His muscled physique and those massive hands made sense now. She had known that the earl had just returned from abroad, and that he had inherited the title about a year ago upon his elder brother, the former earl's death. The gossip below stairs was difficult to ignore. However, she hadn't realized Stoneleigh had been boxing in America.

Despite herself, she was ridiculously, foolishly intrigued by the notion.

Corliss shook her head, as if doing so might remove all such unwanted thoughts, and turned her attention to her charges. "My ladies, your lessons are commencing. We should leave his lordship and the grooms to their..." Her words trailed off as she struggled to explain the ridiculousness unfolding before her. "Their celebration of Lord Stoneleigh's victory."

There, she reasoned. It was as politely as she could describe the unseemly act of brawling with one's stable hands before one's lady nieces. *Good heavens*, little wonder the girls were all hellions. It clearly ran in their blood.

"Lessons are boring," Lady Mary announced.

"We want to see Uncle's winning blow," Lady Henrietta added.

"It will only be a moment," Lady Alice added.

"Show us, Uncle!" Lady Beatrice encouraged.

A small smile played about the earl's lips, but he was still gazing directly at Corliss. As if he found her reaction to this entire unacceptable affair amusing. As if he were testing her mettle alongside his wayward nieces. And perhaps he was.

"Miss Brinton?" he asked. "Will you allow it?"

Oh, now she was to be held responsible for this outrageous showing? Her parents were unapologetically eccentric, and they had given Corliss and her siblings remarkable freedom, particularly at Talleyrand Park. However, she could honestly say that she had never watched anyone sparring with a groom before. And despite herself, Corliss wanted to see the blow. Wanted to watch the earl's body in motion. To stare at him some more and have it be perfectly acceptable.

She was sure she should not allow it. She should coolly demand that her charges return to the nursery at once.

But there was a challenge in Stoneleigh's expression, and she had never been able to resist one.

"I will allow it," she conceded, before adding sternly. "Just this once."

The earl turned to the groom who was his sparring partner, fists at the ready. "On the count of three, Jack. Give me your best."

The younger man looked uncertain. "Are you sure, my lord?"

"Of course I am," Stoneleigh said easily. "On the count of three, now. One, two, three."

The groom swung wildly, his fist arcing through the air as Stoneleigh effortlessly pranced out of the way. "Excellent attempt, lad," he said. "I'll give you another chance."

A chorus of cheers rose from the assemblage. Corliss's heart leapt in her throat as the groom attempted to land another punch, his movements fast. But once again, Stoneleigh neatly avoided the blow.

"Another," he ordered the groom, appearing to be enjoying himself.

Indeed, the earl was *grinning*.

It occurred to Corliss that he hadn't made any attempt at returning the blows. Instead, he was allowing the other man to give him the full brunt of his swinging punches. The groom's fist flew. The earl feinted left, then right. The groom continued, spurred on by the cacophony of his fellow stable hands. Each blow missed, until finally, the earl hesitated a moment too long, and a punch landed on his upper arm. The entire interaction lasted seconds but seemed to Corliss as if it had been intentional. As if the earl had allowed the groom to punch him.

The crowd jeered and cheered in equal measure.

The groom's eyes went wide. "Oh my lord, I'm so sorry! I didn't harm you, did I?"

"This old hide is hard as steel," Stoneleigh reassured him with a rueful grin. "And now you can remind all these lads that you landed a blow on The Bruiser Knight."

The lad's chest seemed to swell with pride before Corliss's eyes.

"I did, didn't I?" he asked, strutting forward with a new confidence in his step.

Corliss's stare slipped back to Stoneleigh, and their gazes clashed. A prickle of awareness flitted over her skin like a caress. He raised a brow at her and gave her a small grin. It made her belly do an odd little flip. She tamped down the sensation and forced her attention back to her four charges.

"Lady Mary, Lady Alice, Lady Beatrice, and Lady Henrietta," she said firmly, "do come with me now, if you please. We have lessons to attend."

She waited until the ladies were reluctantly marching before her, leaving the stables, and then she turned to go, feeling the earl's stare on her with each step she took.

CHAPTER 3

The hour was early, the air holding a distinctly damp chill that was purely England, but Knight was awake and dressed, performing the exercises he had learned in training that kept his body strong and capable. In the absence of true sparring partners, and so far removed from the boxing tours he had spent the last few years engaged in, he needed some means of maintaining his form. He'd never minded the solitude of dawn, and wherever he traveled, he always endeavored to find a park or other similarly situated place where he could lose himself in the mechanics of his body. Two-mile walks and runs were a part of his daily regimen every morning, without fail.

Knightly Abbey was sufficiently sprawling that he had taken a different route every morning since his arrival, and he had yet to repeat his patterns. The newness helped assuage the restlessness settling into his marrow, along with the fear he might find himself forever trapped in Yorkshire, attending the eternal duties he'd inherited. He hadn't spent this much time in the same place since he'd last trained in

New York. And then, remaining where he was had possessed a true purpose: he'd been training to defeat Billy O'Brien.

And defeat him he had. Only to learn of Robert's death and the duties awaiting him in the place he'd once, long ago, called home. The news had been as much of a shock as a knockout blow. Knight had never intended to return. Yet now here he was, running beneath a gray sky, a world away from the life he'd spent the last decade forging for himself.

Bitterness was acrid in his mouth, like the damp scent of the earth rising in the heavy morning air as he rounded a bend in the tree-lined path and nearly collided with someone who squealed and rushed out of his way. He veered to the left, avoiding the impact with instincts honed from years in the ring, and stopped, his breathing heavy, to apologize.

The person he'd nearly trampled was not just *someone*. She was a feminine someone, wearing a jaunty hat and a scarlet gown peeping from beneath a complementing dolman lined with fur. Fine clothes. An equally fine figure, with a cinched waist emphasizing generous breasts, a graceful neck, creamy skin, and sun-dappled hair peeping from beneath her hat. Recognition dawned in his gut, in a feeling that bloomed low and spread, filling him with heat that had nothing to do with the layers of garments he'd donned to aid in his exercise.

"Miss Brinton," he rasped.

Her gloved hand was pressed over her heart, her brown eyes wide, pink lips forming an *o* of surprise that made him think for one stupid moment about setting his own mouth there and kissing away her startlement.

"My lord," she managed, still pale, the freckles on her nose more pronounced this morning.

Was it a trick of the light? Or was she even lovelier than she had been that day in the stables, blazing with disapproval as she watched his pretend bout with Jack? Was it the boldness of her gown, such a vivid shade of red, peeking through? Was it the confidence in her gaze?

"Forgive me," he managed, irritated that other parts of his body were becoming roused, all by standing here in the six o'clock gloom after running a mile and a half. Irritated that *she* was the source of his cock rising to attention in his trousers. "It wasn't my intention to trample you."

"I don't suppose it was," she said lightly, "or else you would find yourself in need of a governess once more."

Yes, and he couldn't afford that, particularly not when his nieces were such devilish scamps. One of them had tied the laces of all his boots together, which he had discovered that morning as he'd prepared to set out on his daily run. This governess had certainly failed to live up to the promise and praise which had been heaped upon her in the letters which had won her the position. But the only fate worse than a governess who could fail to oversee his hellion nieces was no governess at all. And that was why he had allowed her to remain despite his suspicion that the girls were running wild over Knightly Abbey and Miss Brinton both. Had the praise been an exaggeration, he wondered now?

"I was fortunate indeed to find a governess of your impeccable experience," he said smoothly, unable to resist testing her. "Your letter of recommendation was the most effusive of any that were received for the situation."

The girls were troublesome, it was true. But a governess of her skill should not have lost them twice in as many days.

Her gaze darted to a point over his shoulder, her lips tightening, shoulders stiffening. "Effusive, you say? In what way?"

Knight told himself he shouldn't question her further. He could settle the estate matters and be sailing back to America soon, even if Miss Brinton was rather inept at her position. Mr. Smithson could damn well telegraph him about sheep farmers and tenants whose lands were filled with twitch grass. But the notion didn't settle properly in his gut.

Now that he knew his nieces and they were not indistinct burdens an ocean away, he had discovered tender feelings for them where none had previously dwelled. He loved the wayward girls. They were his flesh and blood, and although they were hoydens, they were *his* hoydens to protect. It was the devil of a coil in which he found himself, torn between two worlds.

"They were flowery," he elaborated. "I recall the letter calling you an angel walking amongst mere mortals, capable of calming even the most recalcitrant of children and encouraging them to excel at their lessons."

Her gaze flew back to his, narrowing ever so slightly. "I do not find it an excessive description at all. I thought it rather heartening of Lord Lindlow to speak of me in such glowing terms."

"Lindlow?" He stroked his jaw, the name bearing a false ring to it. "I thought it was Lindley."

"It was?" she asked, her voice going unnaturally high before she cleared her throat. "It was Lind*low*, my lord. I fear you are mistaken. I assure you that I know the name of my previous employer, having spent several years at my post."

Her initial reaction suggested otherwise.

"Ah yes," he mused, suddenly forgetting all about the rest of his run in favor of interrogating his captivating governess. "How many years were you at that post again, Miss Brinton?"

Years seemed unlikely. She looked to be no more than five-and-twenty. Vivacious and spirited in a way his own governess as a lad most certainly had never been. But then, Miss Bramwell had been altogether joyless and had delighted in administering punishments. Knight had been relieved to be sent away to school and be delivered from the harsh woman's rule.

"Four years," Miss Brinton said, her gaze traveling over his form, curiosity sparkling in those brown depths. "What in heaven's name are you wearing, Lord Stoneleigh?"

He glanced down at the bulky knitted attire he always donned for his morning exercise. "It's a sweater. I wear it whenever I run."

The garment helped him to sweat, aided in hardening his muscles, and kept him in fighting condition. He had about a dozen such pieces, all made in New York by his trainer's wife.

"A sweater," she repeated, her eyes still sweeping over him, overheating him as efficiently as the sweater.

Damn. Perhaps it had been too long since a woman had been in his bed. The adulation of the ladies in the crowd, all seeking to have their piece of The Bruiser Knight, had waned in its appeal after Ida, and he had never been inclined toward relationships of a more permanent nature following her betrayal.

Miss Brinton reached toward him as if to stroke his sweater, and his finely honed boxing reflexes came to life. He caught her wrist in a light grip, keeping her from touching him. And yet, now that he had her in his grasp, he found himself having difficulty releasing her. He was not wearing gloves, and his thumb found its way to the deliciously soft skin of her inner wrist, just over her pulse, which beat a rapid rhythm. White-hot awareness shot through him at that touch, the sensation of her, so warm and yielding, so feminine and alluring.

He forced himself to release her, severing the moment, the madness it had brought to life within him.

She stepped back, a charming flush staining her cheeks. "Forgive me. I didn't intend to be so…"

Adorable, he thought. *Lovely.*

"Forward," she finished lamely. "It is merely that I've never seen anything quite like it."

"My trainer introduced me to the garment," he told her, wondering how they had come to be discussing him when he had been questioning Miss Brinton and her dubious recommendation and experience. "What are you doing venturing out at this time of the morning, Miss Brinton?"

"I was taking the air." Her lips curled upward. "Everything is so still at this hour, quite peaceful. At home, I walk every morning. Being alone with one's thoughts, reveling in the beauty of nature, is a lovely way to begin the day."

All he could think was that *she* was lovely, to say nothing of the day. And God, when she smiled, she made him want to smile back at her. To linger with her in the chill of the early morning's gloom. To flirt with her. To kiss her. But he still had half a mile to run and she was his nieces' governess, and he didn't dally with freckle-nosed innocents.

"Where is home?" he asked, curious to learn more about her.

He told himself it was for good reason. He was responsible for his nieces. If she was lying about her experience, if she was unfit for the position, he would have to find someone else. Just like he would have to review the damned recommendations for tenancies before Candlemas.

"Buckinghamshire," she answered readily, her smile fading. "I hope you don't mind if I take the air, my lord. The girls are not awake at this hour, and I forego breakfast in favor of my walk so that I am prepared to begin the day."

She didn't eat breakfast? He frowned, not liking the notion of her doing without.

"Why should you forego breakfast?"

"Mrs. Oak is firm in her schedule," she said. "I prefer my walk to the meal."

He took breakfast after he returned from his runs, and by

Knight's calculations, breakfasting at half past seven would not interfere with Miss Brinton's daily duties where his nieces were concerned.

"Nonsense," he found himself saying. "You shouldn't have to sacrifice a meal so you can take the air before your day begins. Mrs. Oak hasn't the liberty of being so inflexible with my meals. I dine at half past seven every morning. I insist you join me, starting today, Miss Brinton."

Her lips parted in surprise, and he found himself transfixed by them again—so pretty and pink and lush. Begging to be kissed.

"It would be inappropriate of me to impose on you, my lord," she denied demurely.

But now that the notion had occurred to him, he wasn't entertaining objections. If she dined with him daily, it would be an excellent opportunity to learn more about her and ascertain just how experienced she was. Yes, that was the reason he'd asked her. Not because he wished for her company. Nor because he wanted to watch those gorgeous lips from across the breakfast table.

At least, that was what he told himself.

A bloody sacrificial lamb, he was.

"It's hardly an imposition," he countered smoothly. "You'll be doing me a favor. I'm accustomed to being surrounded by people, and yet since I've returned to Knightly Abbey, I've been forced to endure a great deal of solitude. The company will be most welcome."

What was he saying? Why was he inviting Miss Brinton to dine with him? Now he would be subjected to watching her lovely brightness every morning, knowing he couldn't touch her.

Even so, the thought of her being forced to skip her meals so that she might walk displeased him.

"I suppose I could join you," she relented, her smile

returning. And it was almost shy this time, as if his invitation had pleased her and she didn't know precisely what to make of it.

Well, that made two of them.

"Excellent." He gave her a nod, deciding he must continue with his run before he did something even more foolish than asking the governess to join him for breakfast. Like press her to the sprawling tree trunk behind her and kiss her breathless. His cock twitched again at the thought, and he ruthlessly suppressed the desire attempting to rise. "If you'll excuse me, Miss Brinton, I must continue with my exercise. I shall see you at half past seven."

"Of course, my lord." She dipped into a small, polite curtsy which seemed at odds with the familiarity of their conversation and the privacy they shared, here on the path where no one else could see them.

And before he gave in to temptation, Knight took off into a run, feeling the governess's stare follow him with each step he took.

Stoneleigh had been correct.

Her fictional former employer was, in fact, named the Marquess of Lindley.

The first thing Corliss had done following her unexpected meeting with the earl that morning had been to race to her chamber, extract the manuscript which was in an ever-evolving state of drafting, and search it for the name of the lord who employed her heroine. Whilst she had been careful to match all the information in her novel with the letter of recommendation she had forged for herself—*I won't forget even the smallest detail,* she'd thought, feeling endlessly *clever at the time*—somehow, she had, in fact, forgotten. Lindley had become Lindlow.

As she tucked away her manuscript in its hiding place once more, she found herself hoping the earl would forget their conversation. Hoping, too, that he did not have the letter of recommendation remaining in his possession so that he might check her insistence that her employer had been named Lord Lindlow. Her stomach was heavy with the weight of dread as she dressed in a more subdued fashion.

Governess weeds, she liked to think of them, a reminder of who she was. Of who her character was. Miss Brinton was relegated to grays and blacks and dull browns. Unbecoming colors. Shapeless gowns that a governess forced to live on her annual wages would wear. Corliss saved the few, more colorful and ornate gowns she'd managed to pack away in her cases for when she was alone. Or when she *thought* she'd be alone. Like that morning.

As she fastened the hooks on her ugly brown day gown, her mind flitted back to the sight of the earl running toward her, his high cheekbones flushed with exertion, his dark hair bereft of a hat. He'd been wearing his odd sweater, along with corduroy trousers, and his eyes had seemed extra blue. So much of him had been buttoned up and hidden from view beneath layers. In his bulky training garments, he should not have been nearly so alluring.

And yet, he had been. Her heart had been hammering fast, and it hadn't had a thing to do with the fright he'd initially given her when he had rounded the bend and come racing alongside her, nearly sending her careening into the trees in her startlement. Rather, it had been the earl himself. He was compelling in a way no other gentleman of her acquaintance had ever been. No soft, idle lord. He was a man who used his body and his fists. An athlete. He was all strength and muscle, his form a well-honed machine that made her go a bit weak in the knees whenever she was in his presence, much to her dismay.

Because she was not Lady Corliss Collingwood at Knightly Abbey. And even if she hadn't placed herself in the shoes of her heroine for the sake of her half-written novel, she still had no interest in handsome, rakish, pugilist earls who likely had left a trail of hearts the length of America behind them.

No question of it, the Earl of Stoneleigh was trouble. One look at him was all it required for Corliss to be certain of that. The sort of trouble that induced ladies to ruination. The sort of trouble that made grown women want to throw themselves into his chest just to feel his arms wrap around them and see how firmly muscled he was. The sort of trouble that made thoughts of his kisses and his big, boxer's hands flit through her mind with alarming frequency, until she was staring at her reflection in the mirror, flushed and confused, her bodice still half-undone.

Shaking her head, she hastened to finish dressing. She pulled her hair into a more severe chignon, and glanced at the time on the mantel clock, discovering she had precisely two minutes to spare until half past seven. Which meant she had spent thirty minutes inwardly swooning over the Earl of Stoneleigh, also known as The Bruiser Knight, current boxing champion and far-too-sinfully attractive employer.

"Unacceptable, Corliss," she admonished herself aloud, taking a deep, steadying breath.

She would have to breakfast with him—a kindness she certainly hadn't expected, and one which was perhaps inappropriate—without entertaining any of these improper thoughts. She would have to be in his presence for the duration of her stay here at Knightly Abbey without flushing or staring at his mouth and wondering what it would feel like against hers. One month was all she had in total, the duration of her supposed stay with Aunt Louisa, until she had to return to Talleyrand Park before her mother and father discovered her deception. She could resist the Earl of Stoneleigh's allure for the remainder of that time, could she not?

She told herself so, but by the time she joined him in the dining room, her determination faltered. Stoneleigh stood at a sideboard laden with the sort of breakfast she was accustomed to consuming, rather than the simple below stairs fair she'd had for her few days at Knightly Abbey thus far as governess. Fresh fruit from the orangery, eggs, and bacon called to her surprisingly hungry stomach.

However, she wasn't sure which was more delicious, the earl, or the food.

He had changed out of his bulky sweater and corduroy and was instead dressed informally, his hair damp and combed back from his high forehead. Had he bathed upon his return from his run? It would seem he had, and she tried her best not to entertain the mental picture of Stoneleigh in his bath that longed to arise. The crisp white of his shirt beneath his waistcoat made his eyes extra vibrant. The cut of his clothes fit him perfectly, accentuating his long legs, broad shoulders, and lean hips.

"Miss Brinton," he greeted, a new coolness in his voice as he bowed quite elegantly. "I was beginning to think you had changed your mind."

If she'd had one whit of common sense, she would have. Being alone with the Earl of Stoneleigh was a reckless temptation she couldn't afford to indulge in. Her time here was temporary. She had come to enrich her manuscript. That was all.

She forced a smile. "I wouldn't be presumptuous enough to decline your generosity, my lord. I'm most appreciative."

Unfortunately, she was more appreciative of the earl himself than she was of the sustenance.

"I'll fill a plate for you," he volunteered in gentlemanly fashion.

Also unexpected, much like his appearance on the path during her earlier walk.

"You needn't," she protested, moving toward him and the sideboard.

Drawn by the twin lure of deliciously scented food and seductive earl, it was true.

"Tell me what you prefer," he said, ignoring her objection.

"Eggs, bacon, pineapple, and strawberries, if you please."

The earl obligingly heaped a plate with her requests—far more than she would be capable of consuming, but she didn't think it prudent to offer further opposition. Instead, she thanked him and moved to take the plate, intending to deliver it to her seat.

"I'll carry it for you," he said, once more playing the role of gentleman all too well.

What an enigma he was, a man who fought with his fists and engaged in fisticuffs in the stables, and yet who fretted over his governess's breakfast. One who questioned her and yet also showed her unexpected kindness.

"Thank you, my lord," she offered demurely, following him to the place setting where he deposited her laden plate.

He pulled out a chair for her to seat herself. "My pleasure, Miss Brinton. It is the least I can do after nearly trampling you on my run."

There was no reason for a shiver to travel down her spine at the low, deep rumble of his voice. Nor for her pulse to hitch at the word *pleasure*. And yet, both happened. She busied her hands with preparing a cup of tea, telling herself not to watch the way Stoneleigh's shirt pulled as his shoulders moved and doing it anyway.

More than once.

Silence fell between them for a time, until his lordship was settled at his own place setting at the head of the table and Corliss several chairs away, his plate heaped with fresh fruit, oatmeal, bacon, and eggs. Enough to feed three men with ease, she thought. But then, when a man trained as rigorously as the earl did, it was only to be expected that he worked up a corresponding hunger. Little wonder he had filled her own plate so high.

"How are you finding it here at Knightly Abbey?" he asked, breaking the stillness of the room.

Surprising her, it was true. She didn't expect that most earls inquired after their governess's comfort at their homes. But then, she didn't expect they regularly breakfasted with their governesses either. Perhaps this was merely his way of making small talk, to lessen the stilted air of the dining room.

"It is lovely," she said with forced cheer.

In truth, it was certainly not as comfortable as the sprawling Talleyrand Park, but she hadn't expected it would be. Her room adjoined the nursery, and it was quite cold at night, despite the fireplace. The servants were cool and unfriendly, and she was dwelling in a strange world in which she was not quite a servant and yet decidedly not in the same sphere as her charges.

But she wasn't about to confess any of that to the earl.

"That is a rather generous assessment of a drafty, tumble-down Yorkshire estate," he said. "Do you truly think it lovely, or were you only saying so for my benefit? Because I assure you, you'll not hurt my feelings at all if you are brutally honest."

What to say?

She took a sip of her tea, carefully formulating her response. "You are not happy to be home, my lord?"

It seemed to her that there was a bitterness underlying Stoneleigh's words. Perhaps resentment too, as if he was not pleased about his return.

"This is not home, Miss Brinton," he said smoothly, before taking a bite of pineapple.

She watched him chewing—finding his lips oddly mesmerizing again—when she knew she must not. *Oh, Corliss.* This month was going to prove interminable if she could not control herself.

She cleared her throat, turning her attention to her plate, which was a much safer place to look. "What place *is* home, my lord, if I may be bold enough to ask?"

"I don't suppose I've called anywhere home," came his answer, his tone wry. "I've been traveling America for these last many years. Railcars and hotels have been my home. But even those felt far more like a place I belonged than here."

His honesty drew her gaze back to him. He was watching her with an odd expression on his countenance, as if he were every bit as startled as she at the revelations he had just made to her, a veritable stranger who was new to his home, and one in his employ, at that. This was no societal call, and even if she was dining at his table as if she were one, she was most certainly not the Earl of Stoneleigh's guest.

And still, she found herself wanting to know more about him. Wanting to know why he didn't feel at home at his own estate. Having been raised by doting parents who were a love match, and growing up surrounded by siblings who loved her, she couldn't fathom not feeling as if Talleyrand Park was her home.

"Were you never lonely?" she couldn't resist asking, forgetting herself yet again. "Traveling as you have done for so long?"

He was quiet for a moment, as if considering her question, before responding, "I've always been surrounded by others."

Corliss noted it was not truly a response. "One can be surrounded by others and still be quite lonely, however."

His gaze caught and held hers, and for a few heartbeats, it was as if he were peering inside her, seeing some part of herself she hadn't known would be visible to another. "Touché, Miss Brinton. In addition to being an angel walking amongst mere mortals, it would seem you are also wise beyond your tender years."

His response nettled her, and her spine stiffened. Before she could hold her tongue, she was speaking again. "Are you mocking me, my lord?"

The corners of his lips curled upward, twitching as if to suppress a hint of mirth. "I was mocking your former employer, Lord Lindley, Miss Brinton. Or was it Lindlow? I confess, you have me confused and wondering if I don't have the wrong of it."

Was he toying with her now? Had he referred to her letter of recommendation upon his return? It didn't seem likely he would have had enough time to do so and then bathe as well.

"I suppose it hardly matters now that I am no longer in his lordship's employ," she said primly instead of answering, thinking that two could play at his little game.

"Hmm," was all he said, before returning his attention to the food awaiting him on his plate.

She continued with her breakfast as well, the silence irritating her until she could bear it no longer. "Lord Stoneleigh, I wish you would share your thoughts. The silence grows almost insupportable."

So much quiet made her anxious, it was true. If he were to meet her boisterous family, he would understand. She was one of five siblings, each more original than the next. None of them the solemn and stoic sorts.

The earl was silent for a few moments more, before lifting his gaze to hers, and she felt that gaze as strongly as if it were a touch. Striking blue blazed into her.

"I was only thinking, Miss Brinton, that you are nothing like any governess I have ever met before," he said, giving her a slow smile now that could only be called charming.

Warmth blossomed inside her, unfurling like the petals of a spring bloom eager for sun. Being in his presence had her at sixes and sevens. It grew increasingly difficult to remember who she was, so effortlessly did he hold her in his thrall. But she had to recall, for the sake of her novel and the future she was planning for herself. This book was meant to be her means of ultimately proving to her parents that she didn't need to marry. She couldn't afford to jeopardize everything she had been working toward, the life of independence she longed for, not even for a handsome earl.

"I am not certain if that is an insult or a compliment, my lord," she said carefully. "But I choose to believe it is the latter rather than the former."

His lips twitched. "I had a notion you would."

The remainder of the breakfast continued in a comfortable silence until Corliss excused herself to see to her charges. Stoneleigh rose to his feet when she did, helping her with her chair in gentlemanly fashion. She would be lying if she said she did not feel the heat of him at her back, seeping through all the layers of her undergarments and hideous governess gown to sear her. And she would also be lying if she said she did not wish that she had been Lady Corliss so she might have lingered in the breakfast room, stealing more covert glances at the handsome, vexing Bruiser Knight.

But she was Miss Brinton, governess. And so she politely and somberly took her leave instead.

He told himself he wasn't happy to see her.

"Miss Brinton," he greeted.

"Lord Stoneleigh." She returned his smile, hers guarded and hesitant.

Breakfast the day before had ended in rather a stalemate. Since the moment they had literally collided in the nursery several days before, he had been torn between desiring her and distrusting her.

He couldn't act on the desire, because she was the governess and he was her employer. And whilst he had earned his living and his fame with his fists, he was still a gentleman, and he possessed a gentleman's honor. As for the distrust, it, too was suspended for now. He'd attempted to search out the letter of recommendation to no avail the night before. Not every female of his acquaintance was as deceptive as Ida had been, but given his past, it was difficult for him to have faith in any woman.

But here he stood anyway, drinking in the sight of Miss Brinton in a becoming gown and matching dolman, wondering about her. Pleased to have his run interrupted for the second day in a row.

He cleared his throat, aware that he had been staring for far longer than was polite. "I didn't expect to cross paths with you this morning."

"Nor I you," she said softly, catching her succulent lower lip in her teeth before continuing. "If you would prefer your solitude, I would be more than happy to take a different path."

Common sense told him to agree. To tell her that yes, indeed, she should walk elsewhere. Seeing her once a day at breakfast was already temptation enough.

"Of course not," he said instead. "You are more than welcome to walk wherever you wish."

Her gaze flitted over him, and he resisted the urge to

stand taller beneath her scrutiny. "Do you truly run every day?"

"I do."

"Do you enjoy it?"

He pondered her question. She was an inquisitive thing. But unlike the many journalists who had peppered him with questions over the years in interviews—Ida included—Miss Brinton's interest felt different somehow. Genuine.

"I enjoy the way it makes me feel," he answered.

Her brow furrowed, as if it was not the response she had anticipated from him. "And how does it make you feel?"

The query was almost intimate.

He was damp with the mist and perspiration from the mile and a half he had already covered. And yet, he was not at all chilled. He was overheated from the layers he had donned for his training, and now in a different way from her.

From her nearness, her presence, her bold perusal and probing questions. A breeze rustled in the trees overhead, carrying her scent to him. Rose with a hint of bergamot. His stupid cock hardened.

He thought again of her question. She was awaiting his answer, head tilted, gaze fixed firmly upon him.

"It makes me feel strong and healthy," he said. "Capable of defeating any opponent."

"How many opponents have you faced?"

"Forty."

Her eyebrows rose. "My heavens. That is rather a lot of matches."

It was. And at three-and-thirty, he was growing too old for many more. His body was telling him so. But his body was going to have to bloody well wait because Knight wasn't finished yet.

He rolled his shoulders, feeling the old injury giving its customary tweak of pain. "I love the sport."

Unfortunately, the sport did not always love him, but that was the nature of the beast. An athlete suffered pains, injuries, and whatever other troubles faced him all for the chance for one more round. One more victory.

"I confess, I don't know much about boxing, but it seems a rather violent, almost frightening sport. And I find myself curious. Why would the son of an earl leave England to become a prizefighter?"

It was a question a governess had no business asking her employer. A question he had been asked before by many a reporter. A question Knight had always refused to answer directly. Instead, he had dodged it, much as he did blows in the ring, feinting with words. Offering carefully scripted replies.

Despite his fame, he was an incredibly private person. He guarded his personal life with rigid care after he had allowed one woman to grow far too close to him. He'd fancied himself in love with the beautiful, spirited lady reporter named Ida Dawson, and she'd used his trust in her against him, printing salacious reports of his debauchery that had nearly upended his career. He'd learned his lesson in harsh, cutting fashion. He knew better now.

And yet, there was something about Miss Brinton that managed to slip past his defenses and unlock that part of him. To make him give her an honest answer.

"Because I hated every moment of being the second son. My father only gave a damn about my brother because he was the heir. My mother died when I was a lad. There was nothing tying me here save resentment. I finished the requisite schooling and left for America as soon as I was able. I had always excelled at football and cricket when I was at Cambridge. But when I saw my first bare-knuckle prizefight in New York, I knew I was meant to be a boxer."

Words couldn't convey the depth of his reaction at

witnessing the fight. It had been visceral, a feeling to his marrow that he'd finally found the place in life where he truly belonged for the first time. He'd begun training the next day. Within weeks, he had fought his first match and won.

And now, here he was, back in the place he had left. Still bitter. Still feeling as if he didn't belong. Haunted, it was true, by the ghosts of the past.

There was a hand on his arm, at his elbow. Breaking him from his thoughts. He glanced down to realize it was Miss Brinton, comforting him through the thick layer of his sweater. And something inside him warmed even further. There wasn't a hint of seduction in her touch. It was purely heartfelt.

"I am so sorry your family didn't treat you as you deserved," she said softly.

It struck Knight that no one had ever told him that before. To the world, he was the coddled son of an aristocrat who had never known a day of suffering in his charmed life. A man who had gone on to achieve fame and fortune on his own.

There wasn't a trace of pity in her eyes, in her voice. Only understanding. She looked at him as if she saw him. *Truly* saw him. Not The Bruiser Knight, not the Earl of Stoneleigh, but the man beneath all the trappings. His true self.

He wasn't sure he liked it.

Knight swallowed hard against a rush of new emotion. "Thank you. I suspect we all have our burdens to bear. My albatross has been my family."

"And now you have your nieces to look after," she said, her hand still on his arm.

The gesture was too bold. Too familiar. He ought to take a step away, break the connection. But he couldn't.

Didn't wish to. Liked her touch. Liked the gentle weight of it, the meaning implicit. That she *cared*.

And that was every bit as absurd as not shaking free of her hold. Because he scarcely knew the woman before him, and likewise, she did not know him.

"Not through any fault of their own," he said, thinking of his wayward nieces who, to their credit, were nothing like Robert in the least. "The girls are handfuls. However, I do think we are beginning to find some common ground."

Miss Brinton released him, as if reminded, belatedly, of their difference in stations. "In the stables as you engage in bouts of fisticuffs, do you mean? Forgive me, Lord Stoneleigh, but I cannot think it proper for ladies to be exposed to boxing in such fashion."

Of course, it likely wasn't. He hadn't thought about it at the time. He wasn't accustomed to being responsible for anyone aside from himself, and most certainly not young ladies. That was what Miss Brinton was here for, after all. Not to comfort him on the path in the morning and make him long for something more from her.

Something he could never have.

"If you hadn't lost your charges again, they wouldn't have been in the stables," he pointed out, more harshly than he had intended after she had just shown him such kindness.

But he could not forget who they were. Why she was here. That the entire reason for Miss Brinton was so that he could make certain she was a suitable governess for his nieces, allowing him to return and defend his title and resume the life he preferred. Far, far away from here.

"I did not lose them," Miss Brinton countered, her tone cooling, her shoulders drawing back in that same defiant posture also so unlike a governess. The one that made him want to pull her into his arms and kiss her. "I allowed them a break. Now that I understand their proclivity for wandering from the main house during respites, I have made rules accordingly. Chief amongst them, no visits to the stables without proper chaperoning."

He offered her a tight smile. "Capital idea, Miss Brinton. Yet another reason you are an angel amongst mere mortals."

He was taunting her again, and it was rather small of him, he had to admit. But she had made him feel things he hadn't felt in…a long time. And remember emotions he had tamped down years ago, emotions which hadn't been stirred since Ida. He didn't like it. Couldn't afford any of these distractions —emotions, memories, responsibilities, *her*—to keep him from what mattered most.

His training. His title. His return to America. His fame. His fortune.

For a moment, he recalled all the days he'd spent training and traveling in railcars, surrounded by reporters and hangers-on and women who only wanted him for one reason. Thinking again of Ida, who had used his feelings for her against him, of how he had shown her a side of himself he never would have allowed a ruthless reporter to see. God, her betrayal had been gutting.

And then he thought of Miss Brinton's words the day before at breakfast.

One can be surrounded by others and still be quite lonely.

"I am so happy to provide you with the reminder," the governess said, giving him one of her more ferocious smiles.

One that made him think she was far more stubborn and bold than he had yet realized. An equally matched opponent. One that made him think about what else he could do with that pretty pink mouth.

"Until breakfast," he bit out, needing to put an end to this madness before he did something he would regret.

Something like smooth away the curl that had flown across her creamy cheek, or haul her body against his, or—

God forbid—tell her he appreciated the way she looked at him and spoke to him as a man rather than a second son or an earl or a prizefighter.

She curtsied as she had the day before. "Until breakfast, my lord."

And then, he was running again. But this time, he was running for more reasons than just his training alone. Running until his heart was pounding and his breath was ragged and all the inconvenient feelings inside him had been tamped down where they belonged.

Running until he finally stopped, gasping, doubled over, struggling to pull cold, misty Yorkshire air into his lungs.

"To hell with Knightly Abbey," he muttered into the cold autumn dirt.

But no one heard him, because this time, he was truly alone. And he felt every bit as lonely as he had in all those railcars taking him across America and on the ship bringing him back to England. Every bit as lonely as he ever had.

CHAPTER 5

*C*orliss was surrounded by the mischievous laughter of her four young charges.

And covered in feathers.

Lots and lots of feathers.

Also, treacle. The treacle had come first, poured over her head from a pail over the door, which was important to note, because it was what had rendered her transformation from governess to avian monster complete.

"Why Miss Brinton, you look like a bird," Lady Henrietta said with a poorly disguised chortle.

"What manner of bird do you suppose she is?" asked Lady Beatrice, chuckling behind her hand.

"An albatross," Lady Alice suggested shrewdly.

"A swan," Lady Mary shouted a second later.

It was silly, truly. But as Corliss stood at the threshold of the nursery, coated in a bucket of treacle and the remnants of four feather pillows, all she could think of was three things. The first was Stoneleigh, who had, in a rare moment of confidence, told her several mornings ago on her morning walk that his family was his albatross. The second was that it was kind of Lady Mary to at least choose a graceful, regal bird for her resemblance, despite the girl taking part in the prank.

The third was that she was going to get even with the four laughing hellions who had unleashed the treacle and feathers upon her.

"Is this your idea of a joke?" she demanded sharply.

The girls' laughter died. Feathers were yet floating in the air, catching the autumnal sunlight which had replaced the last few days of gray mist and rains. One drifted as she watched, landing atop Lady Henrietta's dark hair.

No one answered her.

She hadn't expected them to, of course. There was no good answer to her question. But inside, she was seething.

Humiliated.

Miserable.

Being a governess was not nearly as easy as she had supposed when it had been a fanciful notion visited upon her from the haven of her writing desk at Talleyrand Park.

She didn't know if she wanted to cry or shout or stomp her feet.

Instead, she stood stiff as a ramrod, refusing to show the devious wretches before her a hint of vulnerability.

"Lady Henrietta, have you a response?" she asked the eldest girl.

And was rewarded no more response than the slow blinking of eyes similar to her uncle's.

"Lady Beatrice?" she tried next, trying to ignore the stickiness of the treacle on her gown, her face, her hair. Rolling down her skirts to pool on her shoes.

There was a feather stuck to the bridge of her nose, impeding her view unless she cocked her head at an unnatural angle, which she also refused to do.

No answer.

"Lady Alice?" she prompted, raising her brows, an action that only served to make a feather droop over her eye.

Lady Alice's large eyes watched her.

"Lady Mary?" she asked finally.

The youngest of the four looked down at her shoes, scuffing them along the carpets.

"I held my tongue concerning the pepper I found sprinkled on my pillow yesterday morning," she continued. "I scarcely chastised you for the banister races, the indecorous display in the stables, the toad in my bed, or my missing drawers—" she paused at the snicker which rose from one of the girls at the mentioning of her spare undergarments, which she still had yet to recover, before continuing— "however, this outrage is quite enough. I will be speaking to your uncle about this. And make no doubt about it, his lordship will *not* be pleased when he discovers you have showered your governess in treacle and the insides of your pillows!"

"They weren't *our* pillows," Lady Mary said, as if the distinction mattered.

But then, knowing the hellions before her, perhaps it did.

"They were Mrs. Oak's pillows," Lady Henrietta admitted. "She keeps all the nicest ones for herself."

Was that true? Knowing the housekeeper, Corliss didn't doubt it. And for a shameful moment, she found herself reveling in a hint of satisfaction at the thought of the unpleasant woman retiring to her quarters only to find all her pillows had been thieved. But she tamped it down immediately as unworthy.

Besides, she had more important matters to attend just now.

"Papa gave them to her," Lady Beatrice said suddenly. "He was having an amour with her."

Corliss's mouth dropped open in shock. The former earl had been engaging in trysts with his housekeeper? And where had Lady Beatrice learned of such a word, let alone discovered her father's shameful secret?

"My lady," she chastised the girl, "that will be enough."

"Yes, Miss Brinton," Lady Beatrice offered with a curtsy, looking suddenly younger than her eight years, her lower lip trembling as if she were about to burst into sobs.

Something in Corliss's heart shifted, breaking away the hard shell of anger that had previously coated it at the antics of the young girls before her. They hadn't a mother or a father. They had chased away every governess who had occupied the position before her. They had a bachelor uncle who had only recently arrived from abroad, a housekeeper who had been carrying on an affair with their father, and what had to be a great deal of loneliness and pain they hid behind their ceaseless pranks.

What a tangled mess she had fallen into, unbeknownst to her. This situation was not at all what Corliss had supposed it would be when she had made the decision to deceive her parents and live in the world of her heroine for one month's time.

She moved forward, impeded, it was true, by her treacle- and feather-bedecked skirts, and stopped before Lady Beatrice. "You needn't cry, my lady. I merely wished for you to know that such matters are not for the ears of young girls like yourself and your sisters. It is not an appropriate topic of conversation."

But Lady Beatrice's chin was still quivering, and the sheen of tears had begun in her bright-blue eyes. "Are you going to leave? You may as well. All the others have before you."

Yes, they had, hadn't they? And so had everyone these girls had loved. Sadness crept over her, entirely replacing the indignation. With it came guilt, for she would leave them as well, in less than a month's time. Corliss knew she had to do everything in her power to help the girls heal while she was here. She owed them that much, and already the notion of leaving them and Knightly Abbey behind filled her with dread.

She instinctively reached to pat the girl on the shoulder and then thought better of it when she realized her hand, too, was covered in treacle and feathers. "No, Lady Beatrice. I'll not be leaving just yet. I am made of far sterner stuff than that. It will take more than treacle and feathers and a bit of pepper on my pillow to send me running to the train station."

"What in God's name is the meaning of this?"

At the outraged male roar behind her, Corliss spun to find the Earl of Stoneleigh at the threshold of the nursery, his handsome face a mask of shock and fury. His gaze landed on her, his lips parting. She could only imagine the picture she presented, covered in sticky treacle and feathers. Treacle she'd forgotten in her trudge to Lady Beatrice's side, the evidence of which remained in the form of wet, feathered footprints on the Axminster.

The girls squeaked in unison.

Lady Henrietta stepped forward, drawing the earl's attention. "Forgive us, Uncle, we played a—"

"It was an experiment," Corliss said, feeling an absurd need to defend the girls from their uncle's wrath.

Five pairs of eyes swung to her.

Stoneleigh raised a brow, looking unfairly debonair in his country tweed whilst she was…well. She didn't want to think about how she appeared at the moment. She had done her best to wipe the bulk of the offending syrup from her face, but she had no doubt she looked nothing short of dreadful.

"An experiment," he repeated, his tone incredulous.

Corliss had seized upon the first excuse that rose to her mind, attempting to blunt some of the earl's ire by casting the blame upon herself. Her father was an inventor, and she had spent a great deal of her youth in his workshop, where Mama had relegated all Papa's inventions following the disastrous occasion when he had set the library on fire whilst perfecting his burglar alarm. That particular incident had caused the loss of dozens of books, along with the curtains, Axminster, and Mama's writing desk.

However, although she had enjoyed poking through Papa's contraptions and watching him work, she had never been much interested in such matters herself. Her older sister, Elysande, was the true scientist of the family.

Now, she searched her mind frantically for an experiment which might have required treacle and feathers.

"We have been researching birds," she said lamely. "And in the absence of bringing one into the nursery, I attempted to...model one. Our experiment was to determine whether the mere donning of feathers would render one capable of flight." More than aware of how ludicrous her explanation sounded and yet having nothing else to offer, she flapped her arms at her sides. "If you were wondering, my lord, the answer is no."

Stoneleigh stared at her.

And stared.

Stared as if she were mad.

Perhaps she was, defending the hellions who had doused her in treacle. But seeing Lady Beatrice's trembling chin and watery eyes had affected her. Corliss had already been humiliated. If she must face the wrath of his lordship for the ruined Axminster, then so be it.

She held his stare, daring him to question her.

At length, he turned a stern look upon his nieces. "Is Miss Brinton's explanation as to her current state the truth, my ladies?"

"Yes, it is," chirped Lady Mary with a grin, quite quick to throw her governess beneath the carriage wheels.

"No," Lady Henrietta said then, looking shamefaced and guilty. "It is not, Uncle. Miss Brinton is trying to protect us. We treacled and feathered her as a prank."

"Treacled and feathered," Stoneleigh repeated grimly.

Corliss bit her lip to suppress a sudden, inappropriate burst of laughter. The scene, the phrase, the feathers tickling her nose, the stickiness of the syrup, the sweetness of it on her tongue, the expression on the earl's face, it was all too much. But she was also aware that the earl would be furious with her. For even if she had not been responsible for the ruined Axminster directly, she had failed in her task of keeping her unruly charges in order, and now they had slathered treacle and feathers all over his carpets and her person.

"It was my idea," Lady Beatrice admitted, her chin resuming its quivering.

"And you have treated Miss Brinton in such abominable fashion, yet she has defended you?" he demanded.

"Yes, Uncle," all four girls replied in unison.

He nodded, his gaze flicking back to Corliss. "Miss Brinton, please go to your room. I will ring for a bath. We will speak of this matter in private later. Girls, come with me."

"Yes, Uncle," they repeated.

Corliss wanted to argue, but she knew her position was already tenuous at best. And she couldn't afford to be sacked yet. Not when her time here had been so short. She'd scarcely learned anything of what it was truly like to be a governess, and she needed her novel to possess an air of veracity that could only come from true-life experience. But more than that, she was beginning to feel as if the girls needed her. And that she needed them, too.

So instead, she attempted a curtsy—no easy feat given her present condition—and echoed the dutiful response of his nieces. "Yes, my lord."

KNIGHT WAS in Robert's study, glass of whisky in hand, when a knock sounded at the door. It was his second whisky, and he rarely imbibed. The liquor was undoubtedly the reason warmth began burning like a hot coal in his belly, why every part of him felt suddenly aware.

It had nothing to do with the woman on the other side of the door.

"Enter," he called, rising, the glass still in hand.

It wasn't polite to swill whisky before a female. Particularly not one currently in his employ. But his eye was still twitching, and his head thumped as if he had taken another punishing right from Billy O'Brien directly to the jaw. Who would have known that children were more fearsome than facing fully grown men who intended to pummel him into defeat?

Not Knight.

The door opened, and Miss Brinton entered with a cautious air. Her golden hair was still wet from her bath, though thankfully bereft of the sticky brown substance that had previously coated the luxurious strands. Not a feather to be seen, either. He would be lying if he said he hadn't harbored a thought or two about assisting her with the removal of all that sticky treacle and the wretched feathers.

"Miss Brinton," he greeted, disappointed that she was wearing another somber day gown that hung about her figure as if it were a sack.

Where were her colorful morning dresses? And why did he note their absence, let alone give a damn what the governess wore? Clearly, all the responsibilities heaped upon him were beginning to have an adverse effect on his brain. Either that, or he had received one too many fists to the old knowledge box.

"Lord Stoneleigh." She dropped into a curtsy, leaving the door open at her back.

The lack of privacy irritated him, and not just because he didn't wish for prying servants to overhear their conversation. Also because he liked the notion of having this lovely, sparkling woman to himself, just as he did each morning on his runs and later again at breakfast. Strange that she lived beneath the same roof, and yet he saw so little of her.

"The door," he said, gesturing with his glass of whisky. "Close it, if you please."

She caught her lower lip between her teeth, her expression turning worried, but did as he asked. He wondered at the cause and thought some more about her previous situation. The idea of a married lord forcing himself upon her made his gut twist and rage rise.

"You needn't fear being alone with me," he said.

She turned back to him halfway across the chamber. "I don't, my lord."

"Good." He felt stupid for saying it. Of course she must know he would not make untoward advances. They breakfasted together every day. "Your former employer did not take advantage of you, did he?"

Her golden brows rose, and her hands, small and dainty much like the rest of her, clasped together at her waist, though she remained safely by the now-closed door. "No, Lord Stoneleigh. He did not."

Relief washed over him. Thank God. The idea of anyone harming her filled him with protective rage the likes of which he had never felt before. But then, he had never known a woman who had been so mistreated—a pail of treacle dumped upon her before being covered in feathers— and yet defended those responsible. Nor one who looked at him with the light of curiosity in her eyes, one who asked him questions about himself rather than his accomplishments, one who seemed to somehow understand him even whilst she scarcely knew him.

He took a drink of whisky. "That is reassuring, Miss Brinton. You had seemed apprehensive upon entering. I misread you, I suppose."

"I am apprehensive, my lord." Her voice was quiet. Almost sad. "I fear the punishments my charges have received."

Again, concerned with others far more than herself.

But then, that was the role of the governess, was it not? To put the care of others first.

"My nieces have received the tongue lashings they deserved," he told her. "They will be asking your forgiveness later this evening, and you are to have the rest of the day to yourself, to do with as you like, as my way of offering an apology of my own for their despicable behavior."

"They are young girls who are lonely and sad," Miss Brinton surprised him by saying, moving toward him.

Bringing with her the sweet scent of temptation—rose and bergamot. Accompanied by a sweetness he suspected was the lingering effect of the treacle.

"They are terrors," he countered. "You may not be aware, Miss Brinton, but my nieces have chased away every governess previously engaged at the position. I can scarcely countenance that you have remained after today's outrage."

A stupid thing to say, perhaps. He didn't wish to chase this woman off. He had begun to be persuaded that she was, in fact, a capable governess. The girls appeared to be learning their lessons, they hadn't drawn on his face in his sleep, and nor had they been racing down the banisters since the first day.

All improvements.

"I was told below stairs," she said quietly. "But I have begun to feel that they are acting as they have for good reasons."

His brows shot upward, for he couldn't begin to understand her. "Good reasons for upending a pail of treacle on your head and covering you in feathers?"

"After the incident, Lady Beatrice made some statements that suggested so," Miss Brinton replied. "Everyone close to them has left them. Their mother, their father, their governesses. I suspect they fear being abandoned again, and to face that fear, they act out, attempting to chase away their governesses on their own."

Good God. What a selfish arse he'd been, so focused upon what he had lost in coming here, rather than having a thought for his nieces and what they had endured. Thinking of them as nothing more than unwanted burdens, troublesome hoydens instead of children with wounded hearts. Just because Knight had despised Robert didn't mean his nieces had. Robert had been their father, after all. One would hope he had been as decent a parent to them as he'd been capable of. And the girls had lost both their mother and their father. Meanwhile, Knight had been across the ocean, a stranger they had never met. A stranger who intended to leave them again soon. Guilt lanced him.

And yet, he still didn't quite follow her assertion. It hardly made sense to him that his nieces would fear another abandonment so much that they *caused* it. Why chase all their governesses away for the last year? Why continue their campaign of pranks and insolence against Miss Brinton?

He shook his head slowly, remaining astounded that she would so defend the four young ladies who had done nothing but undermine her from the moment of her arrival at Knightly Abbey. "Forgive me if I fail to understand your logic. You are saying they fear being abandoned again, and yet they act so abominably that everyone close to them has no choice but to flee."

"Yes," Miss Brinton said, drawing to a halt with a

respectable distance between them. A distance he longed to close but knew he could not. "They are attempting to take back the control they have lost over their own lives. I suspect that in their minds, if their governesses leave them as everyone else has done, at least *they* are responsible. *They* made the choice instead of being powerless."

Bloody hell, when she put it that way, it made sense. Was it possible that his nieces' behavior was rooted in the fear of abandonment? And if so, what would it mean when he left once more as he planned?

Something constricted inside him, going painfully tight. He had spent so much time estranged from his family that he had forgotten they were, indeed, still his family. And his nieces no less so. Now, he was all they had, and they were all he had as well.

"My lord?" Miss Brinton prodded, once again catching her lower lip in her teeth, as if she were worried.

"I…" he began, only for the words to trail away, impossible to say. His throat was suddenly clogged with too much unfamiliar emotion. The weight of responsibility had never felt more like a boulder than it did now. "Thank you for your kindness to them, Miss Brinton. After what they did to you today, they are not deserving of it."

That much was true, even if what Miss Brinton suggested was accurate.

"You needn't thank me." A becoming flush stained her cheeks, and he couldn't help but wonder how far it extended, his view currently hampered by her dreadful prim gown with its high, buttoned collar. "I was initially furious with them myself, but then Lady Beatrice was so near to tears, and all my anger melted away. It has been easy, I'll admit, to see them as my nemeses rather than girls in need of some constancy in their lives."

Constancy.

And who was going to give that to them? Not Knight. Not if he wished to defend his title.

"You are surprisingly tenderhearted for a governess," he remarked softly. Too softly, perhaps, for the moment. Not at all businesslike, as he had intended. As would be appropriate.

He wasn't certain how it had begun, but gradually, the carefully defined walls between them were lowering. He had been aware of her as a woman from their first meeting. The attraction had been instant and undeniable. And yet, over the course of the last week, what he felt for her had, quite unbeknownst to himself, flourished into something more. He had run the same path for a sennight in the hope he would see her. Spent each day looking forward to their breakfast and the chance to spend another half hour in her presence.

Her smile was quick and sunny. "Are governesses not meant to have hearts?"

"I'm reasonably certain mine didn't when I was a lad," he quipped, and then discovered the hint of a feather in her dark-gold braids.

Before he could think twice, he reached out and plucked it from her coiffure, his fingers mistakenly grazing over the silken shell of her ear in the process. The contact was electric, like a jolt of pure fire coursing through him. Miss Brinton seemed to freeze, her lush pink lips parting, eyes fastening upon his.

He could drown in those eyes.

Lose himself in them.

Lose himself in *her*.

"What are you doing, my lord?" she asked, her voice hushed and breathless.

At this proximity, he could discern the warm hues in the depths of her eyes, cinnamon blending with the rich brown. Her pupils were wide and dark.

"You had a feather in your hair," he explained, forcing

himself to maintain his composure as he withdrew his hand and held up the feather for her examination.

"Oh." She flushed again. "Thank you. There were rather a great deal of them. The treacle proved most persistent in its refusal to be washed from my hair, in particular."

And there he was again, thinking about Miss Brinton in the bath. Naked. Washing. *Glorious.* Thinking about how the full breasts hidden beneath her drab, gray gown would have strained above the water as she washed her hair.

He damn well ought to have bedded someone before rusticating in the country. Perhaps he wouldn't be so desperately enamored of the one woman he couldn't have.

Knight swallowed. "Once again, I am sorry. Take the remainder of the day to do as you wish."

"That is generous of you." Another small smile flirted with the corners of her lips. "I appreciate your consideration, especially given what happened to your Axminster."

The chambermaids were doing their utmost to remove all traces of the sticky stains from the carpets as they spoke. If the damage was too stubborn, he would likely have to have a replacement installed. Yet another duty to add to his list of unending obligations.

"The fault is my nieces' and not yours," he repeated, wondering then if the hesitancy he had sensed in her upon her arrival had been concern for her position. "Rest assured I do not hold you responsible for their actions."

"I hope you will not be overly harsh with them beyond the reprimands you've already given," she said, and he nearly groaned when she caught her lower lip in her teeth this time.

She was torturing him, plain and simple. And those four hellions were going to eat her alive if she didn't take care.

Tamping down all inappropriate desire, he inclined his head. "I'll consider what you said, Miss Brinton. Thank you for meeting with me." He paused as an utterly stupid idea occurred to him. One he absolutely should not consider, let alone give voice to. "Would you care to join me for dinner this evening?"

"Dinner?" she repeated, her gaze searching his.

"You needn't feel obligated, of course," he rushed to say, feeling like a callow youth who had just propositioned his first woman. Good Christ, his ears were hot. When was the last time he had flushed? Not in at least a decade, he was sure. "But if you wish to join me, I would appreciate the company."

Perhaps she would politely decline and spare him the misery of sitting across from her, watching that luscious mouth of hers, knowing he could never know it beneath his.

But she smiled instead. "Thank you, my lord. I would enjoy that."

So, he feared, would he. Too much.

She gave him a proper curtsy and departed Robert's study. He watched her go, gaze following the feminine sway of her hips, calling himself a fool in every language he knew. Four, as it happened.

When he was alone again, he glanced down at the feather, still captured in his fingers. Bemused, he tucked it into his waistcoat pocket, intending to keep the thing.

And he couldn't begin to imagine why.

CHAPTER 6

$\mathcal{C}$orliss preceded the Earl of Stoneleigh into the music room, all too aware of his presence at her back, his stare upon her, searing her as surely as any flame. If agreeing to dinner with him had been unwise, then joining him after the meal had finished was the height of lunacy. She had no doubt it would result in more hostility from the domestics, and tongues would be fiercely wagging.

But dining with him had meant more time alone with him. More opportunity to study the fascinating man who was The Bruiser Knight. More chances to speak with him. To chance the merest brush of touches.

And all those reasons were exactly why she had accepted his second invitation of the day.

The risks had thus far proven more than worth the reward. Dinner had been as informal as breakfast was, attended by a footman who had been summarily dismissed aside from the removal of courses. How odd it had felt, being served after serving herself below stairs. A luxury she had taken for granted all these years. The footman had eyed her coolly, making her wonder if the dinner would cost her more of Mrs. Oak's wrath.

The earl had regaled her with tales of his travels across America over the last ten years he had been gone from England. Bereft of their customary roles, she had allowed herself to slip, just for those stolen moments, into her own shoes. Had forgotten she was a governess, and that he was an earl. Instead, he had charmed her as the many friends who paid calls to Talleyrand Park each summer did, when propriety was relaxed and everyone was free to do as they wished.

Despite her best intentions, she could not deny that she found Stoneleigh desperately charming when he wished to be. And handsome, too. She had never been given to romantic fancies as her elder sister Isolde had been. Her interests had lain solely in travel and writing. Hearing the tales of Stoneleigh's time abroad had lit the fires of yearning inside her once more.

But Papa and Mama wished for her to marry, of course. Although they were eccentric in their own ways, they still believed firmly that all their children should wed. It was why Isolde and Elysande were married now, though they had both been fortunate enough to fall in love with their husbands.

It was also why Corliss had deceived her parents into believing she was staying at her aunt's country house in Yorkshire, why she had kept the books she had published thus far, and her aspirations of gaining her financial independence with her latest novel, a secret. She had told no one but her twin, Criseyde. If Papa and Mama discovered she was playing the role of governess at Knightly Abbey, she shuddered to think of their reaction.

She wandered toward the piano occupying the far wall, drawn from her whirling thoughts by the majestic display of gilt and hand-painted scenes. As she drew nearer, she realized there were cherubs displayed in mischievous poses, captured in elaborate detail.

"This is an extraordinarily beautiful instrument," she said, for as fine as the piano at Talleyrand Park was, it could not compare to the one before her, with its intricately carved scroll legs and floral garlands.

"It was my mother's prized possession," Stoneleigh commented, his low voice far closer to her than she had realized. "My father had it shipped for her as a wedding gift, all the way from Paris, painted by an artist who was known for his skill with miniatures."

"A precious instrument then, as well," she said softly, her fingers itching to glance over the cool smoothness of the ivory keys even as she restrained herself.

"Precious to her, I reckon." He was at her side now, but he was not looking at the piano.

His gaze was trained upon Corliss. Something in the air between them shifted, and whether it was the muted light of the low lamps in the music room, the lack of footman hovering over them, or the hushed quiet of the chamber, she couldn't say.

"The piano is lovely," she blurted, intensely aware of him as a man rather than as her employer, and feeling unusually awkward.

While Lady Corliss was so sure of herself, Miss Brinton couldn't spare herself the indulgence.

"I've seen far lovelier things in my day," he said simply, still watching her with a hooded stare, his expression one she couldn't decipher.

Her heart beat faster. She allowed her fingertips to graze over the keys, telling herself it was to distract. To ground herself. Being in his presence felt akin to riding in an ascension balloon. Dizzying and dangerous.

"I'm certain you must have seen much, traveling across America as you have," she managed to say.

His jaw tensed, and his gaze flitted down to her fingers as they strayed over the piano. For a moment, his own hands flexed at his sides, as if restraining himself, and she wondered if she had overstepped. But then his stare returned to hers, and he smiled politely, making her wonder if she had mistaken the heaviness in the air after all.

"You play, do you not, Miss Brinton?" the earl asked.

"I do." Of course he would know that. It had been mentioned in the letter she had written to obtain the situation as governess. But perhaps he had invited her to the music room for just this purpose. "Would you care for me to play?"

She was not the most accomplished pianist, but she could certainly offer a tune. Still, she had never done so for a lone audience of a sinfully handsome earl before. There was something about doing so that felt distinctly intimate. Dangerous to her virtue, even, merely because of how his presence affected her. Made her want to do foolish things.

"I would," he said simply.

And she promptly forgot about the danger and the intimacy of singing and playing piano for Stoneleigh, in favor of pleasing him. Corliss settled herself on the bench, all too aware of him moving to a chair near the hearth so that they faced each other.

"Do you have a request, my lord?" she asked.

A small smile played with his lips, his eyes glistening in the light of the gas lamps. "Whatever you wish to play is what I want to hear, Miss Brinton."

He had been referring to her thus from the moment they had met that day in the nursery, of course. She ought to have grown accustomed to it by now. After all, it was the name of her heroine, a surname she had invented by using the name of her brother-in-law, the Duke of Wycombe's, country seat. And yet, the earl's deep, pleasant baritone with its accent that was strangely musical, devoid of the crisp accents of his peers from his years abroad, calling her *Miss Brinton,* nettled.

But then, she had not come here to throw her cap at Lord Stoneleigh. She had come here to immerse herself in the world of her novel's heroine. To lend veracity to her prose. How could she truly write the life of a governess without a notion of what it was like to be one?

No, best to remain Miss Brinton. She had a novel to finish writing. She had a future awaiting her, resting on the sales of this latest book. She'd already worked so painstakingly hard to forge a name for herself as C. Talleyrand. Her publisher, Elijah Decker, had been very pleased with how well received the first three had been.

She nodded to the earl and set her mind to the task, telling herself she must stop gawking at him as if she had never seen a handsome man. She was sure she had seen plenty; merely none who had been *him.* There was music before her, but a song had risen in her mind, one that was hauntingly lovely.

"If you do not oppose, I should like to sing *Annabelle Lee,*" she said. "I sing it often with my sister."

Thinking of Criseyde now reminded Corliss of how much she missed her. It was only with Criseyde's help that Corliss had managed to plot her month away.

All for the good of her book, she reminded herself sternly.

"You've a sister?" Stoneleigh asked.

And she instantly realized her error. She should not have spoken of her family at all. She was sure she had written in her letter that Miss Brinton was alone in the world. Heavens, she ought to have kept a copy of the letter for her to reference. She hadn't supposed she would find it so easy to forget.

But then, she also hadn't supposed the earl who would employ her was a dashing prizefighter with muscles honed from daily physical exertion and sky-blue eyes and a mouth that made her think wicked thoughts.

"Three sisters," she said, knowing it was too late for prevarication now. Like her unintentional confusion of her previous employer's name, this oversight too would hopefully go unnoticed by the earl. "Now, I should play the song, my lord, before the hour grows too late."

And before she said anything else that was unwise, or before she spent any more time losing herself in Stoneleigh's gaze.

"Of course," he said, resting his big, boxer's hands on the arms of the chair. "By all means, go on."

She settled her fingers on the keys and, with a deep breath, began playing *Annabelle Lee* the song by Henry David Leslie which had been set to an Edgar Allan Poe poem. The melody unfurled, and though she was keenly aware of Stoneleigh's gaze upon her, Corliss found her voice.

"*It was many and many a year ago,*" she began, "*in a kingdom by the sea...*"

The sad tale of Annabelle Lee and the man who loved her unfolded, one of longing and heartbreak and loss. It was a song that never failed to move Corliss, both for its compelling story and the beauty of the music itself.

"*But we loved with a love that was more than love,*" she sang on, finding her way through the song by memory, for she had played and sung it many times before. "*And so, all the night-tide, I lie down by the side of my darling—my darling—my life and my bride...*"

When she had reached the final sad note of the song, she became newly aware of Stoneleigh's eyes upon her. His expression, like his gaze, possessed an intensity that stole the breath from her lungs. And then he was applauding her with the hands that had won him a championship and the name The Bruiser Knight.

"That was hauntingly lovely," he said, but it wasn't his words as much as the way his eyes had dipped to her lips that had heat rising to her cheeks and warmth seeping low into her belly.

The air between them seemed suddenly charged with some force that was larger than the both of them.

"Thank you, my lord." She rose from the bench, breaking his gaze to straighten her skirts.

Not because they were wrinkled, but because she needed an excuse to look away from him. A distraction to keep her from crossing the chamber and doing something dreadfully inappropriate. Something a governess had no business doing. Something not even a lady had any business doing.

She glanced up at motion in her peripheral vision. The earl had risen from his chair, and he was moving across the room with long-limbed strides and graceful intent.

"My turn," he said, surprising her.

Somehow, a man who was a prizefighter and yet could also play and sing seemed at odds. And yet, as she had reason to discover over the last week at Knightly Abbey, the Earl of Stoneleigh was a complicated, intriguing man. A man she longed to know better, although she knew she could not. She needed the remaining time she had left for the sake of her book, and she had no doubt that if she confessed her lies to him, he would no longer wish to know her.

She moved to take her seat, but he caught her elbow in a gentle grasp, staying her.

"Will you sing whilst I play?" he asked.

His request startled her, but not nearly as much as his touch did. Warmth crept over her cheeks, and she hoped he could not sense the effect he had upon her.

She forced a bright smile to her lips. "Of course, my lord."

He released his light hold on her and returned her smile with a grin of his own, one that made him look almost boyish. "Excellent. I can assure you that you wouldn't wish to hear my warbling attempts."

Corliss was sure that his singing would be as velvety and pleasing to the ears as his voice was, but she joined him at the bench anyway, careful to keep her skirts from touching his delightfully muscled thighs. No easy feat given the size of the bench. She perched stiffly at the end, the scent of him—soap and citrus with an underlying note of musk—curling around her.

They settled upon another song that was familiar to the both of them, and then Lord Stoneleigh's fingers were moving over the same ivory hers had. He was incredibly skilled, the melody flowing with ease and bringing her into the song. Like the last, it was a tale of forbidden love and heartache. The longing was almost palpable as the words hung in the air, and as the song drew to a close, Corliss turned toward the earl to find him watching her.

Their gazes collided again.

The urge to kiss him was wild and strong within her. She told herself to tamp it down and gather her wits. But her body had a mind of its own, and it was swaying toward him. Her heart was pounding restlessly. And being reckless had never been more alluring.

"Miss Brinton." His voice was low, like a caress.

"Yes?"

"I would like to extend my sincerest apology."

She blinked, confused. That was not what she had expected him to say. Was she alone in this simmering desire, threatening to overwhelm her? It had been sparking between them like electricity from that day on the path. Or so she had thought.

"For what, my lord?" she asked, a defeated feeling creeping slowly up her throat to make her cheeks burn.

"For kissing you."

Her breath arrested in her chest, heart beating suddenly faster, molten warmth pooling between her thighs. And all at the mention of kissing, not even the act.

"But you haven't kissed me, Lord Stoneleigh," she pointed out softly, stating the obvious, still feeling as if she were walking a slippery path and trying to maintain her footing.

She wasn't a governess. The barriers between them were unfamiliar to her. Had she been at Talleyrand Park, she would have been flirting with Stoneleigh madly. Attempting to catch him in every corner of the estate just to talk.

"I intend to," he said then, his stare dropping to her lips, before rising again. "I'm giving you fair warning. If you linger, the apology will most definitely be owed to you."

She should leave the bench and flee the music room. Never again allow herself to be alone with the wickedly handsome, tempting earl before her. He was a renowned prizefighter. Handsome and mysterious. A champion. And in his eyes, she was but a governess in his employ, someone who would never be his equal.

Besides, she needed to keep this situation for the next three weeks. When Mama and Papa discovered what she had done, they would never allow her to escape their watchful eyes again. It was her only chance to immerse herself in the world of a governess and write the most realistic heroine for her novel that she could.

Yes, for all those reasons, flitting through her mind, she should go with all haste.

She held his gaze instead, because despite all common sense, despite logic and reason, she would never forgive herself if she were to grow old one day, never having known this man's lips upon hers.

"I accept your apology, my lord," she said boldly, and in that moment, Miss Brinton fell away.

She was Corliss again. And this was not a role she was playing.

The look he gave her was unlike any she had ever received. The mask of politeness had fallen along with Miss Brinton. The expression on his countenance was one of frank appreciation and raw, unabashed desire. The boundaries between them, which had been incrementally lowering day by day, had gone.

Slowly he slid his thigh over the bench until it was pressed against hers. Although they were separated by layers of cumbersome skirt and undergarments, she hissed out a breath she hadn't realized she'd been holding at the connection. His right hand left the piano and found hers, their fingers tangling, hers lacing through his of their own accord. Such a simple act, and yet it brought with it so much feeling. The shock of his bare skin on hers was deliciously potent.

His head lowered just a fraction, his stare hot upon hers. "You are still here."

"Yes," she whispered, thinking herself every kind of fool for lingering with Stoneleigh. The Bruiser Knight. A man who believed she was someone else.

"You needn't fear for your position if you refuse me," he said, his brow furrowing as if the thought had just occurred to him.

As if she wouldn't want to kiss him, when she was reasonably sure she would die if she did not.

"I don't fear for my position." She had come to know Lord Stoneleigh well enough to understand he was an honorable man. He had been nothing but a gentleman to her thus far, and she knew instinctively that if she but said the word, he would continue in that same vein, never again broaching the subject.

No, she wanted him to kiss her. Longed for it quite desperately, in fact.

"Damn it to hell," he cursed, and then winced, stroking his jaw with his left hand, giving her fingers a squeeze with the other. "Are you certain, Miss Brinton?"

In the intimacy of the evening, their fingers entwined, thighs pressed together, the promise of a forbidden kiss hanging heavy in the air, the name *Miss Brinton* in his deep timbre felt wrong.

"Corliss," she told him. "If you please."

"Corliss," he repeated.

And good sweet heavens, but she liked the way her name sounded on his lips.

Her head tilted toward his. Waiting. Desperately wanting. "I'm certain."

He gave her a wry grin. "This is the first time I've…"

She didn't know what he had been about to say. Kissed a governess? It didn't matter. Nothing else mattered but what was about to happen next. What she was going to *make* happen next. Because when would she ever again have the chance to kiss this bold, handsome, intriguing man?

Corliss closed the last of the distance separating them, and then her mouth was on his.

∿

SHE HAD KISSED HIM FIRST.

Her lips were soft. Full and lush.

Hot.

He wanted to drown in them, in her. A possessive instinct hit Knight with sudden, undeniable intensity. He wanted to take her in his arms and carry her away. For the last week, they had been circling each other in feigned politeness. And all the while, he had been wanting her. Longing for her. Telling himself he could not have her.

He had her now.

Or, at least, her mouth.

And Lord above, heaven and hell, what a fucking mouth it was. Sweet and responsive. Tentative at first. Lips moving against his as if in question. He answered her with a groan, his hand leaving hers to find its way to her nape as he slanted his mouth over hers and deepened the kiss. Her warmth seared his fingertips, the soft, smooth swath of skin like velvet.

She tasted sweet, with a hint of the wine they had taken with dinner. His tongue moved against hers and she responded in kind, a sinuous glide, a small, heady sound of need emerging from low in her throat. For a moment, they grappled with who was in control. Corliss clasped his neck- tie, pulling him nearer, her lips moving faster, her teeth catching on his lower lip as if she were as suddenly ravenous as he felt. How like her to want to take charge, and this, too, made him appreciative.

And harder than a stone.

He shifted on the bench, willing his trousers to give him some relief, and found none. Because she was filling his senses, all summer roses and bergamot and vibrant, beautiful woman. Soft and supple in his arms, turning into him more fully now, her breasts crushing into his chest. He'd never wanted to savor a woman the way he did this one.

He had known she would be a temptation. But he hadn't understood how she would make him feel. It was akin to the first sun-kissed days of spring, when the world was becoming vibrant and green again, trees and grasses and even flowers transformed. The world coming back to life after the dormant, gray winter. That was how Knight felt, basking in the pleasure of Corliss's kiss. Revived. Renewed. No other kiss had ever moved him more.

The intensity of his reaction startled him. He had to recall who she was. The governess. Not for him. And yet, with her curled into his chest as if she belonged there, her lips beneath his, she felt as if she had been made for him alone.

She felt like *his*.

Dangerous sentiments.

Attempting to assuage the ferocity of his need, he withdrew from her mouth. But when he told himself he could end the kiss, he was reluctant to leave her, to sever their connection. He kissed the corner of her lips instead and then strung more along her jaw. Her head tipped back, giving him more access to her throat above the sternly prim collar of her ugly gown.

What a travesty it was, a woman as lovely as her, hidden beneath drab colors and plain, ill-fitting garments. She ought to be in silk that clung lovingly to her every curve. She deserved bright, vivid colors like those she donned on her morning walks. He'd never bought a gown for a woman before, and he didn't have the slightest inkling of how to go about doing so, but she made him want to travel to Paris, surrender a fortune to the House of Worth. Shower her in the finest gowns money could buy.

His mouth traveled down her throat instead, his other hand cupping her face and jaw, his thumb traveling along the plumpness of her lower lip. Her breath whispered over him, a molten temptation like the rest of her. He sucked on her skin, completely aware that he could leave a mark in his wake. He wanted to see that mark by the early-morning light, wanted the satisfaction of it from across the breakfast table. His hand dipped, fingers finding the buttons of her high collar. Pulling them from their moorings.

He dragged his cheek over her, using his whiskers to rasp

over her skin, and then his lips were on the hollow at the base of her throat which he had revealed, absorbing the frantic beats of her pulse. The hand that was at her nape slid lower, following her spine all the way to the small of her back. One firm press brought her closer still. She molded against him, all pliant, feminine curves and seduction. The hand on his necktie moved, and then her arms were twined around his neck, her fingers in his hair.

He wanted to take her up in his arms, lay her on the plush Axminster, and cover her with his body. Wanted to use his lips and tongue and every other means at his disposal to make her spend, and then he longed to sink inside her. To take her. To lose himself in her and be as free as he hadn't been in...perhaps ever.

When had he ever wanted someone more? If he had, he couldn't recall. He wanted Corliss Brinton more than he wanted to defend his champion's title. Wanted her so badly that his cock was thick and hard and rude, tenting his trousers. So much that his teeth ached.

But he couldn't fuck his governess on the floor of the music room.

Correction: he could, but to do so would be the act of a true scoundrel, and he did not think himself so far gone that he would ruin a woman in his employ merely because the need to be inside her surpassed every other urge he'd ever had.

With great reluctance, he tore his mouth from her satiny skin, drinking in the sight of her. She was flushed and lovely, lips swollen from his kisses, tendrils of golden hair escaping her severe chignon to curl around her face, four tiny buttons undone. His mark on her throat, the tender skin pinkened from the rasp of his beard. Her eyes were glazed, pupils dilated.

"Forgive me," he forced himself to say, his voice emerging

husky from pent-up desire. "I never should have been so familiar."

Familiar.

It was a stupid thing to say. A pale, tepid means of describing the passion that had flared to life between them. He regretted it the moment it emerged. And yet, he could not recall the words.

She flinched, as if coming back to wakefulness after a deep and dreamless sleep. "I must apologize, my lord. I don't know what… It was never my intention…"

Her words trailed away in a sigh as she released her hold on him, whisking herself from the piano bench and putting hated, much-needed distance between them. He felt the loss of her warmth and delicious curves as if it were a blow from an opponent's fist in the ring.

Still shaken from their encounter, he forced himself to rise to his feet. "It was unconscionable of me. I assure you, Miss Brinton, that it won't happen again."

Couldn't happen again, he warned himself.

Because if it did…he was not altogether certain he could force himself to stop at the mere undoing of buttons and a few stolen kisses. No, indeed. He would want more. And he couldn't have more. Not of this alluring, altogether forbidden woman.

"Of course it won't," she agreed stiffly, her fingers flying to her buttons, struggling to force the small discs back into place. "Thank you for dinner, Lord Stoneleigh."

She hadn't managed to refasten all four buttons before she dipped into a curtsy and fled the music room, leaving him to stare after her, haunted by the scent of rose and bergamot and the promise of what else they might have done, had they both been reckless enough to revel in the unknown.

CHAPTER 7

*C*orliss threw herself into the task of instructing her charges and avoiding her handsome employer. It had been a surprisingly uneventful week, without any pranks. Her spare drawers had miraculously reappeared. No feathers, nary a hint of treacle. No pepper. No muffled laughter as the girls waited for her to blissfully fall into their trap.

No morning walks and no shared breakfast. She took her meals below stairs instead, where it was far safer despite Mrs. Oak's grim mien and sour disposition.

No chance of crossing paths with Stoneleigh.

No more temptation of kissing him.

No need to awkwardly avoid eye contact so he wouldn't see how desperately she'd been longing for his mouth to drift over hers again. For those big, knowing prizefighter hands to touch her with such gentleness.

Indeed, her every day had been routine and calm. Boring. Careful. Measured. But she told herself that the ennui settling over her was necessary and needed. Not even halfway through her month-long stay, and she had already discovered that being a governess was utterly grueling work, even when the four demanding ladies in her care were perfectly well-behaved.

A bit too well-behaved, if you asked Corliss. She had taken to crossing every threshold with a careful eye to the ceiling so that she could avoid tipping pails. And yet, on every occasion thus far, there had been no need for the vigilance.

Yet.

No, indeed. The only vigilance she needed to assert was in making certain she stayed far away from the Earl of Stoneleigh. Which was why she had decided to wait until the afternoon of her scheduled day of rest to venture from the haven of her chamber. She had spent all the morning hours at the small writing desk in her room, penning the next two chapters of her novel.

To her dismay, the story had changed from the original conception which had previously been rooted in her mind. Miss Brinton's employer was no longer a dastardly villain. Instead, he was kind and charming and handsome. Rather a bit too reminiscent of a certain earl Corliss was doing her best to keep her distance from.

But she decided she wouldn't think about that as she bundled herself in a wrap, hat, and gloves, and ventured outdoors for an afternoon walk. She missed taking the air in the morning, but eschewing the routine had been necessary. The notion of meeting Lord Stoneleigh on the path during his own running sessions had been enough to make her go hot with longing.

Longing she must not—under any circumstances—allow herself to entertain. The air outside was brisk, the gravel of the Knightly Abbey approach crunching smartly beneath the soles of her walking boots as she went. The scent of drying leaves and autumn mud hung heavy about her. But it felt good to be outside again, in the fresh, cool afternoon, the sun beating down.

Good to take a break from writing. As much as she loved the story she was crafting, her bottom had grown sore after so many hours spent sitting. Corliss was lost in her thoughts, traveling along the approach until Knightly Abbey was obscured by the rising swell of the gently sloping hills preceding it. She walked for so long that she failed to take note of the sun's disappearance behind ominous-looking clouds until the heavens had opened to unleash a torrent.

The deluge was instant and overwhelming. Cold rain soaked through her wrap and bit into her skin despite the layers of her gown and undergarments. Of course, she had chosen a most impractical blue silk for her walk, and she was regretting it immensely as she turned to hasten back in the direction she had come from.

Her molars were clacking together as she shivered, the sound so loud that at first, she didn't hear the horse's hooves approaching her. Freezing and drenched, she turned to see a figure approaching on a mount. A tall, broad-shouldered figure she recognized all too well.

"Miss Brinton," he called as he neared her and reined in his gray roan. "What are you doing?"

"Taking the air," she replied above the din of the slashing rain.

"You're shivering." He offered her a gloved hand. "Come, ride with me."

Ride with him? Nestled against him?

She was certain that braving the cold rain for the long return walk would be far wiser.

Corliss stared at his extended hand, remembering the way that hand had felt, cupping her nape, then stroking down her spine. "I shall walk, my lord. You needn't concern yourself with me. A bit of rain shan't hurt."

"Nonsense," he said, frowning down at her. "This is more than just a bit of rain, and you're too far from the main house to return by foot in this storm."

Knightly Abbey was still well beyond sight, and she knew that he was right. The longer she lingered here, arguing the matter with him, the more soaked and chilled she would become. It was her fault for not taking care with how far she had traveled, and not keeping an eye upon the sky. If she had, she would have turned back well before now.

"I shall be fine," she insisted stubbornly, her pride telling her to carry on with her walk.

Along with her sense of self-preservation. Because if she were seated astride his mount, his arms wrapped around her, she was not certain she could escape from this latest brush with Stoneleigh with her ability to continue resisting him intact.

But he was persistent. "There is an empty home not far from here. I've come from there myself. I'll ride to the house, and you'll at least be warm until the storm is over."

Still, she hesitated. The last time they had been alone, she had been ready to surrender her virtue. Accompanying him anywhere was a terrible idea. But then, so was continuing to walk in the rain, which was falling ever more vigorously, the longer she tarried.

"If you refuse, I'll have no choice but to haul you across the saddle and take you there against your will," he said grimly. "Don't think I won't. Anything to keep you from catching your death in this miserable downpour. You're shivering like a leaf."

The wind roared past them, sending icy raindrops to pelt her face beneath the brim of her soaked and bedraggled hat. And at last she relented, because she hadn't a better choice. She settled her hand in his.

"Very well, my lord."

He pulled her into the saddle before him, hauling her from the sodden ground below with ease. She scrambled to adjust herself, trapped in saturated skirts. But he was a reassuring presence at her back, wrapping his arms around her and lowering his lips to her ear.

"Hold on tight. It isn't far."

She tried to ignore the way his lips accidentally grazed her as he spoke. Tried to ignore the jolt of sheer awareness that coursed over her at the simple touch, chasing some of her chill. The ride was bumpy and hurried, a misery of icy droplets slashing against her face. And yet, his arms were surrounding her, protective and strong. She was nestled against his chest as if it were the most natural place for her to be.

They reached the house in a blur of wind and rain.

"I'll see you inside and then I'll tend to my horse," he told her.

She managed a nod, chin quivering, teeth chattering.

"Christ, you're frozen, aren't you? Can you hold on to the saddle while I dismount?"

"Y-yes." *Clack, clack, clack* went her teeth.

"And you wanted to walk the whole bloody way back to Knightly Abbey," he grumbled, before swinging from the roan and landing on the ground. "You are too stubborn for your own good, woman."

Before she could offer any further complaint, he reached up and caught her waist in his capable hands, plucking her from the saddle as if she were a doll. Instead of lowering her to the muddied ground, however, he swept her into his arms, holding her tight as he walked them through the rain.

"I can walk," she protested weakly as his long-limbed strides ate up the distance between them and the house.

"Not a chance," he said grimly, shouldering his way into the quiet house before depositing her on the floor.

He was every bit as wet as she was as he held her gaze. "I'm going to settle the horse in the stables and I'll be back in a trice to light a fire and warm you."

She nodded, grateful for his presence, his rescue.

Even if it meant she was alone with him again.

Dangerous territory indeed. He swept back into the raging storm outside, leaving her dripping in the entryway of the darkened home. The only sound was the rain thrashing against the roof and windowpanes, everything so eerily quiet and still. She took off her soaked wrap and hung it from a hook at the door, adding her hat to another, before removing her gloves. Her chignon was truly ruined, trailing halfway down her back, pins lost or sticking out at odd angles from her wet hair. She plucked a few free, allowing her hair to fall loose around her shoulders.

The door opened, signaling the return of the earl.

His hat dripped with water, his coat and country tweed darkened with rain. Beyond him, the rain showed no sign of slowing down its relentless persistence. The door closed at his back, surrounding them in quiet and shadows.

"My God, what a storm," he said, plucking the hat from his head and taking off his coat and gloves. "I hadn't expected it to rain when I set out today. Nor, I expect, did you."

"I'm afraid I wasn't paying much attention to anything," she admitted, ending the confession with another violent shiver.

"You're cold." He took her hands in his. "Colder than ice. Come. I'll light a fire."

"Do you not think the owner of the house would m-mind?" she asked on another shiver, allowing him to lead her into a small parlor just the same.

They were both leaving wet footprints in their wake. A dreadful mess for someone to clean up.

"He cares far more about your welfare than he does about some muddied carpets," Stoneleigh assured her.

"You know him, then?"

She still felt dreadfully rude, dripping in someone's parlor. And heavens, her boots *were* muddied, even though the earl had carried her to the door.

Stoneleigh gave her a wry grin, his dark hair glistening with droplets of rain. "I am him. My steward informed me it's in need of a new tenant, having been empty for some time. I rode out to inspect the house and fields before the rains came. So you needn't worry yourself over the matter. I'll start a fire, and then you can warm yourself by it."

Another shiver wracked her, so she simply nodded, suddenly too cold and weary for more. And reassured that it was Stoneleigh himself who owned the house, as well. She tried not to read too much into his assertion that the owner cared about her welfare. He had certainly not meant it as a compliment, nor a reference to those tender kisses they had shared in the music room. He was merely being polite.

She watched as he bent before the fireplace, his trousers hugging his muscled thighs and bottom as he set about preparing a fire. And my, what a fine bottom it was, as nicely formed as the rest of him.

In no time, the logs in the grate were alight, warmth blazing to life from the crackling flames. She moved nearer, lured by the promise of heat with her soaked gown and petticoats plastered to her skin.

Another shiver seized her. Her teeth went *clack, clack, clack.*

Stoneleigh rose to his full height, frowning down at her. "You're cold. And soaked to the bone. You'll need to get out of that gown before you can warm yourself."

Get out of her gown?

Despite her chill, a flush stole over her. "I cannot."

"I'll turn my back."

"I'll still be u-unclothed," she protested as yet another shudder went through her.

"Miss Brinton," he said. "Corliss. I don't want you to take ill."

"I'm perfectly warm now that we have the fire," she lied for his benefit.

She had already kissed him. Allowed him to unbutton her collar. His tongue had been in her mouth. She couldn't remove her gown before him. This empty cottage was different than the music room. More isolated. No servants. No one to overhear them or stop them.

"If you won't do it, then I will," he warned grimly.

"My lord, that would be most inappropriate."

"Then do it yourself."

It was a command. An order. Part of her knew he was right, and that she would not be truly able to chase the cold unless she removed her wet outer layers. But another part of her knew that lingering anywhere with her handsome employer whilst she was in a state of dishabille would offer enough temptation to ruin a saint.

Lady Corliss Collingwood had never been a saint.

As evidenced by the fact that she was lying to the man before her about who she was and why she had come to Knightly Abbey. Another sting of guilt pricked at her conscience. He had kissed her, and she was lying to him.

She told herself it was remorse, along with the need to shed her sodden garments, that had her complying with the earl's demand.

"Very well," she relented. "Turn away, if you please."

He obliged her wordlessly, spinning to face the fire.

Her trembling fingers moved to the buttons on her gown. Plucking them free was not easy in the best of conditions, and the soaked fabric and her chilled state didn't render the task any simpler. Somehow, she managed to peel open her bodice, then step out of her cumbersome skirts, shedding her petticoat and bustle along with them.

She looked about for a place to drape them so that they could have a better chance of drying. The room was partially furnished with two armchairs. Corliss chose one and layered her garments over the arms and back of the worn upholstery. Unfortunately, her corset was every bit as sodden as the rest of her garments, and her chemise and drawers and stockings had fared little better. But she was not going to strip herself of any more clothing, for fear that her chemise would be rendered entirely transparent from the rains. All she had to preserve her modesty was her scarlet silk corset.

She glanced down at herself to make certain she was as covered as she could be in her present state, before shivering again.

She rubbed at her arms, which were cold and damp. "I don't suppose there is a blanket at hand?"

"I haven't an inkling." His back was still presented to her. "I can search about for one, if you would like."

"Yes, please," she agreed, before belatedly taking note of the wetness on his tweed and slicking his hair. She had been so caught up in her own chill that she had failed to consider the state of his own clothing. "But you must be cold as well. Perhaps you should remove some of your wet garments, my lord, before you attend to me."

"I am reasonably certain that taking off any of my garments in your presence would be nothing short of disastrous," he drawled. "Besides, I assure you that not even the rain and cold could chill me."

"Of course." She rubbed at her arms again, feeling quite wretched and damp. "You are close to the fire, after all."

"It hasn't a thing to do with the fire, Miss Brinton."

Her lips parted with shock at the suggestion in his words.

Surely he didn't mean to suggest he was warm because they were alone together and because she had removed her gown. Did he?

Her foolish heart leapt at the notion.

"Oh," she said, feeling suddenly breathless.

And wishing the rain would carry on forever so that she could remain here with him in the charmed world of the firelight's glow. No one and nothing else to come between them. But that was even more foolish.

"May I turn?" he asked her. "You ought to come nearer to the fire."

Corliss took another glance down at her drenched self. Her corset was on full display, her drawers and boots peeping from beneath the hem of her sodden chemise. It was nothing short of scandalous. But what was she to do? Demand that he keep his back to her for the remainder of their stay at this cottage?

"You may," she said, catching her lip in her teeth and worrying it, knowing the picture she would present when he did so.

Slowly, he spun, the intensity of his gaze burning into hers as brightly as the flames at his back.

"Come," he said, extending his hand to her again, just as he had on his roan. "Stand by the fire while I go and take a look about."

Corliss's teeth chattered as another violent shiver over-took her. No more delaying now. She went to him, shivering as gooseflesh rose on her arms.

"Your fingers." He caught them in his, lifting them for his inspection. "They're stained with ink."

His hands were warm, far warmer than her own.

Oh, how she wished his touch, so casual, as if it were a trifling matter, as if she were an impervious object he had chosen to discuss instead of weak flesh and bone, did not affect her. But sparks had skittered to life, skipping from her fingers to her wrist, and then higher, past her elbow. Warming her along with the licking heat emanating from the fire as he pulled her nearer.

"From working on their ladyship's lessons," she lied, not wanting him to guess at the true reason.

She had quite forgotten about the mess she always made of her fingers when she spent hours writing. Here was another unwanted reminder of the lies she had mired herself in so firmly. Governesses did not secretly pen books. Questions would be asked.

She tugged at her fingers, but he didn't release them. Instead, his grasp tightened, his thumb finding a callus on her middle finger and swirling over it.

"You write frequently," he said, more observation than question. "Why were you penning their lessons on your day to yourself?"

His concern struck her every bit as profoundly as his touch did. "I needed something with which to occupy my mind," she said, diverting her gaze away from his searching one to stare into the flames, a far safer place to look.

The guilt was rising, constricting her throat. The earl appeared genuinely nettled by the notion of her toiling away on one of her few free days, when his nieces were looked after by their nursemaid, Miss Wofford, instead. And in truth, she had not been working herself into a frenzy over lessons. Instead, she had been working on the true reason she had come.

What a wretch she was, deceiving him so.

"You're quite chilled," he said instead of addressing the matter again, releasing her hand and taking a step in retreat, putting some much-needed distance between them. "I'll search for a counterpane."

"Thank you, my lord," she murmured, keeping her eyes settled upon the flame, dancing orange and hot.

At the muffled thumps of his booted footsteps receding, she finally exhaled the breath she hadn't realized she had been holding. She couldn't afford for him to discover the truth, to lay bare all her deceptions. Not when she still had a little more than a fortnight of time remaining.

Nor, she realized, could she bear for him to gaze upon her with the wounded look of a man who had been deceived. A man whose lips she had kissed and whose trust she had broken. With another shudder, she held her ink-spattered fingers to the fire, awaiting Stoneleigh's inevitable return.

KNIGHT COULDN'T FIND a damned blanket anywhere in the cottage. By the time he returned to the parlor and Miss Brinton, she was shivering again, the fire having burned lower in the grate than he had expected. There was no more dry wood to be had; he'd been fortunate to find the old, wizened pieces left behind by the cottage's former occupants. And the weather showed no sign of relenting any time soon, the wind beyond howling, sending sheets of rain to pelt the windows and roof.

"You're still cold," he said, trying not to allow his gaze to linger on her undergarments.

But Christ, it was difficult. Her corset was a thing of beauty, scarlet satin trimmed with blonde lace, lifting her breasts high. The damp linen of her chemise and drawers was nearly transparent, even in the low light. Her dark-gold hair was unbound, cascading down her back in soft waves he itched to run his fingers through. He had never been more tempted in his life.

She turned partially toward him, her ink-bedecked

fingers still spread toward the dwindling flames. Her gaze dipped to his empty hands. "I suppose you weren't able to find a blanket, then."

Her teeth chattered as if to conclude her observation.

He hated seeing her suffer. It was a different kind of pain, though it certainly rivaled any punch he'd ever received in one of his matches. Before he could consider the wisdom of his actions, his booted feet were moving. Eating up the distance between them.

"I'll try to stoke the fire," he said, dropping to his knees at her side, his every sense heightened by her proximity.

There was the fresh, damp scent of her—rain, roses, and bergamot. The smoke from the fire. The warmth creeping over him, awareness tingling down his spine. He felt her gaze on him, watching him as he worked, as surely as any caress. He reasoned that if his hands were busy, they couldn't be tempted to touch her.

But there was only so much he could do for the fire. The meager, dry wood had already nearly burned itself to ash.

"It burned quite quickly," she said, her voice husky and soft.

He clenched his jaw and tossed her a look over his shoulder. A mistake, because with the glow of the fire illuminating her, her beauty struck him in a new way. One that almost sent him toppling to his arse. Her arms were crossed over herself, and she was rubbing them, the action pressing her breasts together so that their creamy swells spilled over the top of her chemise.

His heart thundered hard. And his cock...well, that was hard too.

Damn it all. He had no control where she was concerned.

"I'm afraid the fire is dying out," he told her, determined to resist his attraction to her, even if it bloody well killed him.

Because unfortunately, there was another fire roaring to life. And like the one in the grate, it was the sort that would burn her if she touched it. But Knight could be a gentleman. He could recall who she was. Who he was. Lusting after one's governess just wasn't done.

Nor was kissing her in the music room and sucking on her throat.

At the recollection, his gaze slipped to her neck, and he saw the faint pink reminder of his mouth on her. His mark.

"Hopefully the weather shall soon improve and we can return to Knightly Abbey," Miss Brinton said, rubbing at her bare arms.

He rose, keenly aware of how he towered over her, how much larger he was than she. He'd never felt like the brute he was billed as on his tours. The Bruiser Knight was a title he wore, a role he played. But he felt as if he crowded her in this small, shadowed room. A protective surge rose before he could tamp it down, and then he was doing the very thing he had told himself he mustn't.

He reached for her, his hands on her forearms, finding them cold as ice. The lust fled him.

"You're still frozen, and the fire is dwindling." He frowned down at her, thinking there was only one way he could provide her with warmth.

"I'm well enough." She gave him a pained smile, and he noted her lips were pale.

He released her and shrugged out of his wet coat, then toed off his riding boots. She watched him, eyes going wide.

"My lord, what are you doing?"

"Removing some of my wet layers so I can share my body heat with you." The last thing he wanted to do was take her in his arms with the two of them scarcely clothed, but he hadn't another option. "With the flames dying and no more wood to be had, we've no other choice."

"You've already done far too much. You needn't fret over me any more than you have," she protested, but then her body belied her words as she trembled.

He cursed. "I haven't done enough. I'll not have you catching a lung infection."

His trousers were next. There was no help for it; they were soaked from the rain. Thankfully, the thickness of the tweed had protected his drawers. Not that he would have removed them. He could strive for honor, but he wasn't a saint. Grinding his molars, he tugged at his necktie, freeing the knot, and then shucked his shirt as well.

Bare-chested, and clad only in his drawers and stockinged feet, he drew her against him, the coolness of her smooth skin a shock to his senses. She was shivering, and she tucked herself against him without any hint of protest.

"I'll make you cold as well," she said.

No chance of that. Not when she was in his arms.

"I've enough warmth for both of us." Knight swallowed hard against the rising tide of desire, telling himself he was doing this for selfless reasons. "I'm accustomed to cold. When I'm training, I often immerse myself in ice baths. I've grown impervious to physical discomfort in a great many ways."

But there was another discomfort he hadn't trained himself to ignore, and it was desire. He'd never had to suppress his needs before. The sensation was novel, but not necessarily appreciated.

"Ice baths?" Her cold palms settled on his shoulders, her head tucked beneath his chin. "That sounds positively dreadful."

"It's good for the muscles, and for helping me to prepare my body," he explained, all too cognizant of the fact that he was speaking of his body and holding her against it, and that said body wanted her very, very much.

He took care to keep the lower portion of his anatomy from intruding, holding himself away slightly as he held her by the fire. His hands came to life again, stroking up and down her arms, before covering her icy fingers. The urge to kiss her crown was strong. He had a visceral reaction to this woman curled into him. So close. Not close enough.

"You are very strong," she murmured, and he felt as if he were ten bloody feet tall. Her cold fingers flexed against his, moving over his bare shoulders as if she were testing his strength. Most definitely his restraint, though she couldn't know it. "I've never met another gentleman so dedicated to honing himself into a machine before."

Knight swallowed. "I never thought of it in such terms. I merely want to be the best at what I do."

"I admire your dedication."

Her quiet words astonished him. He lowered his head, nuzzling her damp hair, unable to resist. "Thank you."

The air in the parlor changed around them, growing heavier. Laden with the electricity that sparked with ceaseless persistence, regardless of how hard he tried to ignore it.

He cleared his throat into the silence. "Are you warming, Miss Brinton?"

She nodded, her damp hair tickling his chin. "Yes."

"Excellent. I know this is terribly inappropriate, but you have my word that my intentions toward you remain honorable."

Because he would force them to be.

Even if doing so required more skill and concentration than prizefighting did.

She nodded, her cool cheek gliding over his chest in a silken caress. "I trust you, Lord Stoneleigh."

Christ.

You shouldn't, he wanted to say. *You're safer in the blasted rain, walking back to Knightly Abbey on foot.*

But no, that wasn't true. She *was* safe with him. He merely wished that they were two different people than who they were, and that kissing her, wanting her, making love to her wouldn't be wrong and impossible.

"About what happened in the music room," he began, feeling deuced awkward, caught as he was between the need to remember that she was in his employ and the need to have her mouth beneath his. "Pray accept my sincerest apology. It was wrong. I'm in a position of power, and although your response to my advances was not dependent upon your continued employment, I understand why you could perceive it thus. It has torn me apart inside, thinking of that these last few days."

Missing her each day. Her absence on his morning runs had been glaring. He had hated the thought he had pressured her into anything she did not want. Although he didn't think he had mistaken her reaction, he wanted to acknowledge his actions had been wrong. Wanted her to know, particularly now that they were both scantily clad and pressed together, that she needn't worry he would attempt to ravish her.

"You've already apologized, my lord," she said, her fingers lacing through his, her breath warm as it whispered over his bare chest. "There is no need to belabor the matter, for the truth is, I welcomed your kisses. I would do so again."

He froze, lust slamming into him and rendering him immobile.

"Corliss." Her name hissed from him.

What else was he to say? To do?

Knight didn't know. But in the next breath, she tipped her head back, and he lost himself in the dark depths of her eyes, forgetting all the reasons why he shouldn't take her lips with his own.

CHAPTER 8

*S*he was doing something foolish.
Something reckless.

She was inviting ruin.

But Stoneleigh was holding her in his arms, wrapping her in his strength and warmth as if she were someone precious to him, and her heart was galloping and the warmth that had begun seeping back into her had only one source.

Her body's reaction to his.

He had been apologizing for their shared kisses, kisses that had haunted her every moment of each hour since his mouth had last been on hers. She couldn't bear for him to believe those kisses had been anything but wanted. So she had confessed the truth. As close to the truth as she dared inch. Revealing just enough.

Too much.

And she had not one single regret as the earl's lips claimed hers. Not a regret as she opened for his questing tongue, as her hands slid into the damp hair at his nape. Not a hint of remorse as she pressed herself flush against his lean form.

Her breasts were crushed wantonly between them and her nipples were hard and aching beneath the stiff boning of her corset. He kissed her fiercely, as if he were starving for her.

She knew the feeling, because there was nothing she wanted more than his embrace, his kiss, his touch. The taste of him on her lips, his tongue gliding against hers, claiming and full and laden with the promise of more. The storm ceased to exist. Consequences be damned.

She inhaled deeply, filling herself with the scent of him— leather and musk, citrus and rain—and surrendered. He softened the kiss slowly, the pressure of his lips gentling, his tongue withdrawing. His prizefighter's hands, capable of such damage and yet the tenderest of touches, cupped her face. His thumbs swept along her cheekbones, tracing the structure of her face, his palms hot and callused.

Stealing her breath.

"Your freckles entrance me," he murmured, looking down at her with an expression of raw, unabashed desire that was still somehow affectionate.

And then he slowly lowered his head, his lips brushing over the bridge of her nose in a kiss she felt to her toes. She had never liked her freckles. During summers at Talleyrand Park, she was forever roaming the countryside without a hat, and the speckles she loathed became more pronounced. She often covered them with pearl powder. But Stoneleigh's mouth was traveling over that most hated part of herself with a reverence that made her sigh.

He raised his head, his eyes taking her in.

"Who am I fooling?" he muttered almost as if to himself. "Every part of you entrances me. No woman has ever entranced me more, and it's the devil of a thing, because you're the one woman I can never have."

His low confession filled her with wonder, leaving her

feeling dizzied and intoxicated. He was still cupping her face, and their bodies were pressed together. It didn't feel as if he couldn't have her in this moment, in the privacy of the cottage as the storm unleashed its fury around them. It felt, instead, as if he *could* have her. She wanted him to. Wanted her sense of responsibility and all the reasons why she must not lose herself in the handsome Earl of Stoneleigh to disappear.

"You can have me," she said, meaning those words.

She felt the way she did when she drank too much wine at dinner. Her head was light, and her capacity for good decision-making had vanished.

"Corliss." Her name was a groan. His head dropped, and he pressed his forehead to hers. "You shouldn't say such things to me."

"Why not?"

"Because it makes me want to do..." He stopped and shuddered, the action making a thick ridge glance over her in a place that felt altogether lovely. Brought to life by the sinful promise of more.

He desired her. She rubbed herself against him, needing, wanting, desperate.

"What does it make you want to do?" she asked, pushing him.

Pushing the both of them.

It seemed that the entirety of her stay at Knightly Abbey had been a dance. Preparation for this interlude as they stood utterly alone in an abandoned cottage, both of them damp from rain, their bodies entwined, their lips so close. The demarcation between right and wrong fading with each second.

"It makes me want to do this," he said, and then he moved his head, his lips grazing the hairline at her temple. "And this." He kissed her ear. "This." His mouth was on her throat now, hot and demanding as it had been before, only different. "It makes me want to make my mark on you again."

Her head fell back. She was drunk, she thought. Drunk on him. On the way he made her feel.

"Do it," she urged, her voice throaty, thick with desire.

He growled, and then he sucked hard, eliciting a whimper of helpless need from her, before delivering a gentle nip with his teeth, and then rubbing the prickly whiskers of his trimmed beard over her already sensitive flesh. He released her face, his hands moving to her waist, fingers biting into her in a possessive hold that felt utterly right. Grinding her more firmly against him as he licked the hollow at the base of her throat.

She shivered, but for the first time since getting caught in the rain, the action had nothing to do with being cold.

He paused, casting a careful glance up at her. "Are you still chilled?"

"No." She shook her head, taking the opportunity to touch him, moving one of her hands to cup his jaw, the prickle of his whiskers kissing her palm. "I'm quite warm."

And so was he, searing her fingertips as she caressed his cheek, his neck, his wide shoulder. He held still beneath her touch, his sole action swallowing. She watched, mesmerized by the protrusion of his Adam's apple, the way it dipped.

"You're certain?" he asked softly.

And she knew he was asking her about more than whether she was chilled. He was asking permission, too. And she was going to give it. Because she wanted him more than she wanted to breathe.

"Certain," she said, her hand trailing over his chest now, where so much of his strength dwelled.

He was all sinew and muscle, his body hardened from ceaseless training. His muscles tensed as her fingertips ventured along his abdomen, following bands of muscle.

What a marvel he was. She had known that the earl possessed a powerful form, but she hadn't imagined the true beauty hiding beneath his sweaters and crisp white shirts. When she reached the waistband of his drawers, he sucked in a breath and stiffened. She paused in her quest, eyes flying to his.

"Is it…do you not like my touch?" she asked hesitantly.

For she had never been nearly naked with a man before, and she most definitely had never touched a man the way she was touching Stoneleigh. Perhaps she had done something wrong.

"I like it, Corliss. I like it far too much." He gave her a wry grin and lowered his lips to hers for another slow, deep kiss.

And she liked his response the same. Liked it far, far too much.

Liked his mouth on hers even better.

Her fingers found purchase in the waistband of his drawers. His skin was smoother than she had expected. So hot and sleek, dusted with a fine trail of hair. She grasped and pulled, needing the friction of him, needing his hardness rubbing over her between her thighs, where her body was aching, all the earlier chill completely forgotten.

With another low groan, he pulled his lips from hers, his ragged breath coasting over her mouth like a phantom kiss. "We shouldn't be doing this."

"We shouldn't," she agreed.

His gaze was fiery. "You should tell me to go to the devil."

But that was the trouble. She didn't want him to go anywhere else. Not ever.

Her other hand crept to his shoulder, testing the hardness of the muscles there. "I like you right here just fine."

He clenched his jaw, his expression torn. She had seen the Earl of Stoneleigh in so many different lights, and he had been beautiful in them all. Early morning, beneath the glow of gas lamps, the outdoors, and now here in the flickers of a waning fire that never could have held a candle to the blaze within her. Now, he was all shadows and mystery and forbidden desire. Warmth and want and dangerous need.

But honor, too. He was as torn as she was between the attraction sparking between them and the inherent wrongness of giving in to the temptation. Their reasons were different, but the sentiment was the same.

"You are in my employ," he said, as if he needed to remind himself of the disparities, the reasons why they should not indulge.

"Does my being a governess give you pause?" she asked.

She was an earl's daughter. How truly ironic it would be to be denied the only man she had ever longed for because he believed she was from a different class. And yet, how sobering, too. How would Miss Brinton feel if she were losing her heart to her employer, only for him to deny their affection because of who and what she was?

Crushed, Corliss was sure of it.

"Yes and no," he said, his hands flexing on her waist as if he wanted to release her and yet could not. "Because you are a governess in my household. Because I am meant to act a gentleman and be honorable where you are concerned. Because you are a woman in a position most vulnerable whilst I am a man who can take whatever he wants."

He could, yes. He was powerful. An earl, a man made of muscle, wealthy, a prizefighting champion. He was all those things. But he was also the man who made her heart pound. Who had been kind to her at every opportunity. The man who had filled her breakfast plate, who had saved her from the rain. Who had been furious on her behalf when his nieces had played their treacle and feather prank upon her. He was the man who kissed her and made her melt.

She didn't fear him, and he was not taking advantage of

her. If anything, she was the one who took advantage of him, because she was deceiving him. And how she hated that deception now, more than ever.

"What if I want you to take me?" she asked, shameless just the same. Longing for far more than she could ever have.

The Earl of Stoneleigh could never be hers, for he would never forgive her once he learned of her deception.

Nor could she be his. But she told herself it was just as well. After this month was at an end, she would return to Talleyrand Park. She would finish her novel. Publish it. Travel the world.

Why did the thoughts that had driven her here to Yorkshire, to her position as governess, now leave her feeling inexplicably hollow?

"I can't," Stoneleigh said, closing his eyes for a moment, seemingly attempting to gain control over his emotions. "Regardless of how much I long for something more with you, it would not be right." His hands left her waist, sliding up her spine, pulling her tighter to him even as he spoke words that would create further distance. "I'm trying my damnedest to be honorable for your sake, and it's the most difficult goddamn thing I've ever done in my life."

"More difficult than beating your opponents in the ring?"

A half smile kicked up the corner of his sensual lips. "God, yes."

His eyes had opened again, and he was staring into her, seeing her. And she was looking back, letting him know how much she longed for him in return. How much she wanted him to tamp down his honor.

This moment would never come again.

But it was already slipping away.

Silence descended, and she realized why it was different this time. There was no longer the lash of rain on the window panes.

"The rain has stopped," she said, regret lacing the observation, quelling all the desire that had swelled inside her like a storm-tossed sea. "We should return to Knightly Abbey before we are missed."

He had yet to release her. His arms banded around her tightly for another few beats of her foolish heart, and then he withdrew, clearing his throat, avoiding her gaze.

"I expect we ought to dress. I'll take my garments to another room and give you privacy."

"Of course," she answered, feeling numb again, but for a different reason this time. "Thank you for your concern, my lord."

He gathered up his boots and the rest of his clothing, striding from the room with all haste. Corliss watched the corded sinew in his brawny back flexing as he walked away from her. And then she turned to her drenched clothing and forced herself to dress, telling herself it was for the best.

The end of the rain had saved them both from folly.

If only it felt that way.

KNIGHT WAS AWAKE FAR TOO late for his customary early-morning run not to be a resounding failure. Lack of proper rest always made his muscles burn and caused his body to fight every step of each mile along the way in the morning. But he couldn't sleep.

He was thinking, it was true, of the governess who was never far from his mind.

Haunted by thoughts of Corliss, of what might have been.

With a muttered curse, he bent over the billiards table, striking his cue ball into the object ball and sending it sailing into a pocket with expert precision. Somehow, playing billiards alone wasn't nearly as satisfying as playing with an opponent.

"That was a wicked word, Uncle."

The small, girlish voice emerged from behind Knight, giving him a start. He jumped and spun about to find the source—his youngest niece, Mary—and couldn't manage to tamp down yet another oath rising to his lips.

"Fucking hell," he muttered, settling the end of his cue stick on the Axminster with a thump.

"That is a worse wicked word," she announced, shaking her head as if he were a disgrace.

He wondered if she was referring to *fuck* or *hell*, and then he wondered how the devil she had come to know any such words at all. She was only five years old, for Chrissakes. And a lady, at that. Knight knew scarcely anything about children, but he knew one at such a tender age ought not to recognize oaths and curses when they were spoken.

"What the…" He stopped himself, raked a hand through his hair, and rephrased. "How do you know which words are wicked?"

Mary was wearing a night rail, her dark-brown hair in a fat braid that had come partially unbound. She looked so small and lonely, wholly lost in the vastness of the billiards room and Knightly Abbey at large. Corliss's words came rushing back to him.

Everyone close to them has left them. Their mother, their father, their governesses.

The pang in his heart was sudden. Yes, these were Robert's children, but they were also his responsibility now. How the devil was he going to leave them too? Four young girls alone in the world could not be managed by a steward. Nor by a governess, regardless of how generous and caring she was. Not even an angel walking amongst mere mortals, he thought wryly.

"Will I get into trouble if I tell you?" Mary asked then, intruding upon Knight's whirling ruminations.

Clever girl.

He sighed, rested the cue stick against the billiards table, and crossed the chamber to her, before sinking down on his haunches so they were eye to eye. "Not if you tell me the truth, poppet."

"Poppet is what Papa called me," Mary said, eyes so like his own welling with tears.

God. The merciless burn of tears hit the backs of his eyes, and he blinked hard.

"Shall I call you something different then, Mary?"

She appeared to consider his query for a moment before shaking her head. "No. You may call me poppet, Uncle."

Uncle. The appellation, his connection to the four spirited young ladies who were at times troublesome and at times sweet, still felt foreign and new. But, in another sense, meaningful. His sole sense of purpose these last many years had been prizefighting. But that had gradually been changing since his return to Yorkshire. Against his will, it was true. But happening, just the same.

"Fine then," he agreed, patting her thin little shoulder. "Poppet it shall be. Will you tell me now how you've heard such words?"

"Henrietta," Mary said.

He might have known it was the eldest of his nieces who was the source. But that did not answer the question of where she herself might have happened upon the knowledge.

"And do you know where Henrietta learned the words?" he prompted gently.

"She said she heard Papa saying them when he was angry with Mrs. Oak once, and when she asked him what they meant later, he said she must never speak them aloud, for they're wicked words and would turn a lady's tongue green and cause it to fall off if she said them too many times."

Frowning, Knight allowed her unexpected and long-winded explanation to settle in. First, why the devil had his brother been so angry with the housekeeper? And to issue obscenities at the woman? Knight didn't like her much on account of her refusal to allow Corliss breakfast when she wished to take it, but aside from that, he hadn't had much interaction with the domestic. For young Henrietta to have overheard the arguments, and then for Robert to offer such a stupid explanation to his daughter as to why she must not do as he had done…

He sighed. "Your papa was right that such wicked words don't bear repeating."

"Put out your tongue, if you please," Mary said matter-of-factly.

Her request startled him. "Why?"

"I want to see if it's green as Papa warned it would become."

Good God.

Obligingly, Knight did as she had asked, showing her his tongue had not, in fact, changed color. "There you are. Satisfied now, poppet?"

"No." She scrunched up her nose as if she were contemplating the weightiest matters in the universe. "Why did it not turn your tongue green, saying those awful things? Does it only happen to ladies? That was what Papa told Henrietta, that it didn't happen to boys, only to girls. But Henrietta's tongue hasn't turned green yet, and she told us all the words."

Well, that was a fine bit of rot Robert had told his daughter. And now, like everything else his brother had left behind, Knight was forced to attempt to answer for it.

"Cursing won't turn anyone's tongue green," he explained. "That's as impossible as a horse sprouting wings and flying."

Mary gasped. "You mean that Papa lied? Oh, why would he lie? Miss Brinton says we must always be honest to each other, and most especially to adults."

The mentioning of Corliss caused him to think for an aching moment of what had almost passed between them in the cottage. But he forced it down.

"Miss Brinton is not wrong," he conceded. "Honesty is one of the most important virtues anyone can claim as their own. In this instance, I suspect your father wanted to frighten Henrietta enough that she would never repeat the vulgar words herself, for it was wrong of him to say them to Mrs. Oak to begin with."

"If it was wrong of him, why did he do it?" Mary's frown deepened. "And why would he lie? Lying is a sin."

He pondered her latest questions, wondering how the devil children were so curious and perspicacious. He hadn't ever had an inkling they could be. Nor had he ever stopped to care.

He sighed. "Sometimes, poppet, people do things they know are wrong. But that doesn't make it right. It's important to know the difference between good and bad, right and wrong. We must always try, all of us, to do our best."

And he, more than anyone, would have to try harder. Try better. To rein in his desire for a woman he could not have and should not want.

"We should also try to never say wicked words or lie," Mary added somberly. "You should try not to say them too, Uncle, even if your tongue won't turn green."

"Very true," he agreed, matching her seriousness. "Worthy endeavors indeed. Now then, would you care to tell me what you're doing awake at this hour and wandering about when you should be fast asleep?"

"I was having a dreadful dream," she said, her lower lip quivering. "I tried to wake Alice, but she told me to go back to sleep and stop being annoying. What are you doing, Uncle?"

"Playing billiards," he answered.

Her brows drew together. "By yourself?"

"By myself," he agreed.

"Aren't you lonely?"

When Mary posed the question, she certainly made him sound rather pathetic. And then he was thinking of something else Corliss—Miss Brinton, he must think of her—had said yet again. *One can be surrounded by others and still be quite lonely.* A wise woman for her tender years. Capable of understanding so much, capable of such compassion, and sensuality too.

He swallowed hard against a rush of emotion he couldn't afford to entertain. "Yes, a bit lonely, I reckon."

"I could play billiards with you," Mary offered shyly. "If you teach me the rules. Then you wouldn't have to be alone."

"I'd like that very much," he said, startled to realize it was the truth. "Come, poppet. I'll teach you the rules."

"TAG!" Lady Alice announced gleefully as she tapped Corliss on the shoulder. "You're *it!*"

Corliss heaved a feigned sigh of disappointment. "Very well. I'll give you all until the count of five to run. One, two…"

She finished counting and then hefted her dull, brown skirts in both hands, lifting them so that she could move more freely. Her charges were scattered across the Knightly Abbey park, cheeks pinkened with exertion, each one of them grinning in childish abandon. The sight of them so carefree filled her heart with warmth.

The day had dawned sunny and unseasonably warm, a

welcome improvement over the previous day's ferocious storms. Whilst they had spent the morning at work on conjugating French verbs, she had decided the girls were in need of some merriment this afternoon, and on account of such fine weather. It was true that she had also grown bored of staring at the walls of the nursery, trying not to think of their uncle.

An impossible feat after she had been half-clothed with him in the abandoned cottage.

She raced after Lady Mary, who was the youngest and slowest of the four, making a great show of attempting to tag the girl and missing. Lady Mary gave a great squeal of victory and carried on through the grass.

"You missed me, Miss Brinton! You'll never catch me now!"

The game of tag was unladylike in the extreme. But it was also great fun in the extreme. She had played it often with her sisters and brother at Talleyrand Park. The memories of those long-ago days still made her smile.

She turned and redoubled her efforts, catching sight of Lady Beatrice racing toward a tree and pursuing her. The older girl was laughing too, quite giving away any attempts she might make at hiding herself, although the trunk of the centuries-old tree was thick enough to shield her. Corliss rounded the tree with a mock sound of triumph.

"I've got you now," she declared, before lunging and intentionally missing the girl, who darted away with ease.

"Miss Brinton missed me!" Lady Beatrice called to her sisters. "She's still *it*!"

Enjoying herself more than she had suspected she would, Corliss raced about the park some more, chasing Lady Alice for a time before finally settling upon the eldest girl, Lady Henrietta, as her target. With a feint to the right, Corliss caught her, tagging her elbow.

"Lady Henrietta, you're *it!*" she said.

"Bloody hell," Lady Henrietta muttered.

At least, Corliss thought that was what the girl said. The words brought her up short.

"My lady, what did you say?" she asked, frowning at the dark-haired girl.

Lady Henrietta leapt forward, tagging Corliss on the arm.

"I said tag, you're *it!*" she said, laughing.

And then she raced off through the grass.

That had been rather ingenious, Corliss had to admit. However, she did intend to speak with Lady Henrietta about her cursing when this game of tag had come to an end. She caught her skirts up and was off running again when a familiar figure brought her to an abrupt halt.

Tall, broad-shouldered, lean-hipped, and well-muscled, striding toward her.

Handsome, devastatingly so.

The man who had kissed her so skillfully, she had felt him on her lips long after they had parted the day before.

"Lord Stoneleigh," she said, breathless from all the running about she had been doing.

But then, who was she fooling? She still would have been breathless at the sight of the earl had she not been running about and playing tag. Her cheeks went hot as it occurred to her what a sight she must present, hair mussed, cheeks flushed, boots and gown splattered with mud. Showing her ankles as she raced over the park like a hoyden.

"Miss Brinton."

They were proper once again. As if they had never touched. As if she had not so recently been in his arms, scarcely any barriers between her bare skin and his. She hated it.

But Corliss dropped her gown and dipped into a curtsy

just the same, belatedly recalling her position. "To what do we owe the privilege of your company, my lord?"

His gaze met hers from beneath the brim of his jaunty hat as he approached, stopping just short of touching distance, his expression impossible to read. "I was in my brother's study, reviewing reports from Mr. Smithson, when I heard squealing."

She winced at his description, fearing they were returned to formality and he was about to reprimand her for running about with the girls in unladylike fashion. "Forgive us for the interruption, Lord Stoneleigh. We shall endeavor to be quieter as we take the air."

"As you *take the air*," he repeated, stroking his jaw, his countenance turning contemplative. "Is that what you are calling this, Miss Brinton?"

So stilted. She wished he would call her Corliss. She wished she wasn't the governess to his nieces. Wished she was Lady Corliss Collingwood, capable of anything. Futile wishes, of course. She had chosen this path for a reason. It was merely his presence—the earl himself—who had mucked it up.

"Uncle!" cried Lady Mary, hurtling past them in a flurry of skirts, her bonnet hanging down her back. "We are playing tag, and Miss Brinton is *it!*"

So much for her attempt at feigning they had been taking a brisk walk. But then, the earl had already said he'd heard the ladies' squealing, as he had so unkindly phrased it, even if the description was apt. And he had likely witnessed them all scattering about, running as if their lives depended upon it. He would know they had not been merely *taking the air*.

"Tag, you say?" Stoneleigh mused, his face an expressionless mask as he propped his fist on his hip. "And Miss Brinton is *it?*"

Guilt rushed over her. Lady Mary was already running

away, peals of laughter trailing in her wake in a most unseemly display. And yet, Corliss could not have a regret for the girls having the opportunity to be *girls*. To laugh and run in the sunshine. To forget the ugliness of the world that had left them orphans.

Still, she had no wish for the earl to be upset with his nieces yet again. To be the cause for further friction.

"If you are displeased with them, I pray you would direct your ire at me," she hastened to say. "Tag may be an unusual lesson for young ladies, I will admit. However, the sun is shining, the air is warm, the sky is blue, and they deserve the chance to remember what it is like to be happy. They deserve laughter and fresh air and the chance to be children."

She finished her impassioned speech, feeling rather foolish as he continued to observe her in a manner she could not decipher. They had parted on awkward terms the day before, his rejection of her still stinging in the deepest depths of her soul, a place she had not known the existence of until he had wounded it.

"Tag is indeed a most extraordinary lesson, Miss Brinton," he said agreeably, still stroking the sharp angle of his beard-stubbled jaw. Eyes to rival the blessedly cloudless sky held her in their thrall. "I confess, I've never heard of a governess playing tag with her charges."

He hadn't? Very well. Neither had she. But she wasn't a governess. Only, he couldn't know that.

She straightened her shoulders, daring him to gainsay her. "It is an important part of their studies. If you wish to chastise anyone, let it be me, for I—"

"I'm not displeased with my nieces," he interrupted before she could make a further impassioned speech.

"You aren't?"

He shook his head, a slow grin curving his lips that

rendered him even more handsome than before. "I'm not. Do you know why, Miss Brinton?"

Oh, dear heavens. No man had a right to look so alluring. Especially not when he had been a prizefighter for so many years. He didn't even have a crooked nose to show for the time he had spent defending himself in the ring. All he had was a body that resembled a marbled sculpture of a Greek god. And it had certainly been pleasant to look upon, and to feel pressed against her. She had thought of precious little else ever since.

Had closed her eyes to find the memory of his taut and carefully honed torso practically stitched to the insides of her eyelids last night. All those muscles. A sin and a benediction wrapped in one delicious parcel. He had been the most alluring sight she had ever beheld. He still was, even dressed in country togs and looking at her in such a strange, unnerving fashion.

"Why, Lord Stoneleigh?" she asked him then, feeling flustered and hot in a way that hadn't a thing to do with the game of tag she'd been playing.

Everything to do with the man she couldn't stop wanting, regardless of the warnings she issued herself every other minute.

"Because I want to play tag as well," he said, cocking his head at her in an almost boyish manner that had her heart beating faster than a butterfly's wings. "And I understand you're *it*."

She nodded, caught in his stare, her body swaying toward his as if she were a spring sprout newly shot up from the dirt and he was the sun. "You want to play tag, my lord?"

Not the question she had supposed she would be asking him. Nor the conversation she wanted to be having with him after the day before. So many questions abounded. But he remained enigmatic, and that was part of his allure.

"I do." His smile deepened, making the corners of his eyes crinkle in a way that melted her heart and another part of her altogether.

She knew a sudden, physical ache in her chest. Or perhaps that was something else, a far deeper, stronger emotion she refused to examine on this bright autumn day as she stood before a man she was deceiving, his nieces darting about and hiding, their every move punctuated by giggles.

There was a lightness in the air. In his face. In her, too.

Infectious. She wanted to capture it, to capture the moment, to hold it forever in her heart.

But she shook herself from such maudlin sentiment which she could not indulge in, smiling back at the earl. "If you want to play tag, then you had better run, my lord. I am *it*, as Lady Mary said."

"Catch me if you dare," he returned, and then he pivoted and began running across the park.

For a moment, Corliss was so shocked by his response that she could do nothing more than stare in awe at the flawless grace of his muscular body moving without the bulky encumbrance of his sweater. And then gradually, she realized that she was *it*. He wasn't angry with today's lesson. Far from it. Rather, he wanted to play along with them.

She would never catch him.

The man was taller than she was, and he ran for miles every morning.

But she caught her skirts in her hands anyway, lifting them high, and began running after him, laughing as she went. Laughing because it was ridiculous, a grown woman chasing a man across the park. Ridiculous, a governess playing a game of tag with her charges and her employer. Ridiculous in the best of ways.

She felt alive and happy and free, just as she did at Talleyrand Park.

Corliss charged after him.

"Uncle, are you playing?" called one of the girls.

"I would never miss the opportunity to play tag," he called back, sounding the most lighthearted she had ever heard him.

His voice made her smile as she ran on, and for the first time, it occurred to her that he, too, deserved the opportunity to be free. To race across the park without a care. To laugh. To bask in the sunshine and the warmth of the late-autumn day. His life was strict and regimented. He trained, he fought, he strove to be the best prizefighter he could be—the champion. The Bruiser Knight. And then, he had been saddled with the weighty responsibility of four young, orphaned nieces. An earldom. A vast estate which came with a ceaseless supply of burdens, expenses, and duties.

He, too, should have a few stolen moments of happiness.

They all should. What was life without it?

"I'll catch you," she called after him, doing her utmost to increase her pace.

It wasn't easy with the encumbrance of her gown, tournure, petticoat, and undergarments. The earl was a seasoned athlete. He could likely outrun the devil himself. But she knew he was not running to his full potential. Instead, he ran before her, near enough that she thought she might catch him if she outsmarted him.

"Tag Uncle, Miss Brinton," called Lady Alice. "You can do it!"

"Get him, Miss Brinton," joined in the other three, an indistinguishable chorus of encouragement.

The earl ran into a grouping of trees ringing the edge of the park. It was farther than the girls had dared to run, but Corliss forgot about the boundaries they had established at the onset of their game in favor of following him. She was determined. Stubborn.

The shade of the trees cooled her instantly as she raced inside, and within the shadows, she realized she had lost him. Her heart was pounding faster than her booted feet falling on the soft ground. Too much running. Her head swam.

She had to stop, doubling over, to catch her breath, the air burning in her lungs as she gulped in great bursts. Walking was her preference. Ladies did not, as a general rule, run. Indeed, she hadn't run so much since she had been a child herself.

"You'll never catch me if you don't try," called the earl from somewhere deeper in the trees.

Her determination was instantly renewed. She dashed off in the direction of his voice. Around a tree, then another, clutching her skirts ever higher. Determined to discover where he was and tag him.

One more tree, and then…

She stopped, astounded.

For there he was, back pressed to the trunk of the tree, smile flirting with his lips as he stood in the shadows, arms crossed over his chest. It was an indolent pose. As if he had been waiting there patiently for her sluggish attempts to find him.

"How do you intend to tag me if you don't come nearer?" he asked softly, a challenge in his tone.

Why would he want her closer? To torture her? She had never, in all her life, wanted to kiss a man so badly that her body ached with the need. Until now.

But this was just a child's game they were playing, and she was *it*. The reminder had her surging forward, tripping on a tree root she hadn't spied until it was too late. Falling forward, her momentum taking her into the earl's chest. She landed there as if it had been her intention all along, for him to catch her so effortlessly, his strong arms wrapped around her, holding her tight to him.

Her hands were on his shoulders, and she was enjoying the feeling of his hard body against hers far too much.

"You're *it*," she managed past her ragged breaths.

"You caught me," he said, his expression serious, gaze intent, palms flattened to the small of her back.

"Actually, it was you who caught me." She forced a smile, hoping he didn't know how deeply he affected her. "Thank you for keeping me from falling, my lord."

"I don't think you should thank me," he said quietly.

"Why?" She searched his bright gaze for answers and found none.

"This is why," he said.

And then his mouth was on hers.

CHAPTER 9

*H*e shouldn't have left Robert's study.

Shouldn't have been lured by the happy laughter of his nieces and their governess.

Definitely should not have decided to indulge in a game of tag on a whim.

Ought not to have run into the trees.

Or kissed the most delectable governess he'd ever met.

But as Corliss responded to his kiss, her soft lips warm and hungry beneath his, Knight didn't have a single regret. Not one.

No, that was a lie. He *did* have one, and it was that he couldn't take her over his shoulder and carry her all the way to his chamber and lay her down on his bed, strip every hideous inch of fabric off her lovely curves, and then worship her as she deserved. That he couldn't simply keep her there, making love to her until he had finally managed to banish this unholy need to make her his.

Yes, he regretted that.

He would have to be content with her lips instead of the

rest of her. His cock twitched as she sighed into his mouth, fingers curling on his chest as if to hold him to her, or bring him closer. He was painfully aware of everything: the hardness of the tree's bark at his back, the breathy sound of need she made as she returned his kisses, the autumnal scent of dying leaves, the richness of damp earth, and above it all, *her*. Roses and bergamot and delicious woman.

A woman he could not seem to get his fill of, whom he could not stay away from, regardless of how fervently he tried to keep his distance. He should stop kissing her. The distant calls of his nieces reached him, a reminder they weren't alone.

But the voices were far enough away that he knew they had time. A few minutes, at least, before an interruption would stop him and hopefully bring with it a return of his common sense and honor both. Because at the moment, he had none of either. He spun them so that she was the one against the tree, and his body was pinning her there, all without ending the kiss, his tongue dipping into her mouth. It turned hungry and wanton, and he wasn't sure which of them was seducing the other, because Corliss's kisses nearly unmanned him.

He had to have more.

Angling his body so that his aching cock rested more firmly against her pliant curves, he broke off the kiss to bury his face in her throat. Her pulse pounded fast beneath his questing lips, and he didn't know if it was from the game of tag or from his kisses, but it didn't matter. Her scent was more pronounced here, and he drank it in, wondering if she dabbed perfume at the base of her throat every morning.

"I thought you didn't want me," she said softly, her breath coming in little pants that made him wonder what she would sound like when he was inside her, thrusting, filling her, making her his in every way.

He'd never know, and the bitter realization made something inside him wither and turn to ash.

His hands slid down her hips, caressing and holding her to him at the same time, aligning their bodies so that he could thrust his cock into her, showing her how badly he wanted her. "Does it feel like I don't want you, Corliss?"

Her head fell back against the tree trunk, eyes glazed with passion beneath the brim of her prim bonnet. "It feels...wicked."

Wicked didn't begin to describe the way she made him feel, the things he longed to do to her. "I want you more than I've ever wanted another. You're all I can think about. All I desire."

He made the confessions against her silken skin, lips grazing her, then his teeth. God, he was voracious where she was concerned. He wanted to eat her up. He couldn't, damn it. Thank Christ they were outdoors, his nieces in danger of happening upon them at any second. He would hear them rustling in the fallen leaves as they approached, however.

He would have warning, time to prepare.

"Then why did you walk away from me in the cottage?" she asked, her voice hushed and husky with the same desire threatening to overwhelm him.

He nuzzled her throat. "Because I'm trying to be honorable."

Her hands were still between them, caressing over his chest, then down his arms in leisurely strokes that were inciting the riotous urge to take her. "What if I don't want you to be honorable?"

Fuck.

The surge of pure, raw lust that slammed through him at her words stole his breath. He was already thinking of all the ways he could pleasure her without taking her. Of how he might sneak to her chamber, steal inside at midnight. Strip her bare and bury his head between her luscious thighs, lick her until she cried out his name.

No, no, no. He couldn't do that. Could he?

His conscience said he couldn't. His randy cock said he could. That he *should*. No one would ever be the wiser. He could slake some of this rampant need...

"You should want me to be honorable," he whispered in her ear. But even as he murmured the warning, his hand was traveling with a mind of its own, gliding from her waist to cup the sweet roundness of her breast, the full glory of which he was denied by all the layers of cloth and boning separating his skin from hers.

He squeezed, wishing he knew if her nipples were hard. Wishing he knew what color they were. Pale pink? Or darker, like crushed summer berries? Would she like it if he sucked on them? Nibbled at them?

He truly was depraved. He shouldn't be entertaining any of these forbidden thoughts, because now he was lost in Corliss. Thrusting his cock against her as if he were inside her, a lewd mimicry of fucking. Outside beneath the sky, pinned to a tree. Where anyone could come upon them. Where his nieces could.

"What we *should* want and what we *do* want are often two entirely separate entities," she murmured, wrapping her leg around his hip.

Once again, she was not wrong. Corliss was wise beyond her years. She saw inside everyone around her in an uncanny way. She saw him in a way no one else had. Saw his nieces beyond their antics and pranks. She was, in a word, remarkable.

And bloody hell. He would give his champion's title, every belt he had been presented with, Knightly Abbey, and all his worldly possessions, just to lift her skirts and bury himself deep inside her right now.

"What do you want, Corliss?" he asked, nipping at the fleshy lobe of her ear.

"You."

One word. So damned profound. His heart thudded hard. Possibilities he should not be contemplating swirled. Dangerous possibilities. Tempting ones.

He kissed her cheek, and then couldn't resist dusting his lips over her nose, paying homage to the freckles that haunted his dreams. She was so perfectly lovely. So kind and good.

"Lindley was right when he called you an angel." He kissed her forehead. "And surely I'm the devil for longing for you as I do."

She caught his face in her gloved hands, and he wished it was her bare skin against his—nothing more than her palms and fingertips, and yet that was how badly he craved her. "Would it be different for you, if I were someone else? If I weren't the governess to your nieces?"

"Yes." He rubbed his cheek against hers, knowing the prickle of his beard would likely turn her sensitive skin pink and not caring in the slightest. Anyone else would think it had been caused from exertion and the wind. It would be their secret, just like everything else that had passed between them thus far. "No." He tried to wrangle his mind, but it was too filled with her. "I don't know."

Honesty was all he had to offer. Knight hadn't a proper answer for her. He was confused and lightheaded with desire. All the blood in his body had rushed to his cock, and there it would remain as long as she was within touching distance.

"What if I told you that I wanted you to come to me tonight?" she asked.

And his world upended. He no longer understood anything about himself. All he knew was that if she issued the invitation, not even God himself was going to stop him from going to her room.

"No good would come of such a visit," he warned tightly, his voice strained with suppressed want.

He kissed each of her temples, the dimple in her chin. His hands were roving once more, touching every part of her he could. Her curves would forever be emblazoned upon his fingertips.

"Would you come?" she persisted.

He wanted to be good. Wanted to be honorable. Wanted to do the right thing, because Lord knew he hadn't always done so in the past, least of all when it had mattered. Corliss mattered to him. Very much. So much it frightened him.

She held him captive in her stare, and he noted the many striations of color within her irises. So many secrets to unlock. So much to know about her. He wanted, quite suddenly and ridiculously, to know everything.

He took her lips in a slow, thorough kiss. Deliberating his answer. Taking time. Telling himself he should say no. Unable to do so.

"Yes," he whispered against her mouth. "I would."

"Is Uncle *it*?"

Little Mary's curious voice behind him shook Knight from the sensual stupor which had enveloped him. Had him disengaging and stepping away from Corliss hastily. He turned to his youngest niece, forcing a smile, pretending as if his world had not just been entirely, irrevocably altered. As if he had not just been debauching her governess against a goddamned tree.

"I am," he told his niece with a wink. "Miss Brinton caught me. And now, I shall catch you."

"You'll never catch me," Mary declared with a giggle, before darting away through the trees.

It was the happiest he had seen his nieces since his arrival, and the sound of Mary's laughter was priceless. All thanks to the woman behind him. Swallowing hard, Knight chased after his niece, leaving Corliss to gather herself and return to the game on her own.

The far more wicked game they played with each other would have to continue.

Tonight.

HE WASN'T GOING to come to her.

By midnight, Corliss was still awake, pacing the floor, her lamp flickering low and casting mocking shadows over the inside of her humble governess's room. It had occurred to her, as she had watched him racing after Lady Mary in the tree grove earlier, that she hadn't directly invited him. She had posed the question in the fashion of what if, testing the waters. And then her youngest charge had suddenly appeared, shattering the molten isolation of the moment.

Perhaps he had been playing a game, like tag. Perhaps he hadn't realized how fervently she had meant those words, that invitation, despite the immensity of the risks they entailed. Or perhaps he had, and he had merely experienced a change of heart. Likely, Stoneleigh was clinging to his sense of honor.

She told herself it was just as well, that indulging in a few ruinous moments of passion with the earl—especially when she was lying to him about who she truly was—would be a perfectly dreadful plan. Her deceptions weighed upon her more heavily with each passing day. When she had painstakingly arranged for her research, she had never imagined she would grow to care for her charges so much and so quickly.

Nor for her employer. Shame made her throat go tight at the thought of how they would all feel when they realized she had been deceiving them.

Yes indeed, she should be thankful he had made the decision for her. In a little over a fortnight, she would be gone, and their paths would likely never cross again. Her heart gave a pang at the thought, at the inevitable farewells she would say, at how it would feel to go. How badly it would *hurt*. Everything had seemed so effortless and tidy in her mind, when she had conceived of her plan. But now, everything was quite the opposite, and her plan was unraveling faster than a ball of twine rolling downhill.

A slight knock sounded at her door.

So light that she paused, thinking she had imagined the sound. Until it came again. She was flying over the carpets before her mind could frantically attempt to make sense of what was happening. She wrenched open the door, breathless, and there he was.

The Earl of Stoneleigh hovered at the threshold of her room. Tall, barefoot, and handsome, his expression fierce, as if he had been waging an inner battle with himself. One that he had lost. He was wearing a dark dressing gown, and somehow the sight was more intimate than him stripping to the waist in the cottage.

Because she knew what it meant. Why he was here. Her belly flipped, heat pooling between her legs.

"Tell me to go," he murmured, voice hushed.

She should. All the warnings which had been so stridently issued by her mind just moments earlier ought to inspire her to proceed with caution. To forget this mad notion altogether.

She stepped back, giving him room to enter. "Stay."

"Wrong answer, Corliss." But instead of leaving as his

words suggested he might, Stoneleigh crossed the threshold and closed the door at his back.

Suddenly, she was in his arms, hauled into his broad, rock-hard chest. He felt so good against her. Her hands settled on his shoulders just before his mouth slammed down on hers in a kiss that was almost bruising in its intensity. He kissed her as if he had been starved for her, as if they had not just kissed earlier in the shade of the trees. And she kissed him back with all the pent-up need swelling inside her like a flood.

All she could think was that he had said her answer was wrong.

But nothing else had ever felt more right.

She lost herself in the hot glide of his lips over hers, the taste of him, the scent of him. Everything that was so deliciously wondrous. Everything she wanted more of. His lips left hers with the same abruptness that they had first claimed them, leaving her bereft.

"This is wrong," he said, but then his lips were on her jaw, stringing a trail of fire in their wake as they traveled down her throat. "I shouldn't be here."

Her head fell back, giving him better access to the skin that was so desperate for his attention. "I want you here."

He growled, kissed the hollow beneath her ear. "I tried to stay away. I tried so bloody hard. I went to my chamber and told myself to be honorable. I drank a whisky. I took a cold bath. But nothing would chase the need for you. You're like a goddamn fire in my blood."

"It's the same for me," she confessed, similarly astounded by the effect he had upon her.

Nothing could have prepared her for how quickly and completely she would fall beneath the Earl of Stoneleigh's spell.

"Last chance to tell me to go to the devil," he murmured into her ear, his breath hot and laced with the whisky he'd told her he had consumed in an effort to stay away.

She was glad it hadn't worked. Glad he was here holding her, touching her. Glad he was every bit as drawn to her as she was to him.

"I don't want you to go anywhere," she said, fingers threading through his soft, dark hair.

He raked his teeth along the cord of her throat, making her shiver. "A better man would have some restraint."

"I don't want that man." She tugged at his hair, urging his head back so she could meet his eyes. "All I want is you, my lord."

"Call me Knight when we are alone together," he reminded her. "The title belonged to my brother, and it still doesn't sit well upon me."

"Is that your true given name?" she wondered, her fingers trailing from his hair to his jaw, unable to resist touching him everywhere she could.

She traced the bow of his upper lip, mesmerized by the shape. By him.

"No." His mouth quirked into a wry grin. "It's Oliver. But no one has called me that in years. I've always hated it."

She wondered why he disliked his name; she thought it suited him. But then, so did Knight, and she wanted to call him whatever he preferred to be called.

"Knight, then," she agreed, her fingertip circling the fullness of his lower lip now.

He caught her wrist in a gentle grasp and held her there, kissing the pad of her finger. "I like my name on your lips. But there are other things I'd like on your lips far better."

A wicked trill went through her. "Such as?"

"Mine," he answered simply, and then cupped her nape

and brought her mouth back to his for another deep, drugging kiss.

His touch roamed freely over her body, caressing, coaxing a response everywhere they traveled. He found the fastenings on her dressing gown and began sliding the line of buttons from their moorings. When his fingers fumbled on a few, he made a low sound of frustration, before grabbing the dressing gown's twain ends. With one jerk, he tore the remainder of the buttons, sending them raining over the carpet.

He broke the kiss, staring down at her, his expression stormy. She wondered if this was how he looked when he faced an opponent in the ring. "Christ, I'm sorry. I'll buy you another. I don't know what I was thinking."

He couldn't buy her a dressing gown. It wasn't proper, and soon, she would be gone anyway. She banished that last bitterness-inducing thought from her mind. She would not spoil the night, for she may never again be in Knight's arms like this. She wanted to make the most of it. Didn't want to ruin a single heartbeat.

"I don't care about the dressing gown," she said, shrugging it to the floor so that she stood before him in only her night rail. The material was fine and nearly sheer, and she had no doubt that even in the low light, it scarcely shielded her from him.

"My God." He inhaled sharply, his stare drinking her in. "You're certain about this, Corliss? You want me here?"

She didn't hesitate. "I'm certain, and I do."

"Take it off for me," he said, his voice low and deep and laden with sinful command.

The throbbing ache in her core intensified. She grasped the fine linen in both hands and drew it over her head, tossing it to the floor along with her dressing gown.

"Fuck, you're beautiful," he said, raw admiration in his voice. "Do you want me to touch you, sweetheart?"

Did the sun rise every morning?

She swallowed, not feeling even a bit embarrassed at standing before him, utterly nude. He made her feel as beautiful as he had said she was.

"Yes," she said. "Please."

He started in the most unlikely of places—both her shoulders. "I've been thinking of nothing but this for weeks. I've been in an agony of want for you."

It had been the same for her, and now that his big, callused hands were on her bare skin and he was alone with her in the dimly lit haven of her chamber, she was aflame. He trailed gentle caresses over her collarbone, then swept his touch lower, taking his time as he drew closer to her breasts.

All she could manage was a murmur of assent. Her mind was too caught up in him, senses overwhelmed.

"You do have more of them," he murmured. "Like little constellations."

He was speaking of her freckles, she realized as his head dipped and he kissed the places where the small spots multiplied every summer wherever her skin was revealed to the sun.

"I've always hated them," she admitted, her nipples hardening as he kissed the upper swells of her breasts and then moved between them, his hands cupping her at last.

"Why? They're bewitching just like you are." His thumbs rubbed a lazy swirl over her nipples, and sensation shot through her at the touch. "Every part of you is glorious."

Her hands had settled back on his strong chest—a favorite place to land. "I'm hardly that."

"Liar." He kissed the side of her breast and then took one of her nipples into his mouth.

"Oh." She arched her back, delighted by the moist heat of

his mouth, the way he sucked and drew on her until she felt an answering echo of need deep inside.

He released her, smiling against her skin. "You like that, don't you?"

"Yes." The admission was torn from her. She was sure she ought to be ashamed for presenting herself to him so shamelessly. For failing to guard her body and her virtue. But she couldn't summon a single drop of embarrassment.

All she felt was desire.

So much. Weighing her down. Pulsing. Demanding.

"Get on the bed, and we'll discover what else you like."

She didn't hesitate. The counterpane had already been drawn back in anticipation of another fitful night of sleep haunted by the man who was never far from her thoughts. But now he was here with her. She slid into the bed, lying on her back, the coolness of the sheets feeling newly erotic in a way they never had before.

"Look at you, lying there naked for me, so damned lovely," he said, the praise heightening her awareness, feeling his heated stare on her as surely as if it were a caress. "Let me see you, sweetheart."

Her sex, she realized, following his gaze to the apex of her thighs where she had instinctively pressed them together in an attempt at easing the ache. He wanted to see her there. She should be shocked. And yet, this was Knight, and everything with him felt so natural, so easy, so right.

She slid her legs apart slowly, showing herself to him.

"We'll never both fit together on that tiny mattress," he said. "Slide yourself to the edge of the bed. Closer to me."

She did as he asked, uncertain of the reason, but trusting him. Corliss positioned herself nearer to him, and then his hands were on her, guiding her, pulling her so that her legs were hanging off the side of the bed, her rump at the edge.

"Fuck," he muttered, dropping to his knees on the floor

between her parted legs. "You have the prettiest pussy, all pink and perfect."

His wicked words had heat creeping over her, making her flush. But she didn't have time to concern herself with it, because his hands were coasting over her legs with reverent awe, and he'd lowered his head to press a kiss to first one inner thigh, and then the other.

But then, he did the most astonishing thing of all.

He pressed a kiss directly upon her mound.

Her hips jerked at the delightful sensation. And when his tongue darted out to lick up and down her folds before finding the bundle of flesh that was so agonizingly responsive, she cried out.

His lips left her for a moment. "Not too loud, love."

Yes, how foolish of her to make noise. It was merely that she hadn't anticipated such an intimate act, nor her body's response to it...

Oh sweet heavens, his handsome face had disappeared, and his tongue was on her again. His lips found her bud and latched on, sucking as he had her nipples. The pleasure made her toes curl into the cool night air. Corliss clawed at the pillow beneath her head and pressed it to her face, muffling her helpless moan of pleasure. How decadent, this beautiful man's mouth on her, his hands stroking up and down her thighs.

He released her with a wet, lusty sound. It was crude and vulgar and made her cheeks heat, but it also heightened the aching need blossoming at her core and radiating through the rest of her. He blew a stream of hot air on her that had her hips twitching.

"Move the pillow. I want to see your face when I make you come."

His low directive sent another shudder through her, along with a helpless bolt of need. She lowered the pillow, mesmerized by his hot stare, hungry and intent on her. What a wicked sight they presented, her naked curves on full display, his face between her legs.

"Better?" she murmured, her fingers twisting in the sheets.

She was open to him, exposed and vulnerable, and it thrilled her. His lips glistened with the evidence of her desire, and as she watched, he licked them, as if savoring the taste.

The slow smile he gave her melted her insides. "Better."

His hands glided over her eager skin, until he was cupping her bottom in both palms, and then he pulled her to him, draping her legs over his shoulders, as if intent upon devouring her. And devour her, he did. First in long, slow licks up and down her folds that had her writhing in his grasp. Then with laps over her bud, his tongue fluttering and swirling over her. His whiskers rasped against her already sensitive flesh, rubbing over her inner thighs and even her sex as he lavished his sinful attentions upon her.

A gasp stole from her, but she did her best to be quiet as he had instructed. Because her room was situated by the nursery. Because she had four charges within listening distance. Because Knight was her employer, and this was wrong, what they were doing. So very wrong.

Why, then, did it feel so wonderfully, wickedly right?

Not just right, but perfect.

Perfect as his tongue glided through her folds before finding her entrance and dipping inside with thrusts that had her making tiny sounds of need in her throat, hips moving restlessly to bring him deeper. She was at the edge of something wild, her entire body drawn tight. Was it the lateness of the hour? The hot wetness of his knowing tongue? His hands on her? The secret, forbidden nature of having him alone with her here, in her space, in her bed, playing with her body as if she were a musical instrument made for him alone?

"Oh, Knight."

"Yes," he growled against her. "Say my name. God, you taste fucking delicious. So perfect and so wet for me."

The praise in his dark, deep voice made the flames inside her lick hotter and higher. He kissed her swollen bud and then sucked again, before giving her a gentle nibble that had her knees reflexively closing on his shoulders, sealing him to her more tightly than ever. She was sure she would regret this, all of this, in the morning. But nothing had ever felt better than his mouth on her. And everything he was doing to her was making her desperate. Desperate and achy, as if there was something deep inside her that needed to be filled.

His lips were still latched firmly to her when one of his hands slid from her derriere. And then his finger was teasing her opening as his tongue had. He sucked hard and slipped that lone digit into her, and the sensation was exquisite torture. Slowly, he worked her, in and then out, light thrusts that became deeper and more demanding, his mouth continuing to lave and suck and nip her at the same time.

Her inner muscles tensed against the newness of the invasion. It felt strange in the best way. There was a fullness, a new pang of pleasure bordering on pain. His finger slid deeper, pressing against a place that made liquid rush from her core.

It was too much.

It was everything.

His tongue flicked over her, driving her beyond the ledge she had been tentatively occupying, just as his finger slipped in and out in another maddening thrust, finding that spot again. Something inside her tightened and then exploded. There was a burst of pleasure so intense that tiny black stars dotted her vision and her ears rang. She hadn't realized she'd been holding her breath, but she had.

She sucked in air and then crooned his name over and over, body undulating beneath his finger and mouth. Came completely undone like a frayed rope that was beyond repair. And as she lay there in the aftermath, body sated and glowing, heart pounding, she knew that, just like a snapped rope, she would never be the same.

CHAPTER 10

*H*e was a fool.

Because while Knight had told himself that going to Corliss's chamber the night before would be a one-time mistake that would never be repeated, all he could think about was doing it again. And again.

And again.

As he stood in Robert's study with his forehead pressed to the cold glass, staring unseeing at the blurred grounds below, he wasn't contemplating the reports spread laboriously over the desk, awaiting his inspection and decision-making. No, he was thinking about having *her* atop them.

Hell, he wasn't only thinking about fucking Corliss atop his steward's careful reports. He was thinking about having her in every room of Knightly Abbey. Going far beyond pleasuring her with his mouth and fingers alone. Thinking about sinking his cock inside her so deep, about making her his.

About his name being the only one that ever fled her gorgeous lips in pleasure.

"You stupid arsehole," he muttered to himself.

Because thank Christ, he was alone, no Smithson present

to witness his humiliating agony as the hours wore on, nor the cockstand tenting his trousers. The cockstand which had been merciless, omnipresent, and insistent all morning. Undeterred by the three separate occasions he had discreetly taken himself in hand to the memory of her hot, dripping pussy tightening on his finger. Of the sweetness of her on his tongue. The way she'd moaned and ridden his face.

Last night had been the single most erotic moment of his life. Not just because her responsive, sensual allure and eagerness had been ridiculously satisfying. Not just because she was beautiful and her body had been fashioned for sin. But because she was a good, kind woman with a generous heart. Because she genuinely cared for his nieces. Because she made them happy.

Because she made *him* happy.

Yes, he was incurably stupid. Only an idiot would have believed he could have Corliss once and it would have been enough. By the grim light of day, Knight could acknowledge that no amount of having her—not once, not one thousand times, not a bloody million—would ever be sufficient. He was starving for her. Desperate for her.

For the first time, he wanted something more than he wanted to win. And it scared the hell out of him. He didn't know what to do with these inconvenient emotions crowding inside him, so much more complex than mere lust. He had forced himself to be content alone, the sole focus of his life prizefighting, his next match, training.

He heaved a heavy sigh and lifted his forehead from the glass, the rolling park below becoming more distinct. The warmth of the day before had given way to a cold, dreary chill and more rain. Not the pelting, driving kind which had stranded him at the cottage with Corliss, but the kind that was slow and unrelenting. A ceaseless drip.

As he watched, a flock of birds winged across the horizon.

He couldn't bring himself off in the study in the midst of the morning. He may have been depraved enough to seduce the governess last night, but he still had some morals. He could, however, seek out Corliss and his nieces. The reports behind him would wait.

He adjusted his trousers and willed himself to think quelling thoughts, taking a few moments for composure's sake before he left the sanctity of the study. And then his strides were eating up the hall and the stairs beyond, taking him to the nursery where the sound of a piano and laughter trailed from the open door. He hovered at the threshold, taking in the sight before him.

Corliss was seated at the battered, old nursery piano, her dainty fingers trailing lovingly over the keys as she played a melody. The girls had partnered with each other to try their hand at the steps of a quadrille. Alice was leading Mary, and Henrietta—Nettie, as he'd discovered she liked to be called—was guiding Beatrice.

"No, Mary, stop trying to lead," Alice complained at her younger sister. "I am the gentleman this time."

"But I want to be the gentleman," Mary protested with a pout.

"Everyone shall have their turn to be the gentleman," Corliss called above the din. "Now do carry on with your dancing, if you please. Ladies, here is where you spin."

All four girls dutifully spun. Mary promptly tripped over Alice's skirts and fell to her rump.

"Alice tripped me!" she exclaimed, her tone accusatory.

"I did not," her sister countered. "You have the grace of a parsnip, Mary."

"Miss Brinton, Alice called me a parsnip."

"I said you had the *grace* of one."

"My ladies," Corliss chided, her fingers stilling, the music going silent as she rose from the piano bench. "Cease insulting each other and root vegetables, if you please."

She spun about, her gaze falling on him standing at the threshold. A jolt of awareness passed between them, and she faltered, her pretty lips parting as if she had suddenly forgotten the rest of what she had been about to say.

"Uncle!" cried the girls in unison, Mary leaping from the floor and jumping up and down whilst clapping her hands in joy.

Their unfeigned pleasure at seeing him made warmth trickle through his chest.

"Lord Stoneleigh," Corliss greeted softly, dipping into a dutiful curtsy that made him long to cross the room and take her in his arms and tell her to never again genuflect to him.

He swallowed hard, brimming with warmth and pleasure both, and forced himself to nod. "Miss Brinton, hellions. Good morning. Am I interrupting?"

The question was silly. He knew he was interrupting. Doing so had been his intent. He had been too tired for his customary morning training, having only left Corliss's bed close to dawn. The last he had seen of her was her golden hair curled over the pillow in the early rays of sun before the rains had set in. Mere hours ago, and yet, it may as well have been a lifetime.

He had missed her.

What the hell was wrong with him?

"We were working on our dancing lessons," she said softly, a charming flush stealing over her cheeks. "I hope we weren't making too much of a commotion and disturbing you."

He found himself thinking of another occasion upon which she had made a commotion. Last night's lusty moan would live on in his mind for eternity.

143

Knight cleared his throat, willing the memory—and his body's reaction to it—to go away. "Of course not. But perhaps I might be of service as the only gentleman in residence."

Hardly a gentleman, he thought with an inward grimace. Last night had certainly proven that as well.

"You would dance with us, Uncle?" Nettie asked, looking surprised.

Of all the girls, she resembled Robert the most. She had the same blue eyes and wavy dark-brown hair, her nose stubbornly tilted upward at the end just as Robert's had. Looking at her now made a pang of regret arc through him. Robert's life could have been different. They hadn't always been enemies. Time and the world around them had rendered them so.

"If it would prove beneficial, I'd be delighted to dance with you," he said, not sure why he was making the offer, other than it afforded him an opportunity to linger in Corliss's presence and make his nieces happy.

Two wins.

The most dancing he had partaken of recently had been in raucous establishments celebrating various victories as he traveled through America on tour. Hardly proper. But he remembered the quadrille. Some skills had been practically born into him as an earl's son, and dancing had been one of them.

"What a relief," Alice grumbled, shooting her youngest sister an irritated glare. "Mary steps on my feet and trips over her hems."

"I do not," Mary denied, scowling back at her. "You pushed me and called me a parsnip."

Knight bit his lip to contain the laugh that threatened to rise. His youngest niece was growing ever more creative with her accusations against her sister.

"I didn't push you or call you a parsnip," Alice argued, fists on her hips in a gesture of supreme irritation.

"My ladies," Corliss inserted calmly. "That is enough argument. If you wish for his lordship to aid you with the steps, you must take advantage of his kind offer. He is quite busy with other matters awaiting him, I'm sure."

Yes, he was. But none of them held a candle to lingering here in the nursery just so he could be near to her and the girls. It struck him that of all the duties facing him at Knightly Abbey, the only one that felt right, that filled him with an overwhelming sense of contentedness, was his nieces and their lovely governess.

"I'm more than happy to be of use," he said, offering an exaggerated bow that had all the girls chuckling, as he'd intended.

When he had first arrived at the estate, they had been sullen and angry, playing an endless stream of pranks upon him and everyone else. But it had been days since he had last been missing a necktie or discovered water had been poured into his boots, or found pepper on his pillow, or discovered holes had been cut in his stockings.

Even with their sibling squabbles, they all bubbled with an inner joy which had been previously absent. All Corliss's doing.

An angel among mere mortals had never been a more apt description. And last night, that angel had come undone for him. That angel had fallen into sin with him. And he had loved every fucking minute of it.

"Lady Mary, as the youngest, you may go first," Corliss was saying, her voice brisk and businesslike.

And meanwhile, here he stood, thinking about her naked and flushed and so gorgeous whilst he…

No, he had to stop this madness. He was here for good, not for more of what had happened the night before. Which had, coincidentally, been far better than good. Words did not exist to offer adequate description.

To atone for his sins, he spent the better part of an hour guiding all his nieces through various dance steps. More than once, his gaze traveled over the head of the niece he was partnering at the moment to meet Corliss's. Each time, the connection between them was as visceral as a bolt of electricity. At last, she took a break from the piano, pleading tired fingers, and rose from the bench.

"Now it is your turn to dance with Uncle," little Mary suggested, all innocent excitement.

He nearly groaned aloud. There could be no greater torture than whirling about with Corliss so close to his body, before a rapt audience of his innocent nieces.

"That would hardly be proper," Corliss demurred gently.

But Alice, Beatrice, and Nettie joined in, apparently thinking Mary's idea a fine one. A cacophony of pleading voices struck up.

"Please, Miss Brinton?"

"It would be so lovely to watch someone who isn't counting all the steps in her head."

"Or falling on her bottom the way Mary does."

"Or being a potato like Alice," Mary shot back, giving her older sister a baleful look.

"Is that meant to be an insult, dearest?" Alice asked, laughing.

"My ladies," Corliss said. "I already told you that there is to be no more disparaging talk of root vegetables. You must be kind sisters to each other, for you are the best friends you shall ever have in the world."

"How should you know?" Nettie asked. "You haven't any sisters."

"I do," Corliss said. "I've even a twin sister, if you must know, and two others. I have a brother as well. So you see?

I've quite a bit of experience where siblings are concerned. No one will ever protect and love you as they do. You must be that for each other, too."

Well, hell. Clearly, her siblings were nothing like Robert. He found himself wondering about her past, her family. Where were they now? Why was she on her own, in such a solitary occupation, earning her living as a governess? He wanted to ask her why the devil they hadn't seen to her welfare if they loved her so much. He wanted to know everything there was to know about her.

But first, he very much wanted to dance with her.

"Excellent advice, Miss Brinton," he agreed, offering her his arm. "And now, I believe you owe me this dance." He turned to his eldest niece, who he knew was more than proficient at the piano. "Play for us, if you please, Nettie."

"Of course, Uncle." The girl moved to the piano, settling herself primly on the bench Corliss had so recently vacated.

"I want to choose the song," Mary volunteered, racing to the bench and seating herself beside Nettie in a distinctly undignified fashion that was more than familiar to him by now.

The girls were each unique in their own, surprising ways. He was deeply ashamed to admit he hadn't spent much time thinking of them at all before arriving in Yorkshire.

"The gentleman must stand here," Alice ordered him, apparently deciding she was taking on the role of teacher.

"And the lady over here, Miss Brinton," explained Beatrice patiently, guiding Corliss into position opposite him.

"Now you must bow and curtsy," Mary yelled from the piano bench.

She was rather akin to a little windstorm, tearing through Knightly Abbey.

"And also take care to avoid shouting indoors," Corliss said pointedly.

"Alice and Beatrice, do get out of the way now," Nettie commanded with a superior air. "I'm going to begin."

The two girls moved away obligingly, retreating to the piano across the chamber. And then it was Knight and Corliss standing together, staring at each other. And he was falling into the brilliant cinnamon and gold flecks in her vibrant eyes.

"Nettie?" Corliss asked him softly, raising a brow.

Ah yes, the pet name he had discovered for the eldest girl.

Knight shrugged. "She prefers it to Henrietta."

He had taken to calling her by the sobriquet after using it a few days ago. She had been pleased, and he had agreed that Nettie suited her far better than Henrietta.

"You've been spending more time with them," Corliss observed, approval lacing her tone.

He inclined his head. "I have."

He had never previously imagined he would take enjoyment in spending time with his wayward nieces. Somehow along the way, they had ceased to be obligations and duties. He didn't fool himself at the reason—if not for Corliss, he would never have begun to understand them. He would never have known where to begin.

A small smile curved her lips. "That is good of you, my lord. They need that."

She was taking care to keep her voice from carrying to the girls. Her concern for them never failed to astound and move him. She was such a good, giving woman. He could not fathom she would wish to remain in a life of servitude, to never have a husband and family of her own. The thought made an odd, tight ache begin in his chest. He tamped it down, refusing to examine it.

"I can be good sometimes," he told her with wicked intent. "And sometimes, I can be quite the opposite."

Her lush lips parted. "My lord."

"What are you two talking about?" Mary demanded, ever the curious and bold one amongst them. "Speak more loudly so we can hear, too."

"I was saying that you need further lessons in remembering not to bellow," he called wryly.

"Uncle, you must bow," Beatrice reminded him then.

"And Miss Brinton, you must curtsy," added Alice.

He sketched an obligatory bow, wishing for a moment that they were beneath the glittering chandeliers of a ball and that he might dance with her in truth. She curtsied, her cheeks stained with another becoming flush that he knew was from the innuendo in his words. She was so damned lovely.

"And now the dance shall begin," Nettie said, spine going straight as her fingers moved over the ivories.

She had chosen a Viennese waltz. Knight linked hands with Corliss and placed the other on her upper back, her left hand settling upon his shoulder. Their gazes met and held. He wished he could hold her closer, to draw her body flush against his, but didn't dare while his nieces looked on. Instead, he turned his attention to the steps of the dance, determined to take all the pleasure he could in touching her, turning with her, and looking into her eyes. They made their way about the nursery effortlessly, spinning and moving sinuously up and down the Axminster until he, who had never enjoyed formal dance, was almost giddy like a school lad.

It was over far too soon, and although he found himself loath to release her, he had no choice. For Nettie, he offered a round of applause, his stare never leaving Corliss. She was looking back at him with an expression he couldn't quite decipher. And he was looking back at her without bothering to hide the admiration for her which continued to grow.

"Brava, Nettie," he called. And then, for Corliss's benefit

added another, quieter word of praise intended for her ears alone. "Brava."

"That is precisely how I saw Papa dancing with Mrs. Oak," Beatrice blurted loudly into the silence which had fallen.

"Hush," said Alice. "You weren't meant to speak of it. Do you not remember?"

And that was the moment that Knight learned Robert had been bedding his housekeeper. And that, much to his ever-lasting chagrin, perhaps he wasn't as different from his brother as he had previously believed.

CORLISS KNEW she had no business wandering from her chamber that night. But that didn't stop her from slipping from her small room, still dressed practically in a dowdy governess gown, her hair bound in a loose braid that hung heavily down her back. It didn't stop her from slipping through the darkened, quiet halls in search of the spare chamber she knew from below stairs gossip had been trans-formed into a training room for the earl.

Because she also knew that, following the disastrous revelation from Beatrice that the former earl had been having an affair with his housekeeper, Knight likely needed someone to confide in. His countenance had gone instantly grim at his niece's words, his surprise evident. The gaiety of the dancing lesson had rendered him even more handsome as he had smiled down at her after their waltz. But with Beatrice's words had come a sudden and distinct change, rather akin to storm clouds darkening a clear summer sky. All the lightness and levity had fled, leaving in its wake the dark shadows of the past.

There had been such aching regret in his expression

when next he had met her gaze that it had nearly split her heart into pieces on his behalf. He already had so much weight on his shoulders, so much unwanted responsibility foisted upon him, and now he would have to contend with the knowledge that not only had his brother been debauching his domestic, but his innocent daughters had known. Not an easy discovery to manage, to be sure.

He had beaten a hasty retreat from the nursery, and Corliss had been left to feign cheer she hadn't felt and distract her charges with more French verbs. The remainder of the day had been noticeably bereft of his company. She had done her best to carry on with her day as if nothing untoward had occurred. As if neither the night before nor the dance had affected her. As if the Earl of Stoneleigh hadn't somehow infiltrated her heart like an enemy soldier who had found his way into her stronghold.

But the truth of it was, she had begun to realize that he had.

And that reason, above all the rest, was why she paused outside the door to the spare chamber, taking note of the strip of telltale light glowing beneath the door. Why she tapped lightly, hoping he would hear above the din of what sounded like his fists rhythmically connecting with a soft surface within.

"Come," he called instantly.

She hesitated for a moment, hoping she wasn't overstepping. Hoping he would not be displeased she had sought him out. After he had come to her chamber the night before, and he had given her such pleasure, they had fallen asleep for a time entwined together. She had awoken to his kiss on her temple as he had slid from the bed before the sun had fully risen. To avoid embarrassment, she had remained still, eyes closed, pretending to be asleep.

And he had gone, only to return in the nursery, sweeping

her around the Axminster as gracefully as if they had been at a ball instead of turning about a shabby nursery with only his four nieces as their fellow guests.

The door opened, and it occurred to her that she must have lingered, questioning the wisdom of her late-night visit, for long enough that his curiosity had won. He towered over her in the doorway, bare-chested and muscular, a fine sheen of perspiration making his golden skin look as if it shone in the light of the lamps within.

Unfairly handsome as ever.

Bright-blue eyes collided with hers. "Corliss. Is something amiss with one of the girls?"

His question was a reminder that she did not belong here, trespassing upon his solitude. Perhaps it had been a mistake to seek him out at all.

"No," she hastened to reassure him, uncertainty washing over her. "They are all sound asleep, having listened to the latest installment of the story I've been reading them."

He glanced over her shoulder, searching the hall behind her, she assumed, before he took a step in retreat and gestured to the chamber behind him. "Come in."

She did as he asked, trying her utmost not to be affected when his muscled abdomen brushed against her arm as he passed her to secure the door and grant them privacy. The moment the portal was closed, she stared at his broad, glistening back, the muscles rippling in his shoulder blades as he rolled them. Awareness washed over her.

"I shouldn't have come," she said, suddenly uncertain. "Forgive me. It was wrong of me to intrude upon your privacy."

Belatedly, she took in the rest of the chamber. There was a leather bag suspended from the ceiling, dumbbells of various sizes scattered on the floor, along with a few unusual-looking contraptions that she supposed must be used in his training. All the bedroom furniture had been moved to one side of the room to facilitate his needs. Everyone below stairs was buzzing like curious little bees about their new master's eccentric habits. But what they saw as eccentricity, she saw as devotion. His determination was commendable but also quite unsurprising, now that she had grown acquainted with him.

"Nonsense. I'm glad you've come." His words warmed her insides, and had her gaze stealing back to him. But then he flexed his hands, revealing battered knuckles. "I wasn't wearing my gloves, which was bloody stupid. It's best that you stopped me. Otherwise, I'd have my knuckles raw, and whenever that happens, I have the devil's own time getting the cracks to heal. They'd likely be ruined for my next match."

His words startled her. "Your next match? But are you not finished fighting, my lord? You're an earl now."

"I was an earl when I fought Billy O'Brien and won," he said, holding her stare, his breaths calmer now than they had been when he had first appeared at the door.

Conversely, hers was the opposite. Her heart was hammering hard at the prospect of him engaging in another bout. At his proximity. At his lack of proper clothing.

"When is this match of yours, then?" she asked, knowing she was prying, and that questioning him about his schedule had not been her intent in seeking him out this evening.

"Three weeks from now. I received a telegram this evening with the challenge, and I've accepted." He raked a hand through his hair, his expression intense. "One could say it hasn't been the best of days, given the news I've received. All of it unwanted."

Three weeks? That was scarcely any time at all.

She frowned. "Surely you aren't intending to return to America for the fight?"

But the moment the question fled her lips, she read her answer on his handsome face. He *was*.

"If I want to keep my champion title, I've no choice. When an opponent calls for the fight and offers the challenge, I must answer it, or forfeit." His fingers passed through his dark hair again. "I'm fortunate I had this long between challenges. My opponent was being a gentleman. Albeit a gentleman who wants to steal my championship away from me."

He said the last wryly. Her mind was swirling with the implications of this unexpected news.

"You are planning to return to America in three weeks?" she repeated.

He nodded, then passed a hand over his jaw, looking suddenly weary. "Sooner than that, of course. I'll need time to travel to Mississippi from New York and for passage across the Atlantic before that."

"But what of Ladies Mary, Alice, Beatrice, and Nettie," she said, using his pet name for Henrietta, who had informed Corliss that she wished to be referred to thusly from now on. "What shall they do while you're gone?"

"They'll remain here," he answered. "With you."

But she wouldn't be here at Knightly Abbey in three weeks' time. She would be gone, returned home to Talleyrand Park. Only, he didn't know that. Which meant the girls would be alone once again. But it also meant that he would be endangering himself. Fighting an opponent. Beating and being beaten with fists. Worry knotted her stomach along with guilt and fear. Worry for Knight, for the girls she had come to care for during her short stay here. They had made such progress.

Somehow, the knowledge that she would leave them hadn't seemed quite as worrisome, knowing they would have their uncle. But if they were to be alone... Her mind whirled, grappling with the thoughts, the emotions.

"It's dangerous, is it not, prizefighting?" she asked, for she could not tell him she would have to leave Knightly Abbey soon to return to her family. She wasn't prepared to admit her deception, to face his questions, and likely, his anger. "And illegal in many places, as well."

"There is a danger in everything," Knight said softly, his gaze traveling over her face in a new way, as if he were committing it to memory. "Traveling by rail, boat, carriage, and horse is dangerous, and yet we must do it or never leave our homes. I'm not afraid to face a man in the ring. I never have been. As for prizefighting being illegal..." He paused, grinning, taking on a charming, rakish air she could not help but to find irresistible. "We find ways to circumvent the law. And if the law finds us, well, it never lasts more than a night."

"Have you ever been imprisoned for fighting?"

"Twice."

He had been arrested?

She gasped. "Was it perfectly terrible?"

He shook his head. "It was tolerable. All the lads truly want is for me to pay the fine and give them my autograph."

His autograph. The reminder of his fame beyond the walls of Knightly Abbey—and even within, if the grooms were any indication—struck her, and not for the first time. But somehow more poignantly. He was a prizefighter, a champion, and he intended to return to America forthwith. She should have guarded her heart far better. The extent of her foolishness was even greater than she had originally supposed.

He was leaving.

"When will you return?" she asked him, telling herself she posed the question for her charges' sakes and not for herself.

"I don't know." His countenance was solemn now, the

boyishness fading. "It may be some time. I'm fortunate to have found you for my nieces. True to the word of your previous employer, you've been an angel among mere mortals. The girls have changed so much since your arrival. I'm indebted to you."

Good heavens, he intended to leave for an indeterminate span of time. And when he returned, she would be long gone. It was likely she would never see him again, and the thought caused a visceral response, a sharp stab of pain, deep within.

She swallowed hard against a rising rush of shame and guilt for her own lies too, the reminder that her letter of recommendation had been forged. The reminder of the falsehood she was living. She should tell him the truth now. She ought to reveal who she truly was, explain to him why she had settled upon this situation, let him know she would not be present for his nieces during his absence.

But with all the new and foreign emotions churning within her, Corliss found that she could not. Not yet. She would have to tell him, and soon, particularly since he intended to return to America for another fight. She would have to find a way.

For now, best to remember why she had ventured to his training room this evening, flaunting propriety and every bit of wisdom she possessed.

"Speaking of their ladyships," she began, hesitant, "I came to discuss what Lady Beatrice said earlier during the dancing lessons."

Once again, his expression shifted, and he rubbed at his whisker-shadowed jaw.

"You knew about my brother and Mrs. Oak." It was a statement rather than a question.

"Yes," she admitted. "And I would wager you did not. The girls had mentioned it to me before. It wasn't the sort of information I felt appropriate to discuss at the time, but I sensed your surprise earlier."

He heaved a sigh and turned away, stalking toward the leather bag across the room. "It would seem I'm no better than my brother, seducing the domestics."

The domestics. Yes, she must not forget. That was all she was to him—a governess. The woman who would shoulder the responsibility of tending to his wards whilst he was gallivanting about America in railcars, signing autographs and charming all the ladies in his path.

Jealousy rose, swift and strong, choking. She took a deep breath, reminding herself she had no hold on him. That theirs had always been a finite relationship. That when she returned to Talleyrand Park, she would no longer have to endure the grueling rigors of being a governess. Instead, she could focus all her efforts upon the completion of her novel, which was just what she wanted.

Wasn't it?

Corliss took a deep breath, attempting to find that balance inside herself she'd once possessed, but which seemed to have fled her the moment she had first set eyes upon the Earl of Stoneleigh.

"It wasn't my intention to make a correlation between our circumstances and theirs," she said quietly. "I merely wished to tell you that I have told the girls they must not speak of it, but to spare you and your family further embarrassment, it may be best for you to echo the sentiment. It would seem they didn't heed my warning. I also wanted to reassure you that the tale will not spread beyond me."

Yes, that was what she had meant to say. Not to moon over his bare chest and then feel her heart shattering at the realization that he was leaving Knightly Abbey and he considered her nothing more than a servant. She hadn't been prepared for how badly that knowledge would sting.

The dull thud of his fist hitting the leather bag shook her from her ruminations. His back was still presented to her. The heavy bag swung, and he delivered another jab, then another in quick succession. With a heavy sigh, he turned back to face her.

"You needn't make excuses for myself or my brother, Miss Brinton," he said grimly. "Nor do you need to think I would worry, even for a moment, that you would carry the tale of my brother's unfortunate infidelities beyond Knightly Abbey. I trust you implicitly. You, however, are the one who should not trust me."

I trust you implicitly.

Oh, how his words were like a dagger cutting through her conscience. What would he do when he discovered she had been lying to him? Anger was pouring off him now, and she suspected it was not directed at herself at all, but rather, toward his dead brother.

Tell him, said a voice inside her. *Tell him the truth now, before it is too late.*

She swallowed hard, summoning the courage. "Lord Stoneleigh, I—"

But he was also speaking. "I shouldn't have—"

They stopped, staring at each other, and her bravery fled.

"I'm grateful for your confidence in me, my lord," she managed instead of the confession she had intended, all too aware that after the raw, wonderful intimacy they had shared in her chamber, they had reverted to formality once more. "I should leave you to your training now. Good evening."

With a hasty curtsy, she spun about, sick with guilt, needing to flee the chamber and his presence both. Needing to make sense of everything she had just learned, of the way he made her feel. Needing to not be within touching or ogling distance of his muscled arms and shoulders, to be beyond the heat of his brilliant eyes that always saw too much.

"Miss Brinton."

She ignored him, tears she hadn't known she'd been holding at bay blurring her vision. She blinked them away stubbornly, her stride unfaltering as she crossed the chamber.

"Corliss. Wait." There was a pause and then the lone word that finally stopped her. "Please."

CHAPTER 11

*K*night released the breath he'd been holding when Corliss halted in her retreat, her shoulders rising and falling as she took a deep breath before facing him. She was so impossibly lovely. Not even her drab dress could take away from her beauty. He shouldn't have stopped her.

He should have bloody well put on a shirt.

He should have some goddamn honor and be a gentleman where she was concerned.

But the telegram he'd received earlier, and the realization he faced returning to America far sooner than he had previously believed, had shaken him. Shaken him because he'd realized he didn't want to leave. That he would rather remain here in the hated place of his youth, just so he could be near to *her*. So he could touch her and kiss her and hold her again. But it wasn't only Corliss, the governess he shouldn't be longing for holding him here. It was also his nieces.

He loved Mary, Alice, Beatrice, and Nettie. More than he had ever imagined possible. And along with them, he had come to care for their golden-haired, kindhearted, angel-among-mere-mortals governess, too.

And now, he was striding forward. Eating up the distance keeping him from her. But he wasn't the only one in motion. Corliss was moving too, meeting him halfway, her hideous skirts rustling as they collided in the center of the chamber. His hands went to her waist, steadying her, keeping her from falling.

"Don't go yet," he said softly, not too proud to beg for more of her time. More of her smiles. More of the tender caring and concern she bestowed upon everyone in her circle. "I'm sorry for what I said just now, about seducing the domestics. You're far more than a servant to me, to the girls. You're..." He faltered, trying to find an adequate means of describing her and failing. "You're an angel. Stay, please, just for another moment more."

Her fingers rested on his biceps, lightly curling into the muscles he had been working hard to build there, using the plethora of dumbbells he'd managed to haul with him from America to train. The dumbbells he would now need to cart back with him for the return voyage. The thought of leaving made his gut clench and tighten with dread.

"It isn't wise," she returned, eyes wide as she stared up at him, biting her full lower lip as if she faced an untenable dilemma.

"You're right," he agreed. "It's not. Staying here with me is reckless and foolish, and I shouldn't even ask it of you, but I find I'm greedy and selfish where you're concerned. And when that telegram arrived today, all I could think was *not yet*. I'm not ready. Not because I haven't been training, but because I'm not prepared to leave you and the girls behind."

"You could take them with you," she said quietly.

Sadly.

He noted she made no mention of herself. Of course not.

Corliss was selfless. She spent all her time caring for others, and not just because her situation as a governess forced her to do so. Because that was how deeply she felt about everyone around her. He didn't think he could ever find a more wonderful woman anywhere in the world. Not for as long as he lived.

Nor would he wish to try.

Belatedly, he recalled her suggestion of taking his nieces to America and gave his head a slow shake. "The journey is long and arduous, and the matches and the company on tour aren't for impressionable young innocents."

The wrong thing to say, he realized, when her lips thinned and she tensed in his arms.

"I'm sure there is no end of ladies who throw themselves at you," she said. "You're quite right. I don't know what I was thinking. No doubt there is a great deal of carousing as well."

There had been, yes. He'd not lie. Nor would he pretend he hadn't enjoyed the women and the celebrations, the accolades and the fame, once upon a time. But the luster had been waning for some time. He'd always thought of himself as a rolling stone, gathering no moss. But for the first time, he wondered if that had ever been as true as he'd believed. What if, all that time, he'd been searching for contentedness, seeking it in all the wrong places and people?

"Jealous?" he asked, making an attempt at lightening the mood and failing utterly.

She remained stiff against him. "Of course not. I have no claim on you."

Ha! He wasn't so damned certain about that. He felt like she did. Like the sweet-natured, gorgeous woman in his arms had set her indelible mark upon every part of him.

"You needn't be," he told her, rubbing slow, steady circles on her waist with his thumbs, wishing there weren't layers of fabric and undergarments keeping him from the sleek softness of her skin. "The only woman I want is standing before me." The confession was torn from him. He rushed on, hoping she wouldn't understand how much he had just inadvertently revealed to her. "And anyway, it's the travel, the pace, I'm worried about where Mary, Alice, Nettie, and Beatrice are concerned. The violence, too. The crowds are bloodthirsty and loud. What would become of the girls if I were arrested, or worse, if something ill befell me? No, they are better served at Knightly Abbey with you. They'll be safe here."

"You're making me feel frightened for you," she murmured, looking stricken.

The flecks of gold and cinnamon in her eyes were more pronounced in this light. Or perhaps they'd been heightened by her emotions. Her eyes glittered with what he suspected were unshed tears.

For him?

His chest went tight, and a surge of desire he had no right to feel had his cock thickening in his trousers.

"I'll be fine," he assured her. "The Bruiser Knight always wins."

"Oh, Knight. It isn't The Bruiser Knight I'm worrying over. It's the man." A tear clung to her lashes and then slipped down her cheek.

Without thinking, he dipped his head, caught the teardrop on his lips. Kissed her cool, pale skin with the wetness of her sorrow between them. "Don't weep, sweetheart." He strung kisses to her ear. "Not for me. I don't deserve your sorrow."

Didn't deserve her, full stop.

Not her decadent curves pressed against him, not her presence in this room, not her sweet concern. Not her goodness and light, her sunshine. Because that was what she was. Corliss was the sunshine to him, warm and

163

radiant and beautiful. Everything he'd never known he needed.

Everything he didn't want to deny himself.

"I'll miss you," she said. "I'll worry over you."

No one had ever said those words to him and meant them. Not ever. But this woman saying them to him...*fuck*. He couldn't speak. Couldn't think. So he buried his face in the soft skin of her neck, nuzzling the hair at her temple, where she smelled so sweetly of bergamot and rose, and he slid his hands to the small of her back, flattening his palms there, drawing her into his embrace. Her arms went around his neck, and they stood there, pressed together and entwined so tightly that he could feel the steady, sure beats of her heart against his chest.

No one had ever embraced him this way either. No one had held him in her arms with such selfless reassurance, such open, tender caring. He was going to miss her, too. He was going to miss her more than words could convey. More than he could have ever fathomed missing another person mere weeks ago.

Such little time had passed, and yet, she had become essential to him. Necessary. Had it begun that first day in the nursery when he'd been soaked from the pail of water? Had it been on the path during his morning training? In the rain-soaked ride to the cottage? He didn't know, and it didn't matter. She had become a part of him.

The best part of him.

He kissed her neck, then back up to her cheek, intending to avoid her mouth. Because he knew if their lips met, he wouldn't be capable of stopping. Not with this frenzied rush of need swelling inside him. Not with his emotions so raw and ragged.

But she turned her head, and their mouths came together, and then with a groan of surrender, he was kissing her fully, deeply, and she was kissing him in return with the same hunger. She opened for him on a soft moan, and their tongues glided together.

Desire licked at him like roaring flames. His cock was rigid, his entire body suffused with heat. The longing rose until it would not be ignored.

"You should go now," he murmured against her lips, trying to warn her even as he clung to her and fed her another series of slow kisses that left them both breathless.

"I don't want to," she said, fingers lacing through his hair, hand on his shoulder, nails biting into his bare skin in a reminder that he wasn't properly clothed.

He dragged his lips along her jaw. "If you stay, I don't know if I'll be able to stop myself this time."

His restraint on every previous occasion upon which they'd been alone had been worn perilously thin. He was in danger of losing it entirely, and the longer she lingered, soft and warm and tempting in his arms, the greater his chance of forgetting he pretended to be a gentleman and taking her.

"Don't stop," she said, a breathy plea that took him over the edge.

Knight didn't pause to think. Didn't give a damn about the repercussions, about the fact that she was the governess and he was leaving soon.

"Last chance," he told her, gazing down into her gold-lash-fringed eyes, the speckles on her nose entrancing him. "Go back to your chamber, Corliss. We can both forget this ever happened. We'll never speak of it again."

"I don't want to forget." She cupped his face, holding his cheeks in her warm, silken palms, holding his gaze, refusing to relent. "Do you? Do you want me to go back?"

"Hell no."

"Good, because I don't want to go back either." Her

thumbs swept over his cheekbones, tenderly tracing. "I want to be here with you, Knight."

He swallowed hard against a rush of pure, unadulterated need so wild that it felt as if his heart would beat out of his chest. "There's a bed here, and I'm going to lay you in it. I'm going to strip you out of that hideous gown until you're naked, and then I'm going to love every inch of you."

She didn't say a word. Just pulled his head down to hers and fused their lips together in another kiss. Every part of him was clamoring to tear her out of her gown. He felt suddenly, fiercely possessive of her. He wanted to make her his, and she had made it more than apparent that she wanted him every bit as much as he wanted her.

He'd never known a woman like her. Had never desired another more. Why not take what she offered, seize this one night to carry him through the next long weeks without her, until he could return? What was the harm?

He would come back to her. Remaining in America was an impossibility now that he had returned to Yorkshire and realized the full extent of his duties here. He would come back, and they would sort out these complicated emotions, this desire, together. He would leave prizefighting. Attempt to become a man worthy of her.

Making love to Corliss wasn't wrong when he intended to do the honorable thing later. It certainly didn't feel wrong when her mouth was on his, demanding and passionate. When she moaned low in her throat and tangled her fingers in his hair. Didn't feel wrong in the slightest when he caught her up in his arms, holding her against his chest, and carried her across the chamber to the bed which had been pushed against the opposite wall.

All it felt was completely, utterly, so very *right*.

KNIGHT SETTLED Corliss on her feet at the edge of the bed which had been crowded by other furniture on the opposite end of the chamber. His hands and lips were everywhere. True to his word, trailing kisses over every new patch of skin he revealed. Her gown was nothing but a puddle of bleak gray on the floor. Her petticoats, too, had been discarded. He stood behind her now, working on the laces of her corset, her fat braid slung over her shoulder to bare her nape to his questing lips.

He kissed her there, nuzzling her hairline. "You smell like sunshine and summer gardens, and I cannot get enough of it, of you."

He sounded almost frustrated as he made the admission, his voice a low, deep growl against her. She knew the moment he had worked the knot free; she had tied it herself, a feat she was steadily growing accustomed to, but on occasion, she still pulled the knots too tightly and they were stubborn. Her laces relaxed, her corset loosening, and she became aware of her nipples, pebbled and hard against the boning.

She arched her back, spurred by the urge to rub herself against him, to have any contact with him she could get. And she could feel him, his hardness, pressed into her, cradled between the swells of her bottom. He rocked his cock against her, sending an answering rush of need to her core where she was already aching for him. Her knees trembled, threatening to give out.

"God, Corliss, the way I want you." He kissed her ear, then caught the upper ridge of it in his teeth, delivering a nip that caused an answering throb between her legs. "I can't wait to be inside you."

His words, low and wicked, delivered directly into her ear with his hot breath coasting over her, made her head fall back to his shoulder. The warmth from his body pierced the thin layer of her chemise and corset. When he licked the whorl of her ear before playing his tongue over the hollow behind it, her knees trembled, threatening to give out.

"Do you want that too, sweetheart? Tell me," he demanded, his hands clamping on her waist and spinning her so that she faced him.

So much bare, muscled chest was on display. She didn't know where to look. Every part of him was perfectly honed and beautiful.

"Can you doubt it?" she asked. "I want you more than I want to breathe."

"Fuck." His curse was vulgar, more growl than anything, and she felt it in her sex just as surely as she had felt his tongue the night before, lapping over her, bringing her to her peak. "I want the rest of this off you."

He grasped her corset and pulled the hooks and eyes apart, dropping it to the floor. Next came her chemise, up over her head and tossed away. She stood before him in drawers and stockings, the kiss of cool air on her bare breasts making her nipples even harder.

"What of you?" she dared to ask, reaching out to trail eager hands over his shoulders, down his strong arms over the bulge of muscle there.

His skin was so warm, velvet-soft, his body a dichotomy of silk and steel, strength and vulnerability. She very badly wanted to see all of him. Naked from head to toe.

His hands settled over hers, guiding them down the ridges of his taut abdomen to the waistband of his trousers. "You do it."

He was giving her permission to undress him. To take what she wanted.

He released his hold on her, his hands going to her breasts, weighing them in his palms, his long fingers gently massaging, thumbs rubbing over her nipples. It was all the impetus she required. Her fingers moved with haste, fumbling at first and then with greater confidence, plucking buttons from moorings. His cock sprang free, thick and demanding. He hadn't been wearing drawers.

And she had never been more grateful to make a discovery. She licked her lips, taking in the length of him, the evidence of his desire, feeling need building to a dangerous crescendo already.

"I want to touch you," she murmured, feeling uncertain. Not knowing what came next and yet needing it.

Needing *him* desperately.

"I'm yours," he said. "Touch me wherever, however, you like."

His words made her heart give a pang and sent a corresponding jolt of lust to the apex of her thighs, where she could feel herself growing slick. She pressed her legs together to quell the need, reminding herself that he wasn't hers. That if he knew the truth about her, he wouldn't be with her now. But she wanted to believe he could be, at least for this fleeting moment, with everyone else asleep. There was no one about but the two of them, alone with a flickering fire, lamps burning low.

She wrapped her fingers around his thickness, gently, testing the way he felt, so hot and sleek. So surprisingly soft, and yet firm. The contrast in his gorgeous body continued here, it would seem, echoed in every part of him.

"I won't break, sweetheart." His gaze was intense on hers. He released her breast with one hand and gripped himself over her fingers, showing her that she could be far rougher with him than she would have guessed. Together they moved, stroking him from base to tip until she was breathless, caught in his stare and in her desire, in the intimacy they shared. "Just like that, love."

His hips moved along with her, and he groaned, his lashes fluttering over his eyes, his countenance going slack. It was as if all the tension had been leached from him. Idly, he thumbed her nipple and cupped her breast, until she reached his cock head and there was wetness seeping from the slit in the ruddy tip.

But before she could investigate further, he gently pulled her hand away. "Enough, or you'll unman me. Let's get you out of these drawers and stockings and get you on the bed."

Together, they made short work of both her garments and his with mutual reverent touches, kisses, and caresses. Knight drew back the counterpane and guided her to the bed, kissing her sweetly as he joined her there, careful to keep his body at her side rather than pinning her beneath the weight of his massive, sculpted prizefighter's form. Although he was a powerful man, one who had earned his reputation with his fists, he touched her with astounding tenderness, with worshipful strokes and careful, light swirls that drove her frenzy ever higher.

He kissed her throat, tonguing the hollow at the base before moving lower, face between her breasts. He kissed her there, before brushing his lips with aching slowness over the inner swell of first one, then the other. As he drove her to distraction, she dragged one hand over his shoulder and back, reveling in his barely leashed strength, his smooth, hot skin. Her other fingers tangled in his hair, holding him to her breast.

He obligingly suckled her pebbled nipple, and she sighed, arching into him, tugging at his hair and raking her nails lightly over his broad back. He moaned and caught the sensitive flesh in his teeth, tugging until she was moaning too, restless and undulating against him. He released her nipple and glanced up at her, catching her braid in a light grasp to tug her head against the pillow and force her to meet his gaze.

"I'm going to taste you again, Corliss." He kissed the

opposite nipple, flicking his tongue over it, leaving her quivering with his words and his actions both. "I need you on my tongue. One day, I want to make you scream. But tonight, you have to promise to be quiet."

One day would never happen. This night, whatever time they had remaining before he left for America, was all they could ever have. She tried not to think of that now, for she wanted to live in the moment. To focus only on Knight and the pleasure he gave her. How wonderful it felt to be with him, truly. To become one with him.

"I'll be quiet," she agreed breathlessly. "But you needn't do *that* again."

Even if she wanted it more than anything else, she longed to pleasure him as well. For their lovemaking to be equal this time. She wanted to make him feel as wondrous as he did her.

He watched her with a hooded stare, a small, wicked smile flirting with his lips. "Oh, but I *do* need, sweetheart."

With that, he slid down her body, delivering a path of kisses as he went. When he reached her thighs, his mouth grazed tantalizingly over the protrusion of her hip bone, and then his hands were on her, guiding her to her back. Coaxing her legs apart until she was open to him, his gaze blazing with desire as it dipped to where she was on display, cool air licking at her sex.

"Just as pretty and perfect as I remembered when I was alone, thinking about you," he praised. "Better, even. Because now I get to have my tongue on you again. I get to see how wet you are for me. Are you wet, sweetheart?"

The breath hissed from her lungs. This sinful side of him did strange, wondrous things to her body. To her mind. She was certain she would do anything he wanted, say anything he wished, just so that he would stay with her and keep pleasuring her with that knowing, sensual mouth and his fingers and his…

He blew on her, the sensation light and airy. A tease that had her hips writhing, tipping from the bed, silently begging for more.

"I'm not going to give you what you want until you answer me," Knight warned. "Now tell me, are you wet?"

He meant *there*. And she was. She could feel the moisture dripping down her folds, partially from anticipation, because she knew what to expect—the pleasure of this man licking and kissing her until she flew apart. But also because of his touch, his heated stare, his proximity. Because he was Knight, and he was the flame, and she would happily cast herself upon it just to burn herself to ash.

"Yes," she hissed. "I'm wet."

"You are, aren't you?" His voice was admiring as he swiped a finger through her folds, gathering some of her dew and holding it up to show her, glistening in the lamplight. "Look at how wet you are." Holding her gaze, he sucked it clean with a moan of pure, carnal enjoyment. "So sweet. Your pussy tastes so good."

A high, strangled sound tore from her. There was something unspeakably depraved and erotic about watching him lick her own juices from his finger. About the way he seemed to savor her.

Before she could utter a word of protest, he ran his forefinger over her sex again, this time using his elbow to pull his body closer to her. He extended his arm and traced along her lower lip, coating it with the evidence of her desire for him.

"Taste how sweet," he whispered, his voice silken yet laden with command.

She opened her lips obediently, and his finger dipped inside, rubbing over her tongue. The taste of herself was musky and foreign, surely the height of wickedness. But she didn't care if what they were doing was wrong. Nothing about it felt that way. She felt more alive than she ever had. Instinctively, she sucked, earning a low growl from Knight.

He withdrew his finger. "The rest is for me."

With that, he settled back between her thighs, widening them farther, holding them to the bed as his head dipped. The first touch of his tongue on her had her gasping and biting the back of her hand. He gave her a few light, short licks on her pearl. Just the whisper of a touch over and over until she could scarcely bear it.

"Knight, please." Her hips were restless, shifting beneath him, seeking more.

"My greedy darling. I'll give you what you want." There was no censure in his voice, only approval, before he latched onto her and sucked hard.

She bit her knuckles until she left the indentation of her teeth in her skin. Keeping quiet was so difficult when he was…*oh*.

His tongue was inside her now, and he was pressing his face into her so firmly that she thought she'd swoon at the pleasure of it, at the rasp of his beard on her sensitive flesh, at the way his groan rumbled into her core. At the way he licked and lapped as if he were intent upon drinking up every last drop of her.

When he moved his wicked mouth back to her pearl, he dipped a finger inside her, gently at first, and then deeper, working in and out, making her tighten on him as delicious pressure built within her. Another finger joined the first. So deep, reaching that same wanton part of her where the pleasure was agony and bliss all at once. He sucked and used his teeth against her, and as he pressed into her with his lips, tongue, and fingers, she came swiftly.

She cried out. Couldn't help herself, though she had been trying to be as quiet as possible. He stayed with her until the last tremor had subsided, before he kissed his way back up her body, lingering on her breasts until she couldn't help but shift beneath him, ready for more. She touched him everywhere she could, reveling in his strength, in his masculine body, so different from hers, sculpted by years of training and dedication.

His mouth dropped to her shoulder, his teeth sinking into the skin there, as he aligned his body with hers. She felt him, thick and hard, against her. They were almost as intimately entwined as two people could be.

His lips moved to her ear. "Are you sure, Corliss? Say the word and we can stop."

She didn't have to ponder his question. Her fingers dug into his shoulders, her legs wrapping around his lean hips in welcome. There was only one word she was interested in telling Knight.

She was more certain than she had ever been in her life. The way she felt for him was inevitable and irrevocable. Even after they parted, she would carry the memory of this night with him in her heart forever.

Corliss turned her head, until they were nose to nose, breathing in each other's ragged breaths, his eyes burning into hers with the same hunger and fire she knew was reflected in her own. "Yes."

He inhaled sharply. His hands left her body to bracket her face, his calluses rough on her skin. He held her as if she were priceless, as if he had to protect her and treat her with the utmost care, and it made her shatter inside, splintering into a thousand jagged shards of herself. The thought, wild and sudden, occurred, that this man had ruined her for anyone else.

No other could ever compare.

"Yes?" he asked, his voice strained and yet hushed.

"Yes," she repeated, wishing she could tell him more. That

the emotions rising inside her could be eloquently conveyed. But they were too new, too raw. And he was leaving soon, and so was she.

This night was all they could ever have. It would have to be enough.

"Corliss." Her name was like a prayer and a plea in his deep, beloved baritone, and then his lips were on hers, and she forgot about the future.

Everything fell away but the moment, his body and hers, the taste of herself on his lips, his hand gliding down her body, smoothing over her waist and hip bone, then caressing her belly before finding the apex of her thighs. The heel of his palm pressed against her mound with such delicious pressure that she squirmed and panted into his kiss. His fingers dipped into her, swirling over her where she was swollen and wet and sensitive.

She gasped, and he caught her lower lip in his teeth, giving her a nip that had her head rolling back onto the pillow. He kissed the corner of her mouth before lifting his head to gaze down at her again. His jaw was clenched even as his touch danced over her most sensitive flesh below, driving her to distraction and making her hips twitch as if to his command.

"Have you ever..." He stopped, swallowing, his Adam's apple dipping in his throat. "Am I your first lover?"

Of course he was. But she found herself staring up at him, breath arrested in her lungs, wondering what was the correct answer. If she told him that he was, would he stop? She very much did not want him to stop.

As if he had read her mind, he kissed the bridge of her nose. "I only want to know how gentle, how soft, how slow."

Oh. He was being considerate. But she ought not to be surprised. During her time at Knightly Abbey, Knight had shown a great deal of consideration for her. He had fretted over her breakfast. Had given her a day of rest when the girls had treacled and feathered her. He had saved her from the rains, had built her a fire. He had indulged in a game of tag and a dancing lesson for the sake of his nieces.

In this, she must be honest. The remaining deceptions between them were like a splinter lodged in her heart, growing more painful by the moment.

"You are," she said.

"Gentle then," he murmured, kissing her cheek. "And soft." He lightened the strokes on her pearl. "And slow." He gave her an agonizingly leisurely caress.

She rubbed her cheek against his and arched her back, pressing her breasts into his chest. "Perhaps not that gentle, soft, or slow."

Indeed, she was quite certain she wanted hard. More. Faster.

Everything.

He chuckled, a sound that slid over her bare skin like velvet, before kissing her temple, her brow. "You're in control, sweetheart. Tell me what you like, what feels good. If you don't like something, I'll stop. If you do, I'll give you more. Yes?"

She kissed his jaw, the crispness of his short beard a delightful abrasion on her lips. "Yes. I like the way you touch me. It feels...wondrous."

"Mmm." He hummed his approval into her ear and his wicked fingers resumed their work, rubbing over her slickness with increased pressure. "I like that word. But I like the way you feel even better. So hot and wet for me. So bloody perfect."

He caught her earlobe in his teeth, nipping. Corliss was baptized in flame. She was incredibly aware of every place they touched, her senses heightened to an excruciating exactness. His soft exhalations painted heat on her throat as his mouth lowered. His fingers whorled over her, slicking her dew up and down her folds, parting her, tantalizing her by dipping into her entrance. As his body moved against hers, her nipples dragged over him, the coarse hair on his chest stimulating the taut peaks.

He kissed her breasts, suckled her nipples, played with her while she began to come apart a second time, his thumb pressing into her pearl as his fingers dipped into her, stretching her deliciously and plunging deep. She felt at once helpless, bound by her desire for him, and also infinitely powerful. All the secrets inside herself had been unlocked, and now there was nothing but pleasure, and she was awash in it. Utterly shameless for him. Hips tilting, thrusting to meet him, fingers tangling in his hair, holding his mouth to her breast as he licked over her nipple.

Begging him.

"Suck please." She heard her breathless request as if it belonged to another. So foreign and husky. Dipped in decadent need.

He gave her what she wanted with a low growl, his mouth closing over the peak of her breast and giving her the lusty, hard suckle she craved. His fingers were relentless, sinking deep, curling, his thumb rotating over her, finding the spot that sent her spiraling.

She threw her head back, gasping as another wave of bliss rolled over her, hitting her swiftly in her core and rippling outward, like a rock tossed into a still pond. She trembled beneath him, heart pounding hard, her spend so exquisite that the edges of her vision turned dark.

He released her nipple with a pop, kissed the valley between her breasts, and then his lips were on hers. The weight of his body shifted, his hand leaving her sex for a moment. There was a new sensation between her legs as he rubbed his cock up and down her seam, lingering on her aching pearl, coating himself in her wetness. His tongue slid into her mouth, his kiss turning ravenous.

When he reached her entrance, he paused, lifting his head to stare down at her with such naked want that a quiver went straight through her. "Are you ready for me, sweetheart?"

"Always."

On a groan, he sank into her, his cock stretching her wide, the sensation so unlike the penetration of his fingers. He was atop her, inside her, his breath ghosting over her lips, his stare pinned to hers.

"How does it feel?" he wanted to know, his voice husky and strained, the cords of his neck pronounced as he hovered there, still and waiting. Taking such care with her.

And now he wanted words? Her hands fluttered to his shoulders, his smooth, bare skin tantalizing her traveling fingertips and palms. She struggled to think. Found one at last that was suitable.

"Incredible"

An understatement, whispered into his lips, which had lowered to graze against hers.

"Good," he said. "Any pain?"

Not pain, precisely. But a stinging sensation. A pinch. This new invasion was bolder than his fingers and tongue had been. And Knight was a large man. Large *everywhere*. She shifted beneath him, feeling restless, needing more.

"Not pain, but it is different, you inside me." As she made the admission, she rubbed her lower lip against his, teasing them both. "I love the way you feel."

And she did. She loved the new way her body felt around his, under his. Loved his leashed strength, his gentleness, the scent of him surrounding her, his eyes holding her in their thrall, his lips hers to take. Loved the sensual way he undulated and filled her more, his thick cock sliding deeper.

He made a low sound of need in his throat before his lips

were on hers. Demanding and fierce, giving no quarter, demanding her surrender. And she gave it. Gave him every part of herself, all she had to give.

Everything except the truth.

It was a dim, painful reminder at the frayed edges of her mind. One she would contend with later. Because now was not the time for thought, for worries. Now was the time to feel.

Knight gentled the kiss and thrust into her again, their hip bones jutting together, his muscled abdomen pressing into the give of her rounded belly. Her legs, which had forgotten what they were meant to do in the overwhelming rush of sensation, lay limply on the bunched bedding, which they had only managed to halfway pull down in their haste, on either side of him. He guided them around his hips again, first one and then the other, and they were locked together, his cock pulsing inside her.

His mouth left hers, his head lifting. "My sweet Corliss. I have dreamed of this moment for weeks."

He had? There was so much tenderness in his expression as he gazed down at her. That warmth, that look. She would never forget it. Not for as long as she lived. She strung a trail of kisses along his jaw.

"Take me, Knight. Make me yours."

"With pleasure." His lips sought hers, and they kissed and kissed as he began to move within her, sliding out and in, finding a rhythm that had her breathless. Her hips chased his as she clung to him, panting into his kiss, breathing in his breaths, making choked sounds of need into his lips.

He devoured them all and devoured her, claiming her body so thoroughly that she knew she would never be able to erase the memory of his possession, of this night of reckless abandon. Not even if she wished to.

The knot of need was drawn tight within her, and when

he angled his hips, pleasure rocketed through her like fireworks in a dark night sky. She was helpless to do anything but give in. She tightened on him, crying out with delirious pleasure, and he continued his relentless pace. Faster, harder, their bodies slick with sweat, holding each other so tightly, as if they each feared the other would disappear if they let go.

She felt him tensing, the muscles in his shoulders growing thick and taut, before he withdrew from her entirely, breaking their kiss to grasp himself. He tugged harshly at his cock once, twice. With a low moan, he spurted his seed all over her belly. She watched, secretly thrilled, to know she had so much sway over this powerful man, to bring him to such a state.

In the aftermath, Corliss lay there breathless, covered in him, heart galloping, and knew she would never again be the same. The Corliss who had come to Knightly Abbey was forever gone. The woman she had become didn't mourn her loss.

Instead, she gathered this beautiful man—hers for one night—into her arms, the stickiness of his seed trapped between their bodies, so raw and carnal and incredible, and kissed him again.

CHAPTER 12

$\mathcal{K}$night paced the cold marble floor in the great hall of Knightly Abbey, his footfalls echoing in the cavernous chamber, where high above, spoils of past hunts still adorned the walls in grisly fashion. He fidgeted with the cuffs of his coat, before sliding a finger beneath his necktie, which seemed far too constricting this morning. He had nearly forgotten Anglesey was arriving today.

A timely reminder from Mrs. Oak that morning after breakfast had spared him the embarrassment of unpreparedness. His interactions with the housekeeper were stilted, now that he knew the secrets of what had transpired between her and Robert. He had asked Smithson to find a suitable replacement for her, with the intention that he would settle a substantial sum upon Mrs. Oak that would allow her to live in comfort for the rest of her days. Robert had left him quite the tangled web.

As Knight awaited his guests, he had ample time to ruminate.

A flurry of questions flitted through his mind, rather like warning shots fired from an enemy infantry. Peppering his already grim mood. Filling him with more dread, weighing him down. Ought he to have shaved? Did he look as if he had scarcely slept? Would his old school chum, the Earl of Anglesey, take one look at him and instantly know Knight had debauched his governess the night before?

What a despicable bastard he was. He never should have allowed himself to get so carried away with Corliss.

Feeling his ears go hot, Knight stopped pacing before the merrily crackling fire which had been lit to ward off the chill of the day. A mistake, for, coupled with his inner shame, it threw enough heat to melt him. He resumed his strides with a heavy sigh, thinking no one could look upon him and know what had transpired. That was ridiculous. It wasn't as if he were wearing a sign that read *I am an evil seducer of innocents.*

Even if it felt as if he were.

Last night had been the best of his life. Not just making love with Corliss, which had been otherworldly in its intensity and pleasure. But every moment of each second they'd shared. From her tears of concern for him to her sensual acknowledgment of her needs. And the way she had given herself to him...

God.

He had been able to think of nothing but her since they had parted early enough for the servants to still be abed, with hushed whispers, quick kisses, and a mutual attempt at restoring each other's garments to rights. She had left him in a rumpled gown he'd have sooner thrown into the fire to watch it burn, tendrils of golden hair loosened from her braid, cheeks flushed, lips swollen. And he had left her with the bitter acid of self-loathing on his tongue and the desperate need to have her again.

And again.

And again.

It was a problem. Or perhaps *he* was a problem. Knight raked his fingers through his hair and exhaled harshly as he completed another circumnavigation of the great hall. Just where the devil *were* Anglesey and his countess, and what was taking them so long to alight and enter? Their carriage had approached what already seemed a lifetime ago, and the pair had yet to pass through the massive old doors before him.

Knight hadn't played host in... Christ, he hadn't been a host to anyone. Not ever. He was every bit as new to being an earl as he was to being an earl in command of a country seat. An earl with responsibilities and duties and nieces and tenants and stewards and domestics and the most tempting, beautiful governess to have ever graced the goddamned earth.

He could acknowledge, even if just to himself, that he wasn't certain of the rules of hosting a friend, of how to be polite. Did one await one's guests in the great hall as he was doing? He searched his mind for memories of what his parents had done, but it all seemed a lifetime ago, and he had locked away much of his past in favor of a brighter, bolder future. The lad who had left Knightly Abbey wouldn't recognize the man he had become.

Perhaps he should have closeted himself away in his study. But if he were honest with himself, he would admit the true reason for his impatience. He needed—badly—to see a friendly face. To have a trusted chum in whom he could confide. Here in Yorkshire, he'd been set adrift. He hadn't anyone save his nieces and their governess to confide in, and four of them were children, whilst the other was the reason he required counsel.

Because he had made love to her.

Last night.

Sweet God.

Knight swallowed hard and nearly tripped over his own feet, and that was when the doors burst open without any fanfare, and the Earl and Countess of Anglesey crossed the threshold. Anglesey hadn't changed one whit in all the time which had passed since they had last been together. Like a golden-haired Adonis, Anglesey—or as their set had once known him before he had inherited, Barlowe—had always been the envy of them all. Adored by the fairer sex. Now happily married, from what his friend had written and from the sheer reverence with which the earl escorted his wife across the threshold.

Indeed, Anglesey was so consumed by the woman on his arm that it took him a few seconds to realize they weren't alone and that Knight was standing there stupidly, feeling like the world's greatest arse for any number of reasons, tugging at his hair. He straightened his shoulders and forced a smile for the benefit of his friend and his friend's wife.

"Anglesey, my lady." To the countess, Knight offered a courtly bow in deference. "Welcome to Knightly Abbey."

Words he had never supposed he would utter.

A place he had never imagined he would return to.

And yet, he had experienced much since his arrival at Knightly Abbey that he had never reckoned he would. All of it had altered him, to the deepest core of his being.

"The Bruiser Knight." Anglesey grinned. "My love, may I present to you one of my oldest chums, the Earl of Stoneleigh, also known as the American champion of boxing. Knight, my wife. Also known as *my wife*."

Knight chuckled, well understanding his friend's protectiveness when it came to the countess. For he felt the same way about Corliss. Only, she wasn't his wife. She was the governess to his nieces, and he had lost himself inside her last night despite the glaring wrongness of doing so. No doubt about it, he was going to hell.

But was there a better reason to consigning himself to the fiery fate of the damned? He could find none that could compare to Corliss and her golden hair, glittering brown eyes, freckled nose, luscious feminine curves, and deliciously responsive body. It was entirely possible he was in love with her.

He had certainly jolted awake that morning with the thought in his mind that he must marry her, and that if he did, he wouldn't regret a single bloody moment of making her his wife and having her at his side and in his bed for the rest of his life.

"Lady Anglesey, it is a pleasure to make your acquaintance," he said politely, sending a wry glance in his friend's direction. "You'll forgive me, I hope, for awaiting you here. You're the first guests we've had at Knightly Abbey since my return, and I've been abroad for so long that I've quite forgotten what is to be done in such matters, if indeed I ever paid attention to it from the start."

Likely, he hadn't. He had never felt as if he were truly a part of Robert's gilded world. Knight had been the spare. Never the heir. Their father had made that more than apparent, and it had been his coldness which had led Knight to leave Yorkshire and England altogether. He'd never been missed.

Not even a damned letter from his father before his death.

Not one.

His family's lack of concern for him had hurt far more then than it did now. He was older, wiser, his parents long gone. Robert, too.

"This is just the thing," Anglesey reassured him, grinning easily. "You're a fine sight to behold, Knight. I've missed you."

He nodded. "I've missed you as well."

It startled him to realize the veracity in those innocuous

185

words. They were politic, and yet so very true. He hadn't known how much he had missed his school chums until he had seen them again. First Grey, the Marquess of Greymoor, on his way to Yorkshire, and now Anglesey as well. They'd been the best of friends. And although time and distance had intervened, Knight couldn't help but to feel that same sense of kinship—a brotherhood unlike any bond he'd ever felt with his own flesh and blood Robert—making him feel at ease. Making him forget some of the turmoil churning in his head and heart.

"It is wonderful to meet another of Anglesey's friends," said the countess, smiling. She had dark hair and eyes the color of moss, and she was undeniably lovely.

But it wasn't merely her beauty that caught his attention. There was something about her mannerism and voice that seemed suddenly familiar, as if he had met her before.

Which was ridiculous, of course. He doubted Anglesey's wife had ever been present in a railcar or at a boxing match in America, and that was where he had spent most of his recent days, aside from when he had journeyed here.

"The pleasure is mine, my lady," he said.

He would have offered some additional small talk, but the bustle of servants began around them, the domestics taking command of the situation in better form than he could ever hope to possess. It was humbling, realizing how little he truly knew about being an earl.

Delighted squeals intruded, followed by a flurry of hasty, small footfalls that warned him his nieces were about to arrive the moment before they stormed into the great hall in most unladylike fashion. Following them was Corliss in yet another drab gown, the dourness of which was relieved by her golden hair, warm eyes that met his instantly, and the pinkness of her cheeks.

She looked utterly delectable, and he wanted nothing

more than to pull her into his arms and devour her, right there in the great hall whilst everyone watched on. He couldn't do that, of course, but he *could* marry her. And marry her was what he was going to do. What he *had* to do.

The knowledge hit him like a blow in the ring as he stared at her, the sunlight streaming in from mullioned windows overhead gilding her Grecian braids. She was kind-hearted, sweet-natured, intelligent, caring, passionate, and lovely. He'd never met another woman who made him feel the way she did. She was genuine and true, no ulterior motive guiding her, unlike Ida and so many others he had known. She loved his hellion nieces as if they were her own. She'd given herself to him without a thought of the consequences. She was selfless and everything that was good. Nary a hint of deception or manipulation, and God how he appreciated that part of her. Appreciated that there could still exist in the world someone so thoroughly unspoiled and true.

"Forgive us for rushing about, Lord Stoneleigh," she was saying to Knight as she held his gaze. She was breathless, looking flushed and embarrassed at the manner in which she and the girls had come flouncing into the great hall. "Their ladyships were excited when they learned guests were arriving, and I'm afraid I couldn't persuade them to remain in the nursery, no matter how I tried."

"Corliss?"

The voice of the Countess of Anglesey, dripping with disbelief, shattered the moment, and Corliss's eyes went wide as she whirled to face Anglesey and his wife for the first time with a gasp.

"Izzy?" Corliss sounded shocked, and there had been no mistaking the expression on her countenance before she'd turned away from him—she was beyond startled. "Anglesey...I...what are the two of you doing here at Knightly Abbey?"

She knew Anglesey and his countess? Knight frowned, looking between his guests and Corliss, trying to make sense of the little drama unfolding before him. Perhaps from her past situation, he mused.

He stepped forward, feeling damned awkward. "You and Miss Brinton know each other?"

"Of course we do." Anglesey's gaze swung from Knight to Corliss and back again, his expression as incredulous as his voice, brows arched. "She is my sister-in-law."

Anglesey's sister-in-law? But that made no sense. Anglesey's wife was the daughter of the Earl of Leydon. Which would make Corliss *Lady* Corliss Collingwood, not Miss Corliss Brinton.

"What are you doing here, Corliss?" Lady Anglesey asked, fracturing Knight's whirling thoughts with her question.

"I…" Corliss's words trailed off, and she sent a panicked look in Knight's direction.

Just what the devil was going on here? A sick sensation curdled his gut.

"She's my governess," he said, unable to shake the premonition that his world was about to be upended.

"Governess?" The countess's gaze was on Corliss, who looked as if she were frozen, rather reminiscent of a lovely butterfly who had been captured and pinned to a collection board. "Mama and Criseyde wrote that you were visiting Aunt Louisa."

"I can explain," Corliss said weakly, guilt etched on her lovely face.

She bit her lower lip in the way that never failed to make him want to kiss her. Except, he didn't want to kiss her now. He wanted to find out just what the hell was happening, and how the sister-in-law to his old school chum had become his governess.

"An explanation would be an excellent notion," he told

her coolly, fighting the sinking sensation of dread. "Now, if you please."

$\sim$

CORLISS WAS SICK, her stomach knotted, dread heavy as a stone in the pit of her belly, as she followed Knight into his study, her sister Izzy and brother-in-law Anglesey following in their grim wakes. The silence that had descended after his harsh pronouncement had been deafening. But it had been his stare, flinty and hard, the rigid angle of his jaw, which had been more alarming than the quiet.

Lady Alice, Lady Mary, Lady Nettie, and Lady Beatrice had been sent to the nursery to work on their sketching with Miss Wofford to oversee. The girls, too, had been quiet and confused, watching her with puzzled expressions as they had been hastily bundled away by Mrs. Oak at their uncle's request. Now, each step she took felt as if it were one step closer to the destruction of the happiness that had been blossoming inside her since the night before.

And it was no one's fault but Corliss's own.

She had done this to herself. She had lied to gain her situation as governess. She had carried on with her ruse, even after she had begun to develop feelings for Knight. After they had kissed, after they had shared intimacies she'd only previously imagined. After he had made love to her.

She had intended to tell him the truth last night, of course. Had almost done so, until her bravado had faltered. All morning since leaving his arms, she had been thinking about ways she might reveal her deception. Hating the inevitable moment when he would look upon her as he had in the great hall, with cold distrust, knowing she had lied to him. It had never been her aim to deceive him in coming to Knightly Abbey. Nor to hurt him. She should have confided the truth last night, before things between them had progressed so far. But she had been so caught up in the moment, in the man, that she hadn't.

He would never forgive her, she knew it. And nor could she blame him. Lying to him had been wrong. She should have put a stop to this farce long ago, but the truth was, she had been enjoying herself too much. She had fallen in love with him and his nieces, and she had been dreading the moment when she would have to leave them all.

The door to the study closed with an ominous thud, and Knight spun to face her, hands clasped behind his back, face inscrutable. "I await your explanation, madam."

His voice was frigid. The careful, tender lover of the night before, the man who had kissed her farewell this morning with excruciating sweetness, and even the elegant lord whose brilliant gaze had clashed with hers in the great hall just before her carefully constructed lies had begun to dismantle, was nowhere to be found.

She cast a glance toward her sister and Anglesey, who were watching her with countenances that were quizzical and confused, respectively. "Perhaps it would be better explained without an audience," she suggested.

She loved her older sister Izzy dearly, and she was also quite fond of her sister's new husband, who worshipped the ground upon which Izzy trod. However, the prospect of revealing the depths of her relationship with Knight before them made her stomach churn.

"On the contrary," Knight countered, his voice icy. "I cannot think of a conversation more suited to an audience. Their presence is a favor to you."

Knight was quietly seething. Corliss could see it. His fury was evident in his rigid bearing, the way he clenched his jaw. He looked as she imagined he might when he faced an opponent in the ring. Tensed, intimidating. Powerful and angry.

She exhaled slowly, tearing her gaze from him and seeking out her sister's instead. Izzy's bright, green eyes were searching.

"I'm sure there is a reasonable explanation for the confusion," Izzy said softly. "Go on, Corliss. Tell us what has happened and how you've come to be here at Knightly Abbey, acting as a governess."

Reasonable? All the guilt and dread eating away at Corliss from the inside suggested otherwise.

She took a deep breath. "I've been writing a novel about a governess. I wanted to know what it truly feels like to be one each day so that I could accurately represent my heroine. I saw an advertisement for a governess needed in Yorkshire, and since it is also where Aunt Louisa lives, the notion occurred to me that I could tell Mama and Papa that I was paying her a visit and instead immerse myself in the life of Miss Brinton."

And immerse herself, she had. Until she had lost herself and her heart in the process.

"Tell me, just who the devil is Miss Brinton, if not you?" Knight asked sharply, bringing her gaze back to him.

How big and powerful he looked, standing in the midst of the Axminster. How handsome and menacing and beloved and alone. To Corliss, it seemed as if he encompassed the entire chamber. He was the sun, brilliant and searing, and everyone else was merely revolving around him.

"Miss Brinton is the name of the heroine in the novel I'm writing," she admitted through lips that had gone numb. "I am Lady Corliss Collingwood."

She was aware of how dreadful this looked. Of what he must think of her, that she had been playing a role for the entirety of her stay here. But that was not the truth at all. Every part of it had been genuine, except her surname.

"Jesus Christ," he said, looking at her as if she were suddenly a stranger, betrayal in his eyes.

Anglesey cleared his throat. "Knight, are you certain this is the best time for this discussion? It's more than apparent that this is a case of mistaken identity. I'm sure that after we've all had some time to digest this bit of news, cooler heads shall prevail."

It was a tactful response, and Corliss could have hugged her brother-in-law in that moment for his compassion on her behalf. Compassion she likely didn't deserve. He was a fine husband to Izzy, but it was apparent that he was also willing to protect Izzy's sister when it came down to it, and she appreciated his constancy, particularly when she hadn't yet grown to know him well. Izzy and Anglesey had only just recently wed.

"There's no better time," Knight said ruthlessly. "I think *Lady Corliss* owes us all an explanation for her deceptions. Now."

The way he called her *Lady Corliss*, with an icy emphasis upon her title, felt more like an epithet than an appellation. He was angry with her. Beyond angry. She'd never seen him so cold and harsh before.

"You are correct, my lord," Corliss managed past the rising lump of shame and sadness in her throat. "I do owe you all explanations and an apology as well. None more so than you. When I first happened upon the notion of posing as a governess for a month's time so that I might research the position and all it entailed, I never imagined I would become so fond of my charges."

Or their uncle.

But she kept that to herself. No need to reveal so much, not with Izzy and Anglesey watching on.

"You might have explained who you truly were at any

moment over the last few weeks," Knight pointed out bitterly. "At *any moment*, my lady."

Corliss read his eyes, his countenance, and she knew him well enough by now to understand that he was referring to the night before. To what had happened between them. Did he regret it now? Surely, he must, and she hated the thought. Because for her, last night had been life-altering in the very best possible way. Nothing would drive the memories from her mind. Not even if he chose to hate her forever for what she had done.

"I wanted to explain," she rushed to say, crossing the distance between them and reaching instinctively for his arm, crushed when he shrugged away from her touch, as if it would burn.

She stopped, cheeks and ears going hot, but knowing she needed to continue. To try to make him understand.

A small, mocking smile pulled at the corners of his lips. Not a true smile. Nor did it reach his eyes. "If you had wished it, you would have done so, Lady Corliss. Instead, you chose to continue deceiving myself, my nieces, and my entire household. Day after day after day. Did it amuse you to do so? I suppose it certainly must have entertained you to forge a letter of recommendation calling yourself an angel among mortals."

Dear God. Her chest was tight and heavy, her lungs aching with each breath. She had expected to be able to reveal the truth to him in her own fashion. Not to have it relentlessly thrust in his face as had happened in the great hall, and as was happening now. Oh, how she hated this.

"Please believe me that it was never my intention to deceive anyone or to cause any harm. I wanted to immerse myself in the role, to make my Miss Brinton as authentic as possible. All I had to draw upon for research were other novels which have been published and my own faded recollection of my girlhood governess. I've already published three other books which have been well-received, but I wanted this one to be the book that truly propelled me and gave me a means of earning my own income. When I began to write, I realized what little I knew about being a governess wasn't sufficient, and as if by fate, Papa left *The Times* on the dining room table, opened to the page with the advertisements for governesses. I saw Yorkshire, and I thought of Aunt Louisa, for she never travels to London, and no one ever would have known. I paid my lady's maid more than enough funds to journey to visit her family and meet me in Yorkshire in one month's time on my return…"

Her words trailed off lamely, for she knew how dreadful they sounded. How heartless and inconstant they made her appear. How selfish. And yes, she could acknowledge it now. She had only been thinking of herself. She had been thinking of her book, of her future.

"Oh, Corliss," Izzy said into the awful silence, her tone steeped in pity. "I always thought I was the wildest sibling amongst us. But you've found yourself in quite a scrape."

"Quite a scrape indeed," Knight said coldly, looking at Corliss as if she were an utter stranger. "I'll see that your belongings are moved into the guest room at once, and Miss Wofford will be taking over your duties with my nieces until a new governess is found."

"You needn't do so," she protested, pressing a hand over her heart as if she could quell the pain dwelling there. "I enjoy being their governess. I would like to continue, at least until you find a suitable replacement."

"A replacement suitable to a liar who hasn't any experience?" he snarled, his voice cracking like a whip in the stillness of the study. "Thank you, but you'll no longer be required in the capacity of governess. If you'll all excuse me, I need to attend to my household. I'll join you later for dinner.

Lord and Lady Anglesey, I pray you'll forgive me for the sorry manner in which you've been welcomed to Knightly Abbey."

He bowed, and without another glance in Corliss's direction, Knight stalked from the room.

As the door slammed after him, Corliss flinched, thinking how wrong her sister was. For this didn't feel like a scrape.

It felt like the worst mistake of her life.

CHAPTER 13

*K*night was on his third whisky now.

Or was it his fourth?

Christ, who knew? Who gave a damn? He had settled his duties with his nieces, all of whom had promptly burst into tears when he had informed them that Miss Brinton would no longer be acting as their governess. There had been much feminine weeping, along with the stomping of small feet, and hands planted on hips, coupled with more pouting than a debutante ball. He hadn't had the heart to tell them the full truth, that Miss Brinton was truly Lady Corliss Collingwood, and that she had been lying to them all through her pretty teeth from the moment she had arrived.

Instead, he had shouldered the blame. Allowed the girls to believe he had decided Miss Brinton was too lenient, that their galloping through the great hall before guests had been the outside of enough, and that he had given her the sack as a result of it. Four pairs of eyes had filled with tears and recriminations.

He had accepted it all.

Because accepting their heartache and anger had been

better than thinking about Corliss's deceptions and what they meant for him. But the inevitable could only be postponed for so long, and thinking about her duplicity was what he was doing now.

And drinking.

He lifted his glass to his lips, staring morosely out the window at the darkened park below. She had fooled him so well. *An angel walking amongst mere mortals.* Ha! What tripe. More like a cunning liar walking amongst trusting dupes. At the moment, he couldn't decide which was the most egregious sin she had committed, deceiving him about who she was, using him and his family as fodder for the bloody book she was writing, or allowing him to make love to her—to take her virginity, for Chrissakes—with such lies hanging over them.

A knock sounded at his study door and he braced himself for the inevitability of facing her again. For the person on the other side to be Corliss.

"Come," he called, tossing back another swallow of amber liquid and relishing the burn.

But the door opened, and although the interloper crossing the threshold was also blond, he was a tall, broad-shouldered peer instead of a dowdy-dress-wearing, beautiful schemer. Knight tamped down the disappointment slicing through him and forced a smile he didn't feel as he raised his glass in toast to the Earl of Anglesey.

"Hullo, old chum," he said. "Forgive me for being the devil's own host. When you had written with your intention of paying a call, I hadn't reckoned the gates of hell would be unleashed at your arrival."

"I didn't intend to unleash the gates of hell with my visit either," Anglesey said wryly, closing the door discreetly at his back and venturing deeper into the chamber.

Anglesey was dressed for dinner, looking dapper as he

always had, his necktie perfectly centered in stark contrast to his crisp, white shirt and smart waistcoat. Knight had never been particular about his mode of dress, but facing his friend now reminded him that he was still wearing his country bumpkin tweed from the morning.

"Hardly your fault, what happened," Knight said, taking another sip of whisky. "I reckon I'm to blame as much as anyone."

After all, he had believed Corliss's lies. He had suspected, initially, that she wasn't a capable governess, had he not? The signs had been there. She had confused the name of her employer. The effusive letter of recommendation, the way she had lost her charges. The bold gowns in the morning that seemed too fine for a governess. And instead of thoroughly investigating his concerns, he had allowed himself to be charmed by her. Smitten by her. She had won over his nieces and himself with such ease.

"This is damned awkward, to say the least," Anglesey acknowledged with a wince. "I'm sorry our visit proved to be the source of so much unpleasantness."

"Again, not your fault." He moved away from the window, striding to the sideboard where Robert kept liquor and glasses at the ready. Likely to seduce Mrs. Oak, perish the thought. "Would you care for a whisky, Anglesey?"

He splashed a bit more into his glass, replenishing the dwindling store of liquid, knowing he would likely regret over-imbibing later and not giving a damn. He was at sixes and sevens over learning Corliss had been lying to him, to his nieces. By God, how would she have explained her inevitable departure to them? She had never intended to stay. She'd had no right to allow them to form attachments.

He thought of young Mary clinging to his leg earlier and tearfully pronouncing, "But Uncle, we love Miss Brinton, and she loves us!"

Ruthlessly, he shoved the memory from his mind. Whisky wouldn't cure what ailed him, but it would certainly make it easier to forget, at least for the moment.

"I suppose one whisky won't do me any harm," Anglesey said, accepting the glass Knight offered. "You look as if you shouldn't be drinking alone."

A bitter laugh escaped him. "I shouldn't be drinking at all. I've a match to defend my championship in three weeks, and I ought to be training for it."

Not agonizing over the woman who had betrayed him.

The woman he had bedded the night before.

"Back to America with such haste?" Anglesey asked, taking a slow, measured sip from his glass, brows raised. "But you've only just recently returned."

Knight shrugged, the pain in his shoulder, which he'd been doing his best to ignore, making itself known once more. "I'm not getting any younger, and my days of boxing are limited. Besides that, I've been challenged, and if I don't defend my championship, I'll have no choice but to cede it. I've worked too damned hard all these years to surrender without a fight."

He told himself that, but the prospect of returning to America and railcars and the journalists who loved to hound him, dodging fists and squaring off against opponents who were younger and perhaps stronger than he was, no longer held the allure it once had. It was a hollow existence in many ways. He'd had the adulation of so many and yet the true companionship of none. Everyone had wanted him for his fame. They'd all wanted The Bruiser Knight. And here in Yorkshire, he'd begun to feel like a man again, rather than a myth steeped in fame.

But perhaps that had been an illusion too, just like Corliss had been.

"You're one hell of a fighter, Knight," Anglesey said,

raising his glass in salute. "I've read every account of your matches I could. Grey tells me it was quite a sight to watch you trample your opponent in person."

The time Greymoor had spent with him in New York had been a blur of fighting, dance halls, and debauchery, what seemed a lifetime ago now.

He smiled at the memory, forever a pleasant one. Thank God for his friends. "There's always the next bout. You and your countess could come and watch if you like."

Anglesey shook his head. "I never thought I'd say it, but I'm enjoying rusticating in the countryside. Domesticity suits me. No trips abroad for now."

"I'm pleased to see you so happy, old friend. You deserve it."

Knight rubbed the back of his neck, thinking again of Corliss. Of what had passed between them. He had ruined her. Had ruined Anglesey's sister-in-law. The shock of Corliss's revelations that morning had left him dwelling upon her lies. But there was far more troubling him than her deceptions. There was also the matter of what was to be done, now that he had bedded her and he knew who she was.

His earlier, lovesick intentions to marry her had burned to ash. But he was still going to have to wed Lady Corliss. The prospect had him taking another hearty swig of whisky.

"Thank you," Anglesey said simply. "I'm happier than I ever imagined I could be. The right woman will do that for a man. I never knew until my Izzy came along."

His friend's maudlin sentiments were making Knight's guts churn. Or perhaps that was the whisky.

"You're a fortunate man," he managed.

"Are you well, Knight?" Anglesey asked bluntly.

Christ no. He was the furthest from well he'd ever been. Because the woman he wanted more than he needed his next breath had been nothing but a chimera. Just like Ida, only so much worse.

"Better than I've ever been," he lied. "Why?"

"You missed dinner, you're swaying on your feet, and you smell like a distillery," his chum said baldly.

Well, there was something to be said for the familiarity and kinship of friends, was there not? If anyone else were to speak to him with such blunt audacity, Knight would toss the offensive fellow on his arse. But this was Anglesey, and the man was akin to a brother to him.

For that reason, Knight took another lengthy draught of whisky before responding. "I missed dinner?"

That was a rather shocking bit of effrontery, his house-hold carrying on with dinner in his absence. Had someone informed him? He couldn't recall.

"Yes." Anglesey was still staring at him with a concerned expression. "It was done over an hour ago, and quite deli-cious, too. Apparently, you told the housekeeper not to keep it for you, that you had some pressing business to attend to. Is that a new American euphemism for getting thoroughly soused?"

Right. Now that he thought upon it, Knight did vaguely remember ordering Mrs. Oak to proceed as planned. Drowning himself in whisky had seemed preferable to facing Corliss over the dinner table. Frankly, it still did.

"Go to hell, Anglesey," he told his friend without heat. "I'm not soused. I'm merely having a difficult time accepting the fact that the woman I regarded as my saving grace has been lying to me, and now I'll be left scrambling to find a suitable replacement before I leave for my next fight."

That wasn't the truth, though. Not at all. Even deep in his cups, Knight could acknowledge it to himself. He was knee-deep in whisky because he'd been falling in love with a woman who didn't exist. And now he was going to have to marry her, even though he couldn't trust her. That was what he earned for trusting a woman. He ought to have learned his bloody lesson.

"Are you certain it's the search for a new governess that has you so overset?" his friend pressed, frowning.

Seeing too much. When the devil had Anglesey become so observant?

"Marriage has rotted your mind," he grumbled.

"Has it? I rather think it's given me a new sense of clarity."

"I'll finish my whisky alone," Knight declared. "Go find your wife and leave me in peace."

"Not yet, I don't think. You look as if you need a friend just now." Anglesey patted him on the shoulder.

The bad shoulder.

Knight winced. Lifting dumbbells yesterday had likely been a mistake. He'd overdone it. Perhaps an ice bath was in order.

"Curse you, Anglesey," he said, scowling and feeling himself sway ever so slightly, as his friend had claimed he had witnessed. "I just want to drink my whisky and go to bed."

"I think that's a plan most unwise," his friend said grimly. "You'll finish your whisky, and we'll ring for something from the kitchens. And while you're eating, you can tell me all about what has happened between you and Lady Corliss."

"I'd sooner eat my hat," he declared, swaying again.

For a man who was always so very in control of his body, being this deep in his cups was damned disconcerting. Knight didn't like it one whit. Not any more than he liked the fact that Corliss had deceived him.

"I'm afraid a hat would be rather dry," Anglesey observed wryly. "Difficult to chew and swallow. No, you'll need some far more fortifying fare."

"You're too young to be my father, Anglesey." He

attempted a sneer, but he wasn't entirely sure he was suitably impressive.

Because the earl laughed at him and reached for his glass of whisky. "Come now, give Papa your whisky. I think you've had enough. You can thank me in the morning when you aren't shooting the cat into the chamber pot."

Unfortunately, Anglesey's reflexes hadn't been dulled by spirits as Knight's had, and he plucked the half-full whisky glass from his fingers with disappointing ease. He carried the whisky away and set it upon Robert's desk, before stalking to the bellpull and giving it a tug.

Part of Knight knew his friend was right. Athletes couldn't over-imbibe as he had done. But he was as wrecked as an overturned carriage inside. He didn't know what to do. Couldn't make sense of the shattering revelation that Corliss had been lying to him, deceiving him as Ida had.

"Christ," he muttered to himself, raking his fingers through his hair. "Was everything a lie?"

Had she kissed him in research for her novel?

Had anything she'd said been the truth?

Who was the real Corliss?

And could he ever trust her again?

Anglesey turned back to him, leaving the bellpull. "I may not be the most observant of chaps, but even a dead man could have seen the tension between you and Lady Corliss earlier. I'd be willing to bet Barlowe Park that something has happened between the two of you. I understand that you're upset with her for deceiving you, but if there's anything I've learned about the Collingwood women, it's that they're as loyal and good as they are spirited and eccentric. I'm sure Lady Corliss had no intention of hurting either you or your nieces."

"Easy for you to say," he said, listing to the right and catching himself on an overstuffed armchair.

Blast, he did need some bloody sustenance.

"It is," Anglesey said. "Because I know them. Have I ever told you how I met my wife?"

Knight wasn't sure he cared, but it wasn't as if he could escape the earl in his current state. "No."

Anglesey grinned. "She was in her cups at a ball, and she kissed me…"

CORLISS WAS STARING at the happily crackling fire in the grate of the new chamber she'd been directed to by a rather perplexed chambermaid. She hadn't had the heart to explain to the curious girl why she was no longer staying in the governess's room. Nor was it any of Emma's concern. However, her sudden change in status was not going unnoticed, nor unquestioned and remarked upon.

What could she say, truly? She had no doubt that everyone below stairs would look upon her with the same distrust and hurt in their eyes that Knight had.

Knight.

At the thought of him, the tears she had been trying—mostly unsuccessfully—to suppress since that morning returned, stinging her eyes. Would he ever forgive her?

A gentle knock at her door told her without needing to ask that her sister had arrived. She had expected Izzy to seek her out following dinner, which she had stubbornly refused to attend. Instead, she had taken a tray she had not even touched in her new room.

"Come," she called, sniffling and hastily dabbing at her watering eyes.

The door opened and Izzy sailed in, wearing one of her more subdued gowns of deep-purple silk that complemented her inky, upswept hair perfectly. She looked lovely as always, but then, marriage to the Earl of Anglesey suited her. There was a sparkling happiness that radiated from her and heightened her natural beauty in a way nothing else could.

"Dearest." Izzy gently closed the door and crossed the cozy chamber, opening her arms. "You look as if you've been weeping again. Come."

Corliss didn't hesitate in accepting her sister's embrace, and not for the first time that day. No, the first had been in the awful aftermath of Knight's departure from the great hall. Corliss's shock had given way to soul-deep sorrow. She'd gone to her sister's rooms and Anglesey had obligingly made himself scarce whilst she had sobbed her troubles into Izzy's travel gown.

She hugged her sister tightly now, grateful for her presence, even if it was what had ultimately caused the destruction of her little tower of deceptions. "You smell lovely," she said to distract herself. "Is that a new perfume?"

"Don't attempt to change the subject, my dear," Izzy chided gently, drawing back to search her face. "We missed you at dinner."

She sighed, the sort of sigh that began in one's toes and went out through one's shoulders. A deep, body-wracking sigh that conveyed just how distressed she was without words.

"I don't suppose Kni—Lord Stoneleigh—missed me," she said, unable to keep the bitterness from her voice.

"I'm certain he would have, had he been present." Izzy issued a weary sigh of her own, her emerald gaze still seeking. "Will you tell me what has happened between the two of you?"

Everything had happened.

She had lost her heart to him. Lost her heart to his nieces. Had forgotten her true reason for coming to Knightly Abbey. And he had made her realize so much about herself. Had shown her passion. Had made her feel so cherished and cared for.

And she had ruined his trust by failing to confess the truth to him until it was too late.

But Corliss wasn't ready to say all that. So instead, she offered, "I lied to obtain this position, and he is displeased by my deceptions because now he will need to find a new governess. I feel guilty that I'll not be able to attend to his nieces for the remainder of my stay here. I've grown quite fond of them, their antics aside."

Izzy tucked her chin down, giving Corliss a knowing look. "I saw the way the earl was looking at you earlier when you rushed into the great hall after his nieces. It wasn't the way an employer looks at his governess. It was the way a man looks at a woman he loves. It was as if you were the only person in the room."

Love? Ha! If only. Knight had never spoken a word of it, and even if he had possessed tender feelings for her, she had no doubt they had been thoroughly dashed by now.

She sniffed, and to her mortification, the sound emerged as a partial sob. Corliss cleared her throat in an effort to cover her embarrassing reaction. "He was glaring at me, you mean."

"That was after he discovered you weren't his Miss Brinton," Izzy pointed out sensibly.

"I've never been his anything." Another sob escaped her, and her eyes were burning.

"I think you're wrong about that," her sister said. "Unless I mistake my guess, you're that man's *everything*, and that's why he's taken this unwise deception of yours to heart."

"You had to call it unwise, didn't you?" she grumbled.

"I'm only being honest. It's my duty as your elder sister."

"I thought stealing my jewelry was," Corliss returned.

"I never stole your jewelry, Corrie." Izzy raised a brow. "I may have borrowed a few pieces upon occasion."

"Without permission," Corliss countered.

Izzy shook her head. "I always returned them. But I'm not the topic of this discussion, am I? It is you, rather, and all your secrets we should be discussing. You've published books. Why did you not tell me? I'd have dearly loved to read them."

Corliss attempted a chuckle, but it turned into another pathetic sound of misery. And now the tears were rushing down her cheeks in truth, her vision desperately blurred by her abject sorrow. She didn't even feel sorry for herself. She was the reason she found herself in this dreadful mess. If she had only told Knight the truth the moment they had begun developing a friendship, she might have spared them all this wretchedness.

"I don't know," she admitted. "I've told Criseyde, but I suppose I feared Mama and Papa would be more determined to see me married if I told them what I wished to do. I wanted it to be my secret, just for a time."

"And what a secret it was. Poor darling. You need to have yourself a good weep." Izzy drew her back into her embrace, her hand smoothing up and down Corliss's back in sweeping, soothing motions. "Believe me, I should know how restoring sobbing can be. When Arthur threw me over for his heiress, I cried nearly every day."

Before marrying and finding love and happiness with the handsome Earl of Anglesey, Izzy had fancied herself madly in love with her childhood chum, Arthur Penhurst. When Penhurst had become engaged to an heiress instead of Izzy, her sister had been devastated. In the end, she had ruined herself at a ball with Anglesey, and their match—initially a marriage made in haste—had turned into quite the love match. Izzy was much the better for it.

"Arthur Penhurst has always been a spineless swine," Corliss pronounced loyally, hugging Izzy tightly as another onslaught of tears shook her.

"I agree completely." Izzy patted her head. "There you are, dearest. Cry it out."

"Oh Izzy," she managed in between sobs. "I don't think he'll ever forgive me."

"Never fear. I shan't tell Mr. Penhurst you consider him a spineless swine."

Her sister's unexpected sally made Corliss laugh and then hiccup. "No, silly. I meant Knight. Lord Stoneleigh. I don't think he'll forgive me for pretending to be a governess and calling myself Miss Brinton. I'm not sure I forgive myself. It was so foolish of me. No amount of research for my novel is worth hurting someone I lo—"

Abruptly, she cut herself off before she said anything more.

But Izzy was far too clever. "Someone you love, Corrie? Have you fallen in love with The Bruiser Knight?"

Taking a shaking inhalation, she retreated from her sister's embrace, dashing at her tears in an attempt to restore her composure and clear her vision. "I didn't fall in love with The Bruiser Knight. I fell in love with the man he is. He's thoughtful and kind and quite wonderful. And passionate about what's important to him. He spends every morning in training, and evenings as well. The way he has softened toward his nieces since coming here, this great, big, powerful man who faces his opponents in the ring with his fists...it's truly a sight, Izzy. Anyone would have fallen in love with him. I was doomed from the start."

"Not doomed, I think," Izzy said thoughtfully. "But you were certainly misguided in coming here under a pretense."

Corliss nodded. "I know that now. But I wasn't certain how

to tell him the truth. I was terrified he would hate me or think I had intentionally set about to make a fool of him. All I wanted was the chance to research for my novel. I never expected to fall in love with the earl. Nor did I expect to fall in love with his nieces. The little hellions set about doing everything in their power to chase me away, from stealing my drawers, to putting a toad in my bed, to covering me in treacle and feathers. But along the way, I realized they were lonely and in need of someone to care about them. That everyone they loved had left them, and they feared it would happen again..."

She allowed her words to trail off when she realized she had revealed so much to her sister. She trusted Izzy implicitly, but she feared that her wiser, older sister would laugh at her for being so maudlin. For falling so hard and so fast, and for making such a terrible muck of the entire situation.

Instead, Izzy gave her an affectionate smile and used the pad of her thumb to wipe away a fresh tear from beneath her eye. "You do love Stoneleigh and his nieces, don't you, dearest?"

Corliss nodded despondently. "I do. But I've ruined it all. I lied to them."

"I'll tell you something that marriage to Zachary has taught me," Izzy said softly, tucking a stray tendril of Corliss's hair behind her ear in a sisterly gesture. "When you truly love someone, you'll fight for them. You'll do everything in your power to show your love, every day. And when you're wrong, you'll admit it and ask forgiveness. Love is quick to anger, but also quick to heal."

Her sister sounded so certain. Corliss wanted to believe her. Wanted to believe that if she fought for Knight, she could earn his forgiveness at least, if not his love.

"What if you fight for someone, and he still lets you go?" she asked, afraid of the answer.

"Then he doesn't deserve you," Izzy said firmly, giving her another hug and holding tight.

"I fear I'm the one who doesn't deserve him," she admitted painfully.

"I wouldn't be so certain of that, Corrie." Her sister paused, giving her another reassuring squeeze. "Treacle and feathers, though. Truly?"

Corliss smiled. "Truly."

"Hellions after my own heart," Izzy said quietly.

"Mine, too." Her smile faded, and she held on to her sister for far longer than was polite, and she managed to smudge her lovely purple silk with tears.

But Corliss didn't care, and neither did Izzy.

CHAPTER 14

 night woke wearing yesterday's tweed, flat on his back atop the bedclothes, mouth drier than the parched earth in the midst of a drought. He woke with regret searing the place behind his sternum, early-morning light filtering around him telling him he'd over-slept. He woke to the shame of having drowned himself in spirits instead of facing his problems directly.

On a groan, he rolled off his bed, wincing at the ache in his head and the terrible taste of last night's whisky on his tongue. At least his stomach wasn't roiling, and wasn't beset by the sudden, awful need to cast up his accounts into the nearest available vessel, thanks to Anglesey's fatherly concern.

Knight crossed the chamber to a pitcher and basin, then splashed cold water on his face. Murky memories of the evening's grim revelries washed over him as he performed some cursory ablutions. The earl had seen a tray sent round for him. He'd eaten whilst Anglesey had waxed poetic about contentment and love and other such rot. He'd also attempted to persuade Knight that Corliss was trustworthy despite her deceptions.

"Trustworthy," Knight muttered to himself, cupping water and bringing it to his face yet again in an effort to regain a sense of lucidity.

What had Corliss intended to do when her month's lark was at an end? Had she even thought of the devastation she would wreak upon the hearts of the girls she had professed to care for so deeply?

And had she thought of him?

Had she thought of the consequences they would both face? He was leaving as well. Christ, what a pair they made. Two people about to dash the hearts of four children. Perhaps he was no better than she was.

One thing was certain. He had to speak with her. There were details which would need to be settled, and swiftly since he was facing an imminent return to America. Knight rang for a bath and spent a solid hour soaking his pathetic hide in a warm tub. Not the ice bath he should have taken, to be sure, but at the moment, he didn't give a damn about training. He dressed with care before descending for breakfast.

Because he had eschewed his customary morning train-ing, breakfast was laid out on the sideboard, and Anglesey and his wife—earlier risers than he today—were finishing their plates when he entered.

"Knight," Anglesey boomed with far too much enthusi-asm. "You're looking as peaked as I reckoned you would this morning. You didn't shoot the cat after all, did you?"

Knight pinned his friend with a glare, passing a hand over his bearded jaw. "You've a way with words, old chum. Good morning to you, as well. And to you, Lady Anglesey."

He offered a bow for the lady's benefit, noting the rest of the chairs were empty.

No Corliss.

Had she taken her morning walk, or was she avoiding him?

"Good morning, Lord Stoneleigh," the countess returned his greeting with cautious solemnity, eying him as if she didn't know what to make of him now.

That made two of them, for he didn't know what to make of himself at the moment. He felt angry and foolish and frustrated and confused and in desperate need of bacon.

To that end, he stalked to the sideboard and heaped a plate with it, deciding the fresh fruit could go to the devil today. He needed fortification. Sustenance. A plan.

With a sigh, he settled at the breakfast table. His coffee awaited him, black and steaming hot as he preferred it. Knight took a sip and scalded his tongue and throat as he attempted to quickly swallow the molten liquid, only for it to burn all the way down.

He winced, thinking he deserved the pain for being such an imbecile.

"The coffee is a bit warm," Anglesey said wryly, apparently taking note of his discomfort.

Knight forced a smile.

"I appreciate the warning," he drawled.

An uncomfortable silence descended during which Knight wondered where Corliss was and whether he had revealed something utterly embarrassing to Anglesey the night before concerning his sister-in-law, such as that he was besotted with her or some other manner of drivel. He didn't think he had, but he had been deep in his cups by the time his old friend had arrived in the study, coming to his rescue.

"Where is Miss Br—" he began, only to cut himself off. By God, this new name of hers would take some getting used to. "Where is Lady Corliss this morning?" he tried again.

"She expressed a wish to take the morning air," Lady Anglesey said.

On her walk, then. Knight took a bite of bacon and decided his stomach could wait. He rose again. "If you'll excuse me, my lord, my lady, I find myself in need of a bracing walk myself."

"Knight?"

Anglesey's voice stopped him.

He turned back to his friend. "Yes?"

"I hope you've been considering our chat."

What little of their chat that he could recall, yes. He seemed to remember something about Anglesey having met his wife when she kissed him at a ball. And the less-than-reassuring mentioning of the eccentricities of the Collingwood siblings.

He nodded. "Thank you for your kindness yesterday, Anglesey. It's always good to have old friends in times of need."

And in times of discovering one had no choice but to marry the woman who had spent the last fortnight deceiving him and essentially trapping him into marriage. But he kept that to himself, for he was as much to blame as Corliss for allowing himself to lose control and bedding her. If he had resisted his baser urges, he wouldn't be in this current predicament.

Anglesey inclined his head. "You needn't thank me, old chum. Were our circumstances the opposite, I have no doubt you'd do the same for me."

With a nod, he abandoned breakfast and his guests. Seeking a coat, hat, and gloves to warm him, he ventured outside into the gray, chilly morning, his long-limbed strides taking him to the walking path where he knew Corliss preferred to take the air. He didn't have long to wait before she came into sight, wrapped in a dolman, her golden hair in a fat braid down her back, a jaunty little cap perched atop her head that was far more suited to the daughter of an earl he now knew she was.

"My lady," he called out to her, his voice echoing off the gently sloping hills surrounding them.

She stopped, spinning about to face him, her blue skirts swirling about her ankles.

She looked every inch a lady rather than the governess she had purported to be. So many details made sense to him —the drab, hideous gowns, the ink stains on her fingers.

"Lord Stoneleigh." She dipped into a curtsy so reminiscent of Miss Brinton that for a moment, he could have easily pretended the last day hadn't happened, and that they were once more as they had been, two lovers who enjoyed each other's company, no secrets or deceptions between them.

But he blinked, and she was still wearing a fine French gown of bright-blue silk and matching hat and wrap, and she was still the woman who had manipulated him so convincingly, just as Ida had done. And he felt the acknowledgment of that betrayal like a punch to his breadbasket.

He had believed her. Had thought she was good and kindhearted, her motives wholly pure, so unlike the last woman who had betrayed him. Had believed that for the first time in as long as he could recall, he had found a lover who hadn't wanted anything from him. A woman who had wanted the man behind The Bruiser Knight.

Instead, all she had wanted was a story. And perhaps, and even more egregiously worse, to leave him no choice but to wed her. Had she entrapped him intentionally? He would need to learn the truth.

Without realizing he had set into motion, Knight was moving toward her, closing the distance between them. Not stopping until she was close enough to touch, and he could see the fetching smattering of freckles on her nose in intricate detail. She was pale, her eyes lacking the brightness they normally possessed, puffy and red-rimmed. And yet, despite the evidence she was not impervious to the misery of their situation, she was astoundingly lovely.

And he still wanted her so ferociously that it was an ache in his soul.

"I would speak with you," he said curtly.

She was solemn. No hint of a smile curving the lush lips that he had claimed as his own more times than he could count.

"You aren't wearing your sweater today," she observed. "Are you not training?"

As if she cared whether he trained. Or was she merely attempting to distract him?

"I am not," he conceded.

And you are the cause of it, he thought bitterly to himself.

"Is it because you are upset with me?" she asked softly, as if she had been privy to what was whirling through his mind.

"It is because I drank too much whisky last night and am in no condition to run," he admitted. "There, my lady. That is raw honesty. Perhaps you ought to try it for yourself sometime."

She winced as if he had slapped her, and Knight found no pleasure in her reaction. All he felt inside was pain. So much of it.

"You have every right to be angry with me," she began.

"You're damned right I do," he interrupted swiftly, his fury taking charge. "You have spent the time since arriving at Knightly Abbey doing nothing but deceiving my nieces and myself. Although you had every opportunity to tell me the truth at any point during this campaign of yours, you chose to continue manipulating and lying instead. But above all this, you have, through your own reckless lies, entrapped me into a marriage I do not want."

She jolted like a startled horse. "A marriage, my lord? What do you mean?"

He laughed, unable to keep the bitterness from his voice. "Pray do not feign confusion now, Lady Corliss. You know as well as I do that we have no choice but to marry, thanks to your machinations. Was this what you had planned from the start? Tell me, does your Miss Brinton's employer ruin her as well? Does he seduce her? Were you conducting more research when you begged me to fuck you?"

Her lips parted, but no sound emerged. Her eyes were shining bright. Tears, he realized as drops slid down her cheeks. She was weeping. But he would not allow himself to feel remorse. *She* had done this to them, not him. And now they would both have to pay the price.

"Nothing to say?" he prodded when she remained silent. "Did you not think of the consequences of your deceptions? No, don't answer me. I can see plainly you did not, or else you'd never have allowed us all to continue believing your falsehoods."

"What happened between us had nothing to do with my novel," she said, dashing at her cheeks before clasping her gloved hands before her in a defensive gesture that resembled prayer. "I never expected for this to unfold as it did. None of it was planned, beyond my coming here and assuming the role of governess for a month's time."

He wanted to believe her, but he didn't trust her. Couldn't trust her. Not after what she had done, not with the wounds still raw and open.

"Regardless of what you intended when you came here, we have no choice but to marry," he told her, doing his utmost to keep even the smallest hint of emotion from his countenance and tone. Drawing no quarter for her as he should have done from the first moment he had ever set eyes upon her, instead of allowing himself to be charmed by her.

"Since I'm leaving soon to return to America, we'll have to marry as quickly and quietly as possible."

"We cannot marry." She shook her head. "Not when you are so cold and angry with me. Believe what you will of me, but entrapping you into a marriage was never my intent."

He shrugged as if her words didn't matter. "We haven't a choice. I took your virginity two nights ago, and you're the daughter of an earl."

"What if I were Miss Brinton?" she demanded, chin tilting up in defiance. "Would you still wish to marry me then, or is an earl's daughter worthy of consideration, whereas a common governess is not?"

He would have married her under either circumstance. It was the right thing to do, and he'd intended to marry her before he'd discovered who she truly was. A man couldn't take a woman's maidenhead and not marry her; he'd known it two nights ago, and he knew it now. He would have married Miss Brinton and been happy. Because that was the woman he had begun to fall in love with, but that woman had also been a lie.

"It's a moot point now," he said firmly. "I have no choice but to marry you."

"No."

He raised a brow at her vehement denial. "You haven't the luxury of denying me. Although I took precautions, you could be carrying my child. I'll be returning to America for an indefinite amount of time. For your own protection, you must marry me before I leave."

She shook her head, a new sheen in her eyes. "No, Knight. I'm not going to marry you. Not like this."

Frustration and fury mingled. Part of him wanted to reach for her. Part of him knew that giving in and touching her would be a colossal mistake.

He clenched his jaw instead. "You're an earl's daughter,

and I've ruined you. If you don't think the tongues below stairs will wag and word won't reach some newspaper or gossip rag, you're a fool. And I'll not have it printed anywhere that The Bruiser Knight refused to do right by Lady Corliss Collingwood."

Her lower lip trembled, and the sight of her sorrow curdled his gut. He shouldn't feel sympathy for her. And yet, his feelings for her—or for the Corliss he'd thought he'd known—were far too complex and profound to merely be banished over the span of one day.

"How should anyone know you ruined me?" she asked. "I'm not about to tell anyone, and no one knows what happened but the two of us."

"You've been below stairs," he countered, determined to make her see reason. "You know how servants gossip."

"Then let them gossip. Gossip is not truth. No one knows the truth but you and I."

She was adamant. Stubborn. And somehow glorious still, after it all. Damn her.

He'd never imagined he'd have to fight her or force her to marry him. He had reckoned their battle would be fought over other matters, like her deceptions and the novel she was writing. He needed to know what it contained. If there was reference to him. After the treatment he'd received in some of the American newspapers, and after what Ida had done, he didn't bloody well trust any writer. And after the lies Corliss had told him, he most certainly didn't trust *her*.

She was no different than all the rest. Just another woman who had wanted something from him. Another who had used him, thinking only of her own gains. Ida's primary concern had been making a name for herself as a reporter, and Corliss's had been making a name for herself as an author.

"Gossip doesn't need to be true," he told her, thinking of

the reporters who had hung on his every word so that they might bend and twist them into a story, and who had interviewed women who had claimed to know him, some even who had claimed to be his lovers. Thinking of Ida, who had used both him and the intimate relationship they had shared together more cruelly than any other. "Even if it's all lies, everyone wonders. They question you. They look at you differently. Gossip is insidious that way. It never even needs to be proven."

And what Ida had done to him—writing of him charming a different woman in every city, elaborating upon his Bacchanalian revelries, accusing him of striking one of his former lovers when it had never happened—Knight knew how evil gossip was better than anyone else. Ida had been willing to do anything to further her own career. He ought to have seen it, recognized the desperate hunger for success and victory at any cost within her, for it boiled in his own blood as well.

The only difference between them had been that he wasn't willing to sacrifice someone he cared for on his way to a championship title. Ida had. But she had never truly cared for him. In the end, she had only ever cared about herself and her steadily growing reputation as one of America's only female reporters. She'd been prepared to do anything to him, regardless of how great the cost was to himself.

He would never forget the bitter lessons he'd learned from her. *Don't allow anyone too close. Don't show another soul your vulnerabilities. Because when you do, they'll use them against you.*

Just as Corliss had.

She frowned at him now, still refusing to bend. "Why should anyone wish to gossip about us here?"

"Because I'm The Bruiser Knight," he bit out. "I've been

written about in the papers before, and I've had to go to great lengths to restore my reputation after some of the damaging stories written about me. I'll not allow all my hard work to be tossed to the dust heap because you're too damned stubborn to marry me."

"Ah yes," she said coolly. "The Bruiser Knight. That is all you care about, is it not? Your championship title. That is why you want to marry me so suddenly. Because you've discovered who I am, and you're afraid it will be worse for you in the papers if you ruined an earl's daughter rather than a mere commoner."

She was wrong about that. Wrong about him. But he had no wish to correct her. The ice in her voice was just what he needed to harden his resolve.

"I have a championship to defend, Lady Corliss." He was careful to affect a sangfroid he did not feel, for inside he was seething and longing for her and hating himself and desperately confused all at once. "That is what matters most. But before I can turn my attention where it belongs, this unpleasant matter needs to be resolved."

"Is that what I am to you, Knight?" she demanded. "An unpleasant matter keeping you from your training?"

No. She was so much more. He couldn't begin to comprehend what she was to him. And that was why it hurt so bloody much, her lies, this sudden, terrible predicament facing them. It was all like a splinter buried deep inside his heart, one that could not be plucked free. There was no relief.

"Yes," he said instead, wanting to wound her just a bit. Wanting to make her suffer as he had ever since yesterday morning when his happy world had been upended by the revelation that she was not Miss Brinton, the sweet-natured governess he had come to so admire. But that she was instead yet another writer using him for her own purposes.

Using his nieces, too.

He must not forget.

"Then I needn't remain here a moment longer," she said, the hurt in her voice crushing something inside him, turning it to dust. "I'll ask my sister and brother-in-law to take me to Barlowe Park immediately. Good day, my lord, and goodbye."

She skirted him on the path and strode toward the manor house.

Knight watched her go for a moment, dumbfounded. And then he hastened after her, because as furious as he was with Lady Corliss Collingwood, he couldn't allow himself to let her go.

OF ALL THE things Corliss had expected from Knight, a marriage proposal—make that demand—on the walking path they had shared together so many times in contented companionship had not been one. He was angry with her, that much she knew and understood. He didn't trust her, and she couldn't fault him for that.

But she was furious with him as she stalked toward Knightly Abbey, furious and hurt and blinking madly at tears that were swimming in her eyes and blurring her vision into a drab, brown Impressionist painting before her. How dare he command her to marry him, all in the name of preserving his precious reputation? And how dare he only want to marry her now that he knew she was truly Lady Corliss Collingwood instead of Miss Brinton? When she was not too distraught to write again, she would implement a similar dastardly twist in her plot.

Perhaps she would rename Miss Brinton's employer Lord Dastard, and she would send him over a cliff in a speeding carriage. It would crash to the rocky shoals below and disappear into the ocean, taking Lord Dastard to a watery grave.

"Corliss!"

Knight was calling her name. Chasing after her.

Oh, she had hoped he wouldn't. She was too upset by half to face him now. She wouldn't give him the pleasure of seeing her in such a state. Sniffling, she dashed at her tears with her gloved hands, refusing to pause or turn around and face him.

"Leave me alone!" she hurled over her shoulder in response.

The response was quite juvenile of her, she knew. It was something she might have hollered at her twin when Criseyde was being particularly trying and dogging her every step.

"Corliss."

His voice was closer now. And curse him, it still sent a shiver down her spine, even after the callous manner in which he had treated her just now. She carried on, taking longer strides. Moving faster.

Not fast enough.

His hand caught her elbow, staying her and spinning her to face him.

He was glowering down at her, tall and powerful and so handsome. But there were plum half-moons shadowing his eyes that suggested he'd had the same fitful sleep that she had. She wanted to believe it was because he was as distressed over what had happened as she was. But her carefully constructed little world at Knightly Abbey—an idyll in its own way from her ordinary life—had turned to rubble. And he had been so angry, his tone biting, his countenance and words harsh and unforgiving. And she didn't know what to think.

"What do you want?" she snapped, glaring at his hand on

her elbow, for his touch seemed to burn straight through his gloves and her layers. "If you intend to pay me further insult, you may as well spare us both the effort. I'm not interested in hearing any more of your oafish demands that I marry you to save you from scandal."

"Why did you lie?" he asked suddenly, surprising her. "Did you know who I was when you accepted the situation as governess?"

She blinked. "Of course not. I had no notion of who the Earl of Stoneleigh was, and certainly not The Bruiser Knight. I'm not an American, nor do I give a fig about pugilism. It seems a most barbaric sport if you ask me."

There. She had said it. And partially to hurt him, yes. To wound him the only way she could, for he was as impervious as a stone. He had hidden the Knight she had come to know away, and in his place was an unfeeling monster, determined to destroy all the good they had known together.

"Barbaric," he said, grinning.

It wasn't a pleasant grin. It was cold and harsh and cutting. Likely, she thought, it was the grin he used to intimidate his opponents in the ring. She didn't like it.

"Yes," she affirmed. "*Barbaric*. But perhaps you enjoy inflicting pain upon others. This morning would certainly support such a conclusion."

"Do not think you are the only one in pain, *Lady* Corliss." His voice was cool and clipped, his gaze assessing and grim. "But regardless of what we feel, we now find ourselves in an untenable position together, of our mutual making. There is only one way out of it, and that's marriage."

It seemed to Corliss that Knight despised her for what she had done. And yet, his concern for his reputation trumped his loathing for her. She had no intention of allowing him to force her into a loveless marriage laden with resentment, all so that he might keep The Bruiser Knight from scandal. She'd had her own aspirations for her future before she'd come here.

"There is another way out of it," she countered, equally determined. "And it is me, leaving Knightly Abbey with my sister. You never need to see me again. I should think that would make you happy. I've told you I won't carry a tale, and I very much doubt the servants will either."

A muscle ticked in his jaw. "What if there is a child?"

Knight's child. She tried not to allow the unwanted yearning inside her at the notion to show on her face. Because she still loved him, even if he was being hateful to her, and even if she deserved his scorn.

"If there is, I'll send you a letter," she said. "You needn't fear I'd ask you for anything in that regard."

Her parents would help her, she knew. They weren't the sort of mother and father who turned their children away. They would find somewhere safe for her to raise the child. Perhaps the Continent.

"And you truly believe I'd want no part of my child's life?" he asked, sounding outraged at the thought. "That you could send me a letter, and I'd forget all about my own flesh and blood?"

She realized, quite belatedly, that his hand yet remained on her elbow. The weakest part of her was enjoying that touch, that connection. She craved it. But she wrenched herself away from his grasp just the same.

"I don't know what to believe of you any longer," she said, unable to keep the sadness from her voice. "I lied to you, and I was wrong for doing so. But your loathing is punishment enough. I don't need to be tied to you in a miserable union for the rest of my life as well. Forget about me. Forget you ever met me. I'll do the same with you."

That was a lie, for she knew to her core that she would never, as long as she breathed, forget him. But her pride was forcing her to say it. Wanting him to believe it was true. Because if she lingered with him any longer, she was afraid that she would break open, and he would see how affected she was, and she couldn't bear for that to happen.

Stifling another sob, she caught her skirts in her hands and began to run toward Knightly Abbey.

This time, Knight didn't follow her, and the silence she left behind was deafening.

CHAPTER 15

*J*t seemed to Knight that every female in his life currently despised him. Beatrice refused to speak to him. Nettie was quietly morose. Alice wouldn't meet his eye when he had entered the nursery earlier. Mary had left a toad loose in his bedchamber at some point after breakfast. And Corliss was being bloody stubborn.

Beyond bloody stubborn.

She continued to refuse to marry him.

And that was why he was resorting to the lowest, last form of persuasion left in his arsenal.

"You intend to blackmail me into marrying you?" Corliss was staring at him with disbelief etched on her lovely face.

It was afternoon, the bitterness of their morning altercation still weighing heavy on his chest. When she had foregone lunch, he had marched directly to her chamber, his superior strength easily allowing him to shoulder his way inside so they could face each other again. The grayness of the morning had given way to bright autumnal sun, and it shone in the window at which she stood, gilding her hair.

He studied her for a moment, wishing he didn't know

precisely how many freckles dotted the bridge of her nose, but he had counted them two mornings ago, and the number would be forever emblazoned upon his mind, much like everything else about her.

Fourteen.

Knight held her gaze, unrelenting. "Call it what you will. If you refuse to see reason, I have no choice but to encourage you to do so, for the sake of myself and the sake of the child you may be carrying."

"What of me?" she asked softly. "What if marrying a man who loathes me isn't in *my* best interest?"

He didn't loathe her. If he did, all this would have been far easier. His emotions would have been far less complex. As it was, he didn't know precisely what it was he felt where she was concerned. Anger, sadness, longing, confusion, resentment. So much.

Knight crossed his arms over his chest, unrelenting. "You should have thought of that before you gave yourself to me."

"You didn't hate me then," she pointed out.

He didn't bother to correct her. "It doesn't matter. What does matter is that we haven't a choice. We must marry, and the sooner you resign yourself to that fact, the better off we all shall be."

"All of us, or you?" She pushed away from the window, stalking toward him with short, determined strides.

Did she think to intimidate him? He had defeated men twice her size in the ring with ease.

"All of us. Tell me, what do you think shall happen if I'm forced to tell Anglesey what happened between us?" he asked calmly, remaining where he was, near the fireplace in her chamber.

The sweet floral scent of her reached him, teasing his senses, and he wanted nothing more than to take her in his arms and forget about this nonsense. To forget about her lies, his anger, everything and everyone but the two of them just as it had been the night they made love.

"Tell Anglesey if you must," she said, her dimpled chin tipping up in defiance. "He is not my father. He cannot force me to marry you any more than you can."

"Of course not," he said agreeably. "However, Anglesey is a man of honor. He'll have no choice but to go to your father with what he's learned. And when your father discovers you've been living here with me for weeks, and that you've shared my bed, do you truly think he'll not insist you marry me?"

She caught her lower lip in her teeth, worrying it, and he knew she was having misgivings. Thinking about what he'd said. Realizing he was right.

"My father would never force me into anything," she said, but there was a lack of conviction in her tone.

He could almost see the inner workings of her clever mind.

"There is a vast difference between forcing someone to make a decision and encouraging it," he pressed, sensing his advantage growing. "I do not doubt your father wouldn't force you into a marriage with me. However, no father who gives a damn about his daughter would encourage her to take the risk she was carrying a man's child without the protection of marriage."

Her eyes fluttered closed, the golden lashes fanning on her cheeks, and she gripped the back of an overstuffed armchair which stood between them. He watched as she took a deep breath, squaring her shoulders. Took in every detail of her form like a man starved for her. Her knuckles stood in pale relief on the upholstery.

When her eyes opened again, the sadness shimmering in their depths stole his breath. "Why do you want this marriage so much that you would leave me no choice?"

"There *is* no other choice, Corliss. We must wed, and it needs to be done before I return to America. But you do have at least one choice here and now. You can choose to agree to marry me, or we shall do this the difficult way, and I'll go and tell Anglesey that I've possibly managed to get his sister-in-law with child. After that, I'll telegram your father as well. So, my dear, which shall it be?"

He didn't like having to force her to this point, but he was running out of time. He needed to protect her and to protect his nieces, too. Marrying her meant they would have some stability in their lives, at least, even if it wasn't achieved in the most ideal of circumstances. And, like it or not, prepared or not, he and Corliss *needed* to wed. Everything he had said to her was true. If he had to take matters into his own hands and be ruthless, he would. She had driven him to it with her obstinacy.

"Will you ever forgive me for deceiving you?" she asked softly, searching his eyes. "Or is it your intention to keep punishing me?"

At the moment, he hadn't an inkling of what his intentions were where she was concerned. He had fallen beneath the spell of the woman he'd believed her to be. But he had yet to discover if the Corliss who had charmed him with such ease was different from Lady Corliss. He didn't know where he stood with her, what to believe. All he did know was that he still wanted her. He still yearned to take her in his arms and kiss her. To carry her across the room, shoulder pain be damned, and make love to her all afternoon. His desire for her burned hotter than the sun, and there was no chance of it diminishing any time soon.

"Knight," she said, her tone pleading. "Please. Tell me there's a possibility of you forgiving me. It's the only way I can countenance a marriage between us."

"I need to know I can trust you," he returned. "I don't know who you are."

"But you do know me. The only difference is that my name is Lady Corliss Collingwood. Everything else I've told you is true. Every word I've spoken, every action I've taken. It was me kissing you, Knight. Not anyone else. I only know how to be myself, such as I am. The only deception was my name and letter of recommendation."

He swallowed hard against a fresh rush of longing. But holding her and kissing her now would only further muddy the waters, and the waters were already murky enough. "I want to believe that."

She jolted as if he'd landed a physical blow. "But you don't?"

Knight sighed, feeling suddenly helpless. For a man of his strength, a man who never lost a match, it was an unnerving sensation. He needed for her to say yes. To agree to marry him. But he also had to be honest with her. The revelation of her deceit was too fresh. He had yet to wrap his mind around the full implications of it.

"I don't know yet, Corliss. But I also haven't the luxury of waiting. I'm leaving for America in days." Seeing his passage booked had been one of the many tasks he'd had to conduct this morning. Along with convincing an erstwhile, lying, governess-turned-lady that she had to be his wife. His proximity to her and the way she looked in the sunlight, vulnerable and yet as beautiful as any mythical deity, quelled some of the righteous fury which had been burning inside him since the previous morning. He gentled his tone before continuing. "We need to see this settled before I go."

"Knight, please," she entreated, still gripping the armchair as if it were the bank of a flooded river and she was about to be swept away. "There has to be another way. I won't marry you in anger."

But he wouldn't relent. Not in this. He knew what had to be done. He told himself it was what was right. He had a responsibility to her, to the possible child he'd put in her womb. He had a responsibility to Mary, Alice, Beatrice, and Nettie, whom he'd believed he was leaving in the tender care of their trusted governess until her deceptions had been revealed. And now, he was struggling to make the best of this confusing coil for all six of them.

Also, he had a match to defend his championship facing him. He needed to be able to focus on his training. He couldn't afford to spend another day in turmoil, drinking himself to oblivion. Sam Williams was a young brute who had been winning every fight he engaged in up and down the eastern seaboard. Knight felt every bit of his three-and-thirty years. He'd been fighting for a decade. He had to keep himself as finely honed as any machine.

He needed to know that his nieces would be taken care of, that he had done the honorable thing by Corliss. *Today.*

"I'm firm on what must be done. If you'll not agree to a union, you leave me no choice. My presence here in your chamber this afternoon will only help my case rather than hinder it." He paused, hating himself more than he ever had as he held her gaze, keeping his face an expressionless mask of indifference. "I'm going directly to Anglesey after I leave this room. What I tell him is at your discretion."

The sadness in her eyes sank between his ribs as surely as any dagger.

"If you force me to marry you like this, I'm not certain I shall ever forgive you."

"This is what we must do," he said, showing no mercy.

For inside him, there was none. She had whittled him away, clear down to the bone. And he was raw inside. She was the one who had deceived him, not the other way around. How dare she make him care for her and then destroy his trust? How dare she make the girls love her, all while planning to leave them? He was justified, curse her.

But he didn't feel justified at all as he took in the fresh glimmer of tears shining in her eyes. Nor in the trembling of her lower lip. Nor in the manner in which she continued to grasp the chair, using it as a shield between them. Did she fear him? My God, surely she would know that he would never strike anyone unless it was an opponent he faced in the ring. Violence was a necessary part of the sport he engaged in, but that was where it ended, in the ring when he was declared the victor.

This battle between them felt nothing like the sparring he was accustomed to.

"Very well," she said at last, breaking the interminable silence, her voice catching. "If you insist upon carrying on in this manner, I suppose you leave me no choice. I'll marry you."

Knight waited for the relief which usually accompanied victory. But all he felt instead was hollowness, along with a sense of relief that his nieces would not be entirely abandoned.

He nodded. "We will apply for the license today. We'll receive it within a day, and after that, we can marry."

Her lips parted. "That quickly? Surely you cannot think to marry with such haste."

"I'm leaving for America in three days, Corliss. We haven't much opportunity before I go."

Her tongue swept over her lips. "But my family. I would want for them to witness the marriage, at least. And they are presently scattered about. It will take several days to assemble them."

Her family. Of course she would wish for them to be present. He hadn't thought of that, being essentially an orphan in the world, with no one save his nieces.

And Corliss, said a voice within. *You will have a wife now as well.*

He wasn't sure how he felt about that. What he ought to feel.

"I'm afraid they won't be capable of journeying to us before I need to depart," he said, aware of how curt and formal he sounded. How stiff and very like Robert. Robert had always been a horse's arse. Was that who he had become now, too?

He scarcely recognized himself.

"Of course, leaving for your match takes precedence over everything else," she said, and he did not miss the biting sting in her voice.

She was unhappy with him. Fair enough. He was unhappy with her as well. The two of them could have a miserable marriage like most of the quality, aligned for all the wrong reasons. And he would not allow her to make him feel guilty for needing to return to America to defend his title. It was an inevitability which had existed before he had ever met her, and that didn't change now that they were marrying.

"You will have Lord and Lady Anglesey in attendance. They will have to suffice. I wish our circumstances were different, but such as they are, we've no other choice." He bowed. "I'll take my leave so you can set about making the preparations with your sister."

He'd never been married, and nor had he been present at a wedding in as long as he could recall. He didn't have an inkling what was required of one at such an affair.

She curtsied in response, finally letting go of the damned chair. "Anything to please you, my lord."

He ignored the taunt in her words. Ignored the way her offering to please him made his cock twitch to attention. Clinging to what remained of his sanity, he stalked from her chamber. If the door slammed with too much force at his back, it couldn't be helped. And if he stormed into his own apartments and kicked over a chair, well, that couldn't be helped either.

At least, that was what he told himself.

"You're marrying the earl in two days' time?"

Izzy stared at Corliss with wide eyes, as if she had just announced her intention to depart presently for a trip to the moon.

She sighed, wishing she had not gone to her sister's chamber prior to dressing for dinner after all, because perhaps she wasn't prepared for this conversation. "Apparently."

Izzy's dark brows rose to her hairline.

"Apparently?" Her sister's voice was high, almost shrill. "It is rather a yes or no sort of circumstance, is it not? Either yes, you are indeed marrying him with astonishing haste, or no, you are not marrying him in an utterly ludicrous span of days. Which is it, dearest?"

When Izzy phrased it thus, there was no good answer. But there wasn't truly a good answer anyway.

"I…" Misery washed over Corliss as she struggled to form a response. Knight's unexpected visit to her chamber earlier had left her with more questions than answers. "Yes."

Izzy shook her head. She was dressed in an afternoon gown featuring her standard outrageousness. The bustle was massive, and little bunches of silk flowers were dripping from her skirts. She resembled nothing so much as an aggressive spring garden. But everyone knew Izzy was eccentric in her fashion choices. It was simply a part of her, even if today's frock was unusually garish.

"I don't understand, Corrie. You're going to have to

explain this to me again. What has changed so suddenly? I know you're in love with Stoneleigh—"

"I thought I was before he blackmailed me into marrying him," Corliss burst out, before biting her lip, wishing she could recall the words.

"He blackmailed you?" Izzy crossed her arms over her chest, frowning mightily, her displeasure so great that it seemed that even the garden bedecking her skirts twitched with vexation. "I'll box his ears." She held up a finger as if it were a weapon. "Better yet, I'll have Anglesey box his ears."

"Sadly, I don't think any of us are capable of boxing his ears," Corliss said, trying to envision Knight, with his powerful boxer's body, allowing anyone to catch him long enough to box his ears, and failing. "He trains rigorously every day. His body looks as if it were carved in marble…"

As she realized what she had just revealed, she stopped herself, her cheeks going hot.

"Corrie!" Izzy gave her a knowing look. "I think I begin to understand. Just what have you been doing whilst in residence here at Knightly Abbey, hmm?"

"Researching for my novel," she defended herself weakly, trying not to think of the night she had spent wrapped in his arms, when their bodies had been slick with sweat and pressed close together, when he had been moving over her, inside her. When he had kissed her so sweetly, and then she had fallen asleep on his chest to the sound of his beating heart.

Izzy pinned her with a knowing look. "What manner of research?"

Corliss turned on her heel and stalked to the window, where the dressings had been pulled back to allow in the dwindling rays of late-autumn sun. Knightly Abbey unfurled below, as beautiful as any painting. Impossible to believe she would make her home here. She'd never thought to marry.

Certainly not to find herself in Yorkshire. What would Criseyde say when she discovered the news? She would miss her twin sister dreadfully. She already did.

They were the best of friends. Closer, even, than they were to their other siblings. They shared a bond that no one else could truly understand.

"Corrie, you didn't answer me. Just what has happened between you and Stoneleigh?"

She turned back to her sister. "I expect it's similar to what happened between you and Anglesey."

Izzy and Anglesey were a love match, but their marriage had begun in a decidedly different fashion. Izzy had been pining after Arthur Penhurst, and she had imbibed too much champagne at a ball. She'd kissed the former notorious rake Anglesey, and he'd taken her home. The result had been imminent ruination and a need for a hasty wedding.

"You became soused and threw yourself at Stoneleigh?" Izzy teased with a self-deprecating smile. "Come now, I thought I was the most scandalous of all the Collingwood siblings. You're going to tarnish my lofty opinion of myself."

Corliss would have laughed had she been capable of mirth. As it was, she had been through so many emotions in the last day, that she felt inexplicably numb. Drained of all feeling.

"I went to him late one night," she admitted, feeling her ears go hot. "He was training, and he wasn't properly dressed. I should have gone at once, but I told myself that I wanted to speak to him about his nieces. And…"

She couldn't force herself to form a full confession. She was sure the answers Izzy sought were written on her face.

"And you and Lord Stoneleigh…"

"Yes," Corliss hastened to agree before her sister could fully give voice to her ignominy.

It hadn't felt like ignominy then, of course. It had felt

wondrous. As if she had been awakened. As if he had dismantled everything she'd believed she'd known about herself, with nothing but his hands and lips and tongue. And another portion of his anatomy as well.

"Oh," Izzy said with feeling.

"Yes, *oh*," she agreed grimly.

Izzy was frowning. "Did he take advantage of you, dearest? From what I understand, Stoneleigh is something of a rake."

"Anglesey is a rake as well," she pointed out, feeling the need to defend Knight despite everything that had happened between them.

"*Was* a rake, dearest." Izzy smiled smugly. "Now, he is all mine. And reformed rakes make the best husbands."

In that moment, she couldn't help but to covet her sister's certainty. Corliss didn't know where she stood with Knight. His words of earlier returned to her.

I'm leaving for America in three days.

There had been no tender persuasion.

No seductive kisses.

The passionate lover who had held her through the night, who had brought her such pleasure, had stood before her, stony and cold. Telling her she had no choice but to marry him, when he intended to abandon her immediately thereafter.

"But you haven't answered my question," Izzy added shrewdly. "Did Stoneleigh take advantage of you?"

"No," she denied softly. "I wanted everything that happened."

She still wanted it, but not when he was so closed off and cold and bitter. She wanted the Knight she'd come to know, not the frigid stranger he had become.

"And do you love him?"

She sighed, for her anger with him hadn't lessened her emotions, despite what she'd said earlier. "I do."

Love was not so inconstant that it could alter in the span of one day. If only it could, perhaps she wouldn't be steeped in so much misery just now.

"Why don't you wish to marry him?" Izzy prodded. "I need to understand everything properly if I'm to give you counsel, which I assume is the reason you've come to me. And what is this blackmail he is using against you?"

"Of course it's why I've come." Corliss began pacing the plush Axminster, unable to keep still with so much restlessness coursing through her. Ordinarily, when she was faced with difficult circumstances, she sought out Criseyde. This was the longest amount of time she and her twin had ever been apart, and Corliss didn't like it. She felt...adrift. "I don't know what to do. Knight has told me that I must agree to marry him or he will tell Anglesey everything that's happened between us and that Anglesey, as a man of honor, must tell Papa. And if Papa knows what has happened here, I'll have no choice but to marry Knight anyway. So I may as well not marry him in ignominy, with everyone knowing what I've done. I fear I would perish of mortification at the thought of Papa ever discovering how reckless I've been, although I do know Mama and Papa were quite scandalous in their day..."

She was rambling, she knew. By the time she reached the end of the chamber, Corliss felt as if she couldn't catch her breath. Her chest was tight, and a terrible anxiousness had seized her. She spun about to pace the length of the room again and nearly collided with Izzy, who had soundlessly followed her.

"Oh," she cried, halting to stay the impending impact.

"Take a deep breath, dearest," Izzy instructed kindly, taking Corliss's shoulders in a gentle hold. "I know you and

Criseyde are thick as thieves, but I hope having me here will prove a boon to you just the same. I may make foolish, reckless mistakes at balls, but in the end, I've found more happiness than I ever dreamed existed. I want that same happiness for you."

"I'm glad you've found happiness with Anglesey," Corliss said, meaning those words to her marrow. "But I fear I'll not be nearly as content with Stoneleigh. Particularly not when he intends to marry me in anger. And yet, he's left me with no good choice save wedding him. Ever since he came to speak with me earlier, I've been at sixes and sevens, trying to figure out what I must do."

"You deserve far better than contentment," Izzy said firmly. "You deserve a husband who worships you and loves you. One who will do anything to see you happy. And if Stoneleigh doesn't adore you for the wonderful, kindhearted, caring, beautiful, stubborn, intelligent woman you are, I'll box his ears myself. And I don't care how much training he does or how many matches he's won. I'm a fiercely protective sister, and I'm a force to be reckoned with."

"You are indeed, my love, and it's one of the qualities I adore most about you." The deep voice of Izzy's husband had them both starting and whirling to face the door to the chamber, which had opened quite soundlessly. Anglesey stood on the threshold, giving them an apologetic grin.

"Forgive me, ladies," he added. "I seem to have intruded upon a private conversation. I assumed Izzy was alone and thought to have a moment with her before dressing for dinner."

From the color creeping up her sister's cheeks, Corliss was certain what manner of *moment* Anglesey intended to have with Izzy. She tried not to be envious of Anglesey's undying devotion for her sister, and yet, it was an impossibility. She longed for Knight to steal into her chamber for such tender intimacy, not to come to her with cold, harsh demands for a marriage neither of them wanted.

"I should go," she said, feeling like an interloper, and grimmer than she had been upon her initial arrival.

"You needn't leave on my account." Anglesey stepped into the chamber and closed the door discreetly at his back. "Am I to wish you happy, Corliss? Knight tells me the two of you will be marrying, and quite soon."

Her stomach felt as if it twisted into another knot. "I…"

"It is complicated," Izzy finished for her, giving her husband a private look laden with meaning that Corliss couldn't decipher. "Corliss doesn't want to marry him because he's being a horse's arse."

"Izzy," she scolded her sister, pinning her with a warning look of her own, for Anglesey and Knight were old friends. "I didn't say Stoneleigh was being a horse's arse."

"Of course you didn't, dearest," Izzy said airily. "I did. Because he is. Someone needs to tell him. He's browbeating Corliss into marriage, Zachary. Did you know that? I'll not stand for it."

"Browbeating?" Anglesey frowned, stroking his jaw as if in idle contemplation, his every motion one of careless elegance.

He moved so differently than Knight did. Knight was all coiled power, a walking wall of muscle, his body honed as if it were a weapon. He didn't just enter a room, he occupied it. He was such a commanding force, with his intense eyes and the strength he exuded, his dark hair and sky-blue eyes an arresting dichotomy. Anglesey, meanwhile, was golden and leonine, prowling about with the skillful grace of a rake.

"Yes, browbeating," Izzy was saying, her tone one of immense irritation. "Any friend of yours is a friend of mine, but I'll not stand idly by whilst he forces my sister into a union she doesn't want."

"She doesn't want to marry him?" Anglesey's brows drew together, his gaze swinging to Corliss. "You don't want to marry Knight?"

It was a question she didn't have a precise answer for. Because part of her *did* want to marry him. She loved him. She yearned for him. The time she had spent with him here at Knightly Abbey had forever changed her, and she wanted more of that. And yet, she didn't want to marry him without an understanding between them. She didn't want to marry a man who was furious with her, a man she'd lied to, a man who intended to leave her for America in a mere three days, with no word of when he planned to return.

The future loomed before her, utterly terrifying.

"Corrie?" Izzy asked. "Do you want to marry Stoneleigh? If you don't, say the words, and I promise you that Anglesey will do everything he must to see that you leave here an unwed woman. Won't you, darling?"

Her sister addressed the last question to her husband, who looked torn. But it was clear where his ultimate loyalty lay, and that was with Izzy.

"I'll do whatever I must," Anglesey repeated gently.

Gratitude swept over her. Gratitude for the kindness of her brother-in-law, for the determined love from her sister. But she knew in the deepest, darkest corner of her heart that this was a problem of her own making. She wouldn't cause tension between Knight and Anglesey. She had chosen to come to Knightly Abbey. She had chosen to be with Knight. She and Knight alone bore the responsibility for this little tragedy they had created.

And only the two of them could find an ending for it. The realization hit her, suddenly and irrevocably. They had to marry.

"Thank you, my lord," she told Anglesey, "but I'll not be requiring your assistance."

"Corliss, you needn't do this because of Stoneleigh's threats," Izzy said, giving her a meaningful stare. "Zachary won't tell anyone, I vow it. Your secret is safe with us. Stoneleigh would have to go directly to Papa, and by then, you could be on your way to the Continent or anywhere else you wish to go. Even if Papa wanted to force your hand to spare you scandal, he wouldn't make you marry the earl. You don't *have* to do this. You don't have to marry him."

"Yes," she said, giving her sister a sad smile. "I do. Maybe one day, we shall be as wildly in love as you and Anglesey."

"Corrie." Izzy's expression turned forbidding, and she shook her head. "Think on what I said."

But Corliss was every bit as determined, and even if she didn't believe the words she'd uttered for a second, she forced brightness into her tone. "I should leave the two of you now. I need to dress for dinner myself. I shall see you downstairs."

"Corliss, wait," Izzy called after her.

She hastened from the chamber, fighting back the tears welling in her eyes and threatening to spill.

CHAPTER 16

$\mathcal{K}$night walked through the door to Robert's study, too deep in his own ruminations to hear the telltale squeaking of the pail above as it tipped and sent water raining down over his head. The water was cold, the shock of it stealing his breath. He stood still, water dripping off the end of his nose, running down into his bloody shoes.

The girls were once more playing their little pranks. It was as if they had traveled full circle, all the progress they'd made since his arrival having been undone. Because of him. Because they thought he had taken Corliss from them.

He sighed heavily. Now that he and Corliss had settled the matter of their impending marriage, he needed to speak with his nieces. And what better time than now, when he was soaked from their tricks?

A stifled chuckle alerted him to their presence. Had he doubted they would watch? Knight spun on his heel and found the door to one of the sitting rooms cracked open, a flurry of movement in the gap telling him precisely where his wayward nieces were to be found. He strode across the hall, the wet sounds of his shoes mocking him as he went, and threw open the door.

All four girls were within, frozen and wide-eyed.

More water dribbled down his forehead, and he dashed it away with an irritated flick of his fingers, pinning them all with his most forbidding stare. "Which one of you is responsible for the pail of water above my study door?"

The girls watched him warily, maintaining their silence.

Knight slicked his wet hair back with his fingers. "I know the four of you are angry with me over…your governess."

He had been about to say Miss Brinton, but that wasn't her name. The reminder was not without an accompanying twinge of bitterness.

"Miss Wofford isn't nice," Mary blurted. "She never reads us stories or plays tag the way Miss Brinton did."

"Miss Brinton was the best governess we ever had," Alice added.

"And you've chased her away!" Beatrice accused.

Nettie remained quiet, simply watching him with a mournful stare that cut into his already raw heart.

He swallowed hard. "She cannot be your governess any longer because she is going to marry me."

"You're marrying Miss Brinton?" Nettie asked.

"Are you in love with her the way Papa was with Mrs. Oak?" Beatrice asked.

Bloody hell. Not Robert and the housekeeper again. His temples were already beginning to throb, and the cold water soaking his shirt didn't help matters.

"Papa wasn't in love with Mrs. Oak," Nettie told her sister. "He loved Mama."

Knight cleared his throat. "Let's return to the original subject of this conversation, shall we? Which one of you is responsible for the pail of water that just dumped over my head?"

"It was Mary," Alice said.

"Alice did it," offered Mary in the same breath.

"You're marrying Miss Brinton?" Nettie asked again, her tone hopeful.

He was marrying Corliss. The finality of it hit him now in a way it hadn't before. He'd been so consumed by ensuring her agreement and making the necessary preparations that he hadn't taken the time to sufficiently think about the enormity of what was about to happen. He, who had vowed to forever remain a bachelor, a rolling stone gathering no moss, was about to marry.

"Yes," he managed past the rising swell of confused emotion. "I am. So you see, you have lost a governess, but you will be gaining an aunt."

And he would be gaining a wife.

The prospect was terrifying and thrilling and infuriating, all at once. Terrifying because not so long ago, he'd never intended to marry, and certainly not now, at this crucial juncture in his life. Thrilling because no one had ever moved him the way Corliss did, and he knew instinctively that no one ever would. His desire for her had not lessened since his discovery of her duplicity. He wanted her more with each passing day. And infuriating because of her lies. Because she had left him without a choice in the matter. His feelings were as painful as any bruise.

"Does that mean we don't have to learn French?" Mary asked hopefully.

Knight couldn't quell his bark of surprised laughter at her question. "You'll still have to learn French, poppet."

"Oh," she said, looking quite crestfallen.

"I am the one who hung the pail of water over your study door, Uncle," Nettie revealed, guilt pinching her countenance.

"But it was all of our idea," Beatrice added.

"We were quite cross with you for giving Miss Brinton the sack," Alice said.

"But having her as our aunt is ever so much better than having her as our governess," Mary chirped, so thrilled at the prospect that she clapped her hands together and performed a little hop, rather like a bird.

"I'm glad you think so," he said, newly aware of the cold, wet garments sticking to his skin and a trickle of water down the back of his neck.

"Of course we do," Nettie said softly. "We've grown quite fond of Miss Brinton."

"We love her," Alice said earnestly.

"We do," Beatrice and Mary said in emphatic unison.

Ah, hell. His throat tightened as he stared at the four young girls before him, their futures resting upon him. The realization hit him that, regardless of what happened between himself and Corliss, marrying her was the right decision for his nieces. They needed constancy in their world. Needed someone who understood and cared for them, and he believed that she did. Especially since he would have to return to America again so soon.

The thought of leaving them—and if he were honest, leaving Corliss—filled his gut with the leaden weight of dread. But he tamped it down, focusing on the present, the faces so like Robert's, but with hints of Martha as well. Before coming to Yorkshire, he'd thought of them as burdens. How wrong he'd been. They were so much more than that. They were hoydens with big, bruised hearts they wore on their sleeves. They were his nieces, his blood, his girls now. And he loved each one of them. Would always love them, even if they dumped a thousand pails of water on his head.

"I'm glad you're fond of her," he managed past the emotions welling up inside him, all of them so hopelessly tangled. So new and foreign. "I know she's fond of you as well."

"Uncle?" Mary tilted her head at him, eyes wide.

"Yes, poppet?" He blinked frantically, discovering his vision blurred by the sudden threat of tears.

"You're still dripping all over the carpet," she pointed out helpfully. "Perhaps you ought to change."

"You rather look like a duck who's been dunking his head about in search of sustenance," Alice added.

"I was thinking he resembles a dog who's been given a bath, and he isn't too pleased about it," Beatrice said.

"Or a surly bear who's just been for a swim in the river," Nettie added brightly.

He glanced down at himself, thinking that whatever beast he resembled, it was definitely a thoroughly drenched one. "I shall indeed go and find some dry garments. But first, I'll have your promises that you'll not be suspending any more pails of water over doorways."

"Ever?" Mary frowned. "That seems a rather long time."

"What if the pail of water is well deserved?" Beatrice wanted to know.

"What happens if we break our promise?" Alice asked.

"If you had told us you were marrying Miss Brinton from the start, we never would have arranged the pail," Nettie pointed out, her tone no-nonsense.

By God, these hellions were going to be the death of him.

"No more," he repeated firmly. "Now, back to the nursery with you, and stay out of trouble."

He took his leave to the twin sounds of water sloshing in his shoes and his nieces' muffled chortles.

～

"TELL US ANOTHER JOKE, oh please do!" entreated Mary, turning her big, wide eyes so blue like her uncle's upon Corliss.

She and the four young ladies who were to be her nieces after her wedding tomorrow were seated on a blanket spread on the grassy knoll overlooking Knightly Abbey. The air possessed an autumnal nip, but the sun was shining brightly enough that they had ventured out of doors for a late luncheon together. Corliss had been eager to escape another stilted meal with Knight where awkward, frigid silence reined. And the girls were happy to escape the nursery and Miss Wofford in favor of some fresh air.

They had feasted on an assortment of foods Cook had packed into a hamper and were now finishing their meal with the sweetness of ripe fruit from the orangery whilst Corliss entertained them with all the silly jokes she could recall from her own formative years. The distraction was just what she needed to keep her from worrying over the future she faced with Knight, and what marrying him on the morrow would truly mean. Reuniting with her four favorite hoydens had been bittersweet. She had missed the girls greatly, and from the ecstatic hugs they had folded her in upon her arrival at the nursery, the sentiment had been mutual.

"Hmm," she said now, tapping her chin thoughtfully as she searched her mind for another sally. "Ah, I have it now. When is the soup most likely to run out of the saucepan?"

"When it spills," Mary guessed, having not quite grasped the concept of a pun yet, but enjoying herself immensely just the same.

"Excellent guess," Corliss said indulgently. "However, that is not the answer. Lady Alice, do you have a suggestion?"

Alice took a bite of nectarine, chewing slowly before shaking her head. "I haven't any idea."

"Tell us," Beatrice commanded, the least patient amongst the four.

"When there's a leek in it," Corliss concluded, grinning.

Nettie groaned. "That was rather dreadful."

"I thought it clever," she said, still chuckling to herself.

Mary clapped in appreciation. "Another!"

"Perhaps one more, and then we ought to begin packing up and returning to the nursery, before Miss Wofford comes looking for you," Corliss allowed, searching her mind for another pun. "Here is another. What is that from which you may take away the *whole* and yet still have *some* left?"

"I haven't any idea," Mary said, frowning.

"Wholesome," Alice guessed.

"You are correct!" Corliss clapped in the girl's direction. "Excellent work."

"That one was too easy for me," Nettie claimed with a sniff.

"According to you," Beatrice said to her sister.

"Do you have any other jokes?" Mary asked, clearly of the opinion that there couldn't be enough of a good thing.

"I don't know," Corliss said with a wink in the youngest girl's direction. "I shall have to think u-*pun* it."

"Think u-pun it!" Mary laughed gleefully. "Oh, I like that one very much indeed, Auntie. When may I call you Auntie? Do I have to wait until you marry Uncle? When are you marrying Uncle?"

The whirlwind of questions took Corliss back to the subject she had most been wishing to distract herself from. The silliness she'd given in to subsided, and her stomach clenched in the manner it did before she did something foolish, like ride her horse too fast or step on the icy surface of a lake in the winter, knowing there was a chance it could break.

"Tomorrow morning," she said, feeling her shoulders go

stiff at the looming certainty of it. "And you may call me Auntie now if you'd like. It will be my great honor to be your aunt."

"Auntie is so much better than a governess," Mary agreed, nodding seriously. "But Uncle says we will still have to learn French. I was rather hoping we wouldn't."

Corliss chuckled, grateful for the girl's candor. "I'm afraid your studies will still be every bit as important, despite the fact that I'll no longer be your governess."

Mary pouted. "*Je n'aime pas de* French."

"*Je n'aime pas le français*," Corliss corrected gently.

"You see?" Mary huffed out an aggrieved sigh. "It's so bloody confusing."

"You mustn't say *bloody* either, my dear," she added, wincing. "It's a vulgar word. Wherever did you hear it?"

"I heard it from Uncle," Mary said cheerfully.

"And when did you hear your uncle say it?" she asked gently.

"When we were playing billiards."

Corliss had been taking a sip of lemonade and nearly choked on it. "You were playing billiards with him?"

"Oh, yes," Mary said emphatically. "Uncle has taught me all the rules and the best strategies. He's quite good at it, you know."

No, she hadn't known. But it didn't surprise her to learn that Knight would excel at anything. What did surprise her, however, was that he had been mentoring Mary in the art of billiards playing. How sweet it was of him to take the youngest, so in desperate need of affection and attention, under his wing. Warmth crept into her heart, and she was reminded of all the reasons she had fallen in love with him.

That had been before her lies had torn them apart, however. She rolled her lips inward, wishing she could undo the knots of pain she had tied so tightly with her deception.

"One more pun, if you please," Mary pleaded, interrupting her weighty thoughts.

Corliss gratefully turned her mind back to the less stressful task of entertaining the girls. "What musical instrument invites you to fish?"

"A harp!" Mary guessed enthusiastically, causing her older sisters to chuckle.

"That makes no sense, Mary," Alice told her.

"What about a *harp*oon?" Beatrice asked.

"Excellent work, the both of you," Corliss commended. "However, I was thinking of the castanet. *Cast-a-net?*"

"Ha," said Nettie, clearly unimpressed.

Corliss had rather thought it one of her more entertaining jokes. But Nettie had apparently decided she was far too old, wise, and important for the silly puns that so amused her youngest sibling.

"Another," cried Mary, impervious to Nettie's disdain.

Corliss obligingly attempted to think of another. Anything to keep her mind from where it wanted to linger most. And anything to make Mary giggle.

"What is the best way to make the hours pass quickly?"

The familiar, deep voice at her back had Corliss's pulse hammering as she turned toward the source. Knight stood a few feet from their blanket, wearing one of his customary training sweaters, his high cheekbones painted pink from exertion above his neatly trimmed beard. The sky was no match for his eyes, which settled on hers with the precision of a touch. He looked tall, strong, handsome, and unreadable, his expression serious, his dark hair combed back from his high forehead, no hat upon his head.

"Uncle!" Mary cried, flying up from the blanket and launching herself at him.

Knight caught her easily in his arms and scooped her up. "Poppet. I'm pleased to see you as well."

His words were teasing, but his eyes, still resting on Corliss, remained cool.

"I know the best way to make the hours pass quickly," Mary said triumphantly.

"And what is that?" Knight asked, settling Mary back on her feet.

Corliss didn't miss his wince as he did so. Something was hurting him.

"To close your eyes and fall asleep," Mary announced proudly.

"That is one way," said Knight, his tone diplomatic as he turned the full force of his attention upon his youngest niece, who obviously worshipped him. "Another is to use the *spur* of the moment."

Corliss couldn't stifle the laugh that fled her. She hadn't expected Knight to play along. But he had. His gaze swung back to her, and she pressed her fingers to her lips, stifling any further levity.

"That was slightly better than Auntie's attempts," Nettie allowed grudgingly, apparently having appointed herself the arbiter of successful puns.

"Auntie," Knight repeated.

And Corliss couldn't tell if there was censure in his tone or not.

"I hope I haven't overstepped," she said, hating the tenseness between them, loathing that she no longer knew where she stood, what to expect from him.

What he thought of her.

"Of course not." His gaze swept over her face and lower for a fraction of a second. Just long enough to make her body sizzle with awareness. "Tomorrow morning, we'll be married."

And then, the following day, he would be leaving.

She tried not to think of his inevitable departure and the

pain it would cause her. Tried not to think of him surrounded by admirers an ocean away, riding in his elegant rail cars and autographing pictures for his adoring public, some of whom would undoubtedly be beautiful women. Did he intend to be faithful to her in his absence?

Corliss swallowed hard and looked away, turning her attention to the scattered remnants of their picnic luncheon. "I should collect our picnic and return their ladyships to the nursery."

"You needn't end your picnic on my account," Knight said, still towering over all of them except Mary, who was now happily flitting about the dying grass in circles, her skirts swirling around her ankles as she went.

"I'm a fairy!" Mary exclaimed. "Look at my wings!"

"You haven't any wings," Alice called after her sister, who ignored her and continued whirling in happy circles.

"We were finished," Corliss told Knight, gathering up the remnants of the fruit and some of the plates and placing them back into the hamper.

"I'll help." Knight knelt beside her, picking up the serviettes which lay discarded on the blanket and tucking them inside.

His sudden proximity had awareness snapping through her. Her heart pounded so fast and hard that she wondered if he could hear it.

The girls were chattering happily around them, completely unaware of the emotions seizing her. Tomorrow, this man would be her husband.

Her husband for a day.

She collected the utensils, tucking them into the hamper, trying to distract herself by keeping her fingers busy. But when she reached for a stack of plates and Knight did as well, their bare fingers brushed, and their heads came up at the same time, their gazes clashing and holding.

She fell into those brilliant depths, all the love she felt for him clamoring up her throat, trying to escape. How she wished she could tell him. How she wished he could forgive her, and they could go back to the Corliss and Knight they had been before.

"Thank you," she told him instead, her voice husky with suppressed longing and emotion.

"It looks as if we'll have rain soon," he said, gesturing to the distant sky, where she had failed to realize menacing-looking clouds had gathered. "The sooner we have the picnic packed away, the sooner we can return before the clouds open and drench us all."

He wasn't aiding her because he longed to be near her. What had she been thinking? It was clear that she was the only one wallowing in this complex yearning, all these pent-up emotions. He had closed himself off to her.

Corliss tried to banish her disappointment. Tried to feel nothing as she forced a polite smile. "Of course. It wouldn't do for their ladyships to be stranded in the rain."

Her mind returned to the last time she had been stranded in the rain, alone with Knight, and her heart gave a pang. Firmly, she banished the memory and forced herself to finish cleaning up the picnic in chilled silence.

CHAPTER 17

*K*night was lifting dumbbells and attempting to drown out the agony and desire clawing him apart inside in equal measure.

Twenty repetitions on each arm.

Then again.

And again, until the pain in his shoulder had flared impossibly and he was gritting his teeth against the sting of muscle pain as familiar as it was severe. Mayhap he was growing too old for boxing. Mayhap this championship fight would be his last. The thought didn't affect him as deeply as he'd supposed it might; he'd always known that one day, he would need to put down his cudgels. Such was the life of an athlete. The body did not remain forever young and agile, and Knight's body was an excellent reflection of that.

But there was another pain, lodged deep inside him, and it rivaled that of his shoulder.

Corliss.

Corliss and her golden hair and her soft, lilting voice. With her ridiculous puns that made Mary laugh and her games of tag. Corliss, who'd been feathered and treacled as the girls would say, and who had staunchly come to their defense just the same. Whose full, pink lips drove him to distraction, whose body was so deliciously responsive. Corliss, who had made him forget he'd been damaged and wounded when he'd arrived in Yorkshire, forget that he should never again trust in a woman enough to allow her the ability to hurt him.

The beautiful, vibrant woman who was going to become his wife in the morning.

Twenty more times for each arm. The barbell pumped up and down in rhythmic arcs. His muscles were burning, but he didn't give a damn. He needed to train, and he needed to keep his mind from wandering back to the wife he couldn't trust and couldn't stop wanting. Seeing her earlier that afternoon, picnicking with his nieces, being near her, catching the seductive floral scent of her perfume on the breeze, their fingers touching... It had been sheer agony. How would he be able to resist her before he returned to America?

Only time and distance could quell the ceaseless ache, he was sure of it. When there was an ocean separating them, and he went back to the business of using his fists as he was accustomed, he would forget all this, forget her until he was forced to do his duty and have an heir. By then, he wouldn't need her so much. Wouldn't be so tempted to surrender to the weakness he possessed where she was concerned.

A knock sounded on the door.

He paused with a grimace, replacing the dumbbell he'd been lifting on the floor of his makeshift training room, before straightening. He was stripped to the waist, as was his wont when he trained. But his shoulder hurt too bloody much for him to shrug back into the garment just now. He'd been punishing himself for the better part of two hours.

"Come," he called gruffly, hoping to hell the door wouldn't open to reveal *her*.

The door creaked open. He'd have to see to it that the hinges were oiled before he left. Just another task to add to his endless list before he departed for America. But thoughts of responsibilities and leaving died a quick death when the paneled wood swung over the Axminster to reveal Corliss standing hesitantly on the threshold, a leather-bound journal in her arms, pressed to the generous swell of her breasts. She was wearing a dinner gown of burnt umber and blonde lace that hugged her curves perfectly, lacing crisscrossing her bodice that begged to be untied.

"May I come in?" she asked.

He should deny her. Tell her no. The memory of what had happened the last time she had joined him in this room still haunted him, hovering on the periphery of his every waking moment. He was desperately tempted to take her again.

He flexed his fingers at his sides. "You may."

Knight didn't miss the way her gaze dipped, clinging to his chest before sliding lower, traveling over his half-naked body like a caress. His cock twitched to life, traitorous prick.

"Thank you." With graceful, if hesitant, motions, she swept into the chamber, closing the door at her back. "I won't take up much of your time. I merely wished to speak to you before the wedding tomorrow."

The wedding.

Their wedding.

An unfamiliar sensation streaked through him at the reminder.

He clenched his jaw, nodding. "What is it?"

She crossed the chamber, stopping near enough to touch. "My novel. You had expressed concern about what I had written in it. I brought my draft, such as it is, for you to read if you'd like. It isn't completed yet, and I shudder to think of all the mistakes I've made that will require correction in future drafts, but I wanted you to read it if you wish." Corliss extended the volume she'd been holding before her as if it were a shield. "Here it is, all within these pages."

He stared at the volume, which was quite handsome, with shells inlaid on the cover and gilt swirls surrounding a dusky-pink rose at its center. "Why?"

"Because I want you to trust me, Knight. I don't want there to be any more secrets between us."

He jerked his gaze from the dainty, ladylike fingers holding the journal, up to her cinnamon-flecked eyes. "It's a bit late for that, *Miss Brinton.*"

She flinched. "Please don't."

Part of him hated to see her looking so wan and sad, so affected. He itched to draw her into his arms, to hold her, to reassure her. But the other part of him, the broken, raw, wounded part of him, wouldn't allow him to soften toward her.

"Don't what?" he asked bitterly. "Don't remind you that you pretended to be someone else for a fortnight and that the only reason you confessed the truth was that your sister arrived, ruining your disguise?"

The hand holding the journal out to him trembled. "Take it, Knight. Please."

He stared hard at the volume, at her fingers curled around the spine. Remembered what those hands felt like on him, what those nails felt like digging into his skin as he was inside her. And he wanted it again. Wanted her again. He was furious with her. He resented her, distrusted her, desired her, needed her.

Fuck.

Knight took the journal, snatching it away quickly. "There. I have it. I'll read it. Good night."

The words flew off his tongue in a rush, that was how desperate he was to be rid of her. That was how little he trusted himself to be alone with her at this late hour, here in the same chamber where they'd made love before. He wasn't sure he could resist her after he'd listened to her laughing and happily chattering with his nieces earlier that afternoon. He couldn't lie—seeing that tender, caring side of Corliss again, the one he'd been drawn to initially—had affected him. It made him think about all the reasons he'd fallen so quickly and so hard for her despite everything. Despite his past, despite the fact that she was the governess to his nieces and he knew he'd have to leave again soon.

She made him hunger for things he couldn't have. And her betrayal felt so much deeper than Ida's ever had. Not even the articles she'd written about him and the realization she'd been cleverly manipulating him for the stories and acclaim she wanted had hurt as badly as Corliss's had.

He realized the reason now, as she stood watching him with a stricken expression on her lovely face. Because he'd never felt for Ida even a modicum of what he felt for Corliss.

"Thank you for reading my novel," she told him, lingering with her scent and her temptation and that beautiful mouth he couldn't stop thinking about, imagining it wrapped around his cock. "You'll see, I hope, that there is nothing within it that reflects upon you in any way. Nor would it ever be my intention to hurt you or the girls. I...care for you all far too much."

She was slipping past his defenses again. Cleverly. Easily.

Knight gripped the journal so tightly that his knuckles ached, and his jaw clenched so hard that his molars hurt. "If you cared for us, you would have told us the truth when you had a choice to do so, not when you were forced to do it."

"You're right," she agreed, her expression mournful. "I should have told you before Anglesey and my sister arrived. I'll never forgive myself for not telling you sooner. But I did intend to tell you, and I never meant to hurt you."

"I've been lied to before, and I cannot abide by it," he said, not sure why he was offering the explanation.

He hadn't meant to. Speaking of Ida, the pain of her betrayal, was still difficult for him despite the time that had passed.

Corliss's brow furrowed, and instead of leaving as he wanted her—needed her—to do, she remained, like a beautiful butterfly hovering nearby. "Who lied to you? What happened?"

Hell.

Holding her journal in one hand, he scrubbed over his bearded jaw with the other. "A reporter. A woman reporter. She interviewed me in New York, and...it hardly matters now. Suffice it to say, she used her relationship with me for her own gains and nearly ruined my reputation in the process."

"Why didn't you tell me this before?"

"Because it doesn't matter." He raked a hand through his hair, exasperation rising, along with old memories that were still sharp as broken glass when resurrected. "The hour is late, Corliss. You ought to go to bed and get your rest for tomorrow."

But as always, the thought of her and a bed made him think of anything but sleeping. He tamped down the rush of desire that surged, unwelcome and ill-conceived.

She didn't move, however. She remained where she was, that searching brown gaze on his, scorching all the fissures and cracks inside him. Making him want her. Making him want to forget the ugliness of the past few days and take her in his arms.

"Did you love her?" she asked softly.

He rolled his lips inward. Because he didn't want to talk about Ida.

"Knight," she prodded. "I want to understand. I'll be your wife tomorrow. Will you not tell me?"

"I was duped by her," he admitted reluctantly. "After her first interview with me, she wrote an article that hailed me as the finest pugilist in the world. I was...flattered, I suppose. And then she asked me for another interview, and another. Our association progressed from there and took on a more romantic nature."

Knight stopped, hating discussing this with Corliss. Tomorrow, she would be his wife. Despite what had happened between them, speaking of his past with Ida felt wrong.

"Go on," Corliss encouraged. "Please. I need to know."

He shook his head. "I'm not sure it matters."

"Someone hurt you, and now I have hurt you." She looked stricken. "Tell me the rest."

Knight still hesitated. He'd never confided the entire, sordid tale to anyone. Ida's betrayal had left him feeling like a fool. After guarding himself so well, he had somehow slipped and allowed her past the armor he'd always worn like a second skin. Had it been Ida's big, bright smile, her boldness, the way she'd shaken his hand at their first meeting? Had it been the way she had publicly lauded him in that bloody article? He'd never know precisely when or how she had managed to steal into his inner circle. But she had, and the destruction she had wrought had been nearly his undoing.

He blew out a long exhalation, struggling to explain. "It took me far too long to discover the true reason she was so interested in me was because she wanted to use me to gain a reputation for herself. I had the fame she needed to get her articles published. It's not easy for women reporters to make a name for themselves or to be taken seriously, and she had aspirations of becoming the most renowned reporter in the world. I learned too late that she was willing to do anything to make that happen. She wrote a series of outlandish articles detailing my drunken revelries and accusing me of striking a former female acquaintance of mine. It was all lies and exaggerations, of course, but the damage had been done."

"What did you do?" Corliss's question was quiet, dragging him back from the bowels of the past.

"I severed all ties with her, and I worked damned hard to prove to everyone that what she'd written about me was lies. It took me three damned years to undo the damage she'd done, but I finally managed it." He'd never seen Ida Dawson again, and he never wanted to. "The lies she told me...I was so stupid to believe her when she said she was in love with me, when she convinced me to allow her into every part of my life, to agree to the interviews. As a result of all this, yes, I am incredibly careful with my reputation, because I almost lost it, and that nearly destroyed me. And that is also why I can't abide by deceptions."

"Knight." She reached for him.

Her bare hand landed on his forearm, and it was like fire licking through him.

He told himself he should shake free of her touch. Told himself he should demand that she go before he did something he would regret. But he couldn't seem to move. Revealing what had happened with Ida left him feeling strangely free instead of vulnerable. And the hunger for Corliss that was never far from the surface of his every interaction with her would not be denied.

He slid an arm around her waist and pulled her into his chest, her book pressed between them. In that moment, everything else—the past, Ida, Corliss's deceptions—fell away. They were nothing more than man and woman, and she was his and he was hers.

And he was going to kiss her.

~

CORLISS'S HEART was breaking for Knight. Breaking for what he'd endured. Breaking for what she had done. If she'd had any notion of his past, how he had been manipulated and lied to and mistreated, she would have told him sooner. She'd never wanted to cause him a second of pain, and knowing that she had was utterly devastating.

But as his arm went around her waist and he dragged her against his rock-hard, muscled body, her tumultuous thoughts and feelings were supplanted by raw and unadulterated need. He was touching her. Holding her close. And the expression on his handsome face was so intense, so filled with longing, that it stole her breath. The journal in which she'd been writing her novel was trapped between them, digging into her through her corset, somehow symbolic. For it was the novel that had brought her here, and it was the novel that had led her down this slippery path to where she was now.

She wanted to tell him how sorry she was. Wanted to ask him to forgive her all over again. But his hand splayed over the small of her back, holding her with such blatant possession, and she felt the thick ridge of his cock pressing into her. His head dipped toward hers, and she forgot how to say the words which had been so ready for her tongue.

He held her stare, his breath fanning over her lips in harsh bursts. He had been out of breath when she had entered from the training he'd been doing, but that had gradually lessened until he'd pulled her close. Now, he was breathing as if he'd run to her. As if the act of holding her like this was painful.

Knight kept her there, surrounding her with his power and strength and warmth, his sky eyes blazing into hers with the pain she wanted to erase and mysteries she longed to learn. His rich, musky scent surrounded her, and when her hands flew to his sculpted chest, the sheen of perspiration made her palms slick. She hoped she would smell like him later, when she was alone and this embrace was nothing more than a taunting memory.

"You should leave, Corliss," he said, his voice a low, delicious rumble.

She slid her hands up his chest, curling them around his neck instead where the silken strands of his dark hair kissed her fingertips. "Not a chance in Hades. You're forever telling me to go. But there is nowhere else I'd rather be than in your arms."

The admission left her before she could think better of it. But after the way he had just divulged his past, she didn't regret her honesty. Her heart was his, and she wanted him to know it, even if saying those three words—*I love you*—terrified her utterly.

He groaned, and it was a sound of anguish and suppressed need all in one, rumbling beneath her fingertips and gliding over her lips. Suddenly, his mouth was on hers, fierce and hot and demanding. It wasn't a gentle kiss. It was an onslaught of passion and emotion, and she clung to him and gave him everything she could, pouring all of herself into that surrender. Into her lips and tongue and even her teeth.

She bit his lower lip and then used her tongue, soothing any sting. She moaned as molten need rushed between her legs, where she knew she was already wet and aching for him. She was melting for him from the inside out.

It didn't matter that he was angry with her. She loved him. Her sister's words of wisdom returned to her as Knight's tongue swept into her mouth. This embrace, this kiss, this moment was Corliss fighting for him. Asking for forgiveness. Understanding him completely for the first time. Needing him more than she ever had.

She would show him with her actions. With her touch and kiss and her body, too. She would surrender herself to him. Anything, everything he wanted.

The hand that was on the small of her back moved, gliding up her spine, to cup her nape, his long fingers tangling in her hair. He grasped a handful and tugged, forcing her head back and ending the kiss. He stared down at her, his expression stormy and smoldering all at once.

"Damn you for making me want you." He lowered his head and brushed a kiss over her jaw, nuzzling her ear with the tip of his nose. "Damn you for making me want to lift your skirts and see how wet you are between those pretty thighs for me." Her legs quivered in response, and she pressed them together in an effort to stifle a corresponding ache at his wicked words and the coast of his lips over her ear. "Is that what you wanted to hear, why you remained when I warned you that you shouldn't?" He licked behind her ear, and she couldn't stifle her moan. "I told you to go for good reason. Because if you stay, I'm not going to be slow or gentle."

His teeth grazed her throat, and she shivered, allowing her head to fall back to give him all the access to her that he wanted. "I don't care."

Her nipples were stiff and tight, and each slight movement made the friction of her chemise and corset against the engorged flesh a potent tease. She wanted more. Wanted his mouth on her. Wanted his lips closing over a nipple and sucking as he had before. She wanted to be naked and wrapped around him, wanted him inside her. The longing that had been building through the past few days of cold stagnancy had reached a stunning crescendo.

No warning he could deliver would induce her to flee.

She was staying precisely where she was. Where she belonged.

"You *should* care," he growled, his lips moving over her throat as the hand holding her novel slid from between them. He placed the journal on a nearby table and in the next breath his hand was free and cupping her bottom beneath her bustle, grinding her against his cock. "You should care very much, because if you stay, I'm going to use you, and I won't feel a moment of guilt about it." He nipped the side of her throat. "I'm going to sit you on this table, and I'm going to lift your skirts." He kissed the bite. "I'll tear your damned drawers off you with my teeth. Is that what you want?"

He palmed her rump as he asked the question.

Oh God. How could she answer him? Was he trying to drive her away? Did he think to frighten her with his frank, lusty words? Because if so, he was wrong. All he was doing was making her want him more. She was throbbing, the need between her legs heightened to the point of painful pleasure, and there was only one way to ameliorate it. She knew now what it felt like to have the thick cock she felt against her inside her, how good it felt for him to fill her, to feel herself stretch around him.

"Say something," he bit out, his fingers digging into her tender flesh through layers of gown and petticoats. "Is that what you want, Corliss? Do you want me to unleash all this pent-up desire and anger on you?"

She rubbed her cheek against his, loving the rasp of his beard on her skin, hoping it would mark her the same as his teeth. "Yes," she whispered.

"A final warning," he murmured, licking along her collarbone as if she were the finest dessert before him and he had to savor her. "Because after I tear off your drawers, I'm going to lick your dripping pussy until you scream. And when you're begging me for it, I'm going to fuck you so hard and so deep that you'll still feel my cock inside you for weeks after I'm gone." He dragged his teeth over her skin, past the edge of her decolletage to where her breast swelled beneath her bodice, and he pressed a hot, opened-mouth kiss over her covered nipple. "But before I come, I'll make you get on your knees and take me in your mouth. And then I'm going to fuck those sweet, perfect, lying lips of yours the way I've been dreaming. And when I come, you're going to swallow me down. Every." He nipped her breast so hard she felt it through the corset. "Last." Again. "Drop."

Corliss felt as if she were drunk on him. Mayhap she was. Because his words had the opposite of their intended effect on her. She shifted, and she could feel how wet she was between her legs.

"You better make good on your threats," she said, giving him a warning of her own. "Because I'm not going anywhere."

"Fuck," he cursed, the sound so violent and sudden that it echoed off the walls of the chamber.

For a moment, she feared she had pushed him too far and that he would walk away from her, leaving her in this desperate state of longing. But he spanned her waist in his big, prizefighter's hands, the hands that had won so many matches, and he lifted her onto the table alongside the novel she'd yet to finish writing.

CHAPTER 18

There was a place Knight reached when he was deep in a boxing bout, a place of intense concentration, where his body took over for his mind. It was a state where he was a machine, moving, acting, doing without thought. And he was firmly in it now, lifting Corliss atop the table, ignoring the pain in his shoulder. Her waist beneath his hands was small and firm, trapped in the confines of her corset. He knew the delicious curves hiding beneath those rigid stays, and he wanted to sink into them. To mark every part of her as his.

But he was also ravenous.

They were locked in battle, and she was the most fearsome opponent he had ever faced because she had so much power over him. The power to crush him. The power to destroy him. Far more power than Ida had ever possessed or wielded. Because of the way he felt for her, so deep and strong, and terrifying. But he intended to win this match. He was going to win, and he was going to take what he wanted from her, and he was going to enjoy every sinful second of it.

She'd had her chance to flee, and she hadn't taken it. Now,

he was going to do everything he had promised her and more.

He caught fistfuls of her skirts and hauled them into her lap. "Keep these out of my way."

Her lips were parted, swollen and kiss bruised, and her eyes were glazed, her pupils black and round. Her golden hair was coming undone from its tidy chignon, little curls springing free to frame her heart-shaped face. She reached for the silk, lace, and petticoats he offered, their fingers brushing as she took the skirts from him. And God, that touch breathed fire into the deepest, darkest parts of him. Made his cock thicken and lengthen in his trousers and his heart pound furiously in his chest.

Their gazes held, words not needed between them. Tomorrow, he would worry about the ramifications of taking her this way, of allowing himself to lose control, of revealing to her the full extent of his sordid past with Ida. For now, he had Corliss precisely where he wanted her.

"Higher," he demanded when she held her skirts in her lap, and all he could see was her stocking-clad legs up to the frilled hem of her drawers.

Silently, she did as he asked, lifting her voluminous skirts and revealing more of her mouthwatering legs to him. Everything about her entranced him, from the turn of her ankles, to her calves and the lushness of her thighs. But it was still not enough. He wanted more.

He stepped forward, between her legs, pinning her skirts between them. His cock was already leaking, ready to be sheathed inside her welcoming heat. But the lacing on her bodice was taunting him, and he wanted what was beneath it. Feeling vicious, he caught her bodice in both hands and tore. The thin silk lacings gave way with ease and satisfying pops.

She gasped, but didn't protest, which was just fine with Knight, because he wasn't finished. He dragged the short, puffed sleeves down the slopes of her shoulders and yanked them to her elbows. And then he tore at her corset cover, until he had her yellow silk corset before him, the creamy mounds of her gorgeous breasts straining over the black-lace trim. There wasn't sufficient room for fretting over her lacings, so he gripped the twin halves and pulled the top three hooks from their moorings. Her bountiful breasts sprang forward, her chemise the last remaining barrier, so thin that he could see the pink circles of her areolas and the stiff peaks of her nipples with ease.

"Knight," she said in breathy protest. "I've only two—"

He tore the chemise down the middle before she could finish.

"—chemises here with me," she concluded.

Too bloody bad.

He experienced not one moment of regret for his actions as he drank in the sight of her, breasts bared and pushed up like offerings, her nipples hard and begging to be sucked.

"You've one now," he said, before lowering his head, latching on to a nipple for a long, hard suck that had her arching into him, the softness of her breast crushing against his face.

He drew on her nipple, flicked it with his tongue.

She moaned. Knight moved to her other breast, sucking hard as he palmed her and caught the nipple he'd abandoned in his thumb and forefinger, pinching and sucking simultaneously until she was writhing against him. He gently caught her in his teeth and tugged before stepping back to survey his progress.

And fucking hell, what a glorious sight to behold she was. Her lips were parted, head tipped back, her breasts were pushed up, nipples wet and taut and pointing erotically toward him above her half-undone corset. Her undergarments and gown were partially shredded, and the silk burnt umber sleeves had her arms trapped at her sides. Her legs were parted, dangling from the table in those white stockings that lovingly delineated her every curve. But her thighs were still pressed together, keeping the view from being utterly perfect in every way.

It was all he could do to keep from pouncing on her and filling her with his cock as he said, "Open your legs all the way. Show me your pussy."

She did as he asked, bringing her full skirts higher, slowly sliding her legs apart. Through the slit in her drawers, he saw glistening pink folds, and that was all it took for him to drop to his knees.

He caressed her hips, the warmth of her burning him through the layer of silk and cotton separating them. She was beautiful. Every part of her astounded him, and just when he thought he could not desire her more, he did. Corliss was like a fever in his blood. Knight moved between her spread legs, the musky sweetness of her mingling with rose and bergamot. He was starving for her.

With another low rumble, he made good on his promise, dipping his head beneath her lifted skirts to catch the waist-band of her drawers in his teeth and yanking. It didn't surrender as easily as her bodice and corset had, so he slid his hands up her inner thighs and made short work of the buttons, before tugging her drawers down her hips. She moved, shifting her weight from side to side to aid him in their removal.

And then his prize was before him, her pussy bared to his avid gaze, the pouting slit an invitation he couldn't refuse, creamy thighs spread open, yellow silk garters to match her corset holding her stockings in place. Knight hooked her knees over his shoulders and didn't waste another moment. He dragged his tongue through her wet folds, lingering on the swollen bud at the top until she was gasping, her hips jerking. The taste of her was sweet and decadent and so good. He teased her with slow, light licks, fluttering over her pearl and up and down her seam, gathering up as much of her wetness as he could.

When he found her entrance, he couldn't resist licking into her, sinking his tongue deep, showing her what he intended to do to her momentarily with his fingers and soon with his cock. Keeping his tongue pointed and flat, he fucked her as his thumb swirled over her clitoris. Her hips pumped beneath him and his name fled her lips as a husky moan.

"Knight."

His tongue still buried deep, he tilted his head back enough so that his gaze could meet hers past the silk and lace she held bunched in a white-knuckled grip. Her golden lashes were low over her dark eyes, fluttering closed.

He withdrew, his thumb rotating with greater pressure over her greedy nub. "Eyes open, Corliss. I want you to watch what I'm doing to you."

She whimpered, thrusting against his thumb, but her eyes remained closed.

He removed his thumb and lightly dragged his nails over her inner thighs. "Look at me, damn you. Look at how wet you are, all over my lips and beard."

She was so drenched that he had no doubt he would fall asleep later to the sweet perfume of her sex on his face. He had no intention of washing the scent of her away. Sweet torture until tomorrow when he finally made her his in the last way he could.

Her eyes opened, meeting his, taking in what she'd done to him. He imagined he looked as wild as he felt, kneeling between her legs, face and lips wet with her.

"Watch," he repeated.

And she did. She watched as he sank his tongue into her pussy again and again. Watched as he returned his thumb to her pearl and swirled over it in fast, teasing strokes. Moaned as he kissed her folds and lightly licked his way to her clitoris, replacing his thumb with his mouth. He suckled her and nipped, and she cried out, her breasts bouncing above her corset as she thrust against him, seeking more.

He gave it to her, sinking two fingers deep inside her where she was slippery and hot. Her inner muscles clenched on him in a grip that made his aching cock jealous. He bit her again, this time with a bit more pressure, curling his fingers inside her and stroking. Another sound escaped her, and she tightened on him instantly, her body shuddering with release as a rush of liquid ran down his fingers until he was dripping, her juices coating his palm and wrist, running along his forearm.

He gave her pearl another light score with his teeth before he raised his head, admiring the sight of her, in such a hedonistic state of dishabille, her pale skin flushed with orgasm, his fingers still buried in her pussy as far as they would go. Wanting to prolong her pleasure, he worked his fingers in and out of her slowly, turning them inside her, stroking her in a way that had her gasping, her body bowing.

"Again," he said, knowing she was close. Needing to take her over the edge again before he would allow himself to find his own release. "But this time, say my name when you come."

He couldn't resist adding a third finger, sinking into her with ease as her inner walls gripped and clung. How perfect she looked, stuffed full of him. Stretched around him. He sank in and out of her in quick, hard thrusts, using his thumb on her swollen clitoris until she was bucking and twisting, crying out helplessly as a second wave overtook her.

And his restraint snapped. If he didn't sink his cock into her soon, he would die. He was sure of it. Knight withdrew his fingers and surged to his feet in the next breath, reaching for the fall of his trousers. His cock sprang free, hard and aching, and he stroked himself with the hand that was soaked from her spend, slicking her dew all over him.

She was breathing heavily, lips still parted, looking beautiful and thoroughly fucked. He pressed closer, notching his cock to her opening.

"Are you ready for me?" he asked, heart thundering so furiously in his ears that he could scarcely hear her hushed reply.

"Yes."

But it was there. Enough. He lowered his head and took her mouth at the same moment he sank his cock into her snug, wet pussy. She fit him perfectly. One thrust, and he was all the way inside her, their bodies joined. He coaxed her lips open, feeding her his tongue, hoping she would taste herself. He kissed her lingeringly, gently. Tenderly almost, some part of him in awe at the way she felt, wrapped around him.

Mine, he thought. *This woman is mine.*

The realization made his ballocks tighten, and he had to summon all the restraint he possessed to keep from spilling inside her. He broke the kiss, his own breathing ragged, and stared down, past the bounty of silk and lace, to where their bodies were joined. He withdrew slightly, watching his cock, slick with her dew, slide in and out of her. He fucked her slowly. So slowly. Controlling himself, working his body as he did when he trained. Because he'd meant what he'd said to her.

He wanted her on her knees. Wanted his cock between those gorgeous lips.

"I want you to come on my cock," he told her.

She made a needy sound low in her throat, squeezing him so tightly that he slipped from her body. He gripped his cock and guided himself inside her pussy again, sinking deep. This time, he kept his fingers there between them, whirling over her pearl again and again until she was panting. He kissed the corner of her lips, increasing the pressure and the pace of his cock and his fingers both.

She came again, crying out in a half gasp, half moan as her cunny pulsed around him, the reverberations of her release milking his cock so deliciously that he almost allowed himself to come too.

He withdrew, gripping himself, and stepped away from her, barely maintaining the leash on his control. "On your knees, Corliss."

She was dazed from her orgasm, but her gaze fell on his cock, and a bit of lucidity seemed to return to her. He squeezed his cock head hard, desperate to hold his own pinnacle at bay, but it was damned difficult as he watched her tugging up her sleeves, her pert breasts swaying with the effort. Wordlessly, she lowered her skirts and slid from the table.

The moment her feet were on the Axminster, she sank to her knees just as he had asked.

Fuck.

He was going to spend in his hand.

"Take me in your mouth," he gritted.

And she did with an obedience that had his blood roaring in his ears, her head dipping, her pretty, petal-pink lips stretching around him. The first touch of her tongue to his cock, and he almost exploded like a steam boiler. She licked him tentatively at first, and then with greater confidence, her tongue playing along the under-side of his shaft as she allowed him to thrust deeper into her mouth. Still fisting the base of his cock in one hand, he grasped her chignon in the other, guiding her head as he fucked her mouth slowly, taking care not to go too far.

The feeling of her lips around him, her tongue, her heat...

it was incredible. But he was greedy, and he still wanted more.

"Suck," he instructed.

And she did. She sucked, and together, they moved, her mouth taking him deeper, before withdrawing, her lips and tongue gliding in sensual torture along his cock. It didn't take long.

"I'm going to come," he warned her.

In the next breath, he lost himself, spilling down her throat, coming so hard that dark stars speckled his vision.

Just as he'd told her to, she swallowed every last drop.

And he was as wrecked as a derailed train.

"Here, let me help you."

Corliss was struggling with her corset, her back to Knight, when his hand fell on her bare shoulder. As always, his touch made her feel so warm and alive, as if he bore a magic that was uniquely his. In the aftermath of their explosive lovemaking, she had been overwhelmed with a sudden burst of confusion and shyness. She had retreated from him, struggling to right the garments he had ravaged so that she could at least attempt to return to her chamber without looking as if she had been thoroughly ravished.

Which of course she had.

But she was also uncertain of where she stood with him. He was still angry with her for her deception, and he was still affected by what had happened to him in the past. Now that the magnificent passion between them had been fed, she was back to wondering what was next.

"Corliss," he said, his voice low and yet soft, having lost the sensual command of earlier.

She turned to face him, holding the rent ends of her

chemise over her breasts. Although he was still bare-chested, he had refastened his trousers, and aside from the flush on his high cheekbones and the fullness of his lips, he bore no outward sign of what had just happened between them. She was not similarly unscathed. Neither inside, nor otherwise.

"My chemise is quite ruined, but perhaps you might help me in hooking my corset," she said, striving for politeness.

As if they had not just torn each other apart in erotic abandon.

Emotions and so many unspoken words hovered between them. An emotion passed over his handsome face. She hoped it wasn't regret, for she wouldn't change a single moment of what had just happened. The only thing she would change was the hurt she had dealt him.

"Forgive me," he said. "I shouldn't have been so rough with you. Did I hurt you?"

"Of course not," she reassured him, still clutching her torn chemise, holding her breath as he took a step nearer and reached for her yellow corset, tugging the sides together with a solid jerk. His fingers grazed a bare swath of skin as he did so, and she couldn't suppress her shiver in response.

"I was a beast," he said, his gaze firm upon his task instead of holding hers. "I warned you I would be if you stayed."

Yes, he had.

"And I remained anyway," she reminded him quietly, wishing he would look up and meet her stare. Wishing she could read him. The impassioned lover who had so masterfully brought her to her pinnacle thrice, and who had done and said such wonderfully vulgar things was nowhere to be found now.

In his place was the same cold, dispassionate stranger who had demanded she marry him. The unforgiving, harsh man who had told her he was leaving her.

He slid a hook into its eye. "I forgot myself."

"Or maybe you remembered me," she said, frustrated with him and this stalemate they seemed to forever arrive at. "Maybe you remembered who I am, and that not one part of the time we've spent together has been a lie except for my surname and my reason for being here."

"A deception of any magnitude is still a deception," he countered, doing up another hook and corresponding eye.

She swallowed against a rush of sadness. For all the intimacy they had just shared, it would seem he was no closer to forgiving her than he had been before. That wasn't why she had stayed, of course. The need to be with him, to touch him, for him to make love with her, had been the reason. However, she couldn't say she wasn't disappointed to see his impersonal mask fall back into place now that their mutual desires had been slaked.

"I am sorry, Knight," she said. "So sorry for what happened to you with that reporter." The woman's name— Ida—felt far too hateful for her to speak aloud. She couldn't do it. "And I'm sorry I lied to you. I'm sorry, so very sorry, that I hurt you. I never wanted to do you or the girls any harm. Please know that, whatever you think of me."

He slid the final hook into place and tugged her bodice up. The lacing that had embellished it, which he had so easily torn asunder, sagged pitifully. Some of the blonde lace lining her decolletage had ripped as well, and listed sadly to the right. Her skirts were wrinkled and misshapen, and she looked an absolute fright.

"Christ," he muttered, taking in her disheveled appearance as well. "It looks as if I mauled you. Are you certain I wasn't too—"

"You were everything I needed you to be," she interrupted firmly. "Except forgiving."

The accusation hung between them, and he jerked his eyes up to hers at last, his brow furrowing. "I do forgive you,

Corliss. I…I *need* you, too. But I also need time. This has all been so sudden and unexpected, and now I'm leaving again. The last year has been a bloody whirlwind but the last three weeks have been a goddamned hurricane, and we've all been caught up in it, spinning about."

It was a description most accurate. But her foolish heart caught on his admission that he needed her. Perhaps there was hope for them yet. She had certainly felt as if there could be when he had been kissing her and pleasuring her. When he had been deep inside her.

She nodded, words caught in her throat, bogged down by emotion, and busied herself by fretting with her gown. Part of the lacings had fallen to the Axminster. She sank low to retrieve them at the same time he did, and they faced each other on their haunches, the brilliant luster of her crushed skirts surrounding them. They froze that way, their gazes clashing, fingers grazing each other as they both reached for the ripped lacing in unison.

"You have carte blanche with purchasing whatever you like," he said. "Buy a new gown and chemise. Buy ten, if you wish. Replace those dowdy governess weeds with something more befitting a countess."

This was not what she wanted to hear him say. Gowns and chemises didn't matter to her. She had an entire wardrobe awaiting her back home at Talleyrand Park. All that did matter to her was winning his heart. Making him see how much she loved him. How vastly different she was from the woman who had betrayed him and used him so callously.

"I don't need gowns," she said quietly, curling her fingers into a ball, the lacing in the center of her palm. "And as for undergarments, I expect the chemise can be easily enough repaired. The tear is only halfway through."

"Buy the gowns and chemises," he urged.

"Do you think that's what I want from you, Knight?" she

demanded, snapping at last, little different from the lacings on her bodice. "Because if so, you're wrong. All I want from you is *you*. Not your fame, not your fortune. I don't give a fig about The Bruiser Knight. I'm not writing a novel for you or about you. I'm writing it for myself, because the story is living and breathing inside me. I came here to Knightly Abbey with one intention, and it was to research my heroine's position. Instead, I fell in love. The mistake was clearly mine."

The last words left her in a rush, and she couldn't bear to wait for his response. She rose to her feet, for once towering over him. And he was still there on his knees, staring up at her as if he were seeing her for the first time. She had revealed far too much. Panic made her throat go tight. Why had she allowed her feelings for him to slip out with such careless disregard for the consequences?

"I bid you good evening," she forced herself to say past lips that had gone numb.

"Corliss," he said, rising too. "Wait. What happened between us just now—"

"No." She interrupted, shaking her head as tears blurred her vision and stung her eyes. "You've said enough."

She hurried from the chamber in her tattered dress, her heart in ruins.

CHAPTER 19

*T*he morning of the wedding had dawned brilliantly sunny, with a whistling wind blowing through the trees and sending cold drafts through all the windows. Corliss couldn't help but to think the howls beyond the walls of Knightly Abbey presaged the grim future of her marriage to Knight as she shivered and dressed in a simple afternoon dress with a high neck. She had never imagined the tan silk gown with green velvet trim would serve as her wedding dress when she had packed it in her trunk before leaving for Yorkshire.

But when she had left Talleyrand Park what seemed a lifetime ago now—how it had only been a handful of weeks, she'd never know—she'd had no notion of what awaited her at all. She couldn't have known she would fall in love with Knight, with his nieces. Couldn't have expected that the wilds of Yorkshire would come to feel like home to her. That she would finally find the other half of herself she hadn't known she had been seeking, only to have it torn asunder by her own recklessness. That she would want a future with him more than she wanted one alone, traveling and writing her books.

She stood before the mirror in her guest chamber, taking in her pale, unsmiling reflection, and thought she scarcely recognized herself. Izzy's lady's maid had worked her hair into an elaborate Grecian braid. A pair of her sister's earrings was the sole adornment to her gown. Purple crescents shaded the skin beneath her eyes, evidence of the tossing and turning and lack of slumber which had plagued her all night long.

After she had left Knight in his training room, she had hastened to her chamber, fortunate that no one spied her in her ruined gown. The house had been quiet, the silence mocking her. Her mind had been filled with the scorching coupling she'd had with Knight, only for him to retreat again behind the walls he had erected around himself. Her body had still hummed with desire, aching in places that were yet new and unfamiliar. And she had never felt more adrift.

To distract herself, she had tried to write a letter to him, thinking that perhaps she could be more eloquent with her pen than she could with her tongue. But the words hadn't seemed right, and she had crossed through draft after draft, until her fingers had been ink stained and she had tossed every last sheaf of paper in her chamber into the fire, watching it burn to ash. By the time she had pitched the last letter into the grate, the hour had been close to the time the sun would rise again.

Exhausted, she had fallen into her bed, only to jolt awake an hour later as the sun filtered through the window dressings. She had risen and bathed, soaking in the tub until her fingers and toes were wrinkled, but the water had done nothing to wash away the worries holding her in their relentless grip. She couldn't shake the fear that nothing she said or did could fix the damage she had done. But by the fresh dawn of a new day, she knew that she had to *try*. Because she loved Knight more than she had ever imagined possible. And she was going to fight for that love. Fight with everything she had.

It was either prepare for battle, or surrender, and Corliss had never walked away from a challenge in her life. She wasn't about to begin now.

A light knock sounded at her door, and she turned away from her reflection, wondering if it was Knight. "Come."

The door opened, and it was not the man she would marry in two hours' time, but rather, Izzy. As usual, her sister was dressed in ostentatious fashion, sporting a gown with tassels and silk flowers and bold, vibrant colors that clashed horridly. And yet, somehow, on Izzy, the whole of it all still looked elegant.

"Good morning, dearest," Izzy said, hastening across the chamber after closing the door at her back. "I've never seen a more Friday-faced bride. You look as if you scarcely slept last night."

Blunt as ever.

"That's because I *did* scarcely sleep last night," she admitted with a heavy sigh.

Izzy took her hands and gave them a sisterly squeeze. "I'll say it again, Corrie. You don't have to marry him. It isn't too late. We'll take a carriage to York and bundle ourselves onto the first train we can find, and ride it anywhere it goes until he's nothing but a memory."

If only it were that simple. Knight would never be nothing but a memory. He was a part of her. She loved him.

She loved him, and he loathed her.

At least they still had desire to bring them together.

Corliss gave her sister a brittle smile. "I'm not running, Izzy."

Izzy's dark brows drew together. "Perhaps you should. I

love you too much to allow you to throw yourself into a marriage that will make you miserable. And besides, Mama, Elysande, and Criseyde will never allow me to hear the end of it if I don't do everything in my power to stop you from such a mistake."

Their sisters and mother were fiercely protective, she knew. And Izzy was no different. Her intentions were nothing but good. But Corliss had used the night of tossing and turning to contemplate the choice awaiting her.

"I love him, Izzy," she said simply. "The only thing that makes me miserable is the fact that I so foolishly set us up for failure by deceiving him. I hurt him, and I'll never forgive myself for that."

"It wasn't your intention to hurt him." Izzy squeezed her fingers again meaningfully. "You had no notion what would be awaiting you here at Knightly Abbey. How could you have done? I will own that your plan of living as a governess was dreadfully shortsighted, but there isn't a malicious bone in your body, and I fail to see why anyone could be so hard-headed and stubborn as to think otherwise."

"He was hurt before, in the past," Corliss explained, not wanting to betray Knight's trust by divulging the full story of what had happened with the American reporter and yet needing to explain. "It's cast a shadow over what happened between us. I hope that, given time, I'll be able to prove myself to him."

"Are you certain he deserves it?" Izzy asked quietly, still apparently unconvinced by Corliss's arguments.

"He deserves my love," she said firmly, "and I intend to give him that. One day, perhaps, he'll return it. Until then, I'll have the girls to keep me company and my novel to finish writing. Perhaps the five of us will go and visit Papa and Mama at Talleyrand Park. I think a change of scenery would do wonders for them, and I have no doubt Mama and Papa will be quite overset with this unexpected news. I'll need to explain everything to them in person so that I'm there to offer Mama her smelling salts if she swoons."

Planning for a future that was so uncertain—Knight's presence in it a mysterious question she'd yet to answer—felt odd and reassuring all at once. Reassuring in the sense that she had realized she didn't want a future without him in it. Odd because she'd never imagined she would marry at all, and certainly not in such haste. She had once dreamt of traveling the Continent, writing her books, and being free.

But freedom felt like a hollow fancy to her now if it meant a life where Knight wasn't hers. Hers to love. Hers to protect. Hers to kiss and touch and pleasure. Hers, she hoped, to fight for.

His trust hers to regain and keep forever.

"Mama will most certainly swoon when she learns you've not been with Aunt Louisa but have instead married a boxing earl who is off to America to fight in his next match." Izzy released her hands, sighing heavily, unsmiling. "You want this marriage, Corrie?"

She took a fortifying, deep breath of her own, looking inside herself to the answer that remained unwavering. "I want this man. I want him to be mine. I don't want to lose him."

"So we'll not be taking a train adventure today after all?" Izzy asked, her tone teasing, laced with a hint of wistfulness.

"Not today." Corliss smiled, tears not far. "Marrying him is the right thing to do, Izzy. I feel it in my heart."

"All I want is your happiness," her sister said. "And if that means marrying Stoneleigh, marry him you shall."

KNIGHT'S NECKTIE felt as if it was choking him. He slid his finger between the collar of his shirt and his neck and tugged to no avail as his steps carried him back toward the looming edifice of Knightly Abbey. Centuries' old stones seemed to mock him, covered in lichens, reminding him of his life's credo.

A rolling stone gathers no moss.

Why did it lack the meaning it had once possessed for him now? Why did the thought of leaving the place he had once regarded a prison fill him with such trepidation? Or was it merely the realization that he would be wedding Corliss in but an hour's time, and that he would leave her and his nieces behind on the morrow?

"Ready to be a married man, old chum?" Anglesey asked, intruding on Knight's weighty ruminations.

At his friend's suggestion, they were taking the air. A walk on the paths he ordinarily ran every day had seemed a reasonable means of distracting himself from the enormity of the commitment awaiting him. But the wind was downright bloody frigid, howling around them with relentless furor, and cold air whipping at his cheeks and cutting through his clothes and coat. He was chilled to his marrow.

"Is a man ever truly prepared for such a state?" he returned instead of answering.

Because the truth was, he didn't know if he was prepared. Not for marriage, nor for the way he felt for Corliss. Certainly not to return to America.

"You're as ready as you'll ever be," Anglesey said solemnly at his side. "Marriage isn't easy, but it is deeply rewarding. There's no feeling like looking at your woman and knowing she's the best part of you. Knowing she's yours and that she loves you more than anyone should."

Love.

Corliss had told him last night that she had fallen in love

with him, and after reading her novel, he knew without doubt she had meant those words. He'd spent the night poring over the draft she'd left with him in his training room. She was an eloquent writer. Although the story she had begun was incomplete, he'd found himself enthralled by the tale she'd begun spinning.

And she had been correct.

Nary a mentioning of The Bruiser Knight within the flowery script on those neatly penned pages. There was nothing but the story of a governess named Miss Brinton facing wayward charges and falling in love with her employer—a love that was hopeless, given their difference in stations. It was their story, and yet it wasn't. He saw bits of himself, pieces of the girls within those pages, fragments buried so deep no one else would know them unless they had lived and breathed the past three weeks as he had.

It was a beautiful story.

A heartrending story.

He'd felt the hopelessness of Miss Brinton's love, captured in stolen glances and accidental meetings in libraries and darkened halls. He'd felt it because he'd known it. He'd known it and fought it and now... Hell, he'd allowed the demons of his past to intrude and ruin it.

Realizing he'd been silent, lost in his thoughts for far too long, he cast a glance in Anglesey's direction, scrubbing at his jaw. "What if you're not worthy of her love?"

His old friend raised a brow in response. "You don't think you're worthy of Lady Corliss?"

"No," he admitted, the word torn from him.

He'd been caught up in his own emotions and fears, and he'd closed himself off from her. But all the while, she had quietly continued loving him. Loving him when she shouldn't. Loving his nieces through all their pranks and trying behavior. Shining light into the darkest moments. Shining light into *him* when he'd least deserved it.

"You're right." Anglesey grinned unrepentantly. "You aren't worthy of her. Nor am I worthy of my wife. But I'm selfish and greedy, and I'm damned glad to have her at my side. And I'll do anything to make her happy and keep her there."

But Corliss wasn't going to be at his side. He'd be across an ocean in America, and she would remain here in Yorkshire, half a world away. Worse, he'd squandered the last remaining days they had together by clinging to his anger over her deceptions.

"I think I've made a mistake," he admitted, feeling as if he'd entered a bout completely unprepared and had just taken a punishing fist to the face.

"What mistake is that?" Anglesey asked, his gaze turning sharp and his jaw going hard. "And be forewarned. If you tell me you've done something to hurt my wife's sister, ancient friendship or no, I'm duty-bound to plant you a facer."

"I deserve one." He sighed. "I've been so caught up in my anger with her, and I've allowed my past to interfere with the way I feel."

And last night, he'd been such a confused jumble of emotions and longing and raw, potent desire. He'd taken her on a table and had told her to get on her knees for him. She had opened her heart to him, telling him she loved him, and he'd been so frightened of those words and their implications, so afraid to believe them, that he'd allowed her to walk away. He wasn't about to confide all that in his friend—there was a limit to gentlemanly confidences. But damn it all, he wouldn't blame her if she hated him.

"Your past will eat you alive if you allow it," Anglesey said. "Christ knows mine almost swallowed me whole. Don't let it do that to you, Knight. Look to the future. To her. She'll be your wife before the day is over, and you have the rest of your life to work out all the knots in your rope."

He nodded, knowing his friend offered sage advice. Corliss was nothing like Ida. He understood that now, after a sleepless night and the bright sun of the frigid day beating down on him. After this head-clearing walk with Anglesey. After reading Corliss's novel.

After hearing her tell him she'd fallen in love with him.

"This entire bloody business is more difficult and painful than a boxing match," he muttered wryly.

"I'll not lie. Watching someone else squirm as I did is rather amusing." Anglesey grinned at him. "But you'll survive. Christ knows I did somehow, and look at me now, a happily married man with the best wife a sinner like me could ever ask for. She loves me as I am, and I love her more than words can possibly convey."

Anglesey was brimming with emotion, and with something else too. Something so impossibly rare and true. It was, he thought, *happiness*. Pure and simple happiness. Longing seared Knight as he wondered if he could ever have with Corliss what his friend had with his own countess. Or had he muddled everything between them so horridly that their relationship was irreparable?

God, he hoped not.

The realization struck him so suddenly and with so much astonishing clarity that he stumbled over his feet and nearly tripped. He hadn't been falling in love with a woman who didn't exist.

He'd been falling in love with Corliss, the woman who had shown the kindness and affection to his nieces that they so desperately needed when no one else had. The woman who had laughed and darted about playing tag, who had endured being treacled and feathered, who wrote so stirringly and had given herself to him so beautifully, without a thought for the repercussions for herself. The woman who kissed him and stole his breath, who looked at him and set him aflame.

The woman who had understood him, from the first, in a way no one else ever had, and who had loved him anyway. Just him. Not The Bruiser Knight. Not his fame, not his fortune, not his championship or what he could bring her or how she might use him to her advantage.

And Knight…

He loved her, too.

He loved her so much. Loved her deeply, which was why it had cut him to the marrow when he'd realized she'd been lying to him. Why the notion that she was no different than Ida had torn him apart and ruined him.

"Knight?" His friend hovered before him, peering into his face with a concerned expression. "Christ, you're not going to swoon on me, are you? You're paler than a debutante whose corset's laced too tight, and I haven't got any hartshorn."

Anglesey's little joke wrung a laugh from Knight, and it felt good, that laugh. "I haven't had a knockout blow yet. You needn't fret over me, Papa."

His friend's drawn countenance gave way to relief. "Very amusing."

"I thought so." He chuckled, before remembering that he still had a wedding looming ahead of him and a lengthy return voyage to America, and his levity faded. He loved Corliss, and he would have to leave her. Their time together was waning by the hour. His gut clenched at the thought. "I suppose I should go inside and prepare to be married."

"You should indeed. And I won't lie, I've always wanted a brother who isn't an arsehole. I'm pleased it's you Corliss is marrying, old chum."

Anglesey thumped him on the shoulder.

And once again, it was the bad shoulder.

Knight winced. "As have I. Mayhap there's something to be said for starting over and second chances after all."

His friend gave him another hearty pat. "I have a feeling you'll find there is. Come, now. Off to your wedding with you."

And indeed, off to his wedding Knight went.

CHAPTER 20

$\mathcal{C}$orliss had spent days agonizing over marrying Knight, and in the end, it happened in a sunlit drawing room with his nieces, Izzy, and Anglesey as their sole witnesses, all in less than an hour. She spoke her vows alongside him, signed her name, and it was done.

She was the Countess of Stoneleigh.

A joyous wedding breakfast followed, surrounded by laughter and much happiness from the girls, who were thrilled for Corliss to officially be their Auntie. Through the celebration, she was all too aware of Knight's gaze whenever it fell upon her, intense and searing. But he hadn't spoken a word to her aside from the vows, and she had no notion of what was going through his mind.

He was a commanding presence at her side, exuding his quiet strength, his broad shoulder nearly brushing against hers each time he reached for his wine glass, their elbows almost grazing, but not quite. It seemed a metaphor for the complexity of their relationship. They had fallen hard and fast, had shared startlingly raw intimacies, and yet, they sat together, husband and wife, untouching, as formal as could be.

"Are you prepared for the match?" Anglesey was asking Knight from across the table, curiosity in his tone. "I saw you wincing when I clapped your shoulder earlier this morning. You're not injured, are you?"

Corliss felt herself tense at the mentioning of his return to America and an injury both. It was inevitable, she knew, and yet, she would sooner pretend that her husband of one day was not abandoning her on the morrow for a return to the life he had been living before they had met. And if he was hurt...no, she didn't want to think about the repercussions of him facing an opponent in the ring when he was not in finest form. Boxing was dangerous. Deadly, even.

She shivered.

"Yes," Knight said softly at her side. "It's an injury I suffered in my last bout. Unfortunately, I seem to have trained a bit too much during my stay here. It's tender, but I have no doubt that it will have enough time to heal during my travels."

She thought of his pained expression when he'd lifted Mary at the picnic, and fear cut through her, sharp and quick.

"It's a dangerous sport," she said, turning to him. "And far more so, I should think, with an injury."

He gave her a small smile. "I shall manage, Lady Stoneleigh, just as I always have. Though I thank you for your wifely concern."

The name was unfamiliar and foreign, but it was hers now. She disliked the formality with which he spoke to her. Disliked the distance in his gaze. There had been a moment, when their eyes had met during the vows, that she had been certain his walls had lowered. She had thought she spied tender emotion reflecting back at her. But then he had turned away, and it had been gone, and now here he sat, as stiff and unyielding as a stranger.

"Of course you will, Lord Stoneleigh," she returned, and reached for her glass of wine, displeased by the subtle reminder that he'd had a life and career in boxing before her, and that nothing would change for him despite their marriage.

"I don't understand why you must go, Uncle," Mary blurted, her eyes wide and glistening with unshed tears. "I'll miss you dreadfully while you're gone."

Corliss could scarcely swallow the sweet liquid past the lump in her throat.

"I'll be back, poppet," he promised solemnly, giving her a wink.

She wanted to ask when he would be back. They hadn't spoken of how long he would be in America. It occurred to her that she should have asked him, but now was neither the time nor the place, with their audience of children and her sister and brother-in-law.

"Perhaps you could all pay a visit to Barlowe Park while Lord Stoneleigh is away," Izzy suggested to the children, smiling brightly. "And from there, we could venture to Talleyrand Park. My father has a workshop filled with all manner of delightful inventions you ladies would likely find most intriguing."

"Yes, and fortunately, not all of them catch the library on fire," Corliss said lightly, doing her utmost to distract herself as well.

The future with Knight in America loomed before her, miserable and lonely. She would worry over him dreadfully. Boxing was dangerous, and she would be a vast ocean apart from him. What if he was hurt? Or worse? What if that dreadful reporter woman sought him out again?

Her stomach knotted and churned.

More wine, she decided.

"Your library caught on fire?" Alice asked, sounding impressed.

"That was merely the burglar alarm," Izzy said breezily. "He has quite perfected it by now, and nothing has caught on fire since."

"Mama was most aggrieved with him over it," Corliss remembered, grateful to turn her mind to another subject aside from Knight's imminent departure. One that was not so painful. "She made him move his workshop from the main house after that. Papa does love his inventions."

"As does one of our sisters," Izzy added to the girls in conspiratorial fashion. "She is currently perfecting an electrical frying pan."

"How does it work?" Mary asked with a sniff, blinking at her tears to clear them.

"You'll have to ask her when you meet her," Izzy said, smiling indulgently. "I haven't an inkling how electricity functions. But I know Elysande would be more than happy to tell you all about it."

"In boring detail," Corliss said with a chuckle, thinking of her elder sister's devotion to her studies.

Elysande's love of inventions and electricity was something Corliss could never hope to understand. Her mind was given to the artistic rather than the scientific. She was at her most content with a pile of books to read and paper and ink to write out the stories inhabiting her mind.

And with the man at her side, though she was about to lose him.

"You see, old chap?" Anglesey said to Knight, giving him a good-natured grin. "I told you that you were marrying into a delightfully eccentric family. Never a dull moment around the Collingwoods."

"My life has been anything but dull from the moment I

first quite literally collided with my wife," Knight said, turning to Corliss.

She felt his regard, heating every bare expanse of skin it touched. Her face, her throat. Heavens, it even touched places hidden from sight. Her breasts tingled and her belly performed an odd little flip.

She angled her head and met his gaze, seeing the same shadows beneath his eyes that suggested he'd suffered a lack of sleep the night before the same as she had. But despite that, he was so handsome that she could do nothing but drink him in for a moment. The bold slash of his jaw shadowed by dark whiskers, his high cheekbones, those sensually sculpted lips that knew just how to claim hers.

The thought occurred to her, a bit sudden and silly.

He is my husband.

She forced herself to respond, to maintain the same composure he currently exhibited, as if this wedding breakfast were as commonplace as any meal, and it was every day that she married the man she loved whilst knowing he was angry with her and intended to leave in the morning.

"Mine has been similarly eventful," she offered lamely, before turning away from him, for looking at Knight too long was akin to staring into the sun.

Blinding and painful.

She loved him so much, it hurt like a physical ache lodged behind her breastbone.

"Tell us about the rest of your family, Auntie," Nettie urged.

"Oh yes, do," Beatrice added. "It is ever so exciting to think we won't be stranded here alone ever again."

"Will you take us with you every time you visit them?" Mary asked. "Please, Auntie?"

Corliss's heart squeezed in her chest. "Of course I will. You have all of us now, girls."

Except for Knight, she thought sadly. Because she couldn't be certain that any of them would ever truly have him.

Izzy sent her a look across the table and launched into a lively tale of one of their father's other inventions, with the girls as her rapt audience. Corliss took another sip of her wine, grateful for the distraction, feeling as if she were on the edge of tears.

KNIGHT KNOCKED on the door adjoining his chamber to Corliss's. She'd been moved for the second time during her stay at Knightly Abbey. For the final time. She was now in the countess's apartments, where she belonged.

His *wife*.

"Come," she called softly, her sweet, husky voice making longing unfurl inside him like a spring bud bursting open beneath the light of the sun after a cold winter.

He took a moment to gather himself. They'd spent the day in a whirlwind, surrounded by others, and it had felt safer that way. Emotions swelled inside him. There was so much he wanted to say. And yet, he was taking a morning train from York tomorrow. He'd told himself, all during the ceremony and the remainder of the day, that it wasn't fair to tell her he loved her and leave her. That he should return to America, defend his title, and come back to her, victorious.

He could tell her then. They could start their life anew. One last fight, and he would retire. His body couldn't withstand many more, and now that he had found Corliss, he knew his heart couldn't either.

When he hesitated, hand hovering at the door, it opened, and there she stood, looking up at him in nothing but a night rail, a question he wasn't sure he could answer in her cinnamon-flecked eyes.

"I wanted to bid you good night," he said formally, longing for her making his throat go tight.

But he couldn't surrender to that debilitating need. Couldn't allow himself that vulnerability with her. Not now, not with so much at stake. He had to think of the match awaiting him in America. He swallowed hard, prepared to close the door and retreat to the quiet safety of his own chamber, where he couldn't be tempted to touch her or tear her out of that flimsy night rail and spend the night between her delicious thighs. He wanted to be atop her, inside her, wanted to kiss her, wanted her breathy sighs and her nails raking down his back.

But he couldn't have those things.

Not now. He'd taken too much from her already the night before.

"Is that all you wanted?" she asked, a crease between her brows, her voice shaded with disappointment.

With her golden hair unbound, falling about her shoulders, and the warm glow of the fire at her back lovingly silhouetting her curves, she looked like a barefoot goddess torn from his dreams. She was achingly lovely, and he wanted her so much that it terrified him. Nothing had dimmed the desire burning inside him for this woman. If anything, those flames had only grown higher and hotter. They were an inferno, raging out of control.

"Yes, of course," he forced himself to say stiffly, fingers flexing at his sides in an instinctive need to reach for her, to touch what was now forever his. "I'll need to rise early for the journey to the train station."

Even if the thought of going left his gut knotted in agony. For so long, he'd been pursuing one dream: victory in the ring. Now, for the first time, he wanted a different dream. He wanted a life with her. Wanted to wake wrapped up in her, to her smiling lips. Wanted to fill Knightly Abbey with more of the laughter and love she'd brought to these old, cold stone walls.

But first, one more bout.

Corliss held his stare, unsmiling. "How long do you intend to punish me?"

Punish her? Christ. Was that what she thought he was doing, punishing her? If he punished anyone, it was himself.

"I'm not punishing you, Corliss," he managed, fingers still moving, itching for her creamy skin. Two steps, and he could haul her into his body, curl a hand around her nape, and take her lips with his. He could kiss her until they both forgot the way they had wounded each other. Until the morning and the parting he dreaded seemed as far away as stars in the night sky, and they were lost in the passion flaring between them.

Her dimpled chin tipped up, her gaze forthright. "Then why are you not joining me on our wedding night?"

Why indeed? Because giving in to the way he felt about her was dangerous. If he made love to her again, how the hell was he going to leave her behind and return to America in the morning? How could he focus on his match and defending his championship? He'd never been more torn in his life.

"I'm trying to do what's best for both of us. I'm..." His words trailed off as he sought to explain and was momentarily distracted by her fingers working on the tiny shell buttons at the throat of her nightgown. "What are you doing?"

"Undressing for bed," she said, those dainty fingers continuing without pause, plucking buttons from moorings.

Ah, hell.

His cock was unbearably hard, pressing against the

placket of his trousers. He had intentionally remained dressed before knocking at her chamber door, thinking it would be easier to resist her if he was fully clothed. But now he wondered why the devil he had knocked on her door at all. Because she was revealing inch after mouthwatering inch of creamy, delectable skin, and the generous swells of her breasts, and all he could think about was how badly he needed her and how much he loved her, and to the devil with everything and everyone else.

Good intentions.

His championship title.

The hurt and pain of the last few days.

His past.

The train he would leave on in the morning.

None of it mattered.

He was moving before he was cognizant his feet had traversed the Axminster. They collided, much as they had that first day on the nursery threshold. His hands landed on her waist holding her tight against him.

"I can't resist you," he rasped, staring down at her, so beautiful. So *his*.

"Then don't," she said, rose and bergamot wrapping around him.

Seducing him as surely as all the lush skin she'd revealed. As surely as the crush of her breasts against his chest and the soft yield of her body curving into his.

Fuck.

He was lost. Lost in her. Lost in the night. Lost and didn't want to be found.

Knight's head dipped, and he took her mouth. He kissed her as he had the night before, with a hunger that threatened to consume him, sinking his tongue past her lips for a taste. Sweet like the rest of her, wine and Corliss, and he couldn't get enough.

She moaned and opened for him, her tongue moving against his, her hands landing on his shoulders, nails biting through the layers he'd mistakenly thought could keep him from surrendering to his desire for her. Lust was a river flooding, threatening to overwhelm its banks. He backed them into her room, over the threshold.

Because the adjoining chamber still felt like Robert's, as if he were an interloper there, whereas her room had been newly resurrected. The furniture had been rearranged, some of it brought down from storage, other pieces brought in from guest chambers so that she had a writing desk by the windows overlooking the rolling park. He'd thought she might like it there. This room felt like her. Felt like them.

There were words that needed to be spoken, but for the moment, they settled on touch. They settled on deep kisses and reverent caresses, stripping each other of the cloth barriers between them. His coat and waistcoat disappeared, and then he was hauling her night rail over her head and throwing it halfway across the room, hoping she'd never find it and he could keep her naked for hours, worshipping her body as she deserved.

When they were naked and lying together on her bed, he tore his mouth from hers to rain kisses on every part of her body he could. Over her shoulders and down her arms to her fingertips. Across her breasts and belly. Down one leg and another, pressing open-mouthed kisses to her inner ankles, her knees and thighs.

How was he going to leave her in the morning?

He never wanted to be apart from her. Not ever. But he wouldn't think of that now.

Knight focused on her body instead, on giving her plea-sure. He coaxed her legs apart, where she beckoned to him, wet and lush and hot, so hot, the heat of her a temptation he couldn't resist. He buried his face in her sex and licked her until she was writhing and gasping beneath him, the taste of her sweet and seductive, making his rigid cock even more painfully hard. The day had seemed one prolonged taunt, their nearness without ever truly touching, all the unspoken words trapped within. And he was ready for her. Desperate for her.

He lapped at her pearl as she made the soft moans that made him wild, her fingers sifting through his hair and clutching at his shoulders. The tentative lover he had first made love to had blossomed quickly into a woman who embraced her sensuality and the needs of her body. He adored the frank way she made love, wholly and passionately, not sparing a thought for modesty. What she wanted, she took, and what he gave her, she welcomed.

Welcomed just like the fingers he slid into her dripping pussy as he nipped the swollen bud he'd been torturing. The slick glide into her heat, her inner muscles gripping him, wrung a groan from him, and he gave himself over to her, to the wonders of her body, determined that this would be a night neither of them would forget.

A night to carry them through all the lonely days they would be apart.

~

SOMEHOW, she had managed it. She had won over the husband who had knocked at her door, his face an impassionate mask of cordiality, to tell her good night and leave her to the misery of her solitary bed. The boldness had come over her all at once, rising along with frustration. As his too-blue gaze had lingered on her, she'd watched the walls he'd erected fall again, just for a fleeting moment. Long enough for her to seize upon it.

She'd begun undressing herself on a whim, hoping it

would pierce his armor, prove to them both that he was a flesh and blood man beneath his cool exterior. That the man who had possessed her with such beautiful fury last night was trapped somewhere within the polite stranger who had given her his name that morning.

And, miracle of miracles, it had worked.

She was taking nothing for granted now, but committing every second, each sensation, every scent and sound and taste to her memory. She knew it would never be enough to tide her over until he returned, but it would be something. And something was more than nothing, even if it was a far cry from the *everything* she wanted from him.

She would settle for this, his raw, commanding desire. His mouth devouring her, head burrowed between her legs as if he wished to remain forever there. And if he did, she wouldn't offer a complaint. She could happily die thus, with his wicked mouth working on her starving flesh, the heat of his breath warming her, the rasp of his beard driving her ever closer to the edge of overwhelming bliss.

Corliss gasped at the delicious glide of Knight's tongue over her where she was already slick and aching for him, at the feeling of his fingers sinking inside her, stroking, building her need to a stunning crescendo so quickly. Two fingers turned to three, and his strokes were faster and harder as he alternated between lashes of his tongue and soothing kisses and stinging little love bites. In and out, he pumped, reaching that place inside her that was the point of such exquisite pleasure that she couldn't control herself.

She came with a cry, fingernails raking the smooth skin of his shoulder and pulling at his hair with the opposite hand, her bottom thrusting up from the mattress, feet planted firmly to angle herself to him like an offering and keep him there. Keep him there forever. She was so mindless that she could scarcely catch her breath. The edges of her vision went black and her heart galloped in her chest.

She lay there, spent and sated, as he withdrew and dropped wet kisses all the way back up her body. Over her thighs and belly, to her breasts. He sucked her nipples, his fingers dipping into her folds to stroke her sensitive pearl, and she clutched at him, holding him to her, their bodies melding into one.

He bit her shoulder, sucked her neck, raked his beard over her jaw. And then his lips were at her ear, his hot breath coasting over her, and he whispered something that she couldn't make out past the ringing in her ears. Something that sounded like what she wanted to hear rather than what he truly would have said. *I love you.* He dragged the head of his cock up and down her folds in a tantalizing rhythm, coating himself in her.

"What?" she asked on a gasp, too afraid to believe she could have heard him correctly. "What did you say?"

"I said that I love you." He kissed her ear, and pressed himself to her entrance.

One hard thrust, and he was inside her, and it felt so good. Even better than his fingers and tongue. She was full of him, so full. And his body was hot and hard and demanding, the weight of him atop her delicious. She held his shoulders and wrapped her legs around his hips.

"Again," she begged. "Please, tell me again."

"I love you." His lips found hers, keeping her from answering, his kiss claiming and ruthless, tasting of herself and dark desire.

She opened for his tongue, her hands going to his face, holding him there, kissing him with all the pent-up love she'd been keeping hidden away inside. He loved her? Impossible. *She* loved *him*. He was still angry with her, hurt by the past.

But it didn't feel that way now.

There was great intent in his every movement. In the slow glide of his cock, withdrawing from her almost entirely only to sink back in to the hilt. His kisses gentled and slowed, and he withdrew for a moment, while he was still fully seated, his cock big and thick and good, so good inside her. His lips left hers slightly, and he rubbed his nose alongside hers in a tender way that made a new longing flare deep in her core. His breathing was as ragged as hers, and when she inhaled, it was Knight's breath she was taking in. Somehow, the act seemed every bit as intimate and necessary as his rigid length buried inside her did.

She stroked his cheekbones, the scrape of his beard against her fingertips impossibly lovely. "Say it again."

"I love you," he whispered, his lips feathering over hers, his gaze molten.

And God, it felt real, those words. His mouth took hers again, and his body started to move, and she moved with it. They moved together, kissing, tongues tangling, hips pumping. Seeking, searching for release but also each other. Finding it, together.

His strokes became faster, harder. His fingers slipped between them, where they were joined, and his thumb fluttered over her clitoris with light pulses that increased in pressure, demanding a response from her that she had no wish to control. She surrendered herself to it, to him, and felt herself tightening around him, the familiar rush of feeling so exquisite beginning in her core and exploding.

She was utterly helpless, still holding his beloved face in her hands as he kissed her deeply, and she moaned her release into the kiss. She repeated in her mind all the words her preoccupied lips and tongue could not say.

I love you, too, my darling man. I love you so much that it hurts. But it's the most beautiful pain I've ever known.

Another thrust, and he was coming undone too, sinking deep. This time, he didn't withdraw, and the warm flood of his seed rushed inside her, sending another wave of pleasure through her. He collapsed against her, their sweat-slicked bodies tightly pressed together, his weight holding her to the bed, and she held him there, never wanting to let go.

CHAPTER 21

The morning arrived too soon, and Corliss awoke in her husband's arms, his body curved protectively around hers, the firm ridge of his cock pressing into the bare cleft of her bottom. But instead of the ordinary stirrings of desire she felt whenever he was touching her or near, all she felt was the icy grip of fear closing on her heart.

He was leaving today.

How she hated the knowledge, the inevitability. In the night, everything had seemed possible. After their first, frantic coupling, they had made love again. This time more slowly. And he had whispered words of love to her as he'd brought her body to life yet again. In those moments of stirring passion, he had been the husband she had hoped he would be.

And now, he would be the husband who left her.

She clenched her jaw, staring at the faint wisps of sunlight curling around the window dressings, willing the tears that threatened her vision to recede. She would not weep now. Sobbing was for later, when he was gone. For this precious moment, he was still here, the warmth of him seeping into her, his muscled arm slung over her waist, his hand curved around one of her breasts.

Corliss took a slow, deep breath, willing the sadness of the day to remain at bay. Willing herself to think instead of how good it felt, being held by him. She tucked his scent—musk and citrus and soap and lovemaking—into her lungs, hoping she would be able to smell him on her sheets when he was gone.

But there she was again, full circle, back to thoughts of him leaving, and the ache in her throat wouldn't be contained. She made a small, inadvertent sound of sorrow, then bit her lip, fearful she had disturbed his sleep and that he would wake and disentangle himself from her.

"Corliss." His voice was a deep rumble that she felt against her spine. He dropped a hot kiss on her shoulder. "Don't weep, darling."

Somehow, his words had the opposite effect on her. Another sob rose, impossible to contain, emerging as a partial hiccup.

"Love." He kissed her ear.

She glared at the sun, growing brighter and lighting the chamber more, it seemed, with each passing breath.

"I'm not weeping," she lied, swallowing hard against another rush of emotion.

"I'm sorry." He nuzzled her cheek.

She wondered what he was sorry for. Sorry that he was returning to America? Sorry he hadn't offered to take her and the girls along with him? Sorry he had been so furious with her?

They hadn't spoken much in the night, aside from words of pleasure and love. She still scarcely knew where they stood. It hadn't seemed to matter when his hands had been on her, stoking the fires of her pleasure ever higher. But it mattered now.

"Why?" she asked.

"Many reasons." He kissed her cheek, the arm wrapped around her waist tightening incrementally. "I'm sorry that I have to go. But I'm also sorry that I allowed what happened to me in the past to taint what we have. I'm sorry I was so caught up in old mistrust that I didn't believe you. Everything you've done over the past few weeks has shown me who you are."

She closed her eyes, blinking furiously at tears that were threatening to fall, grateful that he was no longer clinging to his anger. At least if he must leave her, he wasn't leaving her in fury and resentment and bitterness.

"I understand why you didn't trust me after what happened to you," she said simply, for she did. "Had I known, I never would have—"

"No," he interrupted gently, rubbing his beard over her cheek. "You needn't excuse my behavior. I was wrong, and I'll admit it. I'm sorry it took me this long to realize just how bloody wrong I was. We could have spent the last few days in a far more enjoyable fashion."

She turned her head, eyes fluttering open, catching his gaze. "We both wronged each other."

"Do you forgive me, my love?" His brilliant stare bored into her.

She couldn't look away. "Of course I do. Do you forgive me?"

"Always." He kissed the corner of her lips. "I love you, Corliss. I'm sorry I was too damned stubborn to tell you until now. Too afraid of the way you make me feel."

She cupped his cheek, held him there, the warmth of his breath coasting over her mouth. "What way do I make you feel?"

"As if…" He paused, as if searching for the words before resuming. "As if I found the other half of myself. The half I didn't know was missing until you. And that terrifies me."

"Oh, Knight. I feel the same way." She ran her nose along his. "And it terrifies me, too. We can be terrified together."

Only, they weren't going to be together. Not for long. They had a scant few hours, and he would be gone, off to America, to return she knew not when. It was on the tip of her tongue to beg him to stay with her. To plead with him not to go. But she tamped down the selfish urge, because she would love him anywhere he went, and she would wait however long she needed until he returned. She wanted him to be happy. To defend his title because he had worked so hard for it, and if that meant being without him, well, she would manage.

She would wait.

His head dipped to her throat, and he placed a kiss there, where her shoulder and her neck met. *"And so, all the night-tide, I lie down by the side of my darling—my darling—my life and my bride."*

She recognized the lyrics, the melody, instantly. It was the song she had sung to him in the music room.

"Annabelle Lee," she whispered, tears clogging her throat again. "You remembered."

"I'll never forget." Gently, he guided her so that she was lying on her back, and he was gazing down at her, his dark hair hanging around his handsome face. "That was the day I started falling in love with you."

"You kissed me," she recalled, smiling at the memory. "And that was when I started falling in love with you in return."

She parted her legs in welcome, and he settled between them, kissing her slowly, lingeringly. Kissing her sweetly. She had never felt more cherished than she did then, his body atop hers, his mouth moving with soft seduction over her lips. When he reached between them to part her folds, she was already slick, her body incredibly attuned to his. He rubbed her pearl the way he knew she liked until her hips were bucking and she was panting into his kiss.

His lips never leaving hers, he guided his cock to her entrance and sank inside. They made love until they were both breathless, holding each other tight, lips and bodies locked, as the sun rose higher in the sky and their remaining hours together dwindled.

THE MOMENT he had been dreading had arrived.

Knight's trunk had been packed and loaded onto a carriage that would convey him to the train station. He stood in the great hall of Knightly Abbey, staring at the anguished faces of the five most important females in his life, and knew nothing but an aching sense of despair. He didn't want to leave.

"Must you go?" Mary asked, sniffling loudly, tears staining her face.

He sank to his knees before her, holding her gaze. "I must. Do you promise me that you'll behave for Auntie?"

Sniff. "I promise."

"And that you'll learn your French?"

She wrinkled her nose. "Must I?"

"Afraid so." He ruffled her hair affectionately. "And that you will practice billiards in my absence? Someone needs to make certain dust doesn't gather on the baize."

"I will." She hiccupped a little sob.

His vision blurred, and by God, a tear slipped down his own cheek. Clearing his throat, he rose, using the back of his hand to wipe it away before moving on to Alice.

"And you will also be kind to Auntie?"

"Of course, Uncle." She was quiet and subdued. "We'll miss you."

"I'll miss you all as well," he admitted. *More than you know.*

More than he'd ever thought possible just a few short weeks ago. But this—Knightly Abbey, the people assembled before him—was home now in a way it had never been before. He felt, for the first time, as if he belonged somewhere.

Here.

With them.

But he moved to Beatrice just the same, telling himself it was necessary. One more fight, and he would return.

Beatrice sniffed and her eyes were rimmed with red. "Goodbye, Uncle."

"I trust you will look after the younger girls, being one of the two oldest of your sisters," he said.

"Of course, Uncle," she said, looking as miserable as he felt.

Nettie rushed forward, stepping out of line and throwing her arms around him tightly. "I'll miss you, Uncle."

"I'm sorry to be going with such haste," he said, guilt curdling his gut.

"Everyone always leaves," she said, blinking furiously as she released him and stepped away.

Yes, everyone always had left them, hadn't they? And he was no different.

"I'll return," he promised, throat thick. "And no more treacling and feathering," he added.

"What if it's Mrs. Oak?" Mary asked.

He bit his lip to stifle a chuckle that threatened to rumble free and pinned his youngest niece with a stern look. "None, regardless of the victim."

Mary sighed with obvious disappointment.

And at last, he reached Corliss. Anglesey and his countess had already said their farewells and had given Knight, Corliss, and the girls this moment of final departure to themselves. He was grateful for the lack of audience, and not just because another tear was rolling down his cheek and he knew Anglesey would never let him hear the end of it if he witnessed him weeping. But also because it felt more sacred this way, the six of them—his family—together.

Corliss's eyes were swimming with tears, and God, how he hated the sight. He took her hands in his, raising them to his lips for a kiss. "I'll miss you, my love." He couldn't resist tugging her into his chest and taking her mouth.

Chastely, of course. His nieces were watching. But the chance to have her lips beneath his once more could not be squandered. He kissed her hard, breathing in her scent, before he released her.

"I'll return in a month's time," he promised. "Long enough for the fight, and I'll be home for good."

Corliss nodded, clearly trying to be strong for the girls. "Be safe, my love. We'll be waiting for you."

Emotion choked him. Words failed him. All he could do was give her a jerky bob of his head in return before he turned and walked away, leaving his sniffling family and every piece of his heart behind.

You can do this, he told himself as he strode down the front stairs of Knightly Abbey to the approach where his carriage was waiting.

He thought of his championship title. Of what it would mean for one final match. The champion could not surrender with a challenge offered like this. It simply wasn't done. His boots crunched on the gravel, mocking him all the way to the carriage. He stepped inside and threw himself onto the leather squabs, his chest heavy and his stomach knotted, tears blurring his eyes.

The carriage lurched into motion, swaying over the drive. The sounds of travel reached him, once a calming lull, a balm to soothe him, and now altogether unwanted. The clip-clop of the horses' hooves, the creak of the carriage, the rattling of the wheels. All of it so familiar, and all of it breaking him apart, as if he were a glass thrown to a marble floor.

It hit him with blinding, brilliant clarity.

He didn't have to go.

He didn't have to leave them.

Didn't need to fight.

He'd been fighting for most of his life in one fashion or another. And now...

Now, all he wanted was peace. Peace and the woman who loved him, and his nieces happy and smiling, and bloody hell, even Yorkshire and tenancies in arrears and twitch grass and sheep. He couldn't leave them behind. They were everything. Far more than a championship title.

More than anything.

He rapped on the roof of the carriage. "Stop the carriage."

"Stop, my lord?" asked the coachman, sounding confused.

"Yes, stop," he hollered back, grinning, the weight on his chest already lifting. "Turn around, if you please. There's been a change of plans. I'm not leaving."

"As you wish, Lord Stoneleigh."

The carriage slowed, and the coachman began guiding the horses in a turn that was almost too wide for the approach. And slow. Too bloody slow.

"Another change of plans," he called to the coachman. "I'm getting out."

With that warning, he threw open the door and leapt out of the moving conveyance. He landed on his feet with ease, and there beneath the front portico, he spied his nieces and Corliss watching him depart.

Still grinning like a lunatic, he started running toward them.

Corliss caught her skirts in her hands and began racing to him. "Knight?" she cried. "What's happening?"

"I'm not going to America," he called back. "I'm staying here."

They reached each other, and he pulled her into his embrace, her arms going around his neck.

"But you can't stay here," she protested. "Your championship. How will you defend the title?"

"I won't," he said simply, and how good it felt, those words, the realization. "You're all far more important to me than boxing. You're more important than anything and anyone else."

"You've been training so hard for it," she said, searching his gaze with hers.

"Knightly Abbey needs me. I'll turn my attention to this estate and its people instead." He didn't know why it had taken him so long to realize what had been obvious from his arrival here. "I'm done being The Bruiser Knight. The only title I want now is your husband and the girls' uncle."

A disbelieving smile curved her pretty, pink lips. "Knight."

"*But we loved with a love that was more than love*," he told her, repeating more of the lyrics from the song she had sung to him, what felt like yesterday and a lifetime ago, all at once. "I love you, Corliss. I don't want to be alone any longer. All I want is to be with you."

"I love you," she said, fresh tears streaming down her cheeks as she turned to the portico where his nieces were watching with rapt fascination. "Girls! Your uncle isn't leaving. He has decided to stay!"

Decidedly unladylike whoops of celebration followed as four girls came rushing toward them, enveloping Knight and

Corliss in one big, ecstatic hug in the midst of the Knightly Abbey approach. Grinning, Knight wrapped his arms around them all as best as he could manage.

A rolling stone no more.

EPILOGUE

"Congratulations, my darling."

Corliss looked up from the French primer she had been reviewing with Mary in the nursery at Knightly Abbey to find Knight standing at the threshold with a book in each hand.

"These have just arrived from your publisher, Mr. Elijah Decker," he added when she stared, dumbfounded, at the beautiful leather volumes he bore on each palm.

She blinked. Once, then twice.

And her beloved husband was still standing there in country tweed, unfairly handsome with his broad shoulders and prizefighter's form, grinning at her with so much love, it made her emit a small, unladylike squeal of pure, unadulterated appreciation.

A high-pitched *eee* was what it emerged sounding like.

For a woman who had spent much of her life in words—writing, reading, sighing over both—it was a horridly and woefully inept response. But she was seeing the result of her efforts these last few months before her at last. A miracle, it seemed. Her words, all the thoughts she had labored over, the research and interviews she had conducted, the long nights working into the early-morning hours, forcing herself to put pen to paper even when inspiration was meager and the words seemingly didn't want to come. Those many days, those thousands upon thousands of words, encapsulated in pretty binding.

"Did you say something, love?" Knight asked, still standing there bearing the fruits of their mutual labor.

Mutual, for although she had written the words, he had suffered her moods, her tempers, her frustrations. He had been there, a calming word, a supporting hand at her back, sliding up and down her spine when she was cross and confused. He had answered her questions, championed her at every turn. This magnificent man, all hers, who loved her desperately and was happy to stand at her side and allow her the chance to shine.

This wonderful husband who had told her, both with words and without, how proud he was of her.

God, how she loved him.

"She said *eee*," Mary said, offering a fair imitation of Corliss's inarticulate response.

"Just what I thought," Knight returned, straight-faced, cocking his head at Mary. "Do you suppose it was a happy *eee* or an angry *eee*, poppet?"

Mary cast a knowing glance in Corliss's direction. "A happy *eee*, Uncle. I'll just go and find Beatrice, Alice, and Nettie now."

No doubt, Mary was happy for the interruption to her French verb conjugation lesson.

"We were working on *être*," she reminded her, attempting to achieve a stern tone and failing abysmally.

The new governess was quite adept at her position. The girls had taken to her, even Mary. But despite the change, Mary still insisted upon individual French lessons with

Corliss, and because Corliss would forever have a soft place in her heart for the youngest of the four girls who had become more like daughters to her than nieces, she hadn't been able to deny her.

"*Je suis* going off to find my sisters," Mary announced with a gamine grin. "They're investigating nature with Miss Strain, which I suspect means they're just collecting flowers to press in their books. It looks as if Uncle has rather a lot to say to you, so I'll be on my way."

"Uncle doesn't mind if you stay and learn your conjugation," Corliss said, but Mary was already skipping past Knight, leaving the room.

Her boundless enthusiasm for life never failed to make Corliss smile. She watched the girl go before turning her attention back to her husband, rising from her small chair with a hand to her lower back and a wince.

"I could have helped you up," he said, frowning as he closed the distance between them with long-limbed strides. "You ought to have waited for me."

"I am *enceinte*," she told him wryly. "Not incapable of removing myself from a chair."

Though truth be told, her belly was growing impossibly larger by the day. Hefting herself up to a standing position was growing increasingly more difficult. The thought had occurred to her, more than once, that there was a strong possibility she was carrying twins herself. How Criseyde would laugh if that were true. Corliss's family had embraced Knight as one of their own despite the rather unusual circumstances surrounding their marriage. Yet another benefit of having an eccentric family.

"That doesn't mean I don't wish to help you, my love." He reached her, smelling delicious as always, and ridiculously handsome, carrying her books in each hand as if they were priceless relics pilfered from some ancient tomb. Too precious to touch.

She reached for the books, snatching them both from his hands and staring down at the covers, humbled and amazed. Regardless of how many books she had published, the first sight of her words turned into neatly bound volumes never failed to thrill her. How impossible to think that the feverish musings of her own imagination had wrought two separate volumes large enough to hold in each hand. All those words strung into sentences, from her.

In her left hand, she held a small leather volume bearing the gilt title of the novel she had mostly written during her tenure at Knightly Abbey as governess. *The Goodbye Governess*, it read proudly. And in her right hand was the biography she had written entitled *Reminiscences of The Bruiser Knight*, both by C. Talleyrand.

"The first run of each has sold out," Knight said proudly. "Just as I knew it would."

Swallowing hard against a rush of emotion—gratitude, love, humility—she clasped both volumes to her breast and stared at the man she had married. The man who had given up his championship title to be her husband instead.

"I can scarcely believe it."

"I can," Knight said, smiling at her with such tenderness, she would have fallen in love with him all over again if she weren't already hopelessly in his thrall. "You are incredibly talented, darling. You've only just begun to show the world what you're capable of."

"Thank you." She bit her lip, thinking of all he had given up for her. "Do you ever miss it? Do you ever miss being The Bruiser Knight and traveling in your private rail car across America?"

"Never." He slid an arm around her waist, pulling her close, his gaze and smile unwavering. "An infinitely wise woman I know once said that one can be surrounded by others and still be quite lonely. And she was right. I realized some time ago that surrounding one's self with the right people—people who love you truly and deeply and regardless of all your faults—is where happiness lies."

She remembered that conversation well.

Corliss smiled back at him. "She was right, that woman. Because my happiness is here, at Knightly Abbey with you, with the girls."

His hands slid over her gown, settling on her protruding belly. "And our little Knight and Corliss."

"What if there is only one?" she asked, laughing as she clutched her books and leaned into her husband's deliciously muscled chest.

"Why then, my dear Lady Stoneleigh, we shall have to try for another," he said, waggling his eyebrows at her in comical fashion before taking her lips with his.

And, holding her finished books in her hands between them, secure in the warm circle of her husband's loving arms, she kissed him back with all the love and gratitude she had, thinking of the song that had brought them together that day in the music room.

But we loved with a love that was more than love.

For they did.

THANK you for reading Corliss and Knight's story! I hope you loved their heartwarming happily ever after and the chance to revisit the Collingwood family again. I have a feeling you'll be hearing from them soon.

Until then, join my reader group for early excerpts, cover reveals, and more here. Stay in touch! The only way to be sure you'll know what's next from me is to sign up for my newsletter here: http://eepurl.com/dyJSar.

There is much more to come from me. Have you read my Sins and Scoundrels series? If you haven't, start with book one, *Duke of Depravity*, here. If you have, read on for a sneak peek at the next book in the series, *Viscount of Villainy...*

A brutal phaeton accident left Viscount Torrington's memory in tatters and his body broken. But certain parts of his old life prove easily relearned. Drinking, gambling, and wenching? Check. Torrie is on a one-man mission toward complete debauchery. Anything to distract himself from the misery of the night he lost everything. Until an accidental kidnapping leads him to the woman he'll never forget.

Five. The number of disastrous Seasons Miss Elizabeth Brooke suffered before resigning herself to her fate as a governess. A lady without a dowry can only exist on the benevolence of her relatives for so long before she admits defeat. Zero. The number of scandals she is permitted to cause before she loses her position. Which is why being unintentionally spirited away by a handsome, dissolute lord spells complete and utter ruin.

Torrie has no place in his life for a wife, particularly not one as icy and prim as Miss Brooke. But even he can acknowledge that compromising a governess, albeit by mistake, necessitates getting caught in the parson's mousetrap. He'll marry Miss Brooke and send her to the country so he can continue with his life, uninterrupted. But there's one small problem with Torrie's plan. He neglected to take into account just how tempting his new wife would be. And now, he's about to lose something far more precious than his memory. His heart.

Chapter One

1816

The rear door at the Earl of Worthing's town house, which connected the stables to the main house, had been left unlatched, just as Eugenia had promised it would be. Torrie slipped inside through the familiar halls, a customary routine whenever Worthing was otherwise occupied, leaving his significantly younger wife alone. Fortunately for Torrie, Eugenia's loneliness could be assuaged in any number of ways—all of them infinitely pleasurable—and he was more than eager to accommodate.

Anything to distract him from the demons inhabiting his skull.

Which was why he had come to her tonight at this late hour, dressed in black, bearing the accoutrements for a kidnapping. All in the name of indulging her most unusual whims for the evening.

But then, what better way to celebrate being risen from the dead than drowning one's self in vice? Now that the fragments of Torrie's lost memory were gradually returning, he was all the more in need of distraction. In desperate need to escape everyone who had known him before his accident.

Because he was different now, and even with the pieces of his old life filtering into his mind like sunlight through attic slats, he would never again be the Torrie he once had been. But those who knew the old Torrie were having a damned difficult time accepting that. His sister, for instance, and his mother, too. His old friend Monty, the Duke of Montrose. Every chum and passing acquaintance he'd been forced to face without knowing their mutual history, what he might have said and done in the past, and what terms they had last parted on.

Being with Eugenia was easy in comparison. Comforting, in a sense. She hadn't known him then, the man he had apparently been. A man who was a stranger, even to himself.

Quite naturally, it helped that she had an insatiable appetite in bed. A lusty nature was the one part of himself, aside from his physical appearance, which he hadn't lost.

No servants were about on account of the late hour, and he made his way through the quiet halls with ease, finding the staircase which led to the first floor where he knew the library dwelled. Halfway down the hall, he located his quarry. Beneath a partially closed door, the light of a lone taper flickered, calling to him like a lighthouse beacon.

Torrie paused at the threshold and reached into his sack to extract the rope he'd brought to bind Eugenia at her request. She wanted to feel the fear of being swept away from her lavish town house and carried off to her captor's carriage. Wanted to be ravished as they traveled through Mayfair.

He'd never kidnapped a woman before. At least, he didn't think he had. Past experience aside, he was ready. The notion of kidnapping her didn't titillate him the same way it did Eugenia. Rather, it was the end result when they were safely ensconced in his carriage that did.

He heard the creak of a floorboard within, heralding a footstep. Movement. Knowing Eugenia, she was likely growing impatient as she awaited him. He took another moment to sort out the mechanics of what he was about to do. And then he remembered the cravat he'd brought to muffle her screams. A quite ingenious stroke, he'd thought. Feeling about in the sack, he retrieved the cravat as well.

And then, he pushed into the room just as the occupant blew out the candle, cloaking the chamber in darkness.

"Is someone there?" whispered Eugenia, a convincing tremble in her voice.

She sounded oddly vulnerable and unlike herself. Well, then. Perhaps she was taking this little kidnapping notion of hers seriously.

Ought he say something? No, he decided hastily. That would ruin the illusion for her. Instead, he strode toward the sound of the voice. Moonlight shone through the bank of windows, illuminating her silhouette. Showing him where to find her. She truly had thought about every last detail.

He swooped into action, moving behind her and swiftly wrapping his cravat around her mouth, stifling the sound of startlement she made, and tying it in a stern knot. Another low sound of outrage rumbled form her, but the cravat was doing its work. She tried to spin toward him, but it was futile. He was far stronger, and he caught her with ease, wrapping his rope around her wrists behind her back.

"*Unnnhnnnd mrrrrrr,*" she protested, her words comically muffled as she tugged at her bound wrists, attempting to free herself, to no avail.

Next came the sack, which he draped over her head.

The action appeared to have a quelling effect on her fight. She went still for a moment, and he wondered if he'd gone too far with his preparations. Well, he'd only been aiming to please.

"Eugenia?" he said softly. "You can breathe properly, can you not?"

"*Mrrrr nrrrr rarjera,*" she said, her voice now going high-pitched, as if she were truly terrified.

If she was speaking, one could reasonably assume she could also breathe, despite the cravat and sack.

"Another moment, love," he said, for he had to admit that now that he'd begun this business, it had severely lessened his ardor.

His cock, hard for the duration of the ride to Worthing's town house in anticipation of another night with Eugenia, had gone distinctly limp. But he reckoned she could restore it to its former glory when they were ensconced in his carriage and the "kidnapping" was at an end.

She launched herself at him suddenly, taking him by surprise. But with the sack over her head, she was effectively blinded. She stormed to his left, and Torrie simply bent, catching her over his shoulder. She continued her struggles, much to his aggravation.

Eugenia ought to have recalled the injuries he'd suffered in the accident, which had left him with a back that chose to remind him of his follies with alarming frequency and any change of the weather. He swatted her rump for good measure.

"Damn it, Eugenia," he said, taking care to keep his voice low to avoid any lingering servants overhearing and raising the alarm. "Cease wriggling, if you please."

His warning seemed to only heighten her frenzy. More muffled sounds of protest emerged.

"*Mmmmmrrrr, mrrrrrrrrrr, mrrrrrrrrrrrrr!*"

This was growing tedious. On the next occasion Eugenia sent a note to him telling him her husband would be away for the evening, he was going to bloody well suggest they simply fuck in her bed in the ordinary fashion. He was growing too old for such nonsense.

Or perhaps he'd always been too old for it.

Either way, he didn't care to revisit this particular worm which had somehow found its way into Eugenia's mind. Holding her struggling form to keep her from toppling from his shoulder, he carried her through the darkness. Down the staircase. Through the hall.

By the time Torrie reached the door and ventured through the mews to his carriage, he had nearly dropped her thrice, his back ached, and he was struggling to catch his breath. But he managed to gently deposit his prize within before climbing inside himself and slamming the door closed. Two solid raps on the roof, and they were in motion, the coach rattling over the road.

It was done.

He heaved a sigh of relief, allowing his head to relax against the Morocco leather.

"*Mmmmm, meeeeee, mrrrrr,*" Eugenia squealed, shifting wildly on the squabs in an effort to get her hands free.

Her discontent hadn't subsided as he had expected it would when they were ensconced in the carriage. If anything, her panic had appeared to increase.

"Calm down, love," he cautioned. "You'll do yourself harm."

"*Raaaaaaaaa!*" was her only response.

Not quite what he'd imagined either.

Frowning, he straightened. And that was when he took note, in the flickering glow of the carriage lamp, of what Eugenia was wearing. Which was decidedly unlike anything he'd ever seen her don.

Her breasts were covered. Entirely.

And her bosom was different. Smaller.

Her gown was not just demure, but subdued. And prim. Proper. The color of it was gray, like the sky before it unleashed rains. Her arms were covered. Her figure, beneath that chaste gown, was not at all the same.

"Eugenia?" he asked weakly.

"*Mrrrr!*" she said, sounding frantic.

He swallowed hard against a knot of dread threatening to rise up his throat and plucked the sack from her head. The wide-eyed woman facing him was not Eugenia at all. No, indeed. She was dark-haired instead of blonde, twin patches of scarlet fury painted on her cheeks.

"Oh God," he muttered. "Blazing hellfire."

He'd kidnapped the wrong woman.

"*Unnnhiiiiii neeeee,*" she said, struggling with the wrists tied behind her back.

"If I remove the gag, do you promise not to scream?" he

asked her, wondering just who the devil he *had* absconded with, if not Eugenia.

A servant?

An errant parlor maid?

"*Mmmmfffff*," she said.

Which Torrie took to mean *yes*, she agreed not to scream.

"I haven't any intention of hurting you," he told her, aiming to sound reassuring. No easy feat when he was too aware of how he must look to her, a stranger who had swept into a darkened room, bound, gagged, and spirited her away.

She nodded, telling him something with her eyes, which were brown and quite unlike Eugenia's blue. Or were Eugenia's green? He couldn't recall, and it hardly signified at the moment.

Torrie leaned forward, closing the space between them across the carriage, and made a show of slowly reaching behind her, fingers working on the knot he'd tied with far too much confidence. The blasted cravat was pulled tight. It took him longer than he would have liked for it to loosen, before he was able to slip the gag from her mouth and over her head.

She screamed. A shrill, loud, soul-curdling, ear-destroying shriek.

"Damn it." He cupped his hand over her mouth. "I said no screaming. You promised."

But then, had she? Incoherent sounds likely didn't signal acquiescence. By God, Eugenia would hear from him after this colossal monstrosity.

Suddenly, Torrie felt the sharp nip of teeth sinking into his fingers.

He removed his hand, shaking it, scowling at the mystery woman he had mistakenly absconded with. "Why the devil did you do that? I've promised you I won't do you any harm."

"Untie me!" she cried, ignoring his question.

Torrie watched her struggling with her bindings in an impressive show of temper and bravado. He suspected he would be dodging flailing fists if he surrendered to her demand. And besides, there was something oddly rousing about her pique. He would have found her courage admirable, were the circumstances not so deuced unfortunate.

He shook his head. "I'm afraid that wouldn't be wise. You seem to be in rather a state, my dear. Would you care to tell me who you are?"

"I'm Miss Elizabeth Brooke," declared the woman he'd carried from Worthing's town house. "I'm a respectable governess in the employ of Lord and Lady Worthing, and I demand you return me to his lordship's residence at once."

He stared at her, aghast, a sinking weight of dread lodging heavy as a stone somewhere in the vicinity of his conscience.

Good God, he had stolen a *governess*.

Want more? Get *Viscount of Villainy* here!

AUTHOR'S NOTE ON HISTORICAL ACCURACY

*K*night's American boxing career is loosely based on the careers of several boxers during that era, including Paddy Ryan and John L. Sullivan. Boxing was, just as Corliss points out, outlawed in many of the places where the matches were held, and often did involve either the arrests of the boxers or the athletes running from the law following their bouts.

The late nineteenth century was an era when modern sports as we know them truly began to develop a foothold. Boxers of this era had much fame and many adoring fans and corresponding notoriety.

The scene where Corliss questions Knight's sweater was inspired by an interview between John L. Sullivan and famed reporter Nellie Bly. Although sweaters (or jumpers) existed before the 1880s when this book takes place, they were primarily worn by athletes before gaining popularity later in the 1920s.

Knight's training regimens in the book are all based on those of boxers during the era as well. I'm much indebted to an article on Yorkshire estates in the 1880s for all Knight's estate woes.

As always, I strive to make every book as historically accurate as possible, from language to historical details. To me, accuracy is the most essential component of a historical romance novel, second only to the romance itself. Thank you for reading and for taking time to read the fussy bits about history!

DON'T MISS SCARLETT'S OTHER ROMANCES!

Complete Book List
HISTORICAL ROMANCE

Heart's Temptation
A Mad Passion (Book One)
Rebel Love (Book Two)
Reckless Need (Book Three)
Sweet Scandal (Book Four)
Restless Rake (Book Five)
Darling Duke (Book Six)
The Night Before Scandal (Book Seven)

Wicked Husbands
Her Errant Earl (Book One)
Her Lovestruck Lord (Book Two)
Her Reformed Rake (Book Three)
Her Deceptive Duke (Book Four)
Her Missing Marquess (Book Five)
Her Virtuous Viscount (Book Six)

League of Dukes
Nobody's Duke (Book One)
Heartless Duke (Book Two)
Dangerous Duke (Book Three)
Shameless Duke (Book Four)
Scandalous Duke (Book Five)
Fearless Duke (Book Six)

Notorious Ladies of London
Lady Ruthless (Book One)
Lady Wallflower (Book Two)
Lady Reckless (Book Three)
Lady Wicked (Book Four)
Lady Lawless (Book Five)
Lady Brazen (Book 6)

Unexpected Lords
The Detective Duke (Book One)
The Playboy Peer (Book Two)
The Millionaire Marquess (Book Three)
The Goodbye Governess (Book Four)

The Wicked Winters
Wicked in Winter (Book One)
Wedded in Winter (Book Two)
Wanton in Winter (Book Three)
Wishes in Winter (Book 3.5)
Willful in Winter (Book Four)
Wagered in Winter (Book Five)
Wild in Winter (Book Six)
Wooed in Winter (Book Seven)
Winter's Wallflower (Book Eight)
Winter's Woman (Book Nine)
Winter's Whispers (Book Ten)

Winter's Waltz (Book Eleven)
Winter's Widow (Book Twelve)
Winter's Warrior (Book Thirteen)
A Merry Wicked Winter (Book Fourteen)

The Sinful Suttons
Sutton's Spinster (Book One)
Sutton's Sins (Book Two)
Sutton's Surrender (Book Three)
Sutton's Seduction (Book Four)
Sutton's Scoundrel (Book Five)
Sutton's Scandal (Book Six)
Sutton's Secrets (Book Seven)

Rogue's Guild
Her Ruthless Duke (Book One)
Her Dangerous Beast (Book Two)

Sins and Scoundrels
Duke of Depravity
Prince of Persuasion
Marquess of Mayhem
Sarah
Earl of Every Sin
Duke of Debauchery
Viscount of Villainy

The Wicked Winters Box Set Collections
Collection 1
Collection 2
Collection 3
Collection 4

Stand-alone Novella

Lord of Pirates

CONTEMPORARY ROMANCE
Love's Second Chance
Reprieve (Book One)
Perfect Persuasion (Book Two)
Win My Love (Book Three)

Coastal Heat
Loved Up (Book One)

ABOUT THE AUTHOR

USA Today and Amazon bestselling author Scarlett Scott writes steamy Victorian and Regency romance with strong, intelligent heroines and sexy alpha heroes. She lives in Pennsylvania and Maryland with her Canadian husband, adorable identical twins, and two dogs.

A self-professed literary junkie and nerd, she loves reading anything, but especially romance novels, poetry, and Middle English verse. Catch up with her on her website https://scarlettscottauthor.com. Hearing from readers never fails to make her day.

Scarlett's complete book list and information about upcoming releases can be found at https://scarlettscottauthor.com.

Connect with Scarlett! You can find her here:
    Join Scarlett Scott's reader group on Facebook for early excerpts, giveaways, and a whole lot of fun!
    Sign up for her newsletter here
    https://www.tiktok.com/@authorscarlettscott

facebook.com/AuthorScarlettScott

twitter.com/scarscoromance

instagram.com/scarlettscottauthor

bookbub.com/authors/scarlett-scott

amazon.com/Scarlett-Scott/e/B004NW8N2I

pinterest.com/scarlettscott

Made in the USA
Middletown, DE
14 September 2023

38498197R00203